The Misplaced Englishman

JONATHAN R WADE

ISBN   : 978-1-9191691-0-1 (eBook)
    : 978-1-9191691-1-8 (paperback)
    : 978-1-9191691-2-5 (hardback)

1st edition 2025

Cover design by **Eleanor Horner.**

Acknowledgements

This book wouldn't exist without the story midwives in the Saturday Writers Club - Kandi, Helen, Robin, and especially our mentor Gary Dexter; a thousand thank yous to each for all the encouragement, corrections and feedback that helped get me to 'the end' and persuaded me this book was good enough.

To all the friends and family who read an early draft and were honest and kind and encouraging, thank you.

Any mistakes left in are entirely my fault.

The frankly brilliant cover artwork is by Eleanor Horner, and she deserves all the applause for making the outside look so good.

To my creative and artistic offspring, Imogen and William, who have changed my world and inspire me just by existing; Immi, I can hear your drumming playing on the accompanying soundtrack to this story, and Will, I need your acting talents to narrate the audiobook version (unless Michael Sheen is available).

Dedication

This book is for Sally, who is my everything, and who makes the world better for everyone else too.

Chapter One

Paul Huggins did not like to be described as 'fussy.' He saw himself as precise, methodical, *particular;* and he wanted to be perceived as such. He would manage a smile when his wife Annie lovingly called him an 'old fusspot,' but it slightly annoyed him none the less. He would have been upset if he had known how many of his colleagues in the Department of Health considered him a fussy little man. Professionally this trait worked in his favour; he was the person every Senior Manager, every Director, even the Minister turned to when an important report needed to be written. He could be relied upon to do a thoroughly professional job which made those above him look good when they took credit for his work.

Paul sipped at the tall glass of beer. The Korean Air departure lounge in terminal two of Seoul's Incheon International Airport was luxuriously comfortable, designed to give travellers a relaxing start to their journey. It didn't occur to him that he only had the Elite Lounge pass because he should have been travelling with the Minister. Paul had never encountered such VIP treatment before, and he felt slightly annoyed with himself that he didn't enjoy it more; it seemed to him like an upmarket bar with some expensive chairs instead of the oasis of pampered luxury he had always imagined such places to be. Paul adjusted his tie and checked the sleeves of his suit jacket. He was surprised everyone else was dressed so informally. Unconsciously he tapped his jacket over the inside pocket every thirty seconds or so to reassure himself his passport and ticket was still safely in his possession.

On the whole he was pleased with how his trip had gone. Although he had travelled around Europe for family holidays and the occasional work meeting, he had never visited Asia before. The G20 Health Innovation meeting here in Seoul was his first long haul work trip. As a born and bred Londoner Paul was used to being in a busy metropolis, but so many of the details were different he found it dis-orienting at first; the language of course, but the signs, the lights, the cars, the food, were all similar but *unusual* compared to home. He had been unprepared for the humidity in this city in September, and grateful for the ubiquitous air conditioning. Fortunately, almost all his time had been spent either in the hotel or at the convention centre, although the Minister had managed a bit of sightseeing with his favourite female staff member as well as photo-ops with his Korean counterparts.

The convention itself had been a triumph for the UK Government contingent. The keynote speech by the Minister, stuffed full of Paul's expert details and with the politician's presentational pizzazz, was lauded by the audience and by the journalists reporting the event. Paul had even got a glowing write up in one of the international healthcare journals.

After an hour or so of dull waiting in the lounge, Paul made his way to the departure gate. He hurried past several gift and food shops, only pausing to browse the shelves with professional interest in the one pharmacy he noticed. The gate assembly area was beginning to fill up with passengers preparing for their long-haul flight. Paul squinted at his smart phone, then jabbed at the screen to bring up his wife's phone number. He always tried to speak to his family when working away from home. He considered the time difference -four pm here, eight am back home, they should all be there to pick up…

'Hi Annie! I'm safe and sound at the airport. Just me, the Minister has to fly to Japan tomorrow at short notice. They didn't need…'

"Was the Minister unhappy with you?"

'No, no, no, no, the conference went really, really well. My speech was very…'

"You gave the speech?" She sounded surprised.

'Well of course the *Minister* gave the speech, but I wrote…'

'Why did *you* have to go all that way then, dear, if you weren't giving the speech?'

'We were re-writing the speech right up until the last minute. I co-chaired the roundtable discussion in the afternoon, which was remarkably interesting; officials from twenty national health ministries…' Annie cut him off again.

"When will you be home?'

'Ah…boarding in about an hour, twelve-hour flight, transfer at Schiphol...I'm aiming to get through the door about six am.'

'Try and keep the noise down when you come in, I'll be asleep. I've a busy day ahead, big client meeting! Anyway, I've got to dash and get ready, lots of love, safe travels, I'll see you tomorrow. Here's Jessie.'

Paul called 'Bye! Love you…' but Annie had already gone.

'Hi Dad!'

'Hey Jessie! How are you my lovely girl?'

'I'm good Pops. Why aren't you on video-call? Show me the pictures!' Jessica's passion was photography – life was all about the visual medium for her.

'Err, hang on.' Paul jabbed at the smart phone again. 'There we go.' The image of his older daughter appeared on the screen in front of him. His younger daughter Sophie wandered across the background.

'Hey Sophie, I'm at the airport!' She waved with the hand that wasn't holding her breakfast bowl.

'Reverse the camera dad, so we can see the view.' Jab, jab. 'Ooh, cool!'

Paul chuckled, 'I'm at the departure gate. It'll be a little while before we start boarding yet.'

'Swing it round. So, when will you…OH MY GOD! Sophie look! Dad, go back, go back!'

Confused, Paul slowly panned the camera back across the room.

'There, stop! Soph, its them, isn't it?'

Paul turned down the volume on his phone as his daughters began gabbling excitedly to each other.

'Dad, film them!' squeaked Sophie. 'Click on the video button!' Jab, jab.

'Who is it?' Paul found he was whispering into the phone for fear of drawing attention to himself in an airport full of strangers. Looking over the top of the phone he realised he was aiming the camera at a couple about twenty metres away. Both were tall and beautiful; both casually but impeccably dressed. Her face was half hidden by stylishly massive sunglasses and an iridescent baseball cap; she stood mannequin still. His face however was on full display; he was flashing a shockingly attractive smile at a stewardess who was looking quite flustered. Paul noticed how the man even gave his head a small shake to show off his perfect mane of blonde hair to best effect.

'It's Jasper and Tor!'

'Who? Oh, those people you two always get obsessed about on Insta-thingy?'

'Oh, Dad! They are, like, the biggest influencers on social media. On. The. Planet. I mean, like, wow.'

'He is sooo gorgeous…look at him…and she is a proper supermodel Dad, you know that? They call her the Swan – she is so graceful. All the best models work for her company now.'

As Paul looked up from his screen, he realised Jasper was moving away from the boarding desk. Tor glided ahead of him to a small table and arranged herself elegantly into a chair. Already seated at the table was another woman who had been tapping at her phone but dropped this into her bag and picked up a large camera from the table when she saw Tor approaching. Jasper pulled from his pocket a small bottle which Paul recognised as the expensive vodka available in the Departure Lounges. Jasper drank most of its contents.

'The Swan, eh? Well, she is certainly a bird with a long neck. Who's that with them?' Although Paul had no interest in internet celebrities, he was enjoying this shared moment with his daughters; these had become increasingly rare as they went through their teenage years.

'That must be Charlotte, Jasper's half-sister; I read her blog. It's all very dramatic really, they've only recently met up; Jaspers Dad must have been shagging around twenty-odd years ago, and pretended she wasn't his. She grew up in a small flat in Croydon. Anyway, she travels with Jasper now, acts as his official photographer.' Jessica looked quite cross. 'She really isn't that good at it.'

'Aww, jealous, big sister?' Sophie laughed.

'No! well, yes, but really, she just is not very good - technically I mean. Her Depth of Field is always wrong; she has no idea about lighting and shadow; I'm much better than her.' Sophie laughed at her sister. 'I am!' Jessica protested. 'Lucky for her those two are totally photogenic. They don't take a bad picture. That's all she photo's, then posts it on Jasper and Tor's media sites.'

'Lucky too that her brother is a handsome millionaire internet sensation as well.' Paul realised this sounded quite envious. The girls laughed anyway. Paul looked again at Charlotte. ' Why are her eyebrows painted like that? How much make up is she wearing?'

The teenagers rolled their eyes and groaned. 'Oh, Dad you are so OLD! Everyone wears that much make up now. Besides if I had to sit next to Tor all day long, I'd want a bath full of makeup on my face. How can anyone compete with that? Send me the video, Dad; please?' Jessica gave her father her best 'puppy dog eyes' look. Jab, jab.

Paul let his daughters chatter on for a little while, feeling a warm glow of paternal satisfaction. He continued filming the other passengers as the crowd swelled, trying not to make it obvious that Jasper and Tor were the focus of his attention, although several other passengers were clearly filming the two celebrities as well. After he had sent them all the video footage and the girls had said something about editing software, they chatted on about their day ahead at school until Annie reclaimed her phone and they finished the call.

Paul wasn't much of a people watcher, and the public infatuation with celebrities left him baffled, but he could recognise how strikingly good looking both Tor and Jasper were. Jasper's eyes were an intense ice blue. It was impossible to describe his jawline and cheekbones as anything other than chiselled. His physique was long and toned, and he took every opportunity to run his hands over his torso, trailing his fingers from his sternum down across his six-pack stomach and coming to rest on his belt buckle. Tor was statuesque, an athletic looking physique, six-foot-tall, pale skinned, and her stillness made it seem she was carved from stone. Her facial features seemed symmetrically perfect making her an ideal blank canvas for hair and make-up artists the world over, but when her honey-hazel eyes were captured by a photographer the model could not be mistaken for anyone else.

On top of their physical beauty the pair exuded an air of such complete confidence in themselves that it was easy to see why they and their adoring fans could believe that the world and everything in it existed just for the convenience of Jasper and Tor.

Charlotte was physically different from her half-brother, a whole head shorter, with a sturdy physique and darker of hair and skin colour. Paul did get a glimpse of similarly blue eyes under thick false eyelashes. She was possessed with a nervous energy, constantly fidgeting in her chair, her hands continuously working her camera, her gaze butterfly-flitting around the room without settling.

A short time after finishing the call with his family Pauls' seat number was amongst the earliest to be called to board. Jasper, Tor, and Charlotte had been first.

It was only later, as the plane's engines powered up at the start of the runway and he was pushed back in his seat that he felt a cold stab of guilt as it occurred to him that he may have broken the law. His phone was now on airplane mode, stowed in the overhead locker – there was nothing he could do about it now.

Chapter Two

Paul would have been surprised to learn his prestige seat was not typical for business travellers, especially not for civil servants. This had been a perk of the trip being planned around a government minister who wasn't high ranking enough to get his own jet.

In the seat beside him was a mature white-haired woman in an elegant, dark coloured travel suit. On entering the aeroplane, she had carefully settled herself into the window seat, arranging a book and a bottle of water into the pocket in front of her before leaning back in her chair and closing her eyes, remaining quite still until after take-off. Once in the air she opened her pale eyes, eased off her flat soled lightweight shoes and looked around. After surveying the cabin her gaze settled on Paul. She observed him for several moments and then she spoke.

'Are you a nervous flier? Or are you feeling unwell?' Her voice was clear and steady. Paul was familiar with this type of well-educated English accent; many of his colleagues and seniors in the civil service sounded the same.

'Er, no, flying doesn't bother me.' Paul loosened his tie as an embarrassed flush started to rise across his neck to his cheeks. He nervously rotated his wedding ring and drew in deep breaths.

'Well, something is upsetting you. You haven't stopped fidgeting since we took off. I don't want to sit next to someone who's about to throw up or pass out.'

'No, I'm perfectly well, it's just that... you see, the thing is... actually... um...'

'Spit it out man,' she said, not unkindly.

'Well, I work for the Department of Health and Social Care. I was on an official trip with the Minister of State, it went really well, and I just called the family to tell them I was on my way home and…' Paul proceeded to explain about the video he had sent to his daughters. 'And I've just realised they will be posting them onto social media!' He sighed.

'And?'

'Don't you see? We've had all kinds of training about this, and the consequences they've threatened us with don't bear thinking about.'

'I am still mystified as to what you are worrying about.'

'Personal data! If my daughters have posted the footage online, which I am sure they will have done, and they've put these celebrities' names all over it, I will have been responsible for a clear breach of personal data rules! Storing the information without consent, making it public, identifying the individuals - oh, I'll be in so much trouble!'

'Tell me about your job at the Department of Health.'

Paul began to talk nervously. He described his role as a Senior Public Health Analyst, how he had worked his way slowly up through the Ministry in Whitehall, eventually becoming an advisor to the Minister. He talked about how he had to keep resisting the attempts to move his job to the office in Leeds, and after a while he began to effusively talk about why he felt his job was so important, the benefits he was bringing to the general public, even the government policies he had helped to shape. It occurred to him later that nobody had ever really asked him about his work before. At least not anyone who had waited around to hear the answer.

The woman listened attentively, occasionally asking a few careful questions. Eventually she said,

'Presumably then, your role comes with a certain degree of security clearance?'

'Err, yes – you have to be vetted and have a security level to brief members of the government. Why do you ask that?'

'My name is Cecelia and among other things I used to be a lecturer. I specialised in international politics and law although I've been retired for a year or two. You have nothing to worry about concerning that video; these people live their lives in the public domain, the filming took place in a public space, and if they have their own publicist with them they have probably already posted almost identical videos themselves. They can't complain about similar footage being in existence from other people's mobile phones.'

'Oh! Oh my! Yes of course. Oh, thank you, that is such a relief. Phew! Ha ha!' Paul rolled his eyes and sighed happily.

Cecelia called out to the stewardess. 'Excuse me, could I have a glass of the Veuve Clicquot, and a brandy for my friend here.'

Paul was about to decline the drink when Cecelia said quietly, 'rather than that video you should be much more worried about having spent the last half an hour telling a complete stranger about your very important government job and your high-level security clearance.'

'Oh. Bugger.'

Pauls eyes darted around the cabin while has mind churned over Cecelia's last comment. He noticed several of the seats close by were unoccupied – probably where his colleagues would have been sitting if they hadn't altered their travel plans. A Korean businessman by the opposite window was snoring rhythmically, a small empty wine bottle rolling across his tray table. The other passengers in view were either asleep or immersed in their in-flight entertainment systems. For a while there was silence between them as Cecelia immersed herself in her book and Paul drank his now welcome brandy.

Once his drink was finished Paul turned nervously to Cecelia. 'Could I ask…?'

'Oh, don't worry. Your information is safe with me. Fortunately for you there is no-one else within earshot and I am…' she smiled widely '…the very soul of discretion. But perhaps you should be a bit more cautious in future? Now, back to my book.' She turned away.

'Yes. Thank you so much.' Paul rested his head back. After a few minutes he plugged in his headphones and selected a film from the screen in front of him. Five minutes into the latest Hollywood disaster movie he fell fast asleep.

After three hours flying time Paul was awakened by persistent shaking of his arm. He blinked stupidly as the bright cabin lights came flickering on. He was slightly alarmed by how concerned the steward waking him appeared to be. 'Excuse me sir, we have important announcement from the captain.' Cecelia was bolt upright in her chair, watching every movement of the air crew in and out of the cabin. The steward moved on.

'Wha's going on?' he mumbled, but he was answered with a curt 'shush!'

Over the tannoy came the captains voice, speaking in Korean. After thirty seconds or so he started again in English. 'Ladies and Gentlemen, this is Pilot Captain speaking. I need to inform you of an issue we have with the aeroplane. We have encountered a serious mechanical problem with only one engine. This aeroplane is still ship-shape, but we now will land at the next possible airport for your safety. Thank you.'

'Ship-shape? Are we over water?' Paul asked, craning his neck to look out the window.

'I think he means air worthy.'

The seat belt sign flashed on as the aircraft began to descend quite rapidly. The cabin crew moved hurriedly about stowing equipment and ensuring passengers were safely strapped in. The tannoy buzzed again, a short message in Korean and then repeated in English.

'This is Pilot Captain speaking. We are beginning a direct approach into Manas Airport in Bishkek. Please wear your seatbelt at all times and stay in your seat until we stop. Thank you.'

Paul was staring blankly at the frozen entertainment screen in front of him. Above the panicky chatter from the other passengers throughout the aeroplane he heard Cecelia say very softly, 'Fuck.'

The steep descent caused a sharp 'pop' in Pauls ears as the air pressure changed quickly. From the back of the economy seating section came the mandatory wail of a small child struggling to acclimatise. Paul could sympathise, but he was glad he wasn't in the seat next to that family. After a few minutes of yawning and holding his nose to get his hearing back, Paul turned to Cecelia. 'Are you OK?'

Cecelia had been peering intently out of the window. 'Yes, I'm fine. We don't appear to be in immediate danger after all.'

'But why would you think we were?! The captain said...'

'The pilot may not have chosen to be completely honest with us just in case the truth would cause all his passengers to panic and run riot. Not what you want in any kind of aeroplane at thirty thousand feet. However, from the smooth and controlled descent we can determine the pilot has full control of the aircraft; the aeroplane is not flying erratically so it does seem likely that it the problem really is the fault he has described. It is serious enough though if we have to land so immediately.'

'Oh. I hadn't considered any of that.' Paul took a couple of deep breaths to clear his hearing, and to try and calm his racing pulse. 'Where is it they are taking us?'

'Bishkek'

Paul's forehead creased in puzzlement. 'I've never even heard of a country called Bishkek.'

'It's not a country, it's a city. It is the capital of Kyrgyzstan.'

'I'm not sure I'm any the wiser.'

'Kyrgyzstan is a former soviet republic in central Asia, just to the west of China.' Cecelia explained. 'It is about as remote as you can get, but probably directly under our flightpath, so it would certainly suggest there is a significant problem with the plane if we can't reach any other airport.'

There was a deep rumble followed by a hydraulic whine. Paul flinched and looked around wildly.

'Calm down, that was just the landing gear being deployed.'

'Oh right.'

Paul glanced out of the window. The aircraft was already low to the ground, with patchworks of long straight fields of green and beige interspersed with unswerving roads and occasional villages. Paul could have mistaken the view for the flat verdant countryside of any West European nation until he raised his line of sight to take in the distant white topped mountain range brooding across the horizon.

The ground moved up towards them and everything in view seemed to move faster. A few final wisps of gauzy grey cloud flowed past and then the detail of the countryside below them became clearer, individual trees and bushes becoming distinct in the woods amongst the farmlands. Paul could make out cars and lorries moving sluggishly along the unswerving roads, which threw up a sharp contrast with how fast the aeroplane was still moving. Paul had a panicky perception that the final approach speed seemed much quicker than he remembered from previous flights.

A narrow road and the boundary fence whipped across their view through the window, then tyre smudged concrete moved past below. A sharp bump of the wheels touching down once, bouncing, touching down firmly a second time, and then the sharp deceleration of the plane caused the passengers to strain against their seat belts. The braking seemed to go on and on and Paul found he was holding his breath. Finally, the pressure on the straps eased as the pace dropped to a crawl. The aeroplane, surrounded by the flashing multicoloured lights of emergency vehicles, was escorted off the runway and guided to an area away from the terminal.

'Phew! Safely down, then, ha ha!' Paul slapped his knees with slightly sweaty palms. 'Let's hope it's a quick fix. I think that's quite enough excitement for one trip.'

Cecelia put her finger to her lips and said nothing, turning to stare out of the window.

It took two hours before the unhappy passengers were able to disembark the aeroplane. After another hour in a drab departure lounge the flight crew informed the now quite excitable crowd that the engine was not repairable, and another jet was being summoned to finish their journey. The replacement aircraft wouldn't arrive until tomorrow.

Within six hours of their arrival, they found out that civil war had broken out in Kyrgyzstan.

Chapter Three

Nobody was angrier about the interruption to the flight than Jasper. From the moment the announcement was made that the plane was not immediately repairable he began to harangue the cabin crew, demanding immediate solutions to get them flying again no matter what. Every attempt to pacify him was met with louder and increasingly foul-mouthed shouting by him; ever more senior airport and flight staff tried unsuccessfully to reason with him as his temper tantrum got worse, until it got to the point where he shoved the Airport Director and tried to throw a punch at the Pilot. The scene was gradually the focus of a ring of faces, and as Jasper's voice got ever louder all the remaining passengers had joined the crowd to become passive spectators of the commotion caused by the agitated Englishman. Individuals safely towards the back of the crowd laughed and made a few jokes at Jaspers expense; a few brave souls in the front row occasionally raised their phones to take pictures but no-one decided to join in. There was a collective 'oh!' of surprise when Jasper swung his fist, at which point Tor and Charlotte dragged him away to a quiet corner of the hall. The crowd broke apart, chattering excitedly. Paul watched as Tor shoved him into a chair, placing both her hands on either side of his face with her thumbs over his mouth to keep him silent as she leaned in to urgently whisper to him. Paul thought he looked so furious he might almost be trembling.

No matter how many times Paul tried his phone it resolutely refused to give him a signal, and he couldn't find any sort of wi-fi signal either. The only stewardess he managed to get anywhere close to in the scrum of desperate passengers shrugged helplessly when he asked for help to phone home. He tried an airport landline telephone he found by the main doors but heard only a repeated beeping when he pressed the numbers. After fruitlessly jabbing the buttons for a short while he was shooed away by a frowning airport employee. His linguistically challenged attempts to borrow the phones of three different Koreans were met with smiles, shrugs and head shakes from two of them when they understood his pointing and miming; the third gave him a blank look and turned away in silence. He had more success with a Dutch family from the flight who at least spoke English. The teenage son had a phone adapted for international travel, unfortunately it had run out of battery power in Seoul Airport and as the boy had fallen asleep on take-off it had not been recharged on the plane. Paul noticed the teenager kept stealing glances towards Jasper and Tor – he had obviously recognised them. The father offered to let Paul use the phone once it had been recharged though, but none of their power adaptors fitted the available plugs.

Eventually Paul approached Jasper, Tor, and Charlotte, feeling oddly shy about doing so. His request to borrow a phone to call home with was met by an angry snort from Jasper and a single shake of the head from Tor. Charlotte smiled thinly at him, but she shook her head also. 'Nah, sorry, my phone ain't working here either, otherwise you could've.'

'Oh, damn.' Paul rubbed his forehead with one hand. He noticed Charlotte's camera bag beside her. 'I don't suppose you have a phone charger in there do you? That young lad…' he pointed at the Dutch family 'has a phone that should work OK here but the battery is dead.'

Charlotte looked excited. 'I've got a battery pack that will do the trick. He's welcome to use it if I can borrow his phone.'

Paul hurried over to the family and brokered the deal. The father introduced himself somewhat formally as Hendrik Van der Molen, his wife Agnes, and his son Jordi. Jordi had clearly explained to his parents how famous these people were, and the boy was overjoyed to be introduced to these global celebrities. While Charlotte attached the phone to the battery pack Tor started talking to the star-struck Jordi, treating him to the full supermodel smile. Her Australian accent was a surprise to Paul; he had assumed she was American for some reason. Jasper appeared to be sulking and took no part in the conversation.

'Jordi, is it?' Tor tilted her head slightly to one side as she spoke. 'Good onya for sharing your phone like this. Where ya from, Jordi?' She indicated the empty seat opposite her.

The teenager, flushed and thrilled, perched on the edge of the chair and began chattering away while Tor focussed her full attention on him, smiling and nodding encouragingly. His mother watched on nervously.

After a few moments of watching this exchange Paul realised this was a conversation he wasn't a part of. He turned to Hendrik who was still standing beside him. 'Thanks again for letting us use your sons' phone. Holiday trip was it?'

Hendrik had been frowning as he stared out of the distant window towards the main runway. From here they could see the back of the brightly coloured 'Welcome to Kyrgyzstan' sign over the Arrivals door. The metal framework was slightly rusted, and the bare boards of the sign were ragged and patched with multiple repairs. It took Hendrik a moment to realise Paul was speaking to him. 'I'm sorry?'

'Your visit to Korea – was it a holiday with the family?' Paul nodded towards Jordi and Agnes.

'Ah, not exactly, no. I work in the pharmaceuticals industry; our visit was for a job interview. My family came to see if they would be OK living in Korea for a couple of years.' Hendrik's English carried only a hint of his Dutch accent.

'Oh, I see. Did they like it, then?' Paul asked.

Hendrik shrugged. 'I am not sure yet – we agreed to discuss it when we got home. What do you do, Paul?'

'I, ah…' Paul remembered the embarrassing conversation with Cecelia on the aeroplane… 'I work in healthcare. Err, hospital management actually.'

Paul was quite pleased with his quick-thinking white lie; it was based near the truth without giving away too much about himself. His self-satisfaction waned over the next ten minutes as Hendrik enthusiastically questioned him about medicine procurement procedures in UK hospitals.

Eventually Hendriks questions ceased, and he took to frowning once more at the view through the floor-to-ceiling window. 'Have you noticed that no other aircraft has arrived or left since we got here? It's been a couple of hours now. I wonder if that is usual here?'

Paul puffed out his cheeks. 'Who knows?'

By now the smartphone had enough power in the battery to get working again. The first use it was put to by Jordi was to take a selfie with Tor, which she agreed to with only a slight hesitation. She did put on her trademark sunglasses again for the picture. Jordi instantly posted the image onto his social media accounts. "Wow!!! #tor #jasper #kyrgyzstan"

Tor retrieved the sim card from her own phone and put it into Jordi's device, then punched in two numbers and sent two texts. Once she was sure the messages had been sent she carefully deleted both the messages and the phone numbers from Jordi's device. She did save another number in his contacts file. 'Can't be too careful, right? I couldn't leave my friends number on ya mobile. As a thank you though - I have put my VIP fan club details in here for you!' Jordi blushed and grinned again. Tor removed the sim card and returned the phone.

Charlotte took the phone next, attaching a cable and spending some time uploading some image files to a website. Paul was twitching to get a chance to use the phone, so the extended wait was excruciating. Charlotte then made a call. 'Mum? Its Charlotte! I had to borrow a phone…it's OK, I'm fine, I'm still with Jasper and Tor…nah, we're not there yet, the plane had to make an emergency landing. Manas International Airport in Bishkek, Kyrgyzstan. Bishkek, did you get that? Let the aunties know! They reckon they can't fix the plane, so they'll send a new one for us tomorrow. No, he's…not happy. Have a look at the pictures online OK? I have to go now.' Charlotte looked at Paul who was trying to stop himself from reaching for the phone. 'Bye Mum, see you soon!' Charlotte finished the call.

Paul grabbed the phone and almost whimpered with frustration when he saw the battery was nearly dead again. 'Give it a minute,' suggested Charlotte. Paul closed his eyes and counted to sixty.

It took another two more minutes after that before the phone was back to enough power to make a call and Paul dialled his home number, then redialled it after Charlotte reminded him to use the international dialling codes. He realised when the phone went to voicemail that it must be early afternoon in the UK so nobody would be home. He left a short message about the emergency stopover and saying he would be a day late. He then tried to ring Annie's mobile but again only got through to her voicemail. He was startled to hear her voice even on the recorded message; she suddenly seemed an awfully long way away. Again, he left a brief message explaining his predicament and promising to ring again when he could. He reluctantly gave Jordi back his phone.

When it was clearly understood that the Korean Air jet was not leaving any time soon the crew, with much pleading, persuaded the reluctant airport staff to unload the luggage. Paul watched a little white truck pulling a train of empty trolleys snake its way across the tarmac and come to a stop beneath the rear of the Korean Air jet. One of the Korean flight crew supervised the passenger luggage removal, and Paul could see him shouting and gesticulating at the airport team who seemed to be working with great haste and little care.

More multi-lingual announcements by the air crew informed the restless crowd that the Airline had arranged for them to be fed and sheltered overnight at the airport hotel. In amongst the repeated apologies for the inconvenience they were told they would be moved in groups to be booked into their rooms and then have a meal arranged. In typical airline style, First and Prestige class passengers were called first to collect their bags from the baggage hall. Only one carousel was running. With their recovered suitcases in tow the passengers were shepherded in small flocks into a long, low-ceilinged corridor harshly lit with glaring neon strip lights which led to the Excellence International Airport Hotel. The rattle and rumble of suitcase wheels and footsteps on the rough concrete floor echoed loudly in the confined space. They emerged from this dull, functional passageway into a massive, ornate reception area opulently decorated with gleaming marble on the walls, gold coloured metal fittings and thick, highly patterned carpeting.

The hotel manager had reacted with heroic calm at being presented with two hundred and thirty unexpected guests for the night and swiftly managed to arrange accommodation for all of them. The Korean Air stewardesses marked up their passenger manifest with room numbers and promised to call each of them as soon as they had more information about the new aeroplane before setting off to collect the next batch of passengers. 'Please to be staying in the hotel. We may have to summon you most quickly.' The stewardess seemed nervous but determined.

It was only as Paul stood outside his hotel room and looked down the endless empty corridor of identical doors that he realised that he hadn't seen Cecelia since they had left the plane.

Once inside the hotel room Paul immediately moved to the desk, swung his flight bag off his shoulder, and picked up the telephone receiver. The wall mounted TV set had switched on automatically when the door had opened, and a welcome message was scrolling across the screen. Paul's attempts to dial directly out to an international number were unsuccessful. He rang the switchboard number indicated with a headphone symbol on the keypad, and after a determinedly hanging on for more than a minute managed to speak to the hotel operator. In heavily accented English the female voice apologised that 'no telephones work outside the country. Please to try again tomorrow.' As Paul replaced the receiver with a deep sigh he realised he was still holding his suitcase. Unthinkingly he let go of the handle and it dropped onto his foot.

After a few moments of hopping and spinning while clutching his toes he tried to sit on the edge of the bed but misjudged the distance and slid slowly and inelegantly onto the floor emitting some Anglo-Saxon swearing. He eased off his shoe and massaged his foot. That'll bruise, he thought mournfully.

After a few more moments feeling sorry for himself, Paul heaved himself off the floor. He removed his other shoe and placed the pair against the wall near the door, aligned together most precisely. He carefully removed his suit and arranging the trousers and jacket on separate hangers, he hung them in the wardrobe, straightening them with care. Once this was done he opened his suitcase, took out his large, well-stocked washbag and limped into the ensuite bathroom. Shortly after Paul had turned on the shower the TV screen flickered, and the channel changed to its default international news service. Being an American channel only ten minutes of every hour was given over to news from Asia. When the ninety second report into imminent war breaking out in Kyrgyzstan came on Paul was rinsing shampoo out of his eyes and ears. By the time the same report came up again an hour later Paul was sprawled naked across the bed, snoring resonantly.

Chapter Four

Paul was woken from a frantic dream about Annie insisting on using the wrong colour spanners by a continuous trilling noise. As he rolled stiffly off the bed he wondered blearily what the time was and stumbled to the phone on the desk.

'Is that Mr Huggins?' the male voice spoke in clear English which was not what Paul had anticipated.

'Yes, Paul Huggins speaking.'

'My name is Fitzroy Campbell; I work at the British Embassy in Kyrgyzstan. I need to speak to you urgently. Could you come down to reception?' The refined accent reminded him of Cecelia, oddly.

'Um, yes; yes of course. Just give me five minutes.'

Paul selected the cleanest underwear from his suitcase and hurriedly dressed, putting his suit on again and taking a moment to select his favourite tie. He was meeting someone from the British Embassy after all.

As he rode the lift down to reception he felt a wave of relief wash over him. The Embassy staff would sort out their travel arrangements no doubt. He should probably mention he was a fellow civil servant to Mr Campbell just to make the right impression and to get on his good side. With a name like that he was probably from Scotland, Paul mused, although the voice on the phone had had no trace of a Scots accent. Most likely from a well-to-do family, bundled off to a posh boarding school at an early age, then a degree at an Oxbridge University had all served to instil a cut glass accent in his speaking voice. The Diplomatic

Service always took the brightest and best graduates from the top Universities in the UK but having the right family connections didn't hurt in that career path either. On reflection, perhaps he wouldn't mention his civil service job.

Walking out of the lift Paul scanned the faces to find Campbell. He could see a huddle of locals, either hotel or airport staff, gathered around a TV screen in one corner. A Korean couple he recognised from his flight were hurrying towards the corridor leading to the airport, dragging their small suitcases behind them. There was even an African businessman and a smartly dressed local near the reception desk talking to a grey-haired lady he suddenly realised was Cecelia, but no sign of the diplomat. He made his way over towards them.

'Hello Cecelia, I'm glad you are here. I got a call from some chap from our embassy to meet him down here; you haven't seen him, have you?'

'I'm Fitzroy Campbell, this is my local interpreter, Taalay Maksat.' Maksat smiled politely and bobbed his head. Paul stared dumbly at the black hand extended towards him. He slowly took it and felt a firm grip shake his whole arm.

Paul spluttered in his confusion. The mental picture his imagination had built of a British diplomat did not align with the reality that was standing in front of him. His voice rose to a squeak. 'Oh, ah, right, sorry. When I saw you…I just thought…you'd be…um…Scottish?' Paul would later realise that since he had first learnt to speak, this was the most stupid thing he had ever said out loud.

Paul looked into Campbells' eyes just as his face formed a mask of stillness for the briefest moment; and in that fraction of a second Paul knew he had been marked down as inherently bigoted. He felt the fiery flush of embarrassment rising from beneath his collar to consume his cheeks.

'Do you mean you thought I'd be white? I'm named after my paternal grandfather who emigrated to Britain from Jamaica in the early Nineteen Fifties. My mothers' family came to the UK from Barbados around the same time. I grew up in Nottingham, Mr Huggins.' Campbell had obviously grown used to explaining his heritage; this was a well-practiced diplomats' statement. His face took on a serious expression. 'Anyway, I was just briefing Cee - I mean, Ms **Eriksen** here, about the current situation and now I need to talk to you and the other Westerners still in the hotel. There is a large meeting room in the business centre just through those doors. Please wait for me with the others in there, I will be with you in a few moments.' Campbell turned away with his Kyrgyz assistant and reached for his mobile.

Cecelia turned and walked towards the meeting room. Paul hurried to catch up with her.

'Just then, I didn't mean…' he started helplessly, just as Cecelia reached the glass door. She regarded him coolly for a moment.

'No, I don't suppose you really did. But it isn't me that you need to persuade of that, is it? Its him. Because you just gave a quite good impression of being prejudiced.' Cecelia opened the heavy door and walked through.

The far end of the room was taken up by stylish and uncomfortable looking chairs and sofas. Closer to the door a large solid-looking board room table surrounded by twenty or so plush office chairs took up most of the space. Gathered at one end of this table were the Van Der Molen family, as well as a huddle of four young women Paul didn't recognise. At first glance Paul thought all four appeared to be in their late teens or early twenties. They were dressed in walking boots and fleeces and on the floor close to them was a pile of overstuffed rucksacks and waterproof coats. Two girls looked remarkably similar; both had reddish blonde hair and thickly freckled faces – sisters, he found out later. The third girl was almost a head taller, long limbed, and thin, with her straight dark hair tied back in a ponytail. The fourth girl was a similar height to the sisters, with broader shoulders and a habit of twisting her wrist as she ran her thumb up the inside of the fingers of her right hand.

Nearby Charlotte was applying a dark blood coloured lip gloss to her already heavily painted face. Paul gave a little wave at Jordi who was looking his way, but he got no response; the pale faced boy was actually watching the door behind him. Hendrik did acknowledge him, though. Paul took a seat at one corner of the table. He straightened the desk blotter in front of him, and as he withdrew his hands he noticed the table edge had a loose flap of veneer under which the chipboard material was visible. Paul tried to press the wooden strip back into place. There was a fair amount of tense and nervous whispering going on amongst those around him.

The door swished open again as Tor entered in a perfect catwalk stride, a jacket thrown elegantly over one shoulder. Silence fell as every head was irresistibly drawn to watch as she moved into the room. Paul almost expected her to pause halfway to let some imaginary paparazzi get their photographs, but she moved directly to stand near the table. There was even a couple of gasps from the group of young women as they recognised her. Following behind almost unnoticed came Jasper, looking miserable. He quickly settled into a chair next to Charlotte as a gentle hubbub of conversation resumed in the room. As Paul turned back to the table he noticed Jordi shyly gazing at Tor.

The door had barely closed completely before Campbell pushed it open again. He stepped forward and let the door fully close behind him before addressing the group in a clear and confident voice.

'Thank you for gathering here everybody. My name is Fitzroy Campbell, and I am the Diplomatic Service Officer with the British Embassy in Kyrgyzstan. I am here to ensure you safely manage to leave the country. As you are most likely aware by now the difficult political situation in Kyrgyzstan has deteriorated to the point where civil conflict has broken out.'

Paul's jaw dropped and his mouth opened to form a perfect 'O' as he let out a little squeak of surprise. The lack of response from anyone else made him realise they all knew this already.

Campbell ignored this noise and continued. 'Most of you arrived on the Korean Air jet last night, but unfortunately you won't be able to rely on the airline to get you out again. This airport was closed a few moments ago and no new flights will be allowed in or out for the foreseeable future.'

The room erupted in a babble of voices, with several people jumping to their feet. Campbell raised his hands.

'I will answer your questions in a moment, one at a time please; please! Thank you. Just let me say we are putting a plan into operation to get you out another way. As there are neither Dutch…' (he nodded towards the Van Der Molen family) 'nor Australian..' (He looked at Tor) '…embassies in Kyrgyzstan the British Government have offered to assist with the evacuation of citizens of those countries.' Hendrik and Agnes happily stammered out a grateful acceptance. Tor was still and silent. Campbell paused for a moment as if giving her the opportunity to respond, but when she remained impassive he continued. 'We have been in contact with the Governments of those countries to let them know you are safe and that we are helping you. We have also advised Korean Air that this group of their passengers are now under the protection of the British Embassy.'

Cecelia spoke. 'I expect Korean Air's insurance company will be hugely relieved. What has happened to the other passengers from our flight?'

Campbell replied with a rueful smile. 'All the other passengers were Korean nationals. They and the Korean crew have been evacuated on the last flight to leave a few minutes ago. Earlier today the Chinese government offered safe passage into their country for any Asian citizens wishing to leave Kyrgyzstan; the two countries share a border. It is no coincidence at all that there has been an Air China jumbo fuelled and ready at the end of the runway for two days now; they were anticipating this. The offer of safe passage to China was very pointedly not given to any Europeans or Americans.'

'Are there are any other British nationals still in the country?' Cecelia asked.

'Not that we're aware of. The Cubitt sisters and their friends here…' Campbell indicated the four young women '…arrived at the embassy this morning. Most foreigners have been leaving the country over the last few days…'

Jasper slammed a fist onto the table noisily. 'Enough of this crap. What's the plan to get us home? And why isn't the Ambassador here himself to look after us instead of sending some…*minion*…to sort this out?! Don't you know…' Charlotte grabbed his sleeve forcefully, interrupting his diatribe. Jaspers' head snapped around to look at her, and after a moment of eye contact between them, he subsided into his chair.

Paul shamefully recognised the mask of stillness Campbells face assumed for a moment before the diplomat addressed Jasper directly. 'The Ambassador and most of *her* staff were evacuated when the political situation became too fraught yesterday. The Deputy Head of Mission is next in seniority; he was busy through the night closing up the embassy building, removing sensitive documents, that sort of thing. Along with the last of the embassy protection officers he will have crossed the border by car into Uzbekistan a couple of hours ago. I am the next, ah, *minion* in the chain of command; I volunteered to remain here and get you safely home. And yes, Mr Hood-Dayley; to answer your final question I do know exactly who you are.'

Cecelia drummed her fingers impatiently on the table. 'Mr Campbell, can we focus on the most pressing issue - how do you intend to get us home?'

Campbell paused for a moment, before giving Cecelia a small nod and addressing everyone again. 'There is a military extraction team on its way here now; they should arrive shortly. They will escort us away from the airport and the capital city to a suitable location for a safe airlift out of the country.'

'Hang on, why are we leaving the airport if we are being airlifted out?' Paul blurted out. 'Surely we should just stay here!'

'Exactly!' exclaimed Jasper, waving his hands for emphasis.

'There are three reasons for not staying here.' responded Campbell in an even voice. 'Firstly, no rescue plane can reach us here; the runways already have air defence systems deployed so any unauthorised aircraft attempting to land here will be shot down.'

'Secondly, the airport is a vital strategic target; whoever controls it will have a significant advantage in this war, so there will be heavy fighting around this site starting in the next twenty-four to forty-eight hours. We might end up as collateral damage.'

'And thirdly, if we remain here too long and survive the fighting we are likely to be captured by one side or the other. Both armies would find it most convenient to have some foreign nationals under their control.'

Hendrik looked confused. 'What do you mean "captured"? Why would we be important to them?'

Campbell sighed. 'Look, here's the situation. The current government of Kyrgyzstan has been following a policy of closer links with China; signing trade & investment deals, even military co-operation. This has caused massive rifts with the 'old guard' who still fondly remember the days of the Soviet Empire and want to retain close links with Russia. In simple terms this conflict is between pro-China and pro-Russia forces. The best way for both sides to keep the UN and the rest of the world out of this conflict is to hold foreign hostages. Personally, I would like to avoid spending several months locked in a cellar somewhere being used as a negotiating tool.'

Agnes hand covered her mouth as she gave a little gasp. Hendrik put his arm around her shoulder.

'It won't come to that I assure you' Campbell said quickly. 'Our rescue team will soon be here; they will move us out of harm's way, and we will all leave the country as swiftly as possible.'

Hendrik called out above the rising hubbub in the room. 'What do we need to do, right now?'

Campbell called for quiet again. 'My interpreter is arranging for the hotel to provide a meal for you all; when we are done here I will take you to the restaurant. After that I will ask you to stay in your rooms until the rescue team get here; the hotel telephones are the easiest way to reach everybody. You might consider sorting through your luggage and jettisoning anything that isn't essential; you'll be carrying your belongings around with you for a while so the less weight the better.' His eyes flickered towards Paul for a moment, dressed up in his suit and tie. 'And it would be a good idea to change into your most comfortable travel clothing. Bear in mind at this time of year it can get very cold at night, especially in the mountains. And Kyrgyzstan is mostly made up of mountains.'

Cecelia addressed everyone, her voice cutting across the turmoil of panicky conversations in the room. 'I took a look around earlier on, and I noticed at the front of the hotel there are a couple of shops, at least one of which sells hiking gear.' Her gaze drifted across the room taking in Charlotte, Tor, and inevitably, Paul. 'If anyone needs a coat and some appropriate footwear it would be worth looking there.'

Jasper's anger boiled over once more. 'When did this become a bloody camping trip?' He shouted at Campbell again. 'You should be arranging cars to drive us over the border if we can't fly out of the airport, not babbling on about comfortable clothing! You're fucking incompetent. Do your job man!'

In the sudden shocked silence in the room everyone looked at Campbell. Staring directly at Jasper he spoke softly. 'There are very few main roads out of this country, and all the border crossing points will have been closed off by the time we reach them. They will be considered strategic positions by both sides, keeping foreign soldiers out and supply lines open. An airlift is the safest and quickest route out of the country.'

Cecelia stood beside Campbell and spoke. 'A convoy of cars on the main road to the border will attract attention. It seems obvious to me we need to keep out of sight as much as possible.'

Jasper leapt to his feet. 'I've had enough of this! I'm not taking travel advice from some old biddy and a bloody pencil pusher! We need to get moving, now!'

A booming voice with a strong Welsh accent startled everyone gathered around the table. 'Right! What the fuckin' hell is goin' on here then?'

Everyone turned to look at the man dressed in green camouflage fatigues standing in the open doorway. He was average height with a stocky physique. Black hair and a short beard framed his small featured, slightly weathered face. Grey eyes under heavy dark eyebrows assessed everyone in the room as he stood head up, shoulders back, chest out and feet firmly placed on the floor. He spoke again. 'I am Colour Sergeant Talbot, Forty Commando, Royal Marines.' He raised an angled hand to the edge of his green beret in salute as he looked in Campbells direction. Campbell nodded and smiled briefly but beside him Cecelia cast her eyes down and shook her head. Talbot continued, 'I'm told I swear a lot. I suggest you all get fucking used to it. We've been tasked with escorting all of you safely out of this shithole. I want it clearly understood by each and every one of you we intend to do exactly that. My instructions to you will be clear and precise and for the good of your health you will follow them to the fucking letter. I understand food is being prepared for you. Go and eat, then get your luggage and clothing ready and we will reconvene in the reception lobby in one hour from now. You'll get a proper briefing at that point, so save your sodding questions until then, but we will all be leaving in sixty minutes.' He inclined his head towards the door. 'Now, off you fuck. Mr Campbell, is it? I need a quiet word…'

The effect of this speech on the group was instantaneous. Most people were immediately on their feet, checking their watches and moving towards the exit, an excited chatter sweeping amongst them. Jasper stood open-mouthed for a moment, his particular demands for action overshadowed and forgotten. He looked at Tor who gave an almost imperceptible shrug before she headed for the door. Jasper followed. Jordi scrambled to walk close to Tor, and his parents hurried to keep up with him. Paul let the four backpackers go past his chair before getting to his feet and moving out of the room; this made him one of the last to leave. As he waited for the bottleneck at the door to ease he looked back at Talbot speaking quietly to Campbell and, oddly, Cecelia was still stood with them as well. He realised that Talbot wasn't carrying a rifle, but he noticed a knife sheathed in his equipment belt and a pistol unobtrusively strapped to his thigh. As he moved forward and the noise level in the room diminished he caught a few words spoken by Talbot.

'…a single troop. It means one chopper's enough…' some more words were inaudible and then, '…put a fuel dump in the north country, can't do it on one tank...' then Paul was out the door.

He looked up to see the backs of his fellow travellers as they headed towards a set of large double doors to the right of the reception area. He recognised Taalay waving them over and set off to join them.

The huge empty restaurant was a brightly lit, splendidly decorated room with dozens of tables arranged symmetrically across the floor. Against one wall was a long counter filled with an array of silver tureens with glass tops and gleaming wire racks, most of which were completely empty. One small section had been used to lay out a few varieties of stew and noodle dishes for them. The labelling of each dish was done with a stylish handwritten card, but as this was in Kyrgyz Cyrillic lettering Taalay was calling out the main ingredients of each dish. There was no sign of any hotel staff; presumably, they had prepared the food and then left find safety away from the hotel. Paul realised he was exceptionally hungry as the aroma of the food reached him. The travellers were tightly bunched around the main food bar, but on a separate table close to the door was a huge selection of different types of enticing looking bread of all shapes and sizes. Paul reached out and grabbed a few pieces and started chewing. First he had some small triangular portions that looked a bit like large fortune cookies; Paul was surprised how dry these were. Next he took a large piece that reminded him of an oversized Yorkshire pudding. This was also extremely dry and flaky, and he found it quite tough to tear, but his growling stomach urged him to swallow. The taste and texture resembled stale naan bread. After a few more mouthfuls Taalay approached, looking slightly perplexed.

'Hello again Mr Huggins.' Taalay said politely. 'Bread is important part of Kyrgyz culture and is always offered to visitors to our homes.' He pointed to the large poster above the table. 'This says "Kyrgyz National Bread Selection. For display only. Please collect your food from the counter." This is written in Kyrgyz and in Russian, but I'm afraid there are no signs in English.'

Paul looked at the sign. 'So...does that mean I'm eating the table decorations?'

Taalay nodded. 'Sadly yes. Please...' he indicated the hot food. '...have some fresh Kyrgyz food instead.' Glumly Paul headed to the counter and picked up a large plate.

After two substantial helpings of the different types of stew Paul felt much better. The first was unquestionably lamb, the second might have been beef, but he wasn't quite sure, but with both the noodles went down a treat. He helped himself to some nuts and fruit even tried some fresh Kyrgyz bread and found it to be delicious.

Seated at the table in front of him were the four backpackers. It was impossible for Paul to avoid overhearing their excited conversation, and the rush of young voices talking over each other made him think wistfully of his daughters. Through the course of the meal, he learned a lot about each of the women. The tall girl was Annabel, who barely picked at a small plate sparsely furnished with some nuts and a solitary apple. She spoke little, but her eyes were regularly drawn nervously towards Tor and Jasper a few tables away. From the teasing Annabel received from the others it became apparent she was starting a career as a model and had even been recently signed to Tor's agency; but she was refusing to introduce herself to Tor, to the astonishment of the others. Rachel, the older of the two similar looking sisters was obviously close friends with Annabel and seemed more lenient on her; Belinda the younger sister and Moira were more persistent. Rachel, Belinda, and Moira were enthusiastically wolfing down large amounts of stew in contrast to Annabel's token morsels of food. Apparently Moira and Belinda were about to start degree studies on their return to the UK; their flight home had been scheduled for tomorrow and they talked nervously about being home in time for the start of term. Rachel seemed to take the role of older sister for the group; chiding their table manners when food was spilt, urging Annabel to eat more and Moira to eat more slowly. Paul found the obvious friendship amongst the group uplifting, whilst pangs of homesickness for his own family washed over him with increasing strength.

Eventually, feeling quite bloated, Paul sat back. Most of the rest of the group had finished eating and had left the restaurant but the four backpackers had returned to the serving counter. They were filling some plastic boxes from their rucksacks with leftovers and putting a few apples and apricots into their pockets. This struck Paul as eminently sensible; the immediate future was quite uncertain, and he couldn't be sure when his next meal might be. As the group of four finished and made for the door Paul found a large roll of silver foil behind the counter which he used to wrap up some bread, nuts, and fruit. The lamb stew was all gone, but a lot of the beef variety remained, so he extracted some chunks of meat from it and wrapped them separately. He then bundled all the items into a single large package and headed for his room.

Chapter Five

Paul hurried along the carpeted corridor with his food parcel balanced on one hand, his room keycard clutched in the other. After fumbling the door handle for a moment, he pushed the door open with his shoulder and moved inside. Placing the foil package on the desk, he paused to remove his tie and mop a few beads of sweat from his forehead. After a moment of thought he delicately removed his jacket and placed it on a hanger in the wardrobe, then he picked up his suitcase and heaved it onto the bed, dragging the large zip around three sides and throwing the lid open. One quick look at the contents of the case made him realise he wouldn't be able to take all its contents with him. He grabbed his wallet, pocketed the keycard, and left the room. He paused to ensure the door was locked behind him, took one step away, turned back to check the door again, and then moved off.

The main entrance to the hotel led out to a wide driveway under a brick canopy designed to resemble a round Kyrgyz tent, but at twice the size. The outside of the canopy was brightly painted, but the underside was bare brickwork. Along the front of the hotel were a number of boutique shops built to service tourists. Checking his watch Paul moved through the hotel lobby at a shuffling run. Still thirty-five minutes left before the departure deadline, but Paul could feel a panicky urgency rising inside him. Once through the main revolving door Paul turned left and hurriedly made his way past a gift shop and a tour guide office to get to an outdoor clothing store. All of the shops were deserted. Outside of the air-conditioned hotel the afternoon autumn sun warmed the air, and Paul could feel his cheeks flushing slightly as he hastened along. He was surprised to find the shop door unlocked. A tinkling bell announced his entrance but there were no staff to respond to the warning. Paul scurried through the racks of clothing to reach the rucksacks displayed on the back wall. He randomly picked out the largest one he could see and moved on to the nearby shelves of footwear. He felt prickles of sweat itching his forehead as he bent over, rummaging through numerous shoe boxes. 'More haste, less speed' he muttered to himself and took a deep breath to try and calm the fluttering sensation beginning in his stomach. Finally finding a pair of boots that fitted him Paul stuffed them into the rucksack and moved towards the front of the store to pick out a waterproof jacket. Rejecting as too flashy the neon yellow coat that was the first one he found that was big enough to fit him comfortably, he settled for a dark red coat that was one size too big for him.

As he stuffed the coat into the rucksack on top of the boots he realised he didn't know how much these items cost. Then it dawned on him he had no local currency anyway. His eyes darted to the door, then to the register on the desk nearby, then back to the door. Apart from feeling his eyelids blinking repeatedly, Paul was motionless, paralyzed by indecision. His breathing quickened again, shallow gasps of air revealing his nervousness. He took one step towards the door, stopped, stepped again, stopped.

The inner torment was punishing him even before he committed the theft of goods that he had not, could not, pay for. He felt this to be wrongful and selfish, stealing from an absent shopkeeper; but suddenly he could hear a cold dark thought at the back of his mind to leave and not look back and to hurry up about it. He obeyed the voice of self-preservation. The bright afternoon sun shone directly into his eyes as he stepped out of the doorway. After the relative gloom of the unlit shop interior the glare was dazzling and Paul screwed up his eyes and turned away to regain his vision. He stood still for a moment to master his bearings, shifted his rucksack onto his back more comfortably, and scampered back into the hotel. His shirt was starting to stick to his back from sweat and he felt uncomfortably hot. He wondered if it was as a consequence of feeling guilty.

Back in his room Paul checked his watch again. ten minutes until departure time; he had to hurry. Setting the rucksack on the bed he felt a small wave of nausea rise in him. Was this guilt going to hit him each time he touched the bag? He pulled out the coat and shoes and set them by the door. Now, what to pack? Obviously, the laptop had to go in, no question. Nice and flat, lay that against the back of the rucksack. The power lead as well; this laptop wouldn't last too long without it, it had a rubbish battery. He kept asking for an upgrade at work, but the request never got processed for some reason. He could leave the computer mouse; he wouldn't need that. Phone charger, plug adapter, battery pack, travel towel, travel documents, all of these must be taken with him. His washbag was big and bulky, including as it did bottles of shampoo and conditioner, a can of hairspray, facial cleansing wipes, a tube of toothpaste, a toothbrush, a razor, a can of shaving foam, some rather nice aftershave and a jar of moisturiser along with the fancy grooming kit the in-laws had bought him last Christmas; he put all that at the bottom of the main section of the rucksack. He would need to take a change of underwear and a shirt, actually two of each would be better. He would have to leave the extra shoes though, much too bulky. And the spare jacket. And the spare trousers. But he might need a second pair, so on reflection the trousers go in. Oh, his workbooks! He couldn't leave them behind, they were government property, and these journals of health policy were horribly expensive, so they had to go in. Well two of them went into the now bulging rucksack, the third went into the top pocket. The food parcel went into the webbing pocket on the front of the rucksack. Quick double check. All that was left in the original suitcase was a pair of shoes, a jacket, the rest of his underwear and a computer mouse. He looked again in all the pockets of his suitcase to make sure he hadn't missed anything else. No, all empty.

Paul sat on the edge of the bed and pulled on his new walking boots, hastily tying the bright orange laces which made him think of the neon yellow jacket in the shop and made him feel nauseous again. The shoes he had just taken off he stuffed into the side pockets of the rucksack. He recovered his suit jacket from the wardrobe and put it on and then clawed his way into the voluminous coat. Having zipped his suitcase up and locked it he set it neatly by the bed. He heaved the rucksack onto his shoulder with a grunt and headed for the door.

He had to admit to himself; the rucksack was heavy. Even through the coat and suit jacket the straps pulled painfully on his shoulders and each laborious step along the corridor made the pack thump against his back. He hadn't sorted out the clip at waist level, which was a mistake he decided he would put right later. The walk from his room to the lifts took less than a minute but he could already feel the strain on his thighs and back from the extra weight. Passing a hotel housekeeping trolley Paul helped himself to four small bottles of water and stuffed them into his coat pockets. He felt quite pleased with this piece of forward planning. It did feel less like stealing when taking from the hotel than taking the rucksack did.

As he reached for the lift button the corridor lights went out. A small fizzing sound preceded a battery powered bulb over the Fire Exit sign turning on. The lights on the lift buttons had also gone out. Guessing that power in the hotel had been cut, Paul sighed and headed for the stairs. The stairwell was lit by opaque external windows and a couple of emergency lights. He had two flights to travel down to get to the lobby.

At the turn of the first flight of stairs a sharp gripping pain caused Paul's stomach to heave. Drops of sweat gathered on his temples and he fell to his hands and knees. He rolled the heavy rucksack off his back and a hot wave of dizzying nausea swept over him. He closed his eyes, stretched his neck forward and vomited copiously. He felt a warm splash on his left hand. He opened his eyes to see dollops of sick on his fingers and this, together with the smell of the orange and brown puddle in front of him, caused him to vomit again. His stomach heaved up its contents until it was empty, but still he retched twice more as bile came up to burn his throat. His whole body was convulsed with a trembling shudder as he rolled sideways to lie slumped against his rucksack, one shoe pressing into the small of his back. He laid still; eyes closed again as he tried to recover control of himself. A blistering pain in his head seemed to be robbing him of his senses.

As he started to feel the first semblance of recovery, he heard a noise from the floor below. The stairwell door opened and closed. Paul opened his mouth to call out, but he could make no sound. Rather than hearing disappearing footsteps as expected, rather came the sound of a female voice. The echoing acoustics of the stairwell made it difficult to identify but he knew he recognised it.

'We only have a few seconds, listen carefully. Take this for me and keep it safe. I will make it worth your while.'

'OK' A younger female voice. He had heard that voice before as well, was it one of the British backpackers? Paul wasn't sure; he tried again but still couldn't call out for help.

The first voice spoke again. 'You have to keep it hidden; no one must know about it, or it will ruin everything I'm working on. You have to be determined & see it through, nobody is going to do this for you, you have to take responsibility for getting what you want out of life. Prove to me you have what it takes to stick it out and the sky's the limit for you. We shouldn't be seen together - wait here for a count of ten then come down.' One sets of footsteps walked sedately down the stairs, shortly after the second hurried down.

After a few minutes Paul summoned the strength to reach with a trembling hand for one of the water bottles which had fallen from his coat pocket. He prised it open, rinsed his mouth and spat out the contents. He then took a few sips to clear his throat. It came as a huge relief that the water stayed down. After another sip he capped the bottle and gingerly pulled himself upright. Although his head was throbbing he felt he was now in control of himself, so he slowly and carefully picked up the rucksack and slid it down the stairs. Gripping the handrail to stop himself swaying he moved down one step at a time. He paused on the landing, sipped more water, and repeated the descent process again. Eventually he reached the bottom and pushed through the fire door into the bright sunlit lobby.

Gathered near the main entrance were the rest of the evacuees. Paul was vaguely aware that were several more people in military uniforms than he had seen before. Fitzroy Campbell waved him over. 'Ah, glad you could finally make it Mr Huggins! We were about to leave without you!' A small chuckle ran through the crowd, but no-one was paying Paul any attention. He slumped into a chair as Campbell addressed the crowd again. 'Now that everyone is here Colour Sergeant Talbot will brief you on the evacuation plan. Colour Sergeant?'

'Thank you Mr Campbell. Here's the plan – we will be leaving the hotel immediately and travelling into the mountains to the south. We have identified two possible rendezvous points where we will be able to meet up with the helicopter that can take us safely out of the country, either tomorrow or the day after, depending on the weather. We have procured ourselves a bus from the airport which is big enough to carry everybody. There is a tourist resort in the Ala-Archa valley where we plan to stay the night, and the bus can take us all the way there. That is where the buggering road stops though, so in the morning we will walk further into the mountains to reach our rendezvous co-ordinates.'

'How far will we have to travel tomorrow, Colour Sergeant?' Although Paul couldn't see Cecelia from where he was sitting he recognised her voice. It struck him that hers wasn't one of the voices he had heard on the stairwell.

'The first rendezvous point is eight kilometres up the valley. If that is unsuitable for any reason, the second is a further four clicks beyond that. It's a bit of a hike but we'll make sure we get everyone there in one piece.'

Cecelia's reply was tinged with amusement. 'Don't you worry about me, Colour. I might be getting a bit long in the tooth, but I can cope with a little walk in the countryside.'

'Ah. Yes, Ma'am.'

Jasper called out, 'Come off it Sarge, this is all getting a bit overly dramatic don't you think? This is hardly the evacuation of Dunkirk, ha ha!' Paul could see Jasper sitting off to one side of the gathering, slouched languidly in a soft chair. Even through his dizziness Paul could tell Jasper was inebriated. Just beyond Jasper in Pauls eyeline stood two marines. After Jasper spoke Paul saw them exchange a knowing glance and shake their heads; the taller one puffed out his cheeks, and the smaller, female one rolled her eyes. Talbot stepped quickly over to Jasper and bent over to look him in the eye.

'Listen up, you Pretty-Boy jizzstain. I don't answer to "Sarge" from anybody; my rank is Colour Sergeant. If I like a civilian I let them call me by my first name, which is "Morgan." You? – you can call me "Colour Sergeant."' Jasper flinched and turned away from the ferocious look in Talbot's eye.

Talbot addressed the whole group again. 'Pay careful attention to what I am about to fucking say. Potentially the most dangerous part of this whole operation is the next couple of hours. We have to get away from the airport and the capital city. That's why we have to move at once, before the two armies in this conflict work out what the fuck they are doing and decide to make a dash for this spot. Civil wars are shitshow clusterfucks with nasty little militias popping up all over the sodding place to resolve a few ancient grudges, regardless of the main fight.' He nodded to the marines standing near him. 'Don't be fooled by the armaments these marines are carrying, especially Lincoln over there with that big machine gun on his back. We are not the fucking heroes in some Hollywood movie bollocks come to save the day. We are not here to participate in anybody's shitty war; we are here to get you safely away from it as quickly as possible. Bonus points to us if we can do it without discharging our weapons. Mind you, we can, and we will defend ourselves if it proves necessary. In the meantime, speed is critical, and silence is crucial. we have to do everything we can to be utterly fucking invisible. Do nothing that draws attention to us. We have to move fast and quiet and be gone before they know we were here.'

Campbell spoke again. 'In light of what Colour Sergeant Talbot has just said, I want everyone to turn off their mobile phones and tablets if you have them. Any electronic devices. Even if you don't have a signal in this country, you should disconnect the sim card and battery if you can.' There was a disappointed murmuring from within the group and a loud groan of disappointment from Jordi. 'Your devices might be trackable and could give away our position, even if the phone doesn't seem to work. Any further questions before we get on the bus?'

Paul weakly raised his hand, then stood up so it would be seen. He suddenly felt woozy again as Campbell pointed at him. 'I say, does anyone have an aspirin? I don't feel terribly…oh…' He fell to his hands and knees, pushed his chin forward and vomited what was mostly just water onto the marble floor.

The next few moments were very blurry for Paul as he slumped onto his side, his eyes closed as the thundering pain inside his head consumed him. He heard different voices calling out, most indistinct, but Talbot's was clear as gave out instructions. 'Draws, see to him. Preston, Flo, we need a stretcher, see what you can find. Corporal, you, and the rest of the section get the other civilians on the bus, then take up your positions. Everyone else – gather your things people! Time to leave!'

A few minutes later, having been tended to by the medic Paul was gently manhandled onto a stretcher. As he was being lifted up he heard one marine laughingly say to the other, 'Old 'Double-Tap' doesn't think much of Jasper then?'

'Nope,' came the reply. 'Doesn't seem to be much of a fan of that arsehole. He's quite taken with the Great Dane though.'

By the time Paul was ready to be carried out the rest of the evacuees had begun to embark onto the green Isuzu bus that had been pulled up outside the main entrance under the brickwork tent. A side panel on the vehicle was raised to allow everyone to hastily bundle their luggage in before stepping onboard to find a seat. As Paul was manoeuvred through the wide double doors at the side of bus one of the marines slammed the luggage compartment panel closed.

From inside the airport transit bus Colour Sergeant Talbot grunted as he scanned the approach road ahead. 'Oh, sodding bollocks.' Talbot spoke into his headset. 'Attention squad, we have suspicious vehicle incoming. Defensive positions.' He turned his head towards the female marine in the driver's seat. 'Keep the engine running, Sydney, but put it in neutral. These twats will be jumpy so no sudden movements. Be ready to move off on my command. Take your beret off for now, marine, but don't give up that seat for anybody.' Laid out on the stretcher improvised from a collapsible wooden trestle table which was now strapped to the luggage rack near the front door, and with his rucksack serving as an uncomfortable pillow, Paul had a clear view through the front windscreen. The medication given him by the medic Draws had eased the pummelling in his skull but had left him feeling very weak.

A gleaming Toyota pickup had come racing up the long straight road leading to the hotel and had stopped less than thirty metres away from the bus. Three men had clambered down from the back of the vehicle, and the driver and passenger had joined them in walking abreast along the road. Four of the men carried assault rifles while the fifth who had been traveling as the front seat passenger held a pistol in his left hand. There was an agitated murmur from the passengers as they realised what was happening. Pauls' fevered imagination made him think of black hatted cowboys in the wild west coming into town for a showdown with the sheriff.

Talbot called down the bus, 'Mr Campbell!' and beckoned him forward. Paul managed to hear the whispered question when it came because Talbot was so close to him. 'Do you trust your interpreter?' Without hesitation Campbell nodded vigorously. 'Then I need to borrow him.' Talbot shouted and beckoned again. 'Mr Maksat, is it? Would you come and translate for me please? Everybody else – stay on this bus until I tell you otherwise.' He addressed Talaay directly. 'You will stay behind me at all times. I will keep you quite safe, I assure you.' Talbot moved to the front door, adjusting his green beret. 'Repeat everything I say. Word for word, mind.' He smiled. 'Even the rude words.' Displaying no signs of trepidation Taalay fell into step behind the Colour Sergeant.

As Talbot stepped onto the tarmac, the five men from the pickup were less than ten metres away from the bus in a line across the road, holding their weapons in such a way so as they were not quite pointing at the bus, but could be very quickly. The pickup driver, who was positioned at the end of the line, moved to stand next to the driver's door of the bus. Syd looked down at him through the open window and smiled innocently.

As Talbot and Taalay approached the pistol carrying leader took two steps forward. He clearly hadn't expected to see a man in military uniform in front of him, but he recovered his composure and spoke in a calm manner. Paul could hear his words but did not understand them. Taalay translated quietly, but Paul heard Talbot's parade ground voice loud and clear. Talbot sounded amused. 'Oh, here to protect us, are you? If that's the case you can bugger off, Sonny-Boy, we don't need an escort of any kind, thank you very much. We can look after ourselves. On your way then.'

Sonny-Boy's voice was angrier the second time he spoke. Talbot's tone didn't alter. 'There's no danger round here that I need your help with. You and your little pals get back in your toy truck and run along now.'

Twice more the Colour Sergeant was addressed; twice Talbot replied with a single word 'No.'

For a brief moment Pauls' attention was caught by a movement in his peripheral vision. Turning his gaze slightly he realised he was looking at the drivers' rear-view mirror, and the at this angle he had line of sight of the rear seats of the bus where Jasper, Charlotte and Tor were seated. On the back seat, just like the cool kids on the school bus, thought Paul. The movement he had noticed but which was probably unseen by anyone else had been Tor shakily removing her enormous sunglasses. Paul was struck by how shocked her expression was; her honey-hazel-coloured eyes were wide and staring at the men in the road.

Paul's attention was drawn back to the scene in front of him. Sonny-Boy was shouting now; the pistol being waved energetically. He wasn't brave or stupid enough to point the weapon directly at Talbot. The Colour Sergeant's voice remained calm. And loud. 'Royal Marines! Take aim! Hold your fire!' From either side of the roadway two teams of two soldiers rose from behind the cover that had hidden them from the gang in the road and took the newcomers in their sights. A green land rover that had been parked beyond the Toyota pick-up started up and roared towards the airport bus. Having closed to within twenty metres the vehicle stopped, and the Corporal and another marine leapt out levelled their weapons at the suddenly bewildered men in front of the bus. Sonny-Boy had spun around as the marines appeared; when he turned back to face Talbot he suddenly found he had an extremely close up view of the wrong end of a Royal Marine's pistol. From the driver's seat of the bus, Syd was still smiling at the man in the road, but his attention was taken by the pistol she was now pointing at him. Almost cross-eyed from focussing on the gun, he raised his hands.

'Gently now; stay nice and calm, alright?' said Talbot as he reached down and took hold of the pistol in the hand of the leader. 'Tell your boyos to drop their weapons and move to the side of the bus.' Reluctantly, Sonny-Boy did as he was instructed and silently the men did as they were told. The marines moved in and recovered the dropped rifles before frisking the men and removing further pistols and some knives. 'Corporal! Take a team of four and escort these gentlemen into the hotel and tie them up somewhere. I want to give us a good couple of hours head start before they are on the move again so tie them tightly. Before you go, though…' Talbot leant close and whispered to the leader who hearing the translation snarled and turned away.

The men were led off. Talbot called out to one of his remaining marines. 'Ren, go and move the pick-up into that field. Then drop the keys down a drain and get back here.'

When Talaay climbed back onto the bus he was met by Campbell. 'Are you ok?' asked the diplomat.

'Oh yes. But I do have one question – the Colour Sergeant used a phrase I am unfamiliar with, and I struggled to translate it. What does 'incompetent cockwomble' mean?'

Chapter Six

Paul closed his eyes and drifted off after the gang were led away. After a few

minutes he was awakened by a gentle shaking of his shoulder. He turned his head

to see Cecelia standing next to him, silently offering him a water bottle.

Gratefully he took a small sip, before the bottle was withdrawn. 'Just a little for

now. Nice and easy. You'll soon be right as rain.' She smiled down at him,

briefly, before turning her gaze out through the bus windows. After providing a

second sip of water Cecelia took up the seat next to him.

Within ten minutes Corporal Towne and the other marines had returned. Through

the still open bus door Paul could hear the debrief as all the Marines gathered

around Talbot. Paul turned his head to watch. Towne began. 'Colour Sergeant,

we didn't find any ropes, so we gaffa-taped our friends together in the kitchens.

We didn't cover their mouths, so they were shouting themselves hoarse as we

left. Eventually they will work out they can bite their way free, but it will take

them a while.' He grinned. 'We used a *lot* of tape.'

'Good job. Now Corporal, you and Lincoln take the first Land Rover, call sign

Zulu Two. Jackson, Ren, you are in the second, call sign Zulu Three. The bus is

Zulu One.' There were a few chuckles and murmurs from the Marines that

Talbot ignored. 'Front and rear escort with a rolling roadblock as required. You

know the planned route and destination; we stay away from built up areas

wherever possible but be ready to adjust the route if necessary. We avoid civilian

and especially military contact if at all possible. Porky...' Talbot indicated a tall

slim Marine '...is our designated navigator, all drivers' co-ordinate through him, but keep radio silence unless absolutely necessary – we don't want to draw attention to ourselves.' Talbot glanced at a tightly folded map. 'We have about seventy clicks to travel to our first waypoint at the village of Kaska Suu: then a further eleven to our destination for tonight. If we get separated for any reason rendezvous is the first waypoint in two hours from now. The roads get tougher after that so the second leg will likely take at least another thirty minutes or more. three hours from now it will be getting dark, and we do not want to be travelling at night. Remember; our key objective is safe delivery of the asset out of the country. Any questions?'

'Zulu? Are we doing that one again, Colour Sergeant?' grinned Lincoln. There were guffaws and giggles from several other marines. 'Come on Linc, you know it's my favourite film! 'Talbot chortled.

'Well, if we are doing films again, I have to say, "I love the smell of napalm in the morning!"' The marines laughed; this was obviously a game they had played before. Porky called out in a strong Scottish accent 'they make take our lives, but they'll never take...our freedom!' and Paul realised he could hear laughter inside the bus too; the passengers had all been listening intently to the marines through the open doors and windows. A few more marines called out some quotes. Paul could make out a few – 'Hasta La Vista, baby!' and 'Houston, we have a problem...!'

'Colour!' Ashton, one of the younger marines called out urgently; the others all turned to look at him. He cocked his head and pointed with one finger to the sky. 'I think I can hear something. Can you hear it?'

Talbot turned his head to the north, and everyone fell silent. The only sounds Paul noticed at first was a breeze gently lifting the telephone lines slung between the streetlights near the kerb, the crackle of stiffened leaves on the autumnal trees on the side of the road, and the trilling of finches hopping through the branches. After a few moments of straining to hear he began to distinguish another, more distant sound; every few moments there was a low rumble punctuated with a whomping sound. These came in batches of twos and threes before a period of silence, then they started again.

'Yes, Smoke, I can hear that. That' stated Talbot, 'is shitting artillery fire. That means the fighting has properly started, then.' The quietness inside the bus grew heavier as the atmosphere congealed into a queasy nervousness. The light-hearted banter of the last few moments had been a welcome distraction but the veil over reality was quickly ripped away. The noise of real of warfare was bringing home to everyone the truly dangerous situation they were in.

'OK marines; we are moving.' Talbot gave the instruction and stepped into the bus. Towne and Lincoln jogged off to the Land Rover that had been left in the roadway, Jackson and Ren hurrying in the other direction towards the second vehicle parked behind the bus. The remaining marines boarded the bus and took up vacant window seats, spreading themselves throughout the vehicle. In the driver's seat Sydney checked over her shoulder that everyone was aboard as the doors closed, revved the engine, put the vehicle in gear, and set off. At the top of the windscreen above her head was an image of the Kyrgyz Republic flag, a yellow sun on a red background, with a message in many languages including English "Welcome to Kyrgyz Nation." Paul gripped the edges of his stretcher, suddenly fearful he may be shaken loose and thrown to the floor as the bus accelerated. However the top speed of the bus was quite sedate and after a few minutes he relaxed slightly as it became clear he was safely strapped in. It wasn't the most comfortable position to be in however and he did feel rather foolish to be laid out in this manner. Whenever the bus was in gear the radio seemed to be jammed on or played automatically. Sydney had turned the volume as low as it would go, but there was a non-stop background sound of local and foreign pop songs.

The airport approach road ran in a straight line, heading west for a mile or so, lined on one side with tall, white-barked birch trees and on the other by shorter conifers. The top halves of the deciduous trees were bathed in golden evening sunlight making them resemble burning torches. At random points illuminated advertising boards would appear at the roadside, all written in Cyrillic lettering, mostly with pictures of European looking men and women wearing business suits. The only exception was one enormous poster featuring wrestlers and the smiling face of an elderly man beneath a very tall white hat with a black brim.

Paul could see the Land Rover Zulu Two maintaining its distance about half a mile ahead of them until they reached the intersection with a main road running north to south. After radioed instruction from Porky the second Land Rover overtook the bus and became the lead vehicle while Zulu Two was stopped at the junction. This precautionary roadblock turned out to be unnecessary; no other traffic was on the move so there were no other vehicles to get in their way. Once the bus had passed by Zulu Two followed closely behind.

As the bus swung around the long curve to join the new road and began to turn south sunlight swept across the inside of the bus, flaring off the metal window frames. Once they were on the new road they were driving directly towards the dropping sun which was framed in the centre of the windscreen, almost parodying the image of the flag stuck to the top of the glass. Paul noticed Sydney sliding on a pair of sunglasses. Blinking, he turned his head to the left to avoid being blinded by the glare. As his eyesight began to focus beyond the bus window he saw a flash of orange light in the distance which, for a fraction of a second, he thought was sunlight illumination once more. The flash was followed by a large billow of black and grey smoke that suddenly bloomed into the sky, seemingly froze for a second, and then expanded and drifted slowly with the wind. The point of impact was probably more than a mile away from the road in an empty field. 'Look…look!' he croaked, stretching an arm to point at the explosion, but many of the other travellers were already staring in that direction. About five seconds after sighting the detonation there came a loud crack followed by a rumbling sound. There was a series of gasps and squeals from the civilians. Then came a second and a then a third blast, each in line with the first but the shells landing further north each time and further away from their position.

Most of the other passengers had cowered away from the left side of the bus, and Mr & Mrs Van Der Molen had even thrown themselves to the floor and then dragged a complaining Jordi down with them. Cecelia however was standing, one knee resting on the seat close to the window to get a clearer view. When no more shells were forthcoming she turned to sit down again and caught Paul's eye. As she spoke Paul got the sense she was thinking out loud as much as engaging in a conversation with him. 'They were lining their shots up on the airport I would say. Pretty shoddy marksmanship in my opinion, but they will have found their range now.' She glanced up to see both Campbell and Talbot were within earshot. 'Those shells came from the south. That puts the artillery within the capital city, which means they were government forces doing the firing. It also implies that the government believes the rebels are about to overrun the airport. Good job we left when we did. Thank you for getting us away from there, Colour Sergeant.'

Talbot nodded curtly and grunted. 'Yes ma'am. This makes no difference to our plan though. We avoid the city and get as far south as we can in daylight. '

The small convoy rolled on down the empty road for another fifteen minutes as flat farmland drifted past the window. A couple of tiny villages each of a dozen or so single storied dwellings only briefly interrupted the view of the landscape.

Another large junction, another change of direction and they headed west for a couple of miles before the road curved to the south again. At one point they were approached from behind by a dusty old Mercedes saloon. The passengers on the bus watched tensely as the vehicle drew closer to the rear Land Rover, which moved to block its path around the bus; but when the message came through from Lincoln in Zulu Two that it was clearly a family of locals in the car rather than soldiers or Sonny-Boy and his team the Mercedes was allowed to overtake and accelerate away. As the vehicle moved past Paul got a glimpse of a woman in the front seat hunched over a map and in the back two young children with suitcases and bags piled up around them. No cars passed them going the other way.

After ten minutes or so they approached a T junction onto a wider main road. Porky relayed a message from the lead vehicle to Talbot. 'Zulu Three are reporting a traffic jam heading west, Colour; The map tells me this is one of the biggest roads in the country running from the capital to the border with

Kazakhstan. Everyone is trying to get out of the city I guess. Zulu Three say they can't see the cause of the blockage, but they have caught site of a few uniforms on foot in the road.'

'Fuckin' shit-bollocks. What about the other carriageway? Sydney! Slow down before we reach the junction.'

Porky relayed the question. 'They say there is no traffic heading east, Colour Sergeant, but we would have to get through the traffic jam to reach it.'

Talbot cocked his head slightly. 'Tell them to make a *fuckin'* bus sized hole then, would you? Get Zulu Two to go help.'

The second land Rover sped off as the bus slowed to a walking pace, although the junction was within sight now. The motionless line of cars and vans was visible on the road ahead. Paul could see the two dark green vehicles trying to edge into the traffic, and two of the marines were moving amongst the stationary cars waving and pointing. As he watched he could make out a few drivers standing beside their cars. As the bus came to a stop a few metres away from the main road he noticed three or four men in grey jackets and caps moving through the traffic towards the junction. Talbot spotted them as well and grabbed his rifle.

'Draws, Smoke, on me; we have to intercept potential hostiles in the traffic.' He hurried out of the bus and set off at a sprint towards the main road followed by the two marines.

A voice called out from within the bus and Talaay came running to the doorway. 'Wait, wait! They are policemen, not soldiers...!' He jumped out of the bus and ran forwards. 'I can help; I can help! Salam, Salam!' He waved his hands in the air as he ran. After a moment's hesitation Campbell jumped off the bus and jogged after him.

The policemen who had been cautiously approaching the Land Rover crews were shocked when three more foreign men in military uniforms came running at them with rifles raised. They were totally bemused when a Kyrgyz national, shouting and waving and being chased by a foreigner, followed shortly behind.

The passengers on the bus were all straining their necks to get a view of the scene playing out on the road ahead of them. After a few moments Jasper cried 'Oh sod this, I can't see a thing' and strode off the bus. He was swiftly followed by Charlotte & Tor, and eventually by the rest of the civilians who all stood in the roadway to view the spectacle. Only Cecelia remained in her seat beside Paul on his stretcher. Sydney was still in the driver's seat, Preston, and Orlando, the two other marines remaining in the bus, had taken up firing positions in the middle and rear of the vehicle.

After only a few minutes it seemed Talaay was successful in resolving a potential standoff with the local law enforcement. With placatory gestures and soothing language, he managed to insert himself between the marines and the policemen and with the slightly breathless assistance of Campbell persuaded the local policemen that they were in no danger. As this conversation had continued the stranded drivers and passengers from the nearby gridlocked vehicles had been drawing closer. Soon there were more than sixty faces looking on and straining to overhear the discussions. There seemed to be no panic in the crowd but rather a nervous uncertainty of what to do; caught helpless in a succession of extraordinary and dangerous events this spectacle of the policemen and the foreigner soldiers was almost a moment of light relief and might even offer some sort of resolution to their current impasse. Stoically the crowd of becalmed motorists looked on in near silence. A few who had come from stationary cars further west occasionally looked worriedly in that direction; those from the eastern end of the traffic jam glanced back that way.

Once the police had been persuaded to assist, the marines set to work breaking the traffic jam. Zulus Two and Three formed a temporary roadblock across the road and half a dozen cars were moved to the roadside or rolled forward to create a bus sized hole. The Police managed to get the crowd of onlookers to move out of the way as well and using a few tools from the Land Rovers and a lot of Royal Marine brute strength a section of corrugated metal barrier in the central reservation was removed. As the Marines moved back to their vehicles Paul heard one of them call out 'Hudson! We are leaving!' which garnered the reply 'Ooh! That one's from Aliens, isn't it?'

As Talbot began to jog back the bus passengers stood in the road started cheering and clapping. Talbot was apoplectic.

'Are you fuckin' *SHITTING ME!?* Get back on that *fuckin'* bus immediately you bunch of absolute *SHITTY ARSEWIPES!'*

They jostled and scurried to get back inside like disorderly children caught in the act of bunking off school. The bus moved off, crossing the blocked carriageway while the Kyrgyz police waved them through and then the vehicle headed west along the empty side of the road. Zulu Two and Zulu Three swiftly followed, as did the Kyrgyz cars nearest the gap in the barrier. The policemen continued to direct more traffic through the gap.

After only a short distance the visibility on the road rapidly deteriorated as a thickening cloud of smoke drifted towards them and a pungent acrid smell filled the bus. Less than half a mile along the road the reason for the traffic jam became apparent. Directly in front of the first stationary vehicles in the queue was a huge crater in the road with the twisted and still burning remains of four or five cars strewn around the edges. Some of the vehicles were utterly destroyed, blasted into jagged fragments by the explosion, slavering tongues of fire whipping back and forth from the furnaces at their core. One car, its cabin flaming like an erupting volcano, was oddly unaffected at the front end with the headlamps, number plate and manufacturers emblem clearly visible and unmarked by the blast or the fire. Another vehicle had been hurled into the opposite carriage way onto its now flattened roof, its blackened underside glistening with leaking oil and fuel. Beside it was another mangled wreck. The dead body of a young woman was in the passenger seat of the damaged car; her corpse held upright by the seatbelt although the head was drooping to one side. Long black hair fell across half her face concealing one eye, the hair ends drifting into her open mouth. The visible eye was half open, staring into the footwell. She was wearing a light summer dress, which fluttered at the collar and hem in the breeze. One pale leg was twisted up onto the dashboard from the force of the crash, giving the figure a grotesque appearance of calm relaxation. Sydney carefully manoeuvred the bus around the vehicle wreckage and the remains of the cars' contents that had been blown out in the explosion.

Paul felt the heat from the burning vehicles as the bus passed the crater, and a noxious mix of different burning smells assaulted his senses. The overwhelming odour of burning rubber and molten metal hit him first. He suddenly had a shocking mental image of the two young children surrounded by bags in the back of the Mercedes saloon, but now they were morphing into his daughters at the same age in the back of that car. He shakily put his hand to his mouth and wondered if he was going to be sick again. He perceived the smell of burnt toast and frying steak, realised what had generated the odour, and did indeed throw up.

The other passengers sat cowed and shaken. The Van der Molen family were clutched together for mutual protection, heads bowed, perhaps in prayer and to block out the sights and sounds outside. The hitchhikers sat motionless with wide eyed terrified expressions on their faces. Cecelia sat upright with a handkerchief held tightly over her nose and mouth, eyes narrowed as she closely observed the scene outside the bus. Talaay had turned away, the back of one hand pressed up to his mouth as his body shuddered with silent sobs. His tears splashed onto his wrist and fingers as Campbell tried to comfort him with an arm across his shoulders.

Talbot stood in the gangway at the front of the bus bristling with an ice-cold fury. When he spoke, his voice was quiet but clear. He was more terrifying now than at any time previously. He pointed at the carnage outside. 'Take a good hard fuckin' look. Go on, look! D'ya see the burning bodies? Or rather, the *bits* of fuckin' burning bodies all over the road? This war is fuckin' *real* you stupid *bastards*. As long as we are in this fucking country we are a target. We need to be invisible. You silly twats running around like a bunch of cunts in front of a fuckin' crowd is not being invisible. You fuckin' cunts. From now on you will stay fuckin' hidden. You won't move a fuckin' muscle unless I tell you, and you will treat every instruction from me like the fuckin' word of God. I'm the fuckin' cunt that's gonna get you fuckin' cunts out of this fuckin' country! IS THAT CLEAR!?!'

There was a muted murmur of agreement from the passengers. A movement in the corner of his eye caught Pauls attention. Glancing up he saw reflected above the drivers' head in the rear view mirror the image of Charlotte working her camera; it was positioned surreptitiously in her lap as if trying to avoid drawing attention to herself. Paul couldn't be sure what the camera was aimed at, but he doubted Talbot would be amused at having his picture taken at this moment.

The bus moved far enough past the crater for the smoke to begin to thin, although the stench lingered inside the bus for a long time after they had moved out of the cloud. The intrusion of gleaming sunlight through the windows came as a shock after the near dark of the smoke and ash moments before.

'Colour Sergeant!' Sydney called out. As Talbot turned, she pointed through the front window of the bus at a bloody faced man in the road waving and staggering towards them. Behind him was a severely damaged car that had been caught in the explosion and whose rear wheels were perched on the barrier in the centre of the road. The vehicle was leaking fluids across the tarmac. There were people still inside. Paul could hear Talaay behind him whispering frantically to Campbell.

'Go round him Syd, we are not stopping.' growled Talbot. Paul tried to raise a voice in protest but could only manage a squeaky croaking sound. Cecelia stood up from her seat and took a step forward to bring her close to Talbot. She spoke softly.

'We don't have to stop the whole convoy. But perhaps one of the Land Rover teams...?' Talbot looked at her for a moment, sighed and then nodded. 'Syd, pull to the side of the road.' He spoke into his headset. 'Zulu Two, see what you can do to patch up the people in the banjo'd car ahead of us to the right. THAT CAR

ONLY, is that understood? We are not here to give treatment to every Tom, Dick and Harriet that wanders past. I'm sending Draws to you. You stay for twenty minutes maximum, then you LEAVE and make for the rendezvous.' Talbot turned his head. 'Draws, grab your medical kit, you and Zulu Two see what you can do for those people.'

There was a chorus of 'Yes Colour Sergeant' as the bus slowed again. At the edge of his hearing Paul caught Tor's angry whisper from the back of the bus. 'Why the fuck are we stopping again? They're supposed to be rescuing *us*…'

As Draws made his way to the door Talaay scrambled out of his seat, pushed past the other marines, and ran after the medic. Campbell stood as if to join him, but Talbot put his hand up to stop the diplomat. 'He can help them; you can't. Sit down.' Speaking again into his radio headset Talbot called out to the Corporal. 'Mr Maksat is coming to translate for you. Keep him safe and sound and make sure you get him back to us in one piece, would you?'

Through the front windscreen Paul could see the injured man grasp at Draws for help, then turn to Talaay as the interpreter spoke urgently to him. All three men moved towards the vehicle on the crash barrier as one of the Land Rovers pulled up close by. The second Land Rover, Zulu Three, moved carefully past the bus and continued along the road. Sydney revved the bus engine, put it in gear, and began to move off as the pneumatic hiss signalled the closure of the doors. As they moved on Paul had a fleeting view of the marines and Talaay helping the bleeding passengers to extract themselves from the wrecked car. Zulu Three was shrinking into the distance ahead as the vehicle accelerated quickly away and the bus followed more sluggishly. A number of cars that had followed them onto the carriageway accelerated past them on the wide road including an expensive looking hatchback that recklessly overtook them on the grass verge, bouncing alarmingly on the rough terrain and then swerving wildly in front of the bus once the tyres hit the tarmac. It sped off, its vibrating exhaust pipe noisily belching gusts of dark smoke.

Before they had travelled another kilometre Porky the navigator was giving instruction to Zulu Three, now several hundred yards ahead, to take a turning off the main road. The bus followed shortly after onto what turned out to be a narrow country lane heading south, surrounded by flat fields on either side but heading towards a range of mountains which dominated the skyline ahead. Zulu Three stayed closer to the bus now; they encountered virtually no other traffic for the next hour. Their carefully navigated route took them mostly away from towns and villages. They travelled along several roads that each ran arrow straight for several kilometres before a junction or bend would angle them in a slightly more easterly direction, but always moving south towards the rising, darkening line of peaks that filled the entire horizon. The bus swayed more on the dusty narrow back roads and the journey became noisier. Squeaks and rattles from the seats and window frames inside the vehicle combined with louder tyre rumbles and the wash of gravel bouncing off the underside of the wheel arches.

Shortly before the twenty-minute deadline elapsed there came a static disrupted radio message; Zulu Two was on the move again.

Three quarters of an hour after passing the crater in the road the view of flat strip fields that had been the constant scenery since leaving the airport started to give way on one side to jumbled rocks and brown foothills. The road started to slope upwards, and the bus engine growled with the extra effort of the climb. After another twenty minutes they drove into a village at the mouth of a narrowing valley with bare rock mountains framing the settlement on either side. Below the level of the road a river gushed through a deep ravine, the powder blue water bouncing over the boulders strewn across the riverbed as it rushed toward the plains. At the end of the village they pulled off the road into a car park, just before a large red STOP sign beside two red and white striped mechanical barriers that blocked the roadway into the mountains. Nearby was an intricately carved wooden kiosk only big enough to accommodate one person, and beside this was an enormous faded wooden sign with Russian lettering carved into it. The barest hint of colour around the edge suggested this had once been brightly painted in red, yellow, and black but many seasons of weathering had taken its toll on the decoration.

'I wonder what the sign says?' Paul mused aloud to himself. He was slightly surprised to receive an answer from Cecelia as he hadn't realised anyone was listening.

'It says "Welcome to Ala Archa National Park." In big letters, and "please pay the entrance fee of eighty, ah…somethings… at the kiosk" in the small print underneath.'

'Eighty somethings?'

'My Russian is pretty good, but I couldn't translate the name of the local currency.' Cecelia seemed slightly disappointed at displaying this gap in her knowledge. They both swayed slightly as the bus came to a halt.

Colour Sergeant Talbot called out a series of instructions to the marines. 'Smoke, Flo, back down the hill fifty yards, eyes on the road. Porky, Preston, recce the road ahead about one hundred yards. All of you stay out of sight, bone domes on, safeties off. Jackson, Ren, check that kiosk is empty and get those barriers open.'

As the marines ran off strapping on their helmets he addressed the passengers from the front of the bus. 'This is our rendezvous point. We will wait here for thirty fuckin' minutes or until Zulu three catches the fuck up with us.' He nodded out of the window. 'I am sure we all want some fuckin' fresh air. If you *must* get off the bus *do not* leave the fuckin' car park! It looks like there is a toilet over there for anyone who desperately needs a piss.' There was a scurry of activity as the civilians made for the exits. Paul reached out for Cecilia.

'Can you help me? I really need some fresh air.' Cecilia untied the rope that had been holding him firm to the wooden frame and helped him slowly rise into a sitting position. His head swam for a moment, but it quickly passed. 'Thank you' he muttered. Grabbing a bottle of water he unsteadily made his way off the bus helped by Cecilia on one side and Sydney on the other.

The coldness of the air outside the bus took Paul by surprise. The last hour of their journey had taken them to a significantly higher altitude which was contributing to the lower temperature, as was a chill breeze that was flowing down the valley. The sun remained bright in the sky but was clearly dipping towards the western horizon. Paul was helped to a bench on the grass verge. Once he was safely seated Cecilia headed off towards the toilet on the other side of the road, accompanied by Sydney. Paul took a few small sips of the tepid water and some large lungfuls of the sharp air and tried to clear the fuzziness in his head. He glanced to his left up the valley and noticed for the first time the taller distant mountains were capped with snow, the evening sun shading them to cream and vanilla. He belched softly.

Autumn was more advanced in the mountains than it was down on the plain. The higher slopes that Paul could see around him were dominated by fir and pine trees but down near the road there was more variety of species. Some of the nearby deciduous trees were already bare of their leaves, while most of the rest had begun the autumnal colour change to present splashes of yellow, orange, red and brown all around him. Paul lent back on the bench and closed his eyes as cool gusts of wind played over his face. From the gorge behind him came the occasional rumbling gurgle and splash of the stream. After a few moments he became conscious of the murmuring choir of the wind in the leaves. The gentle chiming hiss washed over him like a soothing balm. The anxious tension that had subconsciously gripped him since the aeroplane had landed was gradually being eroded. He remained motionless for several minutes, lost in the wind and water song.

Slowly rising to the surface of his reverie he opened his eyes again and looked afresh at the countryside around him. He was unlucky to be here in this valley, in this country. It was only because of a series of misfortunes and awful events outside of his control that he was here. He was the wrong person in the wrong place at the wrong time. He had to leave as swiftly as possible, and he wouldn't be coming back. He wanted desperately to be at home with Annie and the girls *right now*. And yet somehow the undeniable beauty of this foreign landscape sparked an emotional response in him. In this moment he felt a pleasure in his surroundings that was unlike any connection to nature he had ever experienced.

He blinked repeatedly, swallowed, and stretched his face to prevent the liquid gathering under his eyelids from spilling onto his cheeks.

Turning to his right, he had a view of the haze rippled plain they had travelled across and some way off to the north there was a haze above the city of Bishkek, the capital that the marines had been so keen to avoid. A few paces away Colour Sergeant Talbot was scanning this view with a pair of binoculars, Fitzroy Campbell stood beside him. Gingerly Paul rose to join them. Talbot passed the binoculars to Campbell and pointed. 'A lot more smoke there now, see? More artillery strikes most likely. I pity the poor bastards underneath that.' Talbot turned to Paul. 'Hello Mr Huggins. Try not to fucking vomit on me, there's a good chap.' Paul shook his head but didn't trust himself to respond further.

In the southern corner of the car park was a small platform, decorated at the back with a crude wooden frame in the shape of a cartoonish mountain range, decorated with a mosaic of tiny gaudily coloured ceramic tiles. Jasper and Tor were cavorting in front of this while Charlotte took pictures. Knowing smiles and 'V' signs from Jasper, enigmatic pouts and the famous 'Swan' pose from Tor; chin up, arms curved out at shoulder height with fingers stretched downwards like feathers on a bird's wing. Charlotte was swapping between her camera and her smartphone to take the photos. 'Incon-*fucking*-spicuous as ever. *Fucking* children.' Talbot muttered. Campbell glanced across, then went back to surveying the landscape below. Looking at Jasper and Tor it struck Paul as odd to choose the fake mountains as the backdrop of the photos instead of the real ones that were all around them.

The other passengers were milling around near the bus, but they were avoiding getting back onboard; there was still a noticeable sulphurous odour lingering inside the vehicle, as well as the acid stench of vomit, even though Sydney had opened all the doors and put the ventilation system on full blast.

'How much further to the resort, Colour Sergeant?' Campbell asked, returning the binoculars to Talbot.

'About another eleven kilometres, straight up this pissing valley. That's about a thirty-minute drive, depending on the state of the road.' Talbot replied.

Campbell turned to Paul. 'How are you feeling Mr Huggins?'

Paul managed a little nod. 'Yeah, improving, thanks. Pleased to be off that bus for a while.'

Talbot grunted. 'Don't get too used to it.' He raised a hand to his ear and inclined his head. The distant growl of a diesel engine echoed faintly up the valley. 'Time to get back on the bus, here comes Zulu two.'

Within ten minutes the second Land Rover had skidded to a stop in the car park. An ashen faced Talaay slowly exited the vehicle and headed silently to the bus. Talbot spoke briefly to the other occupants of Zulu two; Corporal Towne confirmed that the injured survivors from the damaged car had been given first aid and left in the care of the policemen that Talaay had rounded up and shepherded along the road. The Colour Sergeant began barking orders to the rest of the military team.

'Mr Huggins!' Paul looked up to see the Draws, the Marine medic approaching him. '" Double Tap" wants me to give you a quick once over before we get underway. Try and stop you chucking up on the bus again.'

'That's the Colour Sergeant, is it? "Double Tap"?'

Draws grinned. 'Royal Marine tradition to have a nickname – at least, it is in 'C' company. Let's have a look at you.' Draws tilted Paul's head back, gently pulled up an eyelid, then checked the pulse on his neck. 'You're improving I'd say. Pupil dilation is about right, pulse is steady, your temperature has gone down. How do ya feel?'

'Better than I was at the airport. Still a bit shaky and nauseous though.'

'Well, it's been an exciting day. Get some more fluids in you now, some food later on, you'll be fine by the morning.'

Paul nodded towards the medical kit bag slung over Draw shoulder. 'Do you have anything in there to settle my stomach? Perhaps some bismuth subsalicylate? I should be able to keep that down.'

Draws looked at him thoughtfully, re-appraising him. 'Well, yes, I have some Pepto Bismol tablets, that's the same thing. I've not heard anyone else use that terminology since I finished my medical training. Are you a doctor?'

Paul tried not to look too pleased with himself. 'Not a doctor, no; I studied Pharmacology at university.'

'Aah.' Draws handed him a pink tablet. 'Pity we didn't know that before we settled on your nickname.'

'Wait, what? We've all got nicknames?'

Draws grinned at him. 'It keeps us amused.' He glanced towards the civilians across the car park. 'Some are obvious; some are a bit more convoluted. Collectively you civilians are the Herd; we Marines are the sheepdogs.' He indicated Tor, Jasper, and Charlotte. 'She wants to be called the Swan, but you don't get to pick your own nickname, so to us she's 'Goose.' He's 'Pretty-Boy' of course; and he's lucky its only that. And the other one? With that much warpaint on her face she has to be 'Geronimo'.'

 Paul surprised himself by snorting with laughter. 'So, what about me?'

'If we'd have known you were good with medicines, then maybe you would have been, oh I don't know, 'Drug Lord'? 'Pablo Escobar' maybe?' As it is though…' Draws picked up his bag and moved off, '…you're already known as 'Sicknote' I'm afraid.'

'Really? Oh.'

The passengers were herded reluctantly back onto the sour smelling bus by Campbell. Draws made a quick check on each civilian starting from the back seat and working his way forward. Finally he reached Cecelia who was sat directly behind Sydney in the driving seat. Talbot was stood nearby with Campbell and Talaay across the aisle, so Paul dropped into a seat a couple of rows back. The medic seemed to spend slightly longer talking to Cecelia before reporting to Talbot. 'Good to go, Colour. A couple of the civilians are a bit shaky, so I've thrown them some paracetamol for now, I'll check on 'em again tonight. Pretty-Boy is looking a bit pale, but he wouldn't take any pills.' He nodded at Paul, 'Sicknote seems bit better too; nothing to stop us carrying on.'

'Very good. Alright Sydney, get us underway.'

The overworked engine took a few turns of the starter motor to fire into life. Sydney revv'd it a couple of times before putting it into first gear and releasing the hand brake. Land Rover Zulu Two accelerated through the propped open barrier with the airport bus following behind.

Progress up the valley was slow. Although the road surface was mostly well tarmac'd and even, the incline was steep in places and the narrow road twisted and curved, frequently crossing the river on thin concrete bridges set at right angles to the road. The labouring bus had to swing wide and corner sharply to line up safely with each one.

After they had travelled for only a few minutes steep snow-dusted peaks began to loom up on either side of the valley, threatening to cast them into shadow as the sun drooped towards the western ridgeline. No other traffic was moving on the road; they passed the odd parked car as well as the occasional shack used as accommodation shelters in the tourist season, all currently empty. Twice the bus slowed to a crawl as the Land Rover in front stopped to avoid small groups of wild horses meandering across the roadway in front of them. On each occasion the animals were unfazed by the appearance of the noisy vehicles in their territory; they barely glanced at the machines as they plodded onto the strips of grass meadow beside the shallow river.

They drove for several more miles, long enough for Paul to start to feel nauseous again. There came a squawk on the Marines radio, an alert from the leading Land Rover. They were approaching a cluster of low buildings scattered either side of the roadway, all seemingly deserted. They passed one hundred metres further on and the road widened into a car park and then stopped. Another red and white striped metal barrier blocked access to a wide dirt track that continued along the valley. Across the car park was the entrance to a small hotel, built to resemble a Swiss alpine chalet with a steeply sloping red roof that stretched to the ground on two sides and with intricately carved, heavily weathered wooden panels decorating the balconies.

On either side of the concrete steps that lead up to the hotel entrance was a large plinth more than two metres high. Each supported a stone statue. On the right was a huge-horned mountain goat, its head raised as if sniffing the air and surveying the distant peaks. On the left was a Snow Leopard, crouched low on its haunches with its long voluminous tail curling behind it. The head of this sculpture was turned towards the road, its painted eyes staring intently at the approaching travellers. Lamplight was shining through a few of the windows on the ground floor of the hotel, although the windows on the upper floors were dark.

The Land Rover and the airport bus came to a halt a short distance away from the hotel. Talbot's voice cut across the bustle and chatter of people preparing to disembark. 'Sit still!' there was a sudden silence as all eyes turned to the Colour Sergeant. 'No fucker is to get off this vehicle until I say so! Understood? Marines, dispersal positions around the car park except Sydney and Porky, you stay in the bus and make sure no-one from our party tries to wander off. Mr Maksat, Mr Campbell, would you come with me please? It looks like somebody is home, so I might need your help to negotiate a block booking. The rest of you - just sit quietly for few more minutes while we make sure it's safe.'

Talbot chose to ignore the muttered swearing emanating from the back seat of the bus and strode off into the fading blue light of dusk.

Chapter Seven

Although the disappearance of the sun behind the mountains heralded a further drop in temperature, Paul was finding it uncomfortably stuffy in the odorous bus. He stood to open the small vent at the top of the window beside his seat and breathed in the cool fresh air gratefully. Taking another small sip from his nearly empty water bottle he surveyed the view away from the hotel. Close by the car park the power lines that had run parallel to the road all along the valley disappeared into the side of a bulky metal transformer. Beyond this grey box, on a patch of ground cleared of trees and bushes was a sizeable telecoms antenna which must have been as tall as the hotel itself. Two cables came out of the power transformer, one to the antenna, the other to the hotel. Paul guessed that the antenna was placed to have line of site as far up the valley as possible, but it was now getting too dark to be able to see much into the distance. There were no lights showing in the wilderness beyond the hotel.

Others on the bus must have noticed the telecoms antenna too; at least three different mobile phones emitted pings as people surreptitiously turned on their devices and found a network connection.

'Let me remind you, you were told to keep your mobile phones switched off.' Sydney called out from the front of the bus. Paul wasn't sure who all the activated phones belonged to, but judging by the frantic shuffling in his seat and the embarrassed blushing, Jordi's was one of them. His father gave him a few sharp words of admonishment.

A few minutes later a bright light was switched on above the doorway to the hotel and Talbot, Campbell and Talaay came down the steps followed by a man and a woman. Sydney and Porky opened the bus doors, and everyone hurried off the bus. Once the bus was empty Talbot called out 'Listen up! We have arranged food and accommodation for the night, most of you in the hotel, a few will be in the tents...'

'Yurts.' Talaay interrupted.

'What?' Talbot glared at him.

'They are called Yurts.' Talaay said.

'Alright, a few of you will be in the fuckin' - *Yurts* - near the river.' He gave Talaay a sideways glance. 'They look like big round fuckin' tents to me. Mr Campbell can give you some more details. Marines, with me for a briefing.' Talbot stomped off to the far side of the car park followed by his team.

Fitzroy Campbell indicated the two people beside him. 'This is Chingiz and Orla.' On hearing their names, they waved at the new arrivals. 'Unfortunately, they don't speak much, if any, English. They are the *married couple* who run the hotel.' Paul realised the emphasis Campbell had put on their marital status was to prevent any assumption that they might be father and daughter. A quick look at them both revealed there was little physical resemblance between them. Orla was in her mid-twenties, her broad, smooth, and pale features marked her unmistakably as being of Eastern European or Russian descent. Her angular cheekbones were made more conspicuous by the deep dimples at the edges of her constant teeth-flashing smile. Her plump lips framed a surprisingly wide mouth. No part of Orla could be described as thin, but the large pregnancy bump that encircled her body was more prominent even than the substantial bosom that rested above it. In contrast Chingiz was in his mid-fifties, lean and muscular, and could have stepped straight out of a local tourism poster. He was even wearing the traditional Kyrgyz tall white hat. His features denoted a central Asian heritage, the ruddy cheeks and crows' feet around his smiling eyes suggested a lifetime of outdoor work. The lower part of his face was adorned with a long but neatly trimmed grey goatee beard and moustache.

Campbell had begun to explain the arrangements for their stay in more detail when Orla recognised Jasper and Tor with a loud gasp. Ignoring everyone else she hurried over to them and clasped Tors right hand in both of hers. Tor gave her a tight little smile, but then looked puzzled as Orla began speaking quickly at her in a language Tor didn't understand. When Tor eventually pulled her hand away Orla turned admiring eyes towards Jasper and reached out to put a hand on his arm. With a small twitch of his mouth that barely passed as a smile he patted her hand twice and moved his arm away. Talaay began translating Orla's' excited welcoming speech to the two celebrities but Tor interrupted him, 'Yes, thanks very much, can we get inside now?' Talaay translated, Orla blinked once, and then with the huge smile returning to her face she extended an arm to indicate the way in.

Beyond the reception area most of the ground floor of the hotel was taken up with a large room that was part dining room, part sitting area and part open space beside a wall-to-wall window that presented an uninterrupted view up the valley. The far wall was dominated by a huge open fireplace. The wall nearest the entrance supported a glass fronted display case. Paul expected this to be filled with animal head trophies, horns, and antlers but instead the shelves were full of gold and silver medals, cups and figurines on pedestals and framed certificates. The trophies gleamed even though the dates on some of them spanned more than three decades.

Once everyone was assembled in the main room Campbell finished briefing the travellers. Paul was surprised to find he was to share a Yurt with Campbell and Talaay; the only other Yurt accommodation given out went to Jasper and Tor. Charlotte didn't seem happy to be sharing a room with Cecelia on the top floor of the building, but she didn't object. Presumably, she was discontented at being separated from Jasper and Tor and given less salubrious lodgings or perhaps wasn't pleased that the two female Marines were bunking in that room too. The rest of the Marines were given the large dormitory room on the first floor, whilst the two guest rooms on the second floor were shared by the four trekkers and the Van Der Molens, respectively.

A meal was to be prepared for them by Chingiz, but it would take a while get ready. The guests were invited to settle into their rooms and freshen up before returning to the dining room in a couple of hours. Just as Paul was about to follow Campbell and Talaay out to the path that lead to the Yurts he heard someone call his name. He turned to see a smiling Cecelia and a concerned looking Orla approaching.

'I was trying out my rather rusty Russian on Orla here and in the course of the conversation I mentioned that you had been sick. She seems concerned for you.' The young woman waddled up to Paul with a look of great pity on her face, chatting away at him. Before Paul could protest she had grabbed his rucksack out of his hands and began lugging it outside. 'I may have mixed up the words for "sick" and "ill" I'm afraid.' Cecelia called after him. By the time Paul had hurried outside he found that Orla had thrown his overstuffed rucksack into an ancient wheelbarrow and was bouncing down a flagstone path towards the river and the Yurts. She refused his mimed efforts to recover his luggage, and eventually he gave in and followed disconsolately behind her.

The path was lit by solar powered lamps at regular intervals as it wound its way through a small clump of walnut and birch trees before dipping down towards the river. Two round canvas structures with domed roofs were set some distance apart from each other on a high bank above the stony riverbed. Orla trundled past the first, smaller yurt and led Paul to the larger structure. There was a curl of smoke wafting through a small chimney protruding through the fabric of the roof, but Paul noticed another wisp of smoke emanating from behind the Yurt.

Leaving the wheelbarrow by the entrance Orla picked up the bag with a grunt and heaved it inside, dropping it onto the nearest of three beds arranged symmetrically around the room. Orla pointed at a second smaller door and said something to Paul. As Orla turned away to tidy the furniture and stoke the wood burning heater underneath the metal chimney stack he pulled open the wicker framed door to discover a toilet and shower room made of brick adjacent to the tent. Another even smaller doorway led outside; Paul was astonished to see Campbell and Talaay neck deep in a steaming hot tub.

'The shower is icy cold and this looked too tempting.' explained Campbell. 'Come on in!'

'But I've…not got…any trunks?'

'Oh, don't worry about that, I'm sure you can spare a pair of boxer shorts for this. I think we all want to feel clean after…today.' Campbell's sentence drifted to a halt, and Talaay looked uncomfortable.

Paul came to a decision. 'Are there clean towels?'

After stripping down to his underwear and having hung his clothes in the shower room Paul hurried outside, wincing slightly at the damp grass underfoot and the chilly mountain air on his bare skin. As soon as he began to lower himself into the gloriously hot water however a sense of relaxation swept over him. He closed his eyes and began to drift in more ways than one. He had almost started to snooze when the small door opened, and Orla's head appeared. She let out a squeal of pleasure at seeing her guests in the hot tub. She kicked off her boots, pulled her dress swiftly over her head and jiggled up the steps at the side of the tub before lowering herself steadily into the water, groaning happily. Pauls' calm had disappeared in a moment as soon as Orla started to undress. Water cascaded over the sides of the hot tub, displaced to accommodate Orla's body. The hot tub was big enough to accommodate six people, but it seemed suddenly very full to Paul. He closed his eyes to avoid watching how much of Orla's voluptuous body was floating above the surface of the water.

Orla struck up a light-hearted conversation with Talaay, bits of which he translated for the two Englishmen. Her happy enthusiasm for everything was infectious; she was delighted to have unexpected guests this late in the season, truly thrilled to be housing global celebrities like Jasper and Tor, pleased that the new arrivals had escaped harm on their journey from the airport and keen for them to enjoy their stay, brief as it may be. Paul sensed that Talaay hadn't shared with her any of the grisly details they had seen during their time on the bus, but why would he? The atmosphere was relaxed and merry; it was comforting to float in the hot water and listen to the cheerful chatter of strangers in a foreign language under a string of fairy lights strung across the side of the yurt.

'She says she is teaching the baby to swim!' Talaay smiled widely. They all laughed, and then Paul leapt like a scalded cat when Orla's floating foot brushed against his thigh. Orla giggled as more water slopped over the side of the tub, and then a look of concern crossed her face. She spoke to Talaay, but the frequent glances towards Paul left him in no doubt he was the subject of the conversation.

Talaay translated. 'Orla says she was told by the English lady that you are ill. Orla says she had an uncle that died of liver disease; he was bloated with waxy skin by the end, she wonders if that's your condition too...' the look of mortification on Paul's face caused Campbell to diplomatically look away. Fitzroy kept his hand over his mouth until he could trust himself not to laugh.

Paul had never been particularly worried about his physical appearance, and he considered the rather minimal amount of exercise he undertook every week at the gym and the occasional game of squash enough to keep him in good shape. He did have to admit to himself that every year of the last decade had seen an inexorable increase in his weight. His only concession to this reality was every couple of years to buy some larger trousers. To hear a woman twenty years his junior describe him, even indirectly, as 'bloated' came as quite a shock to his optimistic self-image. Too shocked to verbally dispute Orla's supposition he weakly shook his head and tried to sink lower under the water. Talaay and Orla resumed their conversation. Paul judged from the way Talaay was pointing at the surrounding mountains that he was no longer the subject of their chat.

Eventually conceding he was still unable to hide his amusement, Campbell stood up, announced he was heading for the shower and leapt out of the water. Talaay's eyes tracked after him as he left the tub. Watching Campbell hurry into the yurt with water cascading off his skin Paul realised you couldn't describe Campbell as 'bloated.' 'Lean' would be more accurate. 'Athletic' would be correct too. Paul was unhappy with the comparison.

After a few more minutes of conversation with Orla, Talaay climbed out of the water and headed inside. Watching Talaay move away Paul decided he would describe him as more thickset than Campbell but still solid looking; Talaay wasn't bloated either. As he floated in the bubbling hot water Paul reflected for the first time ever on other men's bodies in comparison with his own. Some men were fit for professional reasons – take Talbot and the Marines for example, they must undergo intensive training to maintain stamina and strength. Someone like Jasper, who spent his life being photographed in exotic locations and who's fortune lay in his image, must have dedicated a serious amount of time to getting toned. So really there was no shame in not being as fit as those guys. But finally, Paul had to admit to himself, his physique was far from being in prime condition. Lots of men, including men the same age or older than him, had managed to keep themselves in much better shape than he had. Watching Orla floating in the steaming tub, the fairy lights twinkling above them and their shimmering reflection on the surface of the water Paul considered how he would describe her body. Oddly, he could imagine Annie's disapproving voice saying 'hefty' while his first choice of words would be 'curvy.' He watched the pregnant woman's water drenched figure as they floated together, and he thought of Annie.

He recalled Annie during her first pregnancy. By the thirtieth week her stomach was huge, like a massive cauldron welded onto her front, while the rest of her body was still quite slender. She had been so happy being pregnant; after the third month she had revelled in the surge of hormones coursing through her body. He had thought she had never looked more beautiful than when she was pregnant, and she had never seemed more *alive*. Her sensual experience of life had been amplified; the smell and texture of food was always commented on, as was the feel of fabric on her skin or the wind and sun on her face. Her appetite for everything was increased. He remembered the holiday they took to the south coast a month before she was due, and that hot sunny day on that secluded beach where they had splashed in the water and laughed and kissed and Annie had grabbed his hand and they had scampered to a hidden spot below the cliffs and enjoyed the best sex of their relationship to that point. He thought Annie's bump that day seventeen years ago must have been as big as Orla's was now. He gazed at Orla's pregnant belly as she turned in the water, droplets cascading off her skin and he thought of that moment on that beach, with the summer sun hot on his back and he pictured Annie wriggling out of her bikini as the seawater dripped off her naked skin. As every other muscle relaxed in the hot tub he felt his stiffening erection stretch the fabric of his sodden boxer shorts and poke through the surface of the water. One wide-eyed moment later he was tumbling out of the tub and skidding across the grass to get back in the yurt. He really hoped he couldn't hear Orla giggling.

Paul could only bear a few moments under the breath-catchingly cold shower, but he was more than happy with the effect it had on his groin. He hurried into the main room and rapidly began to get dressed. The shirt he had been wearing that day carried the sour smell of the bus, so he pulled a different one from the rucksack, regretting that there was no opportunity to iron it before putting it on. He was glad to put his ordinary shoes on after a few hours in the stiff walking boots that were already starting to rub his feet sore. He quickly brushed his teeth then announced to Talaay and Campbell that he was heading back to the main building to catch up with the rest of the group. In truth he wanted to avoid bumping into Orla if she came in to use the shower in their yurt.

The sky was now completely dark as he stepped out onto the pathway to the hotel. The gentle glow of the path lights guided him onwards as his breath steamed in the chilly air. He didn't realise it, but his still damp hair emitted a light mist as well. As he approached the second yurt he realised there was another figure on the path ahead of him; the gentle squeak of a wheel confirmed it was Orla pushing her wheelbarrow back to the hotel. He hesitated for a moment, but then decided it was silly not to carry on walking. Their encounter in the hot tub had been completely innocent, and now she was fully dressed he had no reason to avoid her. As she drew level with the small yurt she stopped and inclined her head as if listening. Turning to approach the entrance she noticed Paul and beckoned him over. Somewhat reluctantly, he joined her. There was peculiar rhythmical thumping sound emanating from within.

Orla put her hand on Paul's elbow as she leant forward to put her head through the doorway, leaving Paul unable to resist doing the same. Orla's grip on his arm intensified as they peered into the tent. Paul was close enough to Orla to hear the surprised intake of breath she took as the scene in the Yurt was revealed.

Apart from a steady red light emanating from a mobile phone positioned on a small tripod on the far side of the room, the room was softly lit by a few yellow lightbulbs pretending to be candles positioned around the walls. Jasper was lying naked on his back on the low mattress, his arms spread wide apart above his head, his hands gripping the slats in the bed headboard, his carefully toned muscles straining with exertion. A gloss of sweat across his whole body reflected the flickering light and gave him the appearance of a skilfully sculptured and polished statue. Tor was positioned above him, knees either side of his waist, one hand pushing on Jasper's chest, the fingers of the other hand entwined in his normally sleek blond hair. She leaned over him, her head thrown back with her teeth bared and clenched together. The tendons on her neck were stiff and strained. Her small smooth buttocks flexed, and her tiny breasts shook as her slender thighs rose and fell. There were no words spoken by the pair; Jasper emitted a high-pitched panting sound while Tor was repeatedly grunting with each thrust. The thumping noise that had attracted Orla's attention was the bed stead hitting the wooden frame of the yurt.

After just a few seconds Paul wriggled free from Orla's grasp and hurriedly stepped away from the entrance, but the image of what he had seen was seared in his memory.

Orla turned away from the yurt with her hand to her mouth failing to hide a playful grin. After giving Paul a saucy wink and uttering a few giggly words she recovered her wheelbarrow and trundled off to the hotel. Paul hurried away.

Paul was relieved the large room in the hotel was mostly empty; he needed time

to compose himself. A small table near the door to the kitchen had some cups and

drinks containers on it and he set about making himself a drink. He found a warm

jug containing coffee and poured himself a mug. As he was adding a generous

amount of sugar he was joined at the table by one of the female backpackers.

'Hi!' she said brightly as she set about pouring herself a cup of hot water, then

adding a tea bag she pulled from a plastic bag in her jacket pocket. 'Any milk?'

she asked, pushing her glasses back up her nose. They set about investigating

each of the containers until they found some. 'I'm Moira, by the way' she said as

she added a dash of milk to mug.

'I'm Paul' he said. 'I wish I had some teabags.'

'Oh, did you want one of mine?' Moira began to reach for her pocket.

'No, I've got this coffee now. Next time maybe.' He smiled but could not think

of what to say next.

'Its' the one thing I've missed on our travels, a nice cuppa. You can't always be

sure to get one in some of the places we've stayed so I stocked up when we got to

a supermarket in the city. Do you drink a lot then?' Moira asked.

'What?'

'Tea. Do you drink a lot of tea?'

Paul followed Moira as she headed to the deep leather sofas at the far end of the

room. They settled into a comfortable discussion of the relative merits of tea over

coffee, their preferred types of tea (neither of them liked Earl Grey very much) and they were just getting into a disagreement about whether to put the milk into the cup first when they were joined by the other women from Moira's group. Paul was introduced to Moira's best friend from school Rachel and her older sister Belinda and Annabel, who Belinda had met at university.

'Actually, Annabel and I are a couple.' Said Belinda, tilting her head defiantly, as if to challenge Paul.

'Oh, ok, good.' Paul replied mildly. Annabel and Belinda seemed to relax a little. 'So why are you in Kyrgyzstan? It's a bit off the beaten track.'

Moira replied. 'Rachel and I are off to Uni at the end of the month, so this was a final chance for us all to have a holiday together. Rach and B and me have been on countless family camping holidays, ever since we were kids, so that was a no-brainer. That was mostly Wales or Scotland. It was Annabel's idea to go somewhere more *exotic.*' There was a tiny hint of resentment in Moira's voice. Annabel ignored it if she noticed it at all but glanced over at Paul.

'I'm studying Art History at Sussex,' she said. 'I did a module on Medieval Art on the Silk Road last year and the landscapes and pictures in the course material just looked so beautiful; It inspired me to visit this part of the world. A hiking trip along part of the Silk Road seemed a perfect fit for everybody. Of course I wish I hadn't suggested it now.' She stared miserably at the floor.

Belinda reached over and grasped her hand. 'You weren't to know, babe. Don't beat yourself up about it. We all said it was a great idea at the time.'

Moira and Rachel exchanged a glance, then Moira gave a small shrug and said, 'Yeah, B's right, we didn't have to agree to it.'

Rachel pitched in. 'Come on, until yesterday we were having a brilliant time! A, you were right about the scenery; the hiking trails by the lakes and up in the mountains were so beautiful and everyone we met was so friendly…'

Belinda spoke to Paul this time. 'We did our research, you know; this looked like the safest country along the whole route.' She turned to Annabel again. 'The four of us were never gonna go hiking on our own through Iran, now were we? Or Iraq? Afghanistan? Or even the deserts of China for that matter. This was the best choice. Full stop.' Annabel gave her a little smile.

'Yeah, definitely not Iran.' said Rachel. 'Four women wouldn't be allowed.' With a mischievous grin she added 'especially if two of them are great big lezzers.'

Moira had been halfway through sip of tea at that moment, and her snort of laughter caused liquid to splash over her face. Annabel laughingly threw a cushion at Rachel, while Belinda, straight faced replied 'Annabel's the great big lezzer. I'm the short lezzer. Get your facts right, sis.'

Paul smiled. 'Has that caused you any problems since you've been here though? Being gay, I mean?' He blushed slightly.

'Well, no, but then we haven't had our Pride flags draped around us every day, have we?'

'I'm sorry, I didn't mean to pry…' Paul mumbled.

'No look, its fine. As I said, we did our research; it's not actually illegal to be a lesbian here, we just have to be a bit discreet and avoid public displays of affection that might upset the locals.' Belinda said.

'And to be fair' added Rachel, 'the same rules apply at our Grandma Audrey's house in Nuneaton.' Moira snorted a giggle into her teacup again.

Over the next fifteen minutes or so the other members of their party made their way to the room. Ren and Sydney were the only two marines to join them; they strolled in just behind Cecelia and Charlotte. As more people gathered, the less conversation there was, as if each new arrival became another oppressive reminder of the situation they were in. Last to arrive were Jasper and Tor. Paul looked away to avoid catching the eye of either of them, but they paid him no attention.

The beef goulash prepared by Chingiz was fairly basic, largely due to the limited availability of ingredients for a party of this size, but it smelled enticing as the travellers eventually gathered in the hotel main room. A few baskets of fresh bread rolls were set out to accompany the main course.

Individually the group may have been tired, frustrated, or nervous, but collectively they were all silent. The group took their bowls of stew and settled on the benches around the large wooden table that dominated the room. Chingiz set out several bottles of a local beer in the middle as well as jugs of water and fruit juice. There was an absence of conversation as the exhausted travellers listlessly began to eat. After a few minutes Hendrik nervously got to his feet. A few faces looked up from their food. 'Excuse me everybody! I know it has been a peculiar day, er, a difficult day today I suppose but, well, it is a special day too – you see today is Agnes' birthday! Could you raise your glasses…or raise your bottles…to wish a Happy Birthday to Agnes!'

There was a cry of 'Happy Birthday!' around the table, and, as if a dam of emotion had been breached, a sudden babble of voices and giggles and laughter and a spontaneous sing-along of "happy birthday to you!" Chingiz and Orla lit some lamps and turned off the harsh fluorescent strip lights around the room and suddenly the atmosphere was warm and comfortable and for a few moments at least the perils of the day were set aside. Agnes' face lit up with pleasure at the sudden outburst of happiness. She grasped her husbands' hand and softly kissed his cheek.

More stew was provided and eaten, followed by fruit and cheese and more beer. Chingiz went round the table with a large bottle of vodka, brushing aside any feeble protests as he replaced water glasses with vodka shots. Even when the meal was finished the happy chatter continued, a sudden flowering of camaraderie among the whole group with everyone wanting to talk through the events of the day they had endured together. They all flocked around Agnes to wish her well. Orla, delighted to have an impromptu party to look after, turned on the music system which began playing a variety of pop songs in different languages. After a few songs there was a squeal of recognition from Annabel and Rachel who started to dance. They were quickly joined by Moira and Belinda, who grabbed the hand of Charlotte who was stood next to them and implored her to join in. After a moment of shocked hesitation, Charlotte began to swing herself around energetically before taking hold of Jordi's arm to drag him along too. At this, Hendrik took Agnes by the waist and spun her around, causing her to laugh delightedly. The couple continue to dance hand in hand. Orla whooped joyfully, turned the music volume up and joined her guests wriggling and swaying to the beat. As the music changed others started to dance too; Talaay unexpectedly body-popping, Jasper and Tor swaying seriously to and fro, Campbell moving in a controlled but rhythmical manner, a smile slowly growing on his face. Paul joined in, bouncing along enthusiastically although at one point found himself pressed up against Orla's swollen belly and so dialled down the momentum until he could back up a little. Orla smiled sweetly at him and continued undulating happily around the room. Sydney and Ren were throwing some energetic moves despite their heavy boots. Finally even Cecelia got up from her seat and stepped towards the crowd of dancers. As she crossed the floor her steps changed from a walk to a shimmy, a shimmy to a sidestep, and then to general surprise and delight she was moving beautifully and in perfect tempo with the changing music, arms flowing, her body turning and swaying gracefully. Chingiz, after clearing the table had returned to the large room and reached for one of the light switches. To everyone's astonishment a small glitter ball hanging near the ceiling and lit by two soft spotlights began to rotate, throwing shards of light across the room. Orla clapped delightedly as she danced. Chingiz smiled and watched her contentedly.

The choice of music, presumably a playlist of Orla's, was wildly eclectic. All the music was fast and upbeat, but they danced to Eighties Europop, K-pop singers, Nineties boy bands and Seventies American rock. It made no difference to the enthusiasm of the dancers – there was a common unspoken need for a physical release of tension. They were, after all, in the warm and dry, well fed, and safe.

Just as the dancers began to flag after thirty minutes or so there was a startling change to the music. A slow but dramatic instrumental piece started, played on violin and piano. As the other dancers slowed to a stop Orla and Chingiz made a beeline for each other and meet in the middle of the dancefloor within the first few bars. With practiced ease they adopted a tango pose, as close together as Orla's bumps and curves would allow, and began to march, twirl and glide across the floor. Orla was as agile and sensual in her movements as Chingiz was upright and strong throughout their dance; their synchronised footwork and precise body positions displayed them as each the perfect complement to the other. As the music reached its final crescendo Orla wrapped one leg around her husband's thigh, and Chingiz leant her backwards until her head almost touched the floor. As the crowd yelled and clapped in delighted approval Orla straightened up, threw her arms around Chingiz' neck and buried her face in his chest as he glowed with pride.

By unspoken agreement, the tango drew the dancing to a close, but the buzz of conversation and laughter continued. Jordi was evidently having a fun time mixing with the younger members of the group, enthusiastically chatting with Moira and Rachel whilst making shy glances towards the statuesque Annabel. Paul noticed Talbot leaning comfortably against the door frame at the end of the room. He got the sense that the Colour Sergeant had been watching them for some time. It was only when Corporal Towne came in and spoke to him that Talbot moved.

'Ladies and Gentlemen!' Talbot called out. 'Just a little reminder that we have an early start in the morning.' There was a pantomime groan from the group. 'Breakfast is at seven o'clock, we will be on the move by eight am. We'll be posting guards throughout the night; if you hear any sort of fucking ruckus *stay where you are and keep your fucking head down* - we will come and find you when it is all safe, understood?'

'Are you expecting trouble, Colour Sergeant?' Charlotte asked. The light from the spinning glitterball strobed across her face, giving her still heavy make up the appearance of camouflage. All eyes turned to Talbot; the mood was suddenly serious again. Talbot shrugged.

'It's best to know what to do, whatever the circumstances.' He said. 'I think it's unlikely anything will happen tonight, mind. I can't imagine some random fucking patrol just happening to come all the way up this sodding valley on a whim, can you? That's why we chose this place, its well-hidden. Right then, sleep well; we've got another busy day ahead of us tomorrow, but fingers crossed it'll finish with a nice little helicopter ride. Sydney, Ren, with me.' Talbot turned on his heel and headed into the reception area followed by the two marines.

Shortly after Paul found himself yawning and realised he was exhausted. He said a general 'Good night, everyone,' and headed for the door. There was a scattered murmured response, and a few others began to head towards the exit as well. Hendrik and Agnes were arm and arm as they walked. Paul could hear Hendrik quietly humming a tune as he grabbed his wife's other hand and turned with her in a few steps of a waltz. Agnes laughed. Jordi was still seated at the other end of the room, but Paul could see the teenage eyeroll from where he was, the universal response to embarrassing parents.

The path through the trees seemed longer now as Paul plodded along. He sped up a little as he drew close to the smaller yurt to avoid encountering Jasper or Tor again that evening. Once inside the bigger tent he stripped off his outer clothing and slumped onto his bed. He crawled groaning under the covers and was fast asleep within a few moments. By the time Campbell and Talaay entered the yurt Paul was snoring rhythmically.

Despite his tiredness though, Paul's sleep was fitful. He dreamt he was floating in the air like a party balloon, but he was tethered at the ankle by a foul-smelling ships rope so he could only rise a few feet off the ground. This scene morphed into the inside of a wooden battleship where Paul, still floating and tethered, was trying to explain to the ship's captain why he didn't have the correctly coloured spanners. The captain, who Paul couldn't see clearly, put a hand to their face, and giggled whilst playing with a large pair of scissors.

Paul awoke from his dream with a start. The room was dark. He could hear the regular breathing of the sleeping men in the room. Being close to the river there were continual sounds of little gurgles and splashes as the shallow water ran over the stones. He lay still for a while, half listening, half hoping to fall asleep again. His eyes seemed unable to stay closed however and when a tiny clicking noise from outside reached him he stood up and tiptoed to the door. Cautiously peering out he was surprised to see a thick mist hanging in the air being brightly lit by moonlight. Looking directly up he could see the stars but looking forward he could only see a few yards. His head jerked as once more he thought he could hear something – more distant this time, in the direction of the hotel, more of a thud perhaps. Were they in danger? Perhaps the Marines were on guard duty, and they were making the noises he could hear, but what if it wasn't them? He took a step forward to investigate before the damp chill of the mist on his bare skin reminded him he was only wearing his underwear and so he went back inside to get dressed.

A minute or so later Paul cautiously made his way along the path towards the hotel. The mist obscured his view of everything less than twenty metres high - the tops of some trees some way off were clear to see, as were the mountain ridges on either side of the valley, but ten yards in front of him was a milky whiteness. The small lamps by the path loomed up at regular intervals. Paul's progress was erratic, as he kept stopping to strain his hearing for any new sound, but never being certain he could hear anything new. As he passed the small yurt and the path curved slightly he stepped onto the grass an let out a strangled yelp as a twig snapped underfoot. A distant owl chose that moment to hoot, causing a startled Paul to twitch violently and make a whimpering sound. Having taken a deep breath, he was about to take a step back towards the path when his foot caught on something. Looking down he saw part of a branch about the length and thickness of a baseball bat. Picking it up he set off for the hotel again.

As the path rose away from the river the mist thinned, and the silhouette of the hotel came into view. Paul could see no lights on inside the building. The few leaves attached to the end of the branch he was carrying rustled slightly as Paul pulled open the door. The reception area was silent and still. Paul moved into the dining area, noticing a small bright light at the far end of the room he crept forwards. He realised the light was coming from a mobile phone screen, and in the darkened room this light was illuminating Jordi's face. Paul could see the charger cable stretched out to the socket on the wall. 'Jordi?' he called softly. The boy noticed him approaching and looked up as he pulled out his earphones.

'Oh, hi.'

'What are you doing down here?' Paul asked him, sitting on the edge of a sofa.

'I couldn't sleep. I mean, I couldn't sleep in the same room as my parents.' Paul remembered the eyeroll from earlier. The boy continued. 'It is my mother's birthday, and my father has had some drink, so they were getting - what is the word in English?'

'Er, well, um...'Paul stammered. He had a horrible feeling that he knew exactly what Jordi was trying to say.

Jordi scrolled through a dictionary page on his phone. '*Frisky,*' he said, disgust dripping from his voice. Plainly this teenager believed his aged parents should be beyond such things. 'So, I told them I would sleep down here. Why are you carrying a tree?'

'I thought I heard a noise.' Paul answered, instantly realising this was no explanation at all.

Before Paul could better explain himself the door from the reception area swung gently open and Colour Sergeant Talbot stepped through, helmet on, treading swiftly but softly with a rifle butt pressed to his shoulder and his eye to the sights, focussing through the large window. Seeing Jordi and Paul he silently put one finger to his lips and then pointed to the ground, instructing them to get low. Even as they began to comply there was a series of shouts and yells, the closest coming from the reception area. Talbot spun around and set off at a flat run to the door. Paul expected to hear gunfire but instead heard a series of thuds and crashes. Just as Talbot came back into the room there was a crash as an object was hurled through the glass of the picture window beside Paul and Jordi. A small metal cylinder bounced onto the carpet and rolled towards Jordi, hissing and sparking. Instantly Paul leapt up, reached forward, and grabbed the grenade. He stretched his arm fully back, and flinging his body forward he hurled the device at the broken window.

He missed. The grenade flew high, hitting the solid window frame and bouncing back to hit Paul just above the ear, the sparks singeing his hair. As he was already off-balance Paul was knocked onto his backside, and the cylinder spun towards Jordi again. This time the boy picked it up in his right hand, ran forward a couple of steps, turned his left shoulder towards the window and bowled the grenade, fast and accurately out through the broken pane. As it hit the grass some distance away there was an audible click and thick white smoke poured out. The sudden whiteness illuminated two armed figures facing the window. One had their arm drawn back as if to throw a second grenade. In quick succession there were four surprisingly muffled cracking sounds from Talbot's rifle and both figures staggered and fell. The second smoke grenade fell from the hand of the man on the ground emitting more smoke.

'Those fuckers. They made me fire my fucking rifle.' growled Talbot. 'Fuckers. Right, you two, upstairs, *now*! get in a bedroom, lie down, and stay there.' Talbot vaulted out through the broken window and disappeared into the smoke. Paul and Jordi bent double to run away from the window. Crossing the reception area, they ran past a figure in uniform lying prone on the carpet. It wasn't one of Talbot's marines. There were shouts and yells from inside and outside the hotel echoing around them.

The stairs were carpeted which muffled their running footsteps. Jordi lead the way, heading straight past the first-floor corridor and heading up the next set of stairs. As Paul paused for a moment on the first-floor landing to catch his breath he heard movement on the stairs below him. Looking over the banister into the gloom below he was panicked to see at least two figures moving up the stairs towards him. The lead figure turned to look upwards, and Paul realised with a start he recognised the face. It was 'Sonny-Boy,' the leader of the gang from the airport. Paul set off at a stumbling run up to the second floor.

Jordi had disappeared by the time Paul arrived at the next level. There were three doors on either side of the corridor and remembering Talbot's instructions he ran to the first on the right and grabbed the handle. He tumbled into the room and pushed the door closed behind him.

With the curtains drawn the inside of the room was even darker than the corridor outside and Paul strained his eyes to make out any details around him. As he squinted in the dark a voice quietly said, 'Mr Huggins, four steps ahead of you on your right is a large wardrobe. Go and stand behind it.' It was Cecelia's voice. Paul hurried forward. 'No, Paul, stand the other side of the wardrobe *away* from the door.'

'Oh, yes, sorry.'

Paul could now make out that Cecelia was standing quite still in the shadowed far corner of the room. Charlotte was crouched beside one of the beds furthest away from the door. The sound of running feet in the corridor outside carried into the room, and from the floor above came heavy thuds and scraping noises as if heavy furniture was being dragged about.

As Paul squeezed himself into the space between the wardrobe and the wall the bedroom door opened again. A single figure stepped through with a small torch held out in front. It was Sonny Boy. The torchlight swept the room, travelling over Cecelia on the first pass before turning back to illuminate her. Sonny-Boy advanced towards her. As he began to raise his pistol he hesitated, disturbed by a *click* from the doorway. Looking over his shoulder he saw Sydney and Ren sighting their rifles at him, feet firmly set. In a low voice Sydney said, 'Get away from her, you - BITCH!' Two rifle shots echoed into the room from the hotel grounds. Sonny-Boy twitched at the sound, hurriedly dropped his pistol, turned to face Sydney, and raised his hands. Cecelia stepped forward and scooped up the gun, slipping it into her trouser pocket. She moved behind Sonny-Boy, pushed a foot into the back of one knee none too gently and forced him to his knees, and then shoved him face down on the floor. Grabbing two pillows she pulled off the pillowcases and stretched and twisted one into a rudimentary but effective binding around Sonny-Boys hands, tied behind his back. Kneeling down she pulled the second pillowcase over his head. She looked up at Sydney.

'That line – 'get away from her you bitch' – wasn't that from the film 'Aliens'?' Cecelia enquired.

Sydney gave a happy smile. 'Yes Ma'am!'

Chapter Eight

After a few tense minutes of silence there came a gentle knock on the door and Corporal Towne's voice calling 'all clear!' Sydney returned the call and opened the door. 'Everybody OK? Good. 'Double Tap' wants everybody downstairs, quick as you can.'

'Is everyone unharmed, Corporal?' asked Cecelia.

'Think so, ma'am.' He paused for a second. 'Everyone from our party at least; can't say the same for the other side.' A few thumps sounded from behind the wardrobe.

'Ah, excuse me?' Paul called out. 'I need a little help here; I seem to have got stuck…'

Once the marines had shifted the wardrobe and Paul had wriggled free, they all made their way downstairs, a still blindfolded Sonny-Boy carefully escorted by Ren and Sydney down each step. In the reception area they found Talbot standing over Draws who was tending to the uniformed figure Paul had seen lying on the floor earlier. The man was now sitting upright, clutching a red stained pad to his forehead as Draws bandaged him up. One side of the soldier's face looked swollen and bruised.

'Get him outside with the others.' Talbot told the medic, who nodded.

'We've got a present for you, Colour.' she said, nodding towards the tied up and hooded figure beside her. Talbot frowned.

'It's the gang leader from the airport.' Cecelia told him.

'Right then! I'll have a few questions to ask him in a minute or two. Keep him separate from the others – find a cupboard or storeroom to lock him in.' Talbot headed for the main entrance. The civilians followed him as the marines took their prisoner away.

The exterior lights to the hotel had been switched on, illuminating the lawn and car park. Twenty-five young Kyrgyz men in camouflage combat gear were sitting or kneeling on the grass, hands restrained with cable ties. Several of the marines stood guard over them. A few of the prisoners were bruised or bandaged. Five corpses were carefully laid out on the gravel car park.

Most of the other evacuees were standing huddled together near the hotel entrance. The Van der Molen family had their arms protectively wrapped around each other. As Paul stepped out of the doorway Jasper and Tor appeared on the pathway from the yurts, escorted by two of the marines. Jasper seemed to be shivering in the cool night air and his voice sounded angry as Charlotte hurried over to speak to them. 'What the fuck is going on now? We got woken up by a couple of firework bangs or something, and then these two grunts come along and drag us out of bed...bloody hell!' Jasper had caught sight of the soldiers on the lawn. Charlotte began speaking to them quietly. From the snatches of conversation Paul could hear Jasper and Tor had been oblivious of the assault on the hotel.

Just then an enraged Orla, barefoot and wearing only a nightdress, came flying through the main hotel doors like the figurehead on the prow of a battleship sailing at full speed. She was brandishing a large frying pan and hollering abuse at the attackers. Chingiz came chasing after her. As she approached the nearest group of soldiers they cowered away from her wrath. Once she was close to the men her oaths became more vicious and angrier and before anyone could stop her she swung the pan with all her might. The nearest soldier let out a yell of fear and tried to scramble to his feet. Fortunately for him Orla's swing was impeded by her bump so instead of hitting the man's head as she intended she caught him square in the back, sending him tumbling and rolling across the grass onto the gravel of the car park. The other soldiers began rolling, crawling, and wriggling away from the furious woman. It took the efforts of both Chingiz and Lincoln, the biggest marine, to disarm and restrain Orla as she kicked and flailed at the Kyrgyz soldiers.

'Dear God, that's a sight.' Talbot seemed impressed. 'Linc, for everybody's safety, help get the lady back inside.'

Lincoln glanced at him dubiously. 'Er, me, Colour?'

'Yes, you! Is she scaring you, Marine?'

Lincoln leaned his head away from the furious woman still wriggling in his grip. 'Too fucking right she is, Colour Sergeant.' He and Chingiz managed to drag the still struggling Orla away from the soldiers and with soothing words from Chingiz they persuaded her to return inside the hotel.

'Mr Maksat!' Talbot called. Talaay hurried forwards. 'Please inform our friends here that if they don't comply with my instructions, I will let the pregnant lady loose on them again, possibly with a meat cleaver next time.'

'Ah. Yes, Colour Sergeant.'

'Draws, how is he?'

The medic was attending the still prone soldier. 'He's alive, Colour; Just winded I think, possibly some fractured ribs, but most likely just bruised.'

As Talaay began speaking to the terrified looking soldiers who kept glancing nervously at the hotel entrance Cecelia asked quietly, 'what do you intend to do with the survivors Colour Sergeant?' Campbell turned his head sharply to hear the answer.

'We are in no position to take prisoners…' Talbot began.

'Now just a minute…' interposed Campbell.

'…nor are we executioners, Mr Campbell.' He glanced at the hotel, 'I don't think leaving them within reach of the lady of the house would be a good idea for anybody, so – we'll load them onto the bus and drive them down to the village on the plain and leave them there. Even if they are stupid enough to try and come back again, without any transport they won't get here in a hurry, and we will be long gone by the time they do.'

Talbot glanced at Cecelia and then at Campbell. 'These squaddies are not my priority, so please note this is me making a real effort to *play nice*. These are not spotty little conscripts who can't tell their rifle from their arsehole; these are trained soldiers who knew what they were doing, so don't expect me to read them a bedtime story and tuck them in with a warm blanket, understood? As long as they give me no trouble they will be OK, but I will NOT endanger my team, or this mission, to look after them.'

'Very well.' Campbell replied.

'Corporal!'

'Yes Colour Sergeant?'

Talbot pointed his chin towards the Kyrgyz soldiers. 'Assuming he is still alive, find me their Rupert, I need to ask him a few questions before I speak to old Sonny-Boy. We'll talk to him out here in view of his men; I don't want them getting too excitable if we lead him out of sight. After we are done get this lot loaded onto the bus, undamaged ones at the back, walking wounded near the front, and strap the dead onto the luggage racks. Post a six-man guard until further orders.'

'Yes Colour.'

Paul whispered to Cecelia, 'Who is Rupert?'

Cecelia glanced at him before replying quietly, '" Rupert" is military slang for an officer.'

Corporal Towne moved among the soldiers, stopping in front of one with a small star pinned to his collar. He rose to his feet when beckoned to do so. Towne removed the restraints from around his wrists. The soldier straightened his jacket and, following the corporals unspoken signal, he walked over to Talbot. The Kyrgyz officer was half a head taller than the Royal Marine. He held his head proudly high, but his darting eyes betrayed an uncertainty as to what was about to happen. He seemed relieved when Talbot gave him a formal salute and introduced himself using name and rank. The Kyrgyz officer returned the salute.

Talbot's interrogation was direct but courteous. With Talaay's translation he established the Kyrgyz officer was named Lieutenant Dinar Yusupov; he and his men were soldiers from a Kyrgyz Army infantry battalion stationed in Bishkek.

The Lieutenant glanced anxiously at the Marines standing guard over his soldiers and posed a question which Talaay relayed.

'The Lieutenant wants to know what you intend to do with his men.'

Talbot kept his eyes trained on the soldier as he spoke to the interpreter. 'Tell the Lieutenant that he has my word of honour no further harm will come to him and his men - *provided they behave themselves*. I have a few more questions for him.'

Yusupov seemed to relax when this answer was relayed, and he was content to provide the information Talbot was after. Yusupov had received orders from his Colonel late the previous evening to provide support to an intelligence officer who was going to arrest a group of spies who had been spotted at the airport earlier that day. The Lieutenant admitted he had been relieved to have been given a specific mission to achieve amid the uncertainty of a civil war that was exploding across the country. The briefing he had received from the intelligence officer had said that the suspects included military personnel, but it was clear that Yusupov was angry that he hadn't been adequately forewarned about what was waiting for him at the hotel. Talaay finished his translation by saying 'He says despite the poor intelligence, he led the squad; the deaths of his soldiers are his responsibility.'

Talbot nodded. 'Spoken like a true soldier,' he said admiringly. 'Final question: was the Intelligence Officer who led him here from the Kyrgyz Republic?'

On hearing the question, Yusupov's face went blank, and after a long hesitation, he declined to answer.

'Well, clearly he isn't, then.' Talbot replied. He stood to attention and presented Yusupov with a parade ground salute which the officer returned immediately.

Talbot turned to go when another question from Yusupov was translate by Talaay.

'He asks what happened to the Intelligence Officer?'

Talbot continued to walk towards the hotel. 'Don't answer him Mr Maksat. Corporal, put the Rupert back with his men and get them on the bus.' The evacuees all followed Talbot.

As he strode swiftly towards the hotel entrance Talbot stopped in front of the Van Der Molens. 'I just wanted to say, your son is the absolute dogs' bollocks.' Agnes and Hendrik looked at each other, mystified.

'What did he do wrong?' asked Agnes.

'Nothing! Quite the opposite, in fact - he saved my life just now, and Mr Huggins here too. Proper hero, Jordi was. You should be enormously proud of him.' Talbot clapped Jordi on the shoulder, making him stagger slightly, before the Marine stomped off into the hotel. Agnes and Hendrick stared wide-eyed at their son who was pink cheeked but beaming with joy at the compliment. An excited conversation in Dutch followed, with Jordi chattering and laughing, pointing, and gesticulating, answering questions fired at him by his parents, and then re-enacting scooping up the grenade, and displaying his bowling technique as he showed them how he disposed of it. He mimed the smoke erupting from the canister, then pointed in Talbot's direction and began to raise an imaginary rifle to his shoulder. As he did so he stopped mid-sentence and stared at the corpses still laid out on the lawn. The smile disappeared from his face and his lip trembled slightly. Agnes, her eyes brimming with tears, enfolded him in a motherly bear hug.

Paul stepped up beside the Van der Molens. He wanted to provide some comfort to Jordi, to tell him he that did the right thing, that he wasn't responsible for the death of anyone; but he couldn't find the words. Instead he turned to Hendrik and said limply, 'Jordi was very brave. He saved me and the Colour Sergeant for sure.' A treacherous little part of his mind was relieved that his own ineptitude in that moment of crisis hadn't been mentioned.

Hendrik smiled slightly. 'I am sure he was brave; he is a good boy.' Then he frowned. 'But I still don't understand; what does this have to do with animal testicles?' For the life of him Paul couldn't think how to answer that question.

The civilians gathered in the hotels large main room. They were joined by Draws the medic, and Sydney and Ren, who seemed to have been deputised to act as their bodyguards. Talbot was in discussion with an annoyed looking Campbell; as Paul walked past he overheard the Colour Sergeant say '...I have a few questions for Sonny Boy, but I don't want you in the room...' Talaay and Cecelia were close by this conversation, for their language skills in the upcoming interrogation, Paul presumed. The other Marines who were not guarding the Kyrgyz prisoners had been sent by Talbot on a reconnaissance patrol.

There was a nervousness among the evacuees. Urgent whispered conversations echoed around the room until Agnes, still clutching Jordi tightly spoke loudly towards Talbot.

'How did the soldiers find us?'

Talbot stopped talking to Campbell and turned to look at Agnes, but he didn't answer. Campbell cleared his throat and said, 'As we said at the airport, we think they want hostages…'

'Yes, but they went to a lot of trouble to track us down in the mountains.' This was from Hendrik. 'And now they are sending soldiers, who should be busy fighting the war, and we are still in danger. You said we would be safe here, but we are not. Why do they consider all of us so valuable?'

There was a chorus of agreement around the room, and Paul got a sense of anger from various people as well.

'Is it really all of us?' said Moira. 'I just think, some of us would be considered more valuable to them than others…' Her eyes flickered around the room.

Pauls eyeline slowly drifted up towards the ceiling and his mouth gaped slightly open. A series of images flickered through is mind – Jordi bowling a grenade through a broken window, Sydney and Ren pointing their rifles at Sonny Boy in Cecelia and Charlottes bedroom, Jasper and Tor being escorted from their yurt after the battle. The realisation of what the true reason for the rescue was dawned on him. A moment later it occurred to him why Talbot would refuse to confirm this information to the group.

'It's me!' he said. His voice was squeakier than he intended. He cleared his throat and said again loudly, 'it's me!' The room became hushed as everyone turned to look at him. 'I'm the reason the Marines staged this rescue.' He shifted his weight from one foot to another and nervously rolled his wedding ring with one thumb. Several faces in the room wore expressions of surprise and confusion. 'I-I-I work for a Cabinet Minister you see. The UK Government couldn't leave me in danger.' He gave a little cough. 'Er, yes, you see, er, it-it would be politically embarrassing to have me paraded on television as, er, a prisoner…' there was a shaking of heads and various mutters of disagreement around the room.

Jasper barked with laughter, but Tor looked furious. She strode across the room to confront Paul. 'Oh please. You!? You think *you* are special? You're just a bloody *suit*! You're a cheap empty suit of a man!' Tor's lips drew back in a snarl as she spat out the words. 'You have no importance in this situation; you are a ridiculous, middle aged, middle-management civil servant! You mean *nothing*! These soldiers are obviously here to rescue Jasper and me. *You* are irrelevant. Just be grateful that you happened to be standing close to us when the shit hit the fan and we let you come along for the ride. Ha! It should be obvious even to someone as ignorant as you that we are the only ones here with any real value…I mean, no offence to anyone else, but it's the only explanation. We are *globally* famous - we get millions of hits online every day! Either side of this tin-pot little war would love to have us in front of their cameras.' Tor had been pacing the floor as her angry words had echoed around the room. 'Obviously, the British Government couldn't have us go missing so they sent the Marines to get us out. You better just try to keep up tomorrow; I am not inclined to wait around if you don't make it to the chopper in time!' Oh yes, Paul thought to himself. *That* is a much better cover story. Damn.

Jasper moved close behind Tor and put a hand on her elbow, but she irritably pulled her arm free. He stopped to wipe beads of sweat from his brow. He coughed, once, twice, his breaths short and wheezy. There was babble of excited voices throughout the room.

Talbot's parade ground voice cut across the hubbub. 'Listen up! None of that

bollocks matters! It makes no buggering difference at all why they came after us.

Because each and every one of you is gonna march up this pissing valley with me

in the morning and get on that shitting helicopter and we will all be fucking gone!

Is that clear? We can't leave here until dawn, which is still four hours away, so I

suggest you try and get some kip.'

Suddenly Jasper groaned, clawed at his shirt buttons for a moment, hunching

over, then legs shaking he half collapsed against the wall. Charlotte reached out

to support him as Draws the medic stepped forward and helped him slide down to

sit on the floor. After regarding Jasper for a moment Draws said quietly 'Your

pulse is racing, you're sweating, your muscles are spasming – what have you

taken?' 'Nothing!' snapped Jasper. He shuddered. 'That's the trouble – nothing'

he sighed and closed his eyes. 'I took the last pill I had before we boarded that

fucking plane. I should have been home by now to get some more.' Charlotte and

Tor tried to help Jasper, pushing chair cushions under his head as he slumped to

lay prone on the floor.

'What is it you are on?' demanded Draws. Jasper didn't reply.

Charlotte leaned forward. 'He's taking Fentanyl. It's legit, it's on prescription. I

knew he was on medication, but I didn't realise he was so addicted...' she trailed

off. Tor raised her head and shrugged. ' He had a motorbike accident in Nepal

about a six months ago that needed surgery. There were complications. He uses

the pills to manage the pain, that's all. He's been fine up to now.' Draws fired

questions at Jasper about the dosage he was on and the frequency of use but got

little response. Charlotte and Tor tried to provide what detail they knew about

Jasper's drug use. Draws turned to them. 'Get him a blanket and some water. We need to make him comfortable for a minute or two before we do anything else.' Looking around he noticed everyone else in the room, after leaning away from Jaspers angry tirade moments before where now gathering closer to see and hear what was going on. 'Can we clear the room out please? Give him some space to breathe.' With Talaay's help, Orla and Chingiz began shoo-ing everyone towards the reception area. The Van der Molens hurriedly turned and headed out of the door, along with Moira, Annabel, Rachel, and Belinda escorted by Ren. Sydney stood in the doorway as if on guard duty. Paul made no effort to leave the table. Campbell, Cecelia, and Talbot were in discussion on the far side of the dining room and Draws moved over to them. He shifted uncertainly and glanced at Talbot. 'He is suffering some serious withdrawal symptoms right now. I could give him a morphine injection to alleviate the immediate pain, but that could just make him worse tomorrow and either way he would be in no state to go trekking into the mountains…'

Paul cleared his throat. 'I can help.' Four heads turned to look at him. 'As Jasper says, I am indeed just a civil servant working at the Department of Health, but I have a degree in pharmacology and I have been working on addiction treatment policy for several years now, and some of the details have kind of stuck. Now I'm not a doctor, but I do know what I am talking about when it comes to pharmaceuticals.' The four heads exchanged glances, then turned back to Paul. Campbell spoke. 'What do you suggest, Mr Huggins?'

Paul addressed Draws. 'What medication have you got in your kit?' Draws opened his main medical bag and displayed the contents. 'We used up some of the morphine on the wounded on the road earlier today, but there is still plenty left. Here is the list of other medication.' The medic handed Paul a sheet and he scanned it hurriedly. He looked up. 'There is an ongoing treatment trial about to come to an end in Scotland using a mix of medications to help wean addicts off opioids while still managing their pain relief. Fentanyl is an opioid. The trial has been extremely successful – the results were the highlight of the Ministers speech in Seoul, and the reason I was in Korea – and there are versions of all the ingredients used in the trial included on this list. We can make up a solution that can tide him over for a couple of days until we can get him to a proper doctor. As long as he keeps taking the correct dosage he'll be right as rain.' Paul grabbed a pencil and napkin and began to write out the combination of dosages.

Cecelia looked thoughtfully at Jasper, then at Paul. 'Why not give him an injection of this little mix of yours?' she asked.

Paul shook his head. 'Some of the ingredients won't operate properly if they are injected into muscle, they need to be taken orally, they diffuse into the bloodstream via the digestive tract. The ideal delivery method is a nasal spray, but a liquid solution will do.' Paul looked up, hesitated for a moment, and then inclined his head slightly. 'It might be a little uncomfortable for him, the dosage will be a bit…imprecise. But he will be able to function ok. You'll be able to get him to the helicopter tomorrow.'

After a drawn-out pause, there seemed to be an unspoken agreement between Talbot, Campbell, and Cecelia. Talbot spoke to Draws. 'Set to it then – make up this sodding solution as Mr Huggins directs. But check his workings, eh? Don't want any accidents with the pissing decimal point in the wrong place do we?' Talbot strode off towards the hotel reception, calling over his shoulder 'If it was me, Mr Huggins, I would have made him take it as a shitting suppository – and I'd have rammed it right up his arse while it was still in the fucking bottle…'

Chapter Nine

It took Paul and the medic only a few minutes to assemble the ingredients needed to make up the medication. Draws listened attentively as Paul described the proportions of each element that was needed and followed the instructions on how to combine them. Paul continued explaining how the pilot treatment study had worked, but as he relaxed into giving a lecture about the statistical analysis of the work Draws cut him off.

'Alright, Sicknote, enough with the speeches, let's just stick to treating the patient in front of us shall we? Now, how long will this solution continue to have an effect?'

Chastened, Paul considered before answering. 'We should give him a double dose now, then top ups maybe every four hours or so.'

'Ok. We should make up enough to last him three days.'

'The ingredients in the solution may separate after twenty-four hours or so. Better to make him a fresh batch the following day.' Paul frowned. 'How long will we be walking tomorrow?'

'That depends on how slow you walk.' Draws grinned at him whilst carefully grinding a pill into powder.

Paul sighed. 'I meant…'

'The first rendezvous point is eight clicks along this valley; there is a plateau near the head of the valley with space enough to land a chopper. With unfit civilians, over rough terrain, it will probably take us three and a half hours; maybe four, if 'Double Tap' allows you lot regular breaks.'

'What if it was just the Marines?'

'Even with full pack we'd get a right bollocking if we didn't yomp that in ninety minutes.'

'Oh.'

Draws, having checked the ingredient quantities for a second time, poured them carefully into a small water bottle containing a measured amount of water. Screwing down the lid he swirled the bottle, watching intently until he was satisfied the powders had dissolved into the liquid. He held the bottle up for Paul to see. Paul nodded.

Draws picked up a needleless syringe from his medic back and filled it with the medication. He then picked out a second syringe, inserted the needle and pulled out a small bottle of morphine. He moved over to the prone figure of Jasper.

'We need to get him sitting up.' Charlotte and Tor helped pull Jasper upright. Jasper's eyelids fluttered slightly before they opened fully and slowly focussed on Draws. 'I need you to drink this.' Draws rested the nozzle of the needleless syringe on Jaspers lower row of teeth and slowly pushed the plunger. Jasper's throat convulsed as he swallowed the medication. He coughed feebly but managed to swallow all of the solution. Once the syringe was emptied Draws reached for the second one.

Tor shook her head. 'No.' She stood up quickly, still shaking her head. 'No, no, no. I can't be doing with this!'

'It's just a tiny little shot; it'll help him sleep for a few more hours. He needs the rest before tomorrow.' Draws continued preparing the injection.

'No, no, I can't do needles!' Tor waved a hand dismissively, turned away and hurried out of the door. Charlotte, left supporting all of Jaspers weight on her own and suddenly off balance, grunted as she slid backwards with Jasper sprawled on top of her. Paul helped get Jasper sitting up again, releasing Charlotte.

'Let's get him on the sofa,' Paul said quietly.

Once Jasper was still, Draws swiftly inserted the needle into Jasper's upper arm, and ignoring his whimpering, competed the injection. After a few moments Jasper's eyelids drooped and his head turned limply against the cushion.

'OK, that should do it.' Draws checked his watch. Five or six hours of sleep should set him straight for tomorrow.' Charlotte hurried out of the room and in the now silent hotel Paul could hear her footsteps running up the main stairs. Draws and Paul set about repacking the medic kit. Charlotte returned a short while later with her arms full of bedding. She draped some of the blankets over Jasper, easing off his shoes and set them on the floor by the sofa. Then she settled herself into a large armchair nearby, wrapped up in the rest of the bedclothes.

'I'll stay with him,' she said. She raised the hood of the sweatshirt she was wearing and pulled the blankets up to her face to shield herself from the cool air seeping through the broken window on the far side of the room. The only part of her face that Paul could see were her thickly painted eyebrows and her dark brown eyes. Draws shouldered his kit bag and headed for the reception area. Paul hesitated for a moment and then followed Draws. Something was nagging at the back of his mind as being out of place, but he couldn't work out what it was.

Paul was about to head back to the yurt to see if he could grab some more sleep when his attention was taken by the light emanating from under the kitchen door and the sound of a voices from within. Stepping closer he had to stretch his neck slightly to get a glimpse through the small round window in the centre of the door. Inside the kitchen he could see Talbot standing facing the door, feet planted and hands on hips with his rifle slung over his back. In front of him was a seated figure in a dark leather jacket. Sonny-Boy, Paul realised. The frilly pink pillowcase acting as a hood had been pulled up high enough for him to see his interrogator, but he was tied so securely to the chair that he was only able to move his head and neck. Also in the room but carefully positioned out of Sonny-Boy's line of sight, were Talaay, Campbell and Cecelia. Talaay was providing most of the translation for what sounded to Paul like Russian.

'I know *why*' Talbot said. 'Explain to me *how* you found us. Look at ME, not over there!' Sonny-Boy stopped straining his neck to look over his shoulder. In a deep voice he gave a short reply to the translated question, which Talaay conveyed.

'He says "we followed you."'

Talbot's eyes didn't leave Sonny-Boy's face. 'No, you didn't,' he said thoughtfully. 'Not once we turned off the main road at least. You were too far behind us at the airport to have seen us directly, and there are too few people in this country and too much else going on yesterday for sightings of us to have been passed on. Once we were off the motorway we could have gone up any one of a dozen different valleys in this mountain range, but you came straight to us.' Sonny-Boy listened to the translation but made no further response.

In an effort to get a better view Paul leaned forward. He hadn't realised it was a two-way swing door, and as the door moved away from him he stumbled forward into the room, suddenly finding himself facing the wrong end of Sydney and Ren's rifles. Paul froze; the two Marines lowered their weapons and the door swung back and hit Paul on the shoulder.

Talbot glared at Paul for a few moments then turned back to Sonny-Boy. 'Well, I think we are done here,' he said.

Sonny-Boy spoke to Talbot. Talaay translated again.

'He says, "aren't you supposed to ask me my name, rank and number?"'

Talbot smiled. 'I really don't give a shit about your name and number; and I know your rank already. Only agents who have reached a certain rank in the Russian Intelligence Services get to lead operations like this beyond the borders of the motherland. Isn't that so, Captain? Hey, I said look at ME.'

Turning his head back to Talbot, Sonny-Boy spoke again, his voice still sounding calm and controlled.

'He says "We only came here to get some information…"'

Cecelia interrupted him. 'The way he phrased it means 'to engage in a dialogue.''

Talaay nodded. 'Yes, that's correct, 'dialogue' is most accurate. He only wants a dialogue, nothing else. He says the soldiers behaved foolishly; he did not tell them to start shooting. It was most regrettable, he says. He hopes there were not too many casualties. He is offering to escort our survivors to safety.'

Talbot's smile turned into a harsh grin as he addressed Sonny-Boy again. 'I told you yesterday – we are quite capable of looking after ourselves. It's your boys that need looking after.' He reached forward and pulled the pillowcase down over the man's face. 'Let's go,' he said, untying the ropes on the chair but leaving his hands tied behind him. Hauling Sonny-Boy to his feet Talbot spun him round. With one hand gripping the jacket collar and the other in the small of Sonny-Boy's back he forcefully guided him towards the door. The prisoners muffled voice called out, sounding more urgent now.

'He demands to know what you intend to do with him,' said Talaay. Paul scurried out of the way as Talbot reached the door. 'He'll find out soon enough,' snarled Talbot as he grabbed a linen napkin from a small pile laid out on a tray of cutlery beside the kitchen entrance. Sonny-Boy continued to protest as Talbot marched him through the reception area, escorted by Sydney and Ren and followed by the civilians from the kitchen. Stopping by the main desk Talbot pulled open a draw and grabbed a roll of adhesive tape. Pulling the pillowcase up as far as Sonny-Boy's nose Talbot stretched the napkin into a thin tight strip and forced it into Sonny-Boy's mouth. He then wound the adhesive tape around the other man's head several times to hold the napkin in place before pulling down the hood once more and resuming the march to the front door.

Although the outside lights had been switched off the moonlight was providing some degree of illumination to the space in front of the hotel. Halfway across the lawn Talbot pulled Sonny-Boy to a stop and pushed him face down onto the ground. Suddenly animated, Sonny-Boy began to twist and wriggle, causing Talbot to growl and pin the other man down with a knee in his back. As the prone man continued to struggle Cecelia stepped forward and crouched by the man's head. Lowering her head alongside his she whispered in his ear for a few moments and immediately he went still. Quickly Cecelia stood up and moved away.

'You can get off him Colour Sergeant.' As the Royal Marine stood up Cecelia put her finger to her lips, then pointed at the man on the ground. She said loudly 'I told him if he did as he was told we wouldn't kill him; I said you were only allowed to shoot him if you absolutely had to.' She silently summoned Talbot closer and said in a muted whisper 'I told him that in English and he obviously understood me immediately. So just be careful what you say in front of him from now on.'

Talbot held her gaze for a long moment, then said with a nod 'Yes Ma'am.' He turned to Ren. 'Stand guard over him.'

'Yes Colour.'

'We won't put him with the others just…yet…' Talbot turned to look towards the bus and broke off. 'What the pissbucket shitfuckery is that thundercunt doing *now*?'

Peering towards the vehicle Paul could see two of the luggage compartment doors on the side of the bus were open and the long legs of Tor were sticking straight out from one of them. Corporal Towne was stood nearby watching, and a row of faces were pressed up against the windows inside the bus. On the ground outside was a medium sized pink metal suitcase. As Talbot and the rest of the little entourage approached another similar case was pushed out of the bus, then another, then a fourth. Finally Tor crawled out backwards. The eyes inside the bus watched her intently but she paid them no attention.

'I couldn't leave these all behind Colour Sergeant.' She looked hopefully towards Sydney. 'Now, I need some help getting them to my Yurt?'

Paul was standing close enough to see Sydney suck in her cheeks to stop herself from laughing. Talbot walked up close to Tor bristling with anger. Being a whole head shorter than her he had to raise his head and stretch his neck to address her. 'Whatever shit you take out of here tomorrow is what you and your druggie boyfriend can carry on your own fucking backs. None of this *shit* is getting carried by my team, so I suggest you *fucking* ditch this *fucking* crap right *fucking* now. If you want to take this *shit* to your *fucking* tent, then move them your-*fucking*-self, you lazy *cow*!' He turned away from the open-mouthed woman, checked his watch and addressed the other civilians. 'Breakfast is in seven hours; in eight hours we set off. I suggest you try and get some more sleep until then. Mr Maksat? Would be so kind as to relay to Lieutenant Yusupov and his men that they will remain where they are for the next five hours or so before we take them back down the valley.' Talaay headed towards the bus door as Talbot added with a twinkle in his voice 'and let those soldiers know that Sonny-Boy there blamed them for the failure of their mission, would you?' Talbot looked at Campbell. 'I don't think Yusupov will take that too well; and it doesn't hurt us to sow a little dissention in the ranks of our opponents now does it?' Campbell shrugged and nodded. 'Corporal Towne! Keep the current guard on these men, plus our friend on the lawn over there. At oh-five hundred take a fresh squad of three as prisoner escort and a fourth to drive a Land Rover, take all the prisoners back down to the village at the park entrance, disable the bus and bring the squad back in the Landy. That shouldn't take you two hours, back in time for breakfast. Understood?'

'Yes Colour.'

Talbot stalked back across the car park ignoring Tor who was still motionless beside her luggage. Talaay called out from the bus doorway 'Colour Sergeant Talbot!' The Royal Marine turned. 'The Lieutenant requests some water for his men?'

'Yes of course. Corporal Towne, see to it please?' Talbot resumed stomping back to the hotel, followed by Cecelia and Sydney.

Tor picked up one of her suitcases and looked at Campbell, Talaay and Paul. 'A little help please?' she said icily.

'It is on the way to our Yurt I suppose,' said Campbell and picked up one of the cases. Paul and Talaay did the same and then all three followed Tor as she headed along the path towards the river in the gloom.

Tor barely acknowledged the three men as the placed her cases in the yurt. Pauls eyes flicked quickly over the bed and at the spot where the camera had been. Avoiding looking at Tor he hurried out.

They made their way back to the larger tent and Paul slumped onto his bed. He fumbled to take off his shoes, set them neatly beside his bed, lay back and fell asleep.

Daylight was brightening the canvas behind the wooden lattice frame of the yurt when Paul awoke. He could hear the shower running in the small room next door, presumably being used by Talaay as Campbell was moving around the main room collecting his belongings as he repacked his rucksack. 'Good morning Mr Huggins. Colour Sergeant Talbot sent us a message to be ready for breakfast in about...' he checked his watch '...fifteen minutes.' Paul grunted a response and then ran his tongue around the inside of his mouth, feeling how dry and parched it was. Talaay appeared with a towel around his waist and another wrapped turban-like around his head. Paul hurried into the shower room, before immediately coming back for his washbag and starting again. Attempts to remove the grey flecked stubble that had developed on his face were partly successful despite the lack of hot water, but he was left with numerous small cuts on his neck and a line of bristles under his jawline that he did not notice until sometime later. The cold shower, although necessarily short, did moisten his parched mouth and enliven both his bare skin and his tired spirits.

It did not take Paul long to pick out his clothes for the day as he only had one other shirt and one change of underwear to choose from. He carefully folded the clothes he had slept in and added them to his rucksack before pulling on his walking boots and heaving his rucksack onto his right shoulder. With a quick glance to see that he had left nothing behind, and then a thorough check, and then *another* look just in case, he left the yurt.

Although the light was bright, and the sky was clear the sun had yet to rise above the eastern mountains as Paul set off. Walking through the trees towards the hotel Paul had to keep adjusting the pack resting on one shoulder. If he held his shoulders level it would slip off, if he held that shoulder up the weight would unbalance him and cause him to stagger. He stopped to put his left arm through the second strap and realised he could hear a voice.

'Well dear viewers, I have decided to keep the all-purpose foundation - this one - as well as my all-time favourite clear waterproof mascara which I've shown you before, and these eyebrow pencils. That just leaves which lip paint to take with me...'

Paul was standing a few feet away from the smaller yurt. He recognised the voice as belonging to Tor, and the style of speech was familiar to him as well. As he continued to trudge up the path, he was reminded of the makeup tutorials his daughters watched online.

Walking to the front of the building Paul saw that the two military Land Rovers were in the car park, but the bus and all the Kyrgyz soldiers were gone. There was no prone figure lying trussed up on the lawn either, so he presumed Sonny-Boy had been taken too.

Paul made his way into the dining area of the hotel, wriggling out of his rucksack and adding it to the collection near the door. The window that had been broken the previous evening was now boarded up, making the room darker at one end. Most of the other evacuees were already in the room, either eating or filling their plates from the assortment of foodstuffs Chingiz was laying out on the long side table. It took Paul a moment to realise he could hear classical music playing softly from speakers around the room; it was a gentle and familiar piece, Mozart was it, or Bach perhaps?

Jasper was sitting upright at one end of the sofa that had been his bed the night before. He was obviously looking out for Paul, for as soon as he came in Jasper rose to his feet and came over. He stood by one of the unbroken windows with the daylight illuminating his handsome, tired face.

'Charlotte tells me you were the one who sorted out the medication that put me right last night. So, thank you – I owe you a lot.' Jasper's manner seemed quite shy, but his direct gaze demonstrated an earnestness that Paul had not seen in him before. Paul found he was mildly touched by the obvious effort Jasper was making.

'How are you feeling this morning?' Paul asked, squinting slightly.

'Yeah, OK I guess, all things considered. I had another dose of your stuff this morning, and Charlotte tells me I have to keep taking it every four hours or so.'

'Yeah, that's about right,' Paul said. Charlotte had come up to stand beside them and she gave Jasper a meaningful stare.

Jasper winced slightly as he addressed Paul again. 'Look here, I said some things to you yesterday that were, well, a bit unkind…'

'More than a bit…' muttered Charlotte.

'Well, yes. More than a bit. Anyway, I'm sorry about that, OK? I obviously wasn't feeling well,' he glanced at Charlotte, 'but nevertheless what I said was cruel and unnecessary.'

'Hmm, well, I suppose…' Paul began, but Jasper was looking past him.

'Have you seen Tor today? Oh, there she is…' Jasper moved away to intercept Tor as she entered the room. Charlotte remained with Paul.

'That medication isn't a cure you know – it'll keep him going for a while, but…'
Paul broke off.

Charlotte sighed. 'I know, but we can only deal with whatever day is in front of us, can't we? One day at a time. It'll all be different once we get him home.' She seemed about to say something else but stopped herself. Standing this close Paul once again noticed the volume of make-up she wore.

'Did you get much sleep?' he asked.

'Some.' She yawned slightly. 'Jasper was out like a light after that injection. I drifted off soon after.' She blinked a couple of times.

Paul considered her for a moment. 'Do you mind me asking – do you always wear contact lenses?'

She focused ice blue eyes on him. 'Yes. Yes, I do.' She said abruptly and turned away.

The atmosphere amongst the evacuee's was nervous, with conversation kept to a minimum. Everyone seemed to be keeping one eye out for Colour Sergeant Talbot, but he was noticeable by his absence. By contrast with the civilians, the Royal Marines who were breakfasting in shifts seemed in high spirits. Their banter seemed largely centred around the events of the night before.

The food presented to Chingiz was largely a continuation of the meal from the previous evening – probably the only food remaining in a hotel winding down for the winter season – with the addition of some fresh scrambled eggs. Paul loaded up a plate and carried to the dining table, finding himself next to Cecelia. Paul indicated a group of the Marines sitting further along the table which included Sydney, all laughing uproariously at a tale being told by Preston, the youngest member of the squad.

They're all a bit boisterous, aren't they?' Paul grumbled.

Cecelia looked the Marines and smiled. 'A mission like this is everything they've been trained for. Hostage rescue, escape, and evasion? Night-time ambushes and firefights? Forced marches over hostile terrain? Most people in the military never get to use their skills like this. These guys will be dining out on this escapade for years to come.'

'Well, I suppose. As long as, er, we *all* get home safely.' Paul muttered.

Cecelia regarded him closely for long enough to make him feel uncomfortable. 'Hmm. Their mission objectives aren't achieved yet, that is true enough. But so far so good, wouldn't you say?'

When Corporal Towne had just finished his meal he was approached by Hendrik. 'Excuse me, Corporal. My family and I were wondering, can you tell us what happened to the soldiers that attacked us last night?' Paul could see Jordi and Agnes listening intently for the answer. Judging by Jordi's pale and anxious face the boy was still troubled by what had happened.

Towne looked up. 'Don't worry. We put 'em all in the bus and drove 'em back down the valley just before dawn this morning. We parked up, slashed all the tyres on the bus, threw the keys into the river, and left 'em to it. Them soldiers were all still trussed up when we drove off. Even if they wanted to, I don't think they could get back here any time soon if that's what you are worrying about.'

'No, no, that is not it. We wanted to be sure they were unharmed.'

'Unharmed? Apart from the dead ones you mean. Look, they were in the same condition when we left 'em as they were when we put them on the bus yesterday, OK?'

Hendrik nodded, but his son still looked unhappy. 'Jordi.' Towne beckoned the boy to him. 'As my Jamaican Grandmother would say – "the spider and the fly can't make a bargain." Sometimes two sides can't avoid conflict, no matter how much you wish it were otherwise. At that point – you have to look after yourself and those around you. Which is what you did last night. By the sound of it, you were outstanding.' Jordi gave a tiny shrug of the shoulders and looked thoughtful.

Paul slapped his forehead. 'Hendrik, that's it! They are outstanding!'

'I beg your pardon?' said Hendrik.

'The conversation yesterday about dogs' bollocks - they stand out! They stick out, the dogs' bollocks, they stand out! That's why being called 'the dogs bollocks' means you are outstanding, it's a…play on words…' He stammered to a halt.

The Van Der Molens still looked confused. The Marines grinned. Hamilton looked up from food. 'I was always told 'the dogs bollocks' were good because a dog spends all his time licking 'em, so they must be the best.'

'Yeah, but don't drop a bollock, that's bad,' said Lincoln.

'And talking bollocks, that's bad too,' added Jackson.

'You don't want to *get* a bollocking, either.' called Ashton from the far end of the table.

'You should know, Smoke!' replied Towne, which made the other Marines laugh.

Hendrik threw up his hands. 'English! It is so...confusing!'

'Yeah mate,' replied Flo, deadpan. 'It's all bollocks, mind.'

Chingiz was clearing away the last of the breakfast plates when Talbot returned with the rest of the Marines.

'Listen up everybody! In ten minutes we set off; make sure you are packed and ready to go by then. We have some distance to go, but the rendezvous time is set for four pm, so there is no rush – you can walk at your own pace, but don't get out of sight of everyone else; I do not intend to waste my precious time playing hide and fucking seek with any of you. Corporal Towne will take point, I will be the rear-guard, the rest of the marines will be spread out in-between. Do not get ahead of the Corporal or fall behind me! The route isn't complicated, we just go straight up this valley for eight kilometres or so, but it will be rough terrain and steep in places so we will take plenty of breaks. Make sure you have plenty of water with you; our hosts here at the hotel have prepared some food packs for everybody as well.'

Right on queue Chingiz and Orla appeared carrying large trays piled high with a variety of containers and bags containing fruit, nuts, and bread which they started distributing to everyone.

'Any questions?' Talbot asked.

'Colour Sergeant Talbot?' Tor waved a languid hand to get his attention. 'I know how to use a gun, why not give all of us a weapon in case those soldiers come back?' She seemed to realise both Charlotte and Jasper were looking at her curiously. 'You know my dad was a sheep farmer, of course he taught us how to shoot…'

Talbot snorted in derision. 'None of my team are giving up their weapons for you.'

'What about the guns you took off the soldiers last night? They were all piled up on the grass.'

'We sent them away on the bus too.'

'*WHAT?* You gave them back? Why on earth would you do that? They were trying to kill us!' Tor's accent grew more pronounced when she got angry.

Talbot sighed and glanced around the room. Most of the evacuees looked confused and concerned. Cecelia was staring at the ceiling.

'I don't have to justify myself to you Missy, but out of the goodness of my fucking heart let me explain the situation just this one fucking time. Firstly, those soldiers weren't trying to kill you, they were trying to kidnap you. That will still be their intention if they come back. Secondly, this country is at war with itself. We kept their weapons here they would have two reasons to come back to this hotel. This way they will only come directly back if Sonny-Boy can persuade them they should chase us again, and they didn't seem incredibly pleased with him by the end of the night. More likely they will insist on reinforcements which will take some time to arrive, so we should have gained ourselves several extra hours. Is that clear enough?' Tor sat silently with a thunderous expression on her face. 'As for giving you – or any other civilian for that matter – a weapon; I'm sure you do now how a gun works, but it's not *how* to fire, but *when* and *if* that matters. I don't want any untrained panicky fuckwit firing an AK forty-seven anywhere near me thank you very much. Quite frankly you are all fucking dangerous enough as it is.' There were a few giggles around the room at this last comment, although Paul wasn't convinced Talbot was joking.

'Anyway, we didn't exactly just give them their guns back, right Corporal?'

'No Colour Sergeant. Along with the bus keys we redeployed their arms and ammunition into the river.'

Agnes stood up. She looked worried. 'If the soldiers are coming back here, aren't we leaving these two in danger? Shouldn't they come with us?' She indicated Chingiz and Orla. All eyes turned to look at the lean man and his heavily pregnant wife. The pair looked at each other uncertainly, realising they were the focus of everyone's attention.

'No of course they are not coming with us.' Talbot said bluntly. 'However…' he walked over to Chingiz and held out his hand. Hanging down from it was a set of car keys. 'Mr Maksat, please tell him - thank you very much your kind hospitality and I would like you to accept the Land Rover as recompense for the disturbance we have caused you and your wife. Then tell him it would be wise to leave here for a few days, and they should depart this morning.'

Chingiz stood motionless as Talaay relayed the message. A wide smile broke across his face as he took the keys, and he nodded to Talbot and replied. Talaay translated. 'He says we are most welcome; it has been very exciting having us here!' As Chingiz was speaking Orla gave him an amused punch on the shoulder.

'He says he will take Orla to her family's village across the mountains just to keep her from killing the soldiers if they dare to return…' There was a guffaw of laughter from the Marines who had seen Orla with the frying pan. Chingiz looked more solemn for a moment. 'He wishes us safe travels and hopes we return one day in more peaceful circumstances.' There was a subdued chorus of 'thank you's' from around the room.

Talbot spoke again. 'Mr Maksat.' He gently threw a second set of keys to the Kyrgyz interpreter. 'I understand you are leaving us today. I figured you could use these.'

There was a sense of shocked surprise amongst the evacuees. Talaay said softly 'Thank you Colour Sergeant, you are most kind.'

Talbot shrugged. 'Well, we can't take the vehicles with us, so you might as well have it. Good luck.'

Talaay looked sadly at the civilians gathered around him. 'I am sorry to leave you all, but I must stay in my country. I will go to my family in the east.'

Paul glanced at Campbell whose face was diplomatically blank. Paul got the feeling that the man from the embassy was deeply upset to be leaving the young Kyrgyz interpreter behind.

Talbot pushed out his chin. 'One last thing before we go – you will all surrender your mobile phones and tablets to me, right now. Any communication device you have will go in this.' He tossed a medium sized lightweight bag onto the table. Speaking loudly over the clamour of complaining voices he continued. 'I should have done this yesterday, but I was far too trusting. Because of this error on my part we were tracked to this location and as a consequence of that five people are dead. This is a Faraday Bag; it is designed to block out phone and GPS signals from any electronic device. So no more tracking.' The complaints subsided as he spoke, leaving him to finish in complete silence. Jordi stepped quickly forward, turning off his mobile phone and offering it to Talbot. 'Put it in the bag, my lad.' In ones and twos more people stepped forward and surrendered their devices. Charlotte unloaded two phones and a tablet. Paul recovered his mobile from the side pocket of his rucksack and slid it into the bag. Turning away from the table he was passed by the Cubitt sisters, Moira, and Annabel, who were all holding one device each. Annabel glanced over her shoulder at Jasper and Tor, who after a whispered discussion joined the queue at the table. When their turn came Tor stared at Talbot and said 'I am doing this under protest. Connecting with my fans around the world is crucial to my brand's success so I have to have my phone with me at all times. I insist this is returned to me as soon as possible.'

Paul was expecting Talbot to respond with a profanity laced put down but instead he nodded and said, 'You can have it back the moment I decide it is safe.'

Once Jasper had quietly surrendered his mobile Talbot announced, 'You now have five minutes until we leave.' There was a pause until he said, 'Last chance today to have a piss indoors…' which caused a sudden scramble towards the toilets in the reception area.

Paul did not feel the need to use the facilities so picked up his rucksack and ambled towards the hotel entrance. He paused at the reception desk to straighten the sleeve of his coat; something was catching his arm. On turning the sleeve inside out he found a cardboard shop tag tied through a loop. A flush of guilt swept through him at the memory of taking the items from the airport shop. He grabbed a pen, and a piece of hotel note paper and quickly but carefully wrote out a letter.

Under his home address and date he wrote –

Dear Sir/ Madam

I am writing to inform you of a debt I owe to you of the sum of approximately €400. This is in recompense for the following items which I took from your shop at the Manas International Airport on 24th September this year.

The items concerned were as follows –

1 x Rucksack ('Summit', 90 litres)

1 x pair of Walking Boots ('Empire GTX', size 8)

1 x Waterproof Coat ('Hunter 2' size XL)

I apologize for not paying for these items at the time although the shop was unattended and it was necessary for me to leave immediately. I enclose the product labels for you to update your stock records.

If you would kindly send me your bank details I will arrange a money transfer to recompense you. Once again, my sincere apologies for your inconvenience.

Yours Sincerely

Paul Huggins

Paul grabbed an envelope from the desk and was about to fold the letter into it when another thought struck him, and he added -

P.S. If your company has ceased trading due to the current conflict, please ignore this letter.

He wrote the shop name on the front of the envelope, removed the tags from the rucksack and coat, peeled a slightly grubby one from the sole of his shoe and stuck all three labels on the back of the letter before neatly folding the sheet into three and sliding it into the envelope. He moistened the glue on the flap with little dabs of his tongue. He looked up to see Moira and Belinda watching him with amusement. 'You look like a kitten eating ice cream,' giggled Moira. Paul couldn't think a reply, so he smiled awkwardly and set off to find Talaay.

The young Kyrgyz translator was standing between Tor and Orla next to a pile of Tors suitcases. 'Tell her to send them to this address,' Tor handed a card to a puzzled looking Orla, 'as soon as the mess in this country gets sorted out. I'll pay for the courier of course, how about that?'

Talaay repeated the message, then relayed Orla's reply. 'She says she will try to do that on the condition that she can get some photographs with you and Jasper to put on the wall.'

As Tor summoned Jasper and Orla fished her mobile out of her pocket, Paul tapped Talaay on the shoulder. Campbell, never too far away from Talaay, listened in.

'Um, if you get the chance, would you mind posting this for me?' He briefly explained the contents of the letter as he handed it over. Talaay glanced at the diplomat who nodded. 'Thanks.' Paul said.

Chingiz came hurrying over and began speaking to Talaay but looking at Paul. Talaay listened and then relayed the message. 'Mr Chingiz has a request to make of you.' Paul glanced at the hotel owner who smiled and nodded at him. 'He asks if you would write a review of his hotel.'

'What, now? We're about to leave…' Paul said.

'No, I think he means when you get home. Online.' Chingiz spoke again. Paul recognized the words 'trip advisor' even through Chingiz' accent.

'Mr Chingiz especially asks that you recommend the food,' Talaay said as Chingiz beamed at him.

Paul remembered cowering with Jordi by a broken window while Talbot fired over their heads; he thought of Sydney's rifle aimed at the intruder in the bedroom. 'Yes,' he said. 'I will be delighted to. Just a s soon as I get home.' Chingiz nodded happily, then taking Talaay by the arm headed off towards the Van der Molen family.

Jasper, and Tor were busy posing for selfies with a beaming Orla. Charlotte pulled out her camera and began clicking at the trio.

'How about a group photo?' Annabel called out and hurried to stand next to Tor. The rest of the civilians hurried to assemble. Paul found himself jostled into the middle of the group beside Orla and Chingiz on one side and Campbell on the other as Charlotte adjusted her camera again. Just then Cecelia emerged from the hotel, but rather than joining the group she held out her hand to Charlotte to take the camera.

'Go on, you get in the picture,' she told the young woman. Charlotte moved to join Jasper and Tor who had effortlessly positioned themselves front and centre. 'Say "Kyrgyzstan" everybody.' Cecelia took the photograph.

Talbot stood at the top of the steps. 'Oh, for fucks sake. If you shitmonkeys are done with all this tourist wank, we can get going.'

There was a final round of farewells to Talaay, as well as handshakes and waves for Orla and Chingiz. Orla squeezed Paul's arm and kissed his cheek as he left. He tried to pretend he didn't see the wink she gave him. Campbell held Talaay in a long hug before abruptly turning away and walking up the path. Walking beside him Cecelia patted Campbell gently on the back before adjusting the height of the walking poles she had extracted from her backpack. The four backpackers had formed a small circle, each woman checking the straps on the pack of the woman in front.

The group only got a short distance along the rising path before Cecelia and Campbell stopped and looked back to watch as Talaay climbed into one the Land Rovers in the hotel car park. With one long final wave of his arm out of the window he drove off. The remaining evacuees turned back to the path.

Chapter Ten

The Marines walked in pairs, strung out along the path with little knots of civilians spaced between them. The track started out as wide enough to accommodate vehicles with the occasional tyre mark in the mud to indicate that some motorised transport occasionally came this way. Within a few hundred metres though the footpath took a turn up a steep slope and narrowed significantly.

'Just as well we left the vehicles behind then. We seem to have run out of road already.' Paul spoke a little breathlessly.

Ren turned towards him grinning broadly. 'Roads? Where we're going we don't need *roads*!' She waved an arm around above her head and made a 'wopwopwop' sound.

Sydney pointed at Ren and laughed. 'That's from "Back to the Future"!'

Inspiration suddenly hit Paul from the last family film night he had organised at home. 'Clever girl!'

The two marines, Cecelia and Campbell turned to look at him.

'Don't you think that's a little condescending to these young women?' Cecelia inclined her head to one side as she stared at him.

'No no no! I-I-it's a film quote…it's from Jurassic Park…when the dinosaurs attack…' Paul trailed off as he noticed a small twitch at the corner of Cecelia's mouth. Sydney and Ren both laughed.

'Oh Sicknote,' came Talbot's voice from behind him. 'It's almost too easy to tease you, isn't it? Now move your arse up that path.'

The countryside around them was lightly wooded with a mixture of spiky Juniper and flat leaved Rowan trees. Underfoot brittle dry grass was interlaced with a spectrum of different wildflowers. The morning sun was now cresting the eastern mountains, and its light was smeared through the branches of the larger trees beside the path. Along the valley floor the river was a narrow ribbon of white-water jinking across an expanse of grey weathered stones.

Within twenty minutes of setting off Paul knew he was in real trouble. The other walkers were able to maintain a pace which quickly left him at the rear with only Talbot keeping position behind him. Paul's shoulders and back began to ache from the unfamiliar weight of a rucksack, his thighs and knees were stiff from climbing even gentle slopes and he felt flushed and sweaty from the exercise. Worst of all though was the sharp chafing sensation in both feet from his new walking boots. After forty minutes each step had become a torturous effort which forced an audible wince. The pain from his feet was making each step stiff and tense which worsened the discomfort in his legs and back. Talbot began urging him on with short sharp instructions which got more profane as Paul got slower and slower. After an hour, the Colour Sergeant gave an exasperated snort and spoke into his radio.

'Corporal Towne, find us a suitable place for a short rest. I've got a shitting pack horse here that might need to be shot.'

It took another five minutes before a limping Paul reached the small clearing amongst the trees where the others were already gathered. With sweat dripping into his eyes he stumbled to a halt beside a large evergreen tree and fumbled with the straps and buckles on his rucksack. Talbot grabbed the handle at the top to aid Paul's efforts to escape and grunted as he took the full weight. 'Fuckin' Nora, what arse-slapping shite have you got in here, lead bricks? You're carrying more fuckin' weight than I am.'

Still panting for breath Paul leaned back against the tree and slid jerkily to the ground. His racing pulse was still hammering in his ears as he leaned his head backwards until it rested against the sharp bark of the tree trunk. Heat seemed to be rising across his neck and face from within the heavy coat. He stared upwards as he tried to suck in as much fresh air as he could. Above him he could see a tall thin spruce tree, the dark green needles jutting out from spindly branches which wafted gently in the breeze. The sunlight flickered weakly through the layers of green and brown above him. Focusing on the movement and changes of light for a few moments helped ease the lung burning discomfort.

Looking down again he saw Talbot was emptying the rucksack, muttering expletives with each item that was pulled out. Piled up on the carpet of pine needles beneath the tree the collection of goods seemed ridiculously large. Paul could hear a few muted chuckles from those around him and there were smiles from several Marines and civilians. The good humour drained away as it became obvious that Talbot was truly angry as he paced top and fro beside Paul. 'What the fuck were you thinking, ya silly cunt?' Talbot demanded. 'What is this?' Talbot grabbed the three hardback books from the pile. "Anthology of Governance Approaches to Recovery Management, International Edition." How is an "anthology" gonna help you get up a cocking mountain? "Encyclopaedia of Concepts, Methodologies and Applications of Health Care Delivery"…fuck's sake… "Department of Health Expert Committee Guide to Major Themes Addiction Reporting Standardization"…Jesus Christ! That title doesn't even make bloody sense! Trying to carry all this unnecessary shit is just so…*fucking*….DUMB!' He punctuated his words by hurling the thick books towards the river in the valley below. Feeling the eyes of everyone upon him Paul could find no words in response, his mouth gaping as he panted for breath. He watched as Talbot sent his smart shoes frisbeeing away and then kicked the spare shirts, and trousers into the surrounding bushes. The Colour Sergeant ripped open the washbag, snorting angrily as he flicked the large bottles of shampoo, conditioner, deodorant, shaving foam, aftershave, and hairspray into the undergrowth. He dropped the toothbrush, razor and, oddly, the jar of moisturizer back onto the rucksack before throwing the rolled-up washbag and its remaining contents javelin style into the valley. Only when Talbot reached for the laptop did Paul eventually manage to utter a strangled protest, grabbing the device and clutching it to him. Talbot glared at him for a moment but then relented. 'Sort the rest of this fucking shit out, and ditch most of this bollocks.' He summoned the Marine medic. 'Draws, look him over.' He glared at the other civilians. 'Now listen up! I've had enough of this shit. This is not a fucking game anymore. From here on in, there'll be no more babysitting, no more hand-holding –it's up to each and every one of you twats to keep up with me and my team, or you are fucked – d'ya understand? Any cunt who can't get to the helicopter on time will be making their own way home.' Both Jasper and Hendrik seemed about to protest but Talbot forcefully cut them off. 'No fucking ifs and no fucking buts. This is not a negotiation. You better all be ready to set off again in five minutes.'

Paul felt a rush of panic filling his chest. He was astonished at how painful the walking had become in so short a space of time. Why was he so physically inept? What if it got so bad he couldn't walk any further? Would they really leave him behind to fend for himself? He had a flash of mental images of him crawling shamefully on hands and knees back to the empty hotel, sitting in the dark and waiting alone to be captured. He wanted to be at home. He intensely wished he could hug Annie right now.

A tiny thought zipped through Paul's mind about the expenses claim he had struggled to get signed off for the academic reference books now scattered across the valley below them. They had cost the department nearly five thousand pounds. This concern flittered away as Draws knelt in front of Paul and checked his pulse before offering him a sip of water. 'Let's get your coat off,' the medic muttered and pulled on the heavy-duty zip, revealing Pauls buttoned up suit jacket underneath. 'Oh, Jesus…get that off too. No wonder you're struggling.' As Paul removed the jacket Draws was unzipping the internal fleece from the overcoat. 'For the rest of the day either wear the fleece, or the coat, or the jacket, but not all three. Put the other two in the rucksack, you might need them if it gets cold later on tonight.'

Paul shrugged off his jacket, feeling the relief of cool air over his neck and chest. 'My feet…' he muttered and reached with a grunt for the laces of his walking boots. Draws helped him remove them. Both his heels were slick with a broad smear of blood that looked like tomato paste on a pizza. Blisters had begun to swell under the balls of his feet and over several toes. In several places his thin nylon socks were enmeshed into the swollen skin. Draws quickly pulled off the socks, ignoring the whelps of pain. The medic reached for his kitbag and set to work. After cleaning up the raw skin and burst blisters, then dousing both feet in antiseptic cream, he slapped several padded plasters and gel strips across the most damaged parts. The medic reached into his own pack and tossed a pair of thick woollen socks to Paul. 'My old socks won't smell too sweet, but they will protect your feet better than the cheese graters you were wearing. Don't take them off again until I tell you to.'

Paul nodded, gingerly pulling on the socks and walking boots once Draws had finished. The medic dropped a couple of painkiller pills into Paul's palm which he swallowed gratefully with a swig from his water bottle. Climbing stiffly to his feet he reached for his rucksack, loading the laptop and travel documents. After a moments contemplation he added the towel, the laptop power lead, the phone charger, toothbrush, razor, and moisturizer. Why had the Colour Sergeant left him that? His suit jacket and fleece he folded carefully and pushed inside the pack before finally adding his water bottle and the food from the hotel to the outside pockets. Everything else, including the food parcel from the airport which was now smelling a bit rank and his blood-soaked nylon socks, he arranged into a neat bundle and pushed underneath a bush. As he stood up to pull on his coat he noticed for the first time the rest of the group had already returned to the path. His heart was racing as the prospect of being left behind once more slapped into his mind. He swung the rucksack onto his back quite easily now, the remaining weight barely pulling on his shoulders. Flanked by Draws and Talbot he tentatively began to walk. There was a moment of unutterable relief when he found that his feet were only giving him a dull ache rather than the sharp pain he had experienced before. The realisation that he might be able to keep going hit him with a jolt. He tried to hide a trembling lip with some deep breaths and blinked and squinted to squeeze out the tears that had formed under his lower eyelids. Draws kept pace with him for a few minutes until, satisfied that Paul was moving more easily, the medic moved ahead to check on the other civilians.

Despite the weight reduction in his rucksack and the treatment for his feet Paul was still far slower than the others and for the next hour of the trek Paul continuously fell behind everyone else despite being closely shepherded by Talbot. Although the pain in his feet was less severe now he was more aware of growing discomfort in his muscles and joints through the rest of his body.

"Mind those tree roots on your left. Get your head up; you need to focus your eyeline a further ahead, don't stare at your feet or you're more likely to trip or wander off course. Keep your back straight…" The Colour Sergeant kept up a constant stream of verbal encouragement, but he barked angry instructions at Paul each time he paused or stumbled, "Oi, Soppy Bollocks, what are you stopping for? Get a move on! Up, up, up!"

On the next occasion when the group stopped for a rest Paul had barely caught up with them before they were preparing to set off once more. He sat, slumped over and wheezing, as the others shouldered their backpacks and moved on. There were a few words of sympathy and encouragement murmured in his direction, but the Marines briskly chivvied the other civilians to hurry along. Only when he could breathe without panting would Talbot let him start again by which time the rest of the group where already some distance ahead. When the main group stopped again an hour later to everyone's mild astonishment Paul walked straight past them and continued plodding up the path. Eyes fixed determinedly ahead he merely shook his head when they called for him to stop.

'Go with him, Corporal, so he doesn't wander off the path and get lost,' Talbot called out. 'No doubt the rest of us will catch you up soon enough.'

Being barely able to focus on anything except his physical discomfort Paul hadn't noticed the Royal Marine jog up beside him until Towne cheerily said, 'What's up, Sicknote? Trying to win a race now? Didn't you fancy a rest with the others?'

Breathlessly Paul replied, 'Once I stop…. it's so painful…to start again…I'd rather…keep going…'

Towne's response was gentler. 'Ok then. Just take it one step at a time. On you go…' They moved on, side by side for as long as the path was wide enough, Towne scanning the mountains on either side and the far horizon up the valley, Paul looking just a few yards ahead. It was nearly fifteen minutes later before the fastest walkers, the four backpackers, caught up with him again.

As they drew level Rachel pointed to the sky along the valley ahead. 'Did you know that weather front was coming, Corporal?' The Marine nodded.

'We saw the forecast. We expected to get out ahead of it.'

As the morning had gone on the sun had moved clear of the eastern mountains and drifted across the southern sky in front of them. As noon approached the brightness became dimmed by a velvety haze. Approaching slowly but inexorably from the southwest was a straight edged, vast bank of thick dark cloud that stretched form one side of the horizon to the other.

'I reckon we will be under that within the hour.' Rachel said. 'I hope that helicopter is warm and dry.'

The Marines Hamilton and Lincoln jogged ahead to take lead at the front of the column as the four women moved ahead of Paul and Towne. Moira patted Paul's arm as she passed.

'Keep going!' she whispered. This left Paul feeling strangely disheartened. Over the next ten minutes Paul was overtaken by everyone else. The Marines exchanged a few words with Towne each time but largely ignored Paul, as did Jasper and Tor who loped past him with long legged strides. Charlotte was easily keeping close behind her half-brother even though she had to deploy a scurrying semi-run to keep up. She nodded and gave a sad little smile to Paul as she went past. When the Van der Molen family came past Agnes said a small 'hi!' without looking at Paul; Hendrik had touched the peak of his cap as he passed but had said nothing. Jordi was too busy straining to keep his eyes on Tor further up the path. Campbell seemed to barely notice him as went around.

Last to catch him up was Cecelia who fell into step beside Paul and stayed with him for some time. She had been using two walking poles since they had set off from the hotel, with a hiking style reminiscent of cross-country skiing. She offered a pole to him together with a brisk instruction on how to use it and the best posture to adopt.

"With one pole its best to hold it at more of an angle across your body…." Paul was the passive recipient of the pole and the advice, but he rapidly found using it made the walking easier. Nevertheless it only took a few more minutes before all the rest of the party were disappearing into the distance.

'I think you should walk on now, Ms **Eriksen.** You need to keep up with the others.' Talbot spoke clearly. 'Corporal, Syd, go with her. I'll stay with Mr Huggins.'

'Yes, Colour.' Sydney moved quickly in front of Paul and beckoned politely to Cecelia, who glanced at Paul and sighed.

'Colour Sergeant, I suggest we stop for lunch in the next half an hour or so before that weather closes in completely.'

'That will depend on how far we get in the next half an hour, Ma'am. We still have some distance to go to the pick-up point.'

'Very well.' Without another look back Cecelia set off at a surprisingly fast pace with Towne and Sydney hurrying after her.

Once Cecelia was out of earshot Paul spoke quietly to Talbot. 'If I fall too far behind…'

'Keep putting one foot in front of the other, Sicknote.'

Paul glanced up at the line of dark cloud now obscuring half the sky. Slate grey in places it made Paul think of church roofs and coffin lids. 'I've worked it out, Colour Sergeant. Your mission objectives don't actually include rescuing me.'

'Shut the fuck up and walk, you knobhead.'

'I'm not sure I can keep going…' Every part of Paul seemed to hurt. He couldn't focus his thoughts on anything else suddenly. He felt swamped.

Talbot growled at him. 'Do you actually want me to get you home?'

'What? Yes.'

'Why? Tell me *why* you want to go home.' Talbot had moved swiftly in front of Paul, blocking his path. Paul stuttered for a moment; he couldn't help noticing Talbot had one hand on the grip of the rifle slung across his chest. 'Think carefully now about what you say next.' For a second his mind went blank, and then an image flew across his mind's eye.

'Yesterday, on the bus, I saw a family drive past us on the motorway, and then later I think I saw the same car in the bomb crater.'

'And?'

'And...I am terrified of letting my family down. I really, *really*, want to get home to hug my wife and daughters, Colour Sergeant. I want to be home, safe, with them, to look after them. They mean the world to me."

Talbot stared at him for a moment, then patted him roughly on his shoulder. 'Well then, that there, that is your motivation not to get left behind. Every time you think you can't go on, you think of getting back home to them. You will be astonished at what you can actually achieve. Now go on, get moving.' He pulled Paul ahead of him and pushed him onward.

Paul resumed trudging along the path. After a short distance he turned slightly and asked, 'just then when you said about determining my whole future...you had your rifle...if I didn't have a reason, what would you...er...'

'Oh you dippy twat, I wasn't gonna shoot you.'

'Oh. Of course not.'

'I might fucking reconsider it now if you don't get a move on.'

Every moment of walking for Paul was distorted and stretched by the pain into a timeless zone measured only by each tormenting thudding step. Although it was actually forty minutes before Talbot eventually conceded they should stop for something to eat Paul could have been equally persuaded it had been fifteen minutes or two hours. Paul and Talbot caught up with the others sitting in the shelter of a sheer rockface in the lee of which stood a small thicket of short walnut trees. Seated in amongst the trees the rest of the group had already begun tucking into their food packages by the time Paul arrived. He swung his pack from his back and dropped it to the floor. He stiffly lowered himself to sit straight legged against a tree. He closed his eyes and concentrated on nothing but breathing normally.

After a minute or two he opened his eyes and having confirmed by the continuing pain in his limbs that he wasn't dead yet, he reached for the food in his rucksack. As he retrieved the package he looked up to find an object being waved close to his face. After wiping some perspiration from his eyes he managed to focus on it and recognised it as a water bottle. Paul was mildly surprised to realise it was Tor who was holding it out to him. He reached out a tired arm and clutched it, but Tor didn't let go. She was looking at him intently but with her head turned slightly to one side. Paul tugged again at the bottle but still she held it tight. His smile of appreciation drooped into a look of puzzlement.

'OK, got it,' said Charlotte and Tor let go. Paul juggled his food package and the suddenly loose water bottle, dropping both. Tor moved over to Jordi and held out another bottle. A stony-faced Charlotte line up her camera for the next photograph, taking time to adjust the lens. 'Don't look at the camera, Jordi,' Tor told him. 'Make it look natural.' The young boy smiled happily and held out his hand towards the offered water bottle, keeping it suspended in mid-air for some time until Tor and Charlotte were content they had the image they wanted. They turned next towards Cecelia but were met with an abrupt, 'Do not point that camera in my direction, young lady. And you can keep that bottle of water to yourself.' Tor took one more step towards Cecelia as if to ignore the comment, but then she caught the steely look in the elderly woman's eye, thought better of it, and moved away.

Looking at the group around him Paul had the nagging feeling something was off. In an attempt to distract himself from his various complaining muscle groups he tried to focus his mind on this puzzle as he ate. What was different? Everybody was there, well, all the civilians at least. Some of the Marines weren't with them. Paul had been too self-absorbed to notice this earlier, but four of them were absent. Maybe there would be some scouting ahead or something. That wasn't what was tickling his subconscious though. The Marines that were with them were all facing outwards – either up the valley, or back the way they had come.

Peering through the trees to his right Paul got glimpses of the valley they had travelled along. He hadn't realised how high they had climbed - the mountain tops either side of the valley seemed less high now. Down the valley the hotel was far out of site, the furthest point he could see was the valley floor some miles away which was now several hundred metres below them. He looked closer at those around him.

Seated nearby were the Van der Molen family. Hendrik and Agnes were stretching and flexing their feet and legs to ease tired muscles. A flushed looking Jordi was staring transfixed at Tor even as he rapidly fed small pieces of fruit into his mouth. Tor and Charlotte were reviewing the pictures they had just taken, using Tors long leg as support with the camera resting on the model's bent knee. Beside them Jasper was oblivious to their efforts, leaning back on a rock with his eyes closed. Cecelia and Campbell were talking softly; heads tilted towards each other. Draws the medic was crouched talking to Annabel and, what had the Marines called them? Yes, Legolas and the hobbits. All four of them seemed listless, sitting slumped against a couple of intertwined tree trunks. Draws seemed to be checking the hobbits were all ok. As the Marine stood up Paul called him over.

'How are you gettin' on?' Draws asked. 'How painful are the feet?'

Paul took a moment to gather his breath before speaking. 'Yeah, they are still painful. Really painful.' he nodded towards the dozing blond man across from him. 'Jasper's medicine? Does he have plenty left?'

Draws brow furrowed slightly. 'Really? Are you that bad? I don't think you should be taking any of that...'

'No, no, no, not for me. I was just thinking - we said he should have doses every four hours?'

''Yes, but we haven't quite reached that mark yet.'

'Well, when I calculated the dosage I didn't allow for continuous exercise and increasing altitude. None of the addicts I have dealt with before will have been continuously trekking through mountains six thousand feet above sea level. He is probably getting at a guess, about fifteen percent less oxygen up here…' Paul

paused to take a long breath before continuing, '…so he is having to work much

harder. All his body chemistry will be slightly different.' Paul paused again and

looked around. 'We are all working harder I suppose. Anyway, I think he needs

to take his medicine more frequently, starting right now.'

Draws stared for a moment and then nodded. 'You are full of surprises, Sicknote.

What do you reckon he needs then?'

'Same dose, but every two hours until he sleeps or gets down to an altitude of two

thousand feet or less.'

Draws crossed over to Jasper and shook his shoulder. It took a while for the

young man to blearily open his eyes; he seemed woozy as Draws helped him take

some more of the solution concocted the night before. Paul noticed the bottle was

still mostly full. Good. As Draws tipped the bottle Charlotte turned away from the

camera to look at Jasper. Tor's attention didn't move from the images in front of

her.

As Paul put his remaining food back in his rucksack a blustering draft of wind

agitated the trees around them. A few thick shelled walnuts landed on the grass

nearby with a gentle thud. Paul reached out and gathered them up, then collected

several more that were within easy reach, stuffing them into his coat pockets. The

wind began blowing more consistently, causing the top branches of the trees to

bend and twist. The dark line of the storm front was almost above them now, the

towering clouds billowing and rolling on remorselessly.

'Time to move! Everybody up, up!' Talbot's parade ground volume was needed

now to carry above the creaking trees and buffeting wind. 'It's only two kilometres to the pickup point from here, come on, let's go!' Slowly the group dragged themselves to their feet and hoisting their packs onto their shoulders. By unspoken agreement they waited for Paul to set off first, shepherded by Talbot. Stepping clear of the shelter of trees the full force of the strengthening gale hit them, causing Paul to stagger slightly and lean into the wind, his trousers flattened tightly against his skin. As the wind whirled around him Paul could occasionally hear Talbot muttering 'fucking fucking fuckit…' to himself over and over again.

Progress for everybody was considerably slower. The area around them provided little protection from the elements; the landscape was now devoid of trees, with low tough bushes and short grass the only vegetation clinging to the stony ground. The air blasting at them was cold; Paul felt the sweat on his neck and back rapidly chilling despite his renewed exertions. After only a few minutes he stopped to retrieve the fleece from his pack, nearly losing his overcoat to the wind in the process. Once he had wrestled his way back into both layers of clothing Talbot helped him swing the rucksack on again.

As they resumed walking Talbot spoke into his comms device. 'Porky, have you made contact with Hansel, over?' Paul couldn't hear the response, but the Colour Sergeant was obviously unhappy with the reply.

'Who is Hansel?' he shouted, but the Royal Marine just shook his head at him and spoke again into his headset. 'Porky, you, and Preston make your way to the RV point, over. Say again, over?...no, not in this weather. We should be there in less than an hour, over….OK. Talbot out.'

'Who is Hansel?' Paul called again. Just as he did so something small and cold hit his tongue. He looked around as more shards of snow were flung against him by the express wind. Thick black clouds covered the sky above, sucking the light from the air around them. A churning curtain of driven snow hurried over the landscape towards them, reducing visibility still further. The leading edge of the snowstorm hit them like a physical wave, making most of the walkers pause or stagger. Talbot leaned into the wind and waved them on.

Even in the difficult weather conditions Paul was still the slowest walker and was rapidly overtaken by everyone else. In the reduced visibility the Marines worked to keep the group close together. As Paul was soon at the back of the line this meant Talbot kept stopping those at the front before they got too far ahead to let Paul plod past them to take the lead once more. Eventually everyone just fell into place behind him and let him set the pace.

Within a short time the landscape around them had become frosted white even though the tiny snowflakes were still being driven by the ferocious wind. The narrow paths they had followed for most of the morning had been edged in by precipitous mountain slopes to their left and steep drops into the valley floor to their right. After a while the ground started to level out and widen into a plateau, although the size of it was hard to judge because of the weather conditions. The wind eased a fraction, causing the snowflakes to move diagonally downwards rather than horizontally towards them. This lessened the painful experience of small shards of ice being blasted into their faces. Paul's cheeks were aching from squinting to protect his eyes.

Paul had trudged on and on after they had left the walnut trees, desperate not to stop and delay everyone further, but the pain and tiredness were causing him to stumble to a halt when Talbot called out and pointed ahead. Looking up Paul could make out in the distance two Marines at the foot of a steep ridge crouched under a large aerial on a tripod. The Colour Sergeant ran towards them. By the time Paul and the rest of the group reached the spot the two Marines, Hamilton and Preston, were dismantling the arial and packing it into one of their rucksacks. Although still gusting energetically he wind had diminished sufficiently for Talbot to speak to everybody.

'Situation report. We have managed to make contact with HQ. This storm has moved in quicker than we expected, and it has become more powerful than we anticipated as well. As a consequence we have been advised that the helicopter won't be able to reach us today.' Talbot ignored the tired groans of disappointment and angry expletives from the civilians. 'The forecast is for this to pass through in the next twelve hours or so ahead of the next weather front. Tomorrow morning we will have a window of opportunity to land a helicopter right here and pick us up. You lot can't stay out in the open overnight in this weather, so we need to take shelter. Across the valley there is a building we can use, so we will head there now.'

'Couldn't you have told us that an hour ago? We could have been out of this bloody snowstorm already!' Jasper was waving his arms angrily. Paul noted with slight satisfaction that the medication was still working.

Talbot glanced in Jasper's direction. 'We couldn't get a signal through until we got high enough. The best plan was always to try and get out today.'

'So if we had got here sooner, we'd be on our way home by now?' Tor threw a contemptuous glare at Paul. His face, already flushed with exertion and wind-chill, burned with shame that he might be responsible for delaying their escape.

'No, that would have made no difference; it's this storm that has delayed the aircraft, not our arrival time. Even if the chopper was here waiting for us it would be too dangerous to fly in these conditions.

'Colour Sergeant, I have two questions.' Cecelia had slightly raised a hand as if casting a spell. Everyone turned to look at her. She pulled down the scarf that was covering the lower half of her face.

'Firstly, how far away is this shelter? Personally, I could do without trekking for the rest of the day in this weather.'

'Yes Ma'am. On a clear day you would be able to see it from here.' Talbot pointed to the east. 'As the crow flies it's about a mile and a half away over there on the other side of the valley, but the safest route to get there is to maintain this altitude and follow the ridge line around the top of the valley. That'll be about two miles, give or take.'

'Very well. Secondly, you said we have a 'window of opportunity' tomorrow. How small is this 'window'?'

Talbot looked slightly uncomfortable. 'It's a two-hour window, ma'am. Between nine and eleven o'clock tomorrow morning. Much later than that and the weather will close in again. Or the chopper will run out of fuel on the way back.' There were groans of dismay from the civilians.

'Understood, thank you.' Cecelia pulled her scarf back over her mouth.

'Hang on. Why not take the direct route to that building?' Campbell asked.

'Taking the direct route would mean climbing down this mountainside, traversing a glacier, and then climbing up a steep cliff on the other side. It would take much longer, and it would be much more dangerous.'

'Well, fair enough then. I didn't realise there was a glacier down there.' Campbell stared at his feet.

'No more questions? Right then.' Talbot turned to the Marines. 'Corporal, take Smoke and Jackson and scout ahead; find us a safe path to the lodge. The rest of you keep our guests together and stay in sight. Anyone wandering off on their own will have an uncomfortable evening.' There were some grim chuckles from the Marines as they prepared to set off.

'What do you mean, 'uncomfortable'?' Agnes sounded worried. Hendrik put an arm around her shoulder.

'He means we won't survive the night out in the open.' Jasper shouted. 'He's being a bit over dramatic if you ask me!' He laughed. Agnes looked terrified.

Talbot pushed past Jasper and approached the van der Molen family group. 'We will all be fine; it will be more comfortable indoors in this weather, that's all.' He looked down at Jordi, who was shivering slightly. 'Here.' He pulled off his beanie hat and placed it on Jordi's head. 'Let's go.' The boy smiled and pulled the hat over his ears. Talbot turned away.

'You old softy.' Sydney grinned.

Talbot walked past and didn't look in her direction. 'Fuck off.' The Marines roared with laughter. 'Sicknote, with me.' Talbot put a strong hand on Paul's elbow and pulled him forward.

The wind was less forceful now with larger flakes of snow whirling around them. As Paul gingerly limped onwards he realised his trousers were becoming sodden by the wind-blown snow, the thin fabric sticking to his legs and pulling tightly with each step. Although the snow was settling more thickly on the ground the footsteps of the three Marines leading the way were easily visible even though the figures themselves had become obscured by the cloud fall. As the trail reached the edge of the plateau it continued just below the crest of the ridge which denoted the top of the valley. The ridge curved away to their right and seemed to funnel the wind more powerfully into their faces, with occasional gusts and zephyrs threatening to dislodge them from the side of the mountain. There was little chance of losing the path for the first mile or so as it remained parallel with the ridge arcing above it. After this the footsteps of the pathfinders veered right as the ridgeline took a left turn and merged into a jumble of jagged mountain peaks that disappeared into the cloud. Their route began to descend slightly. Talbot was having to scan the ground more carefully to find path to follow. The settled snow was reaching to ankle height on Pauls boots by now and the footprints were disappearing under the drifting flakes. The going underfoot was becoming more treacherous as the as the white blanket around them camouflaged jutting boulders and sudden holes which caused several people to stumble and fall. Just as Campbell tripped and went sprawling into the snow a figure appeared on the path in front of them. It was Jackson.

'Send us a postcard if you enjoyed your trip!' Jackson chortled. Campbell snorted in disgust as he brushed himself down. Jackson smiled again. 'Nearly there Colour Sergeant – Corporal Towne sent me back to guide you in. He and Smoke are at the RV already.'

'I hope they get the heating going.' grumbled Campbell.

'The smoothest path is a couple of metres to your left, Colour; you've wandered into a field of rocks where you are. The snow was a lot lighter when we first came through. Follow me.' Jackson set off confidently and the civilians hurried after him.

As Paul watched the others move off along the path in front of him, he suddenly felt a sharp griping pain in his stomach. He stumbled on trying to ignore the discomfort when another spasm twisted in his gut, then another. He tried to hurry forwards, tried to break into a shuffling run but more sudden tightening pains in his bowels demanded attention. He wouldn't make it to the unseen building ahead of them; he had to relieve himself now. He hobbled to a pile of broken rocks away from the path and scurried to the far side. Clutching his stomach, he climbed down to a secluded point between two large boulders and wriggled his rucksack off his back. He fumbled for his trousers belt but had to undo his coat before he could reach it to get it undone. In a near panic he pulled down his trousers, roughly peeling the sodden material down over his thighs and knees, whipping down his underpants and squatting down just as with a squirting pain his bowels evacuated. Even as the internal discomfort eased he realised his bare buttocks were stinging with cold from direct contact with the snow beneath him.

He let out a little sigh as the pain eased and he realised he was finished. At that moment there was a small cough from just above him. His head spun round to see Talbot standing on the rocks nearby looking at him.

'What the fuck are you playing at?'

'I-I'm sorry Colour Sergeant, I couldn't wait…I was in pain.'

'Hmm.' Talbot turned his head, cupped his hands around his mouth, and shouted 'Draws! To me!'

'No! Don't…' pleaded Paul.

Talbot ignored him 'Draws! I think Sicknote just shat himself!'

Paul closed his eyes. Talbot addressed him again. 'If you haven't brought any bog roll you'll have to use snow to wipe your arse. Have fun with that.'

Paul didn't have any paper. He stood up and leaned over the edge of the boulder to his right, reaching down to scoop up a handful of snow from the large snowdrift resting against the stone. As his fingers reached into the icy material the texture changed; after the first few centimetres of ice crystals it suddenly became scratchy wool. The whole snow drift leapt to its feet, let out a startled 'baaa!' and jumped away up the mountain side. With trousers and pants still around his ankles an equally surprised Paul stepped backwards and put one heel into his own squishy excrement.

Chapter Eleven

By the time Draws had made his way over to Talbot, Paul had been able to clean himself and pull up his underpants. However his trousers were proving more difficult to recover. Saturated with icy cold snow water the cloth was clinging to his lower legs and thighs and resisting his increasingly frantic efforts to pull them up to his waist. Grabbing the belt with both hands he sprung upwards in a feeble star jump. With a ripping sound the thigh seams on the outside of each leg pulled apart as the top of the trousers finally reached Pauls hips. He quickly buttoned them up as best he could.

Talbot and Draws exchanged a quick word before the Colour Sergeant set off after the other travellers. Draws looked at Paul.

'You are keeping me busy, Sicknote. What is it this time?'

Paul scrapped his heel on the edge of a nearby rock. 'I had… well, an urgent bowel movement, that's all.'

Draws craned his neck to look at the flattened faeces. 'Hmm. When it's that runny, that yellow, and that urgent, I'd says you have diarrhoea, not just a mis-timed bowel movement. I've got some medications that will help sort you out. Come on, we're nearly there.' He turned away. Paul followed, dragging one heel through the deepening snow. Once or twice he thought he could hear a distant 'baaa!'

The path became easier as the ground became less boulder strewn. Despite the thickening snow the footprints of the others were easy to follow, although there were all out of sight in the heavy snowfall. After a few hundred yards the path rose and narrowed to a thin strip with steep slopes above and below. Draws paused to look back at Paul. 'Careful – this looks like a scree slope, nothing but loose stones underfoot.' Paul tried to tiptoe behind the medic but quickly found this too painful. The path sloped downwards after a couple of minutes and soon they were back on flat solid ground.

'There it is – tonight's barracks.' Said Draws. A dark shape came into focus as they approached.

Hunkered below a steep peak was a derelict ski lodge. Surrounded by a low stone wall it consisted of two larger buildings with a scattering of small outhouses behind them. The bigger of the two main structures was a two-storey dormitory, long and narrow, its steep sides encased in slate grey metal cladding which was punctured by small deep-set windows. The badly rusted exterior covering ran across the thin roof and all the way down to the stone foundations. The second equally rusted building was on a single level, as broad as it was wide with large windows on three sides. This had once been the kitchen and social area for the intrepid trekkers and skiers who had ventured this far into the mountains. Although the buildings seemed weatherproof and the windows seemed to be intact the site had the air of having been deserted for several years. Paul was immediately reminded of a youth hostel in Wales he had stayed in on a school trip when he was fourteen. That had been a miserable experience too.

The civilians stood huddled in a group, sheltering by the wall of the dormitory building while the marines conducted a search of all the site. Only once it was deemed to be uninhabited were they allowed by Talbot to go in. Moira and

Belinda ran to be the first up the steps to the door set in a small porch at the front of the building. Moira won, and pulled open the creaking tin door, laughing.

'Always bloody competing, those two.' grumbled Rachael. Annabel took her hand and led her towards the steps.

'Race you!' Annabel shouted and set off running. Rachael squealed and chased after her.

As everyone else followed, Talbot shouted instructions. 'Drop your rucksacks inside, then bring any food and you have and gather in the kitchen over here. Corporal Towne tells me there is a toilet block round the back on the left if anyone needs to relieve themselves.'

Paul got the feeling everyone glanced at him.

Following everyone else he trudged into the building, pausing at the door to kick the snow off his boots and check the heel of his boot for any other material still clinging to it. It seemed to be clean, so he went inside.

Beyond the porch lined with dozens of coat hooks on the walls was a small hallway, to the left of which was a metal spiral staircase with wooden treads. The thunderous sound of running footsteps announced Moira, Rachel, Annabel, and Belinda were making their way upstairs. Jordi was following close behind.

Opposite the main doorway in the hall was a small space containing only a low table pushed against one wall. Cecelia was stood in front of the table staring at a patch of wooden panelling above it. As Paul limped towards her he could make out faded paintwork on the wood she was staring at. The artwork was decades old to judge by how faded it was. There were several figures drawn against a mountainous background, adults, and children, all the females wearing headscarves, the males bareheaded except for a helmeted soldier. The women all wore skirts and waistcoats, the men a variety of working clothes. Every character had their sleeves rolled up to reveal smooth muscular arms, even the children. They all clutched something, whether it was schoolbooks, factory, or farm tools, or even a briefcase. The soldier was cradling a long-barrelled machine gun. Their faces were all turned upwards, chins tilted as they stared collectively into the distance. Most of the facial features had disappeared as the painting had faded and scuffed over time. Cecelia glanced at Paul.

'Soviet era. They call this style 'Socialist Realism.' Full of idealism and hope for a great future. I've always found it rather endearing.' She smiled. 'One of the few good things to come out of communism in the twentieth century.' She turned and headed for a bedroom with Sydney stood in the doorway.

To the right of the hall was a narrow passage with a square window at the far end, with several doors leading off on either side. Paul chose one and pushed open the door to reveal a small room with four bunk beds and a rough wooden table. To his surprise there were thin mattresses on each bed in a variety of faded colours and patterns. He put his rucksack on the table, pulled out the remaining food and the water bottle and went back to the hallway. Campbell emerged from the door opposite.

'Feeling okay?' Campbell asked.

'Umm…not really.' Paul suddenly felt exhausted.

'Just one more day, then we'll be on our way home.' Campbell tried to smile but it wasn't very convincing.

'How about you?' Paul asked. 'You must be missing your friend.'

Campbell had his hand on the front door to push it open but stopped. 'Well…yes. I am missing Talaay actually. Or rather I am just worried that they will be safe.' He stepped outside. 'Not being able to speak to him is the most irritating thing. Once we are out of the country I can at least ring him…' He shook his head. 'Anyway, there is nothing I can do about that just now. I will just have to concentrate on helping get Cecelia, and you, and all the others safely evacuated. But thank you for asking.'

'I'm not sure Cecelia needs too much looking after. She seems to be coping just fine if you ask me.' Paul reached the steps to the kitchen building ahead of Campbell and lifted his leg for the first high step. There was an ominous but thankfully brief ripping sound as his trouser seams gave way a little more.

'Even so, she is in her seventies, we have to be sure she is alright.' Campbell looked at Pauls legs ascending the stairs in front of him. 'I say, you do know you've got a hole, no, two holes in your trousers?'

'Yes I know.' Paul had reached the top step.

'And, er, Talbot said you, ah, had an accident?'

Paul looked at Campbell, annoyed. 'I didn't shit myself, OK? I was just caught short, that's all.' He stomped into the building, wincing as his feet complained at the harsh treatment.

This building was one large open plan space, the back third being a kitchen area with a large wooden sink and empty trestle tables and shelves around the walls.

The remaining area was a mostly empty space with only a large wooden dining table that stretched the length of the room with rough bench seats arranged either side. Dividing the room was a huge oven which doubled as a fireplace with a round metal chimney that ran up to the ceiling. Like the dormitory this building was still weatherproof – the floor and walls were dry with no signs of mould or damp. Smoke and Preston were bringing in armfuls of chopped wood as Ren set about lighting the fire.

'There's a wood store underneath the building.' Preston sniffed. 'Fuck knows where they got the wood from though; there's no trees for bloody miles.'

Ren looked up at him. 'They probably got a donkey like you to drag it up here.'

Preston grinned and pointed at his groin. 'Donkey? You been spying on me in the shower again?'

'Nah, I saw your IQ score.' Ren turned back to the fire.

The young Marine everyone called 'Smoke' playfully pushed Preston's shoulder. 'Come on Eeyore, we better get some more wood.'

The other Marines in the room laughed and shouted 'Eeyore!'

'Oh no, don't call me that!' Preston protested as he and Smoke headed for the door. 'I want a cool nickname like Double Tap, or Florida.'

Ren called after them. 'Smoke, just tell him, 'Eeyore' to know better by now! Get it?' She loaded several pieces of dry wood onto the burning kindling and fanned it, causing the flames to erupt upwards. She closed the vented metal door of the firebox, watching the chimney for a while as the fire grew. There was little sign of smoke escaping into the room. Seemingly satisfied she stood up. She looked at

Paul who was standing near the window in a small puddle of melted snow. 'Hey, Sicknote, come and stand by the fire – you need to get those trousers dry.'

Paul nodded and shuffled over to one end of the stove. He felt the heat start to radiate out from the metalwork. He turned to rest his backside on the edge for a moment, hoping to relieve some of the weight from his abused feet. With a strangled yelp he rapidly stood up again as the heated metal briefly scorched his buttocks. He remained standing as still as he could, as the fire blazed, the room warmed up, and his trousers started to steam slightly. Eventually the throbbing discomfort in his feet became too much, so he lay on his left side with his legs in front of the fire, propping up his head on his left arm.

Most of the other evacuees had arranged themselves at the dining table in small groups, gradually relenting to remove coats and gloves as the room warmed. Three Marines were stationed as lookouts at windows facing east, south, and west, although this struck Paul as pointless as the weather was limiting visibility to only a hundred yards or so. The other marines in the room busied themselves with equipment checks and a concerted effort to boil snow water in a saucepan to make a brew. Draws was working his way around everyone in the room, seemingly undertaking a brief health check on military and civilian alike. He left Paul until last, dropping onto his haunches to get closer to Paul's eye level.

'How ya doin'?' Draws asked, raising his voice slightly above the increasing hubbub of conversation in the room.

'This doesn't feel like my finest hour.' Paul grumbled. 'My feet are killing me, every muscle in my body is sore, I'm not entirely confident of controlling my stomach in either direction, and I think I may have burnt my bum on the stove.'

He glanced at Draws face, saw a flicker of amusement, and couldn't help letting out a guffaw of laughter. 'And it turns out I'm a whiney little bitch as well!'

Draws grinned. 'Yeah, don't forget self-pity on your list of woes. Well, here's another couple of paracetamol to help manage the pain in your feet and your back.'

'Do I need to re-bandage my feet do you think?' Paul swallowed the small white pills with a swig of water.

Draws shook his head. 'Nah, we'll take another look at the bandages this evening. Better to keep your boots on for now in case your feet swell up and we can't get your boots back on. I for one am not carrying you to the helicopter tomorrow.' He checked his medic pack. 'I'll make you up a little solution in a minute to settle your stomach; just lay off the solids for a couple of hours, ok? Talking of solutions, I will need your help again with Jasper.'

Paul looked up sharply. 'What is it, is he alright?'

'He's ok for now, but by dawn he is going to run out of the withdrawal cocktail we made up for him last night, so we need to cook up a new batch to get him through tomorrow.'

'Yes of course.' Paul frowned slightly. 'Is there anything I can do for anyone else?'

'Like what?'

'I, er…. well…um…. oh, I don't know. I just wanted to help the others. And to feel useful I suppose.'

'I think you're keeping the entertained at least. And making them feel better about themselves. In a 'I might be knackered but at least I'm not as bad as Sicknote' kind of a way.'

'Oh good grief.' Paul slumped face down on the floor as Draws chuckled.

'At least from here I can see you haven't burnt your arse – just singed your trousers a bit. From this angle it does look a tiny bit like you've shat yourself though.'

'Oh, for god's sake.' Paul rolled quickly onto his back as Draws laughed and stood up.

'Just kidding! If I think of anything useful for you to do I'll let you know.'

Paul closed his eyes and ran a mental check of each limb and muscle group to try and work out whether anything hurt as much as his feet. He tried to focus on his ankles, then his knees, then hips – they all hurt, but his feet were worse. Concentrate on his back, then the neck, his shoulders, elbows, wrists, …fingers…. Paul fell asleep.

He was woken by a gentle prod from Draws foot.

'Wazza..?' He blinked and squinted, confused there was still daylight showing through the windows. Surely it was the middle of the night by now. 'What time is it?'

'It's about two thirty pm. You've been asleep for about forty minutes.' Draws offered him a mug. 'Here - a potion to keep your stomach settled.'

'Yeah and snoring like a hog for about thirty-nine of 'em!' Jasper laughed at his own joke but no-one else seemed inclined to join in. Campbell the professional diplomat could only manage a polite smile in Jasper's direction which disappeared when he looked away. Everyone else was too engrossed in their own conversations to pay any attention to Jasper. Or at least they pretended to be.

Paul realised laying by the fire had mostly worked. His right trouser leg, the one nearest the stove, was quite dry whilst the left leg was now only slightly damp. There was a water stain on the floorboards marking where he had been laying which was evaporating in the warmth of the room. His ripped trousers felt out of shape and uncomfortable. Stiffly Paul levered himself onto his hands and knees, and then onto his feet, wincing as his blistered skin took his full bodyweight again. He limped over to the bench nearest to him and gingerly sat down.

Through the window in front of him Paul could see there had been a change in the weather whilst he had been asleep. The sky was noticeably less dark, although visibility was still only about a hundred metres or so. The cloud base seemed higher and more broken. Although the snow had settled a thick foam over every nearby landscape feature there were pockmarks appearing everywhere caused by the sleet that was now sporadically dropping out of the sky. There were fewer Marines in the room now; Paul guessed some had been sent out on guard duty, or patrol, or something.

In one corner of the room Hamilton and Preston had arranged their radio equipment with cables feed out of one small window to the aerial that was set up outside. Across the babble of voices in the room Paul could occasionally catch

Hamilton repeating over and over 'This is Shepherd, calling Gretel, come in, over. This is Shepherd…' No response was forthcoming.

Paul returned the mug to Draws and they set about creating more of the medical solution for Jasper. It took the best part of an hour to complete this time. The captive audience in the hut with absolutely nothing else to do gathered around to watch and peppered them with questions at each stage of the process. Paul ended up giving an impromptu science lecture, skimming over elements of chemistry, pharmaceutical medicine, anatomy, and elements of addiction. As they continued Paul notice Charlotte was photographing him as he worked. Jasper seemed increasingly annoyed that his failings were being discussed in the open without him actually being the centre of attention. When Paul made what he thought was an innocent remark about this solution 'keeping Jasper on the straight and narrow' the young man thumped the side of his fist against the wooden wall of the hut and shouted at Paul, 'well at least I didn't shit myself on a sheep, unlike you!' and he stormed out of the door and ran off towards the dormitory building. Charlotte rolled her eyes and sighed, then slowly went after him. Pauls face flushed beetroot red with embarrassment, and he and Draws finished their activity in virtual silence.

When they were done, Draws handed Paul the bottle. 'Keep hold of this until tomorrow, would you? Its best he doesn't get hold of it too soon. I'm not sure his impulse control is all that good.' Paul tucked the bottle into one of the voluminous coat pockets. Feeling embarrassed and irritable Paul hauled himself to his feet again, snatched up the leftover items from the table, shoved them deep into another pocket of the coat and then made for the doorway.

Just in front of the steps Paul found Cecelia surveying the landscape; she seemed to have appropriated a pair of binoculars from Sydney, who was stood beside her. Three Marine sentries were positioned around the perimeter wall still facing east, west and north. Although sunset was still nearly two hours away in the lee of the mountain ridge the light was noticeably poorer. Talbot was nearby, talking quietly with Lincoln. A brief sharp noise followed by the echo of a muffled cry bounced off the metal cladding of the buildings around them. Paul couldn't tell if it was animal or human that had called out. The Marines dropped into crouching positions and aimed their rifles into the gloom. The noise came again, louder. 'Crack! Crack!' Paul sat down hard, tugging at Cecelia's sleeve. 'Shots! Get down!' Cecelia didn't move.

'Hmm…no,' said Cecelia softly. That is not the sound of a gun. It's more like…a whip?' Talbot set off at a crouching run, beckoning Lincoln to follow. Despite the improving conditions the two men were quickly swallowed up by the greyness. One more round of 'crack, crack' was heard and then silence.

It was several minutes later before Lincoln came running back. The rest of the Herd were still inside the lodge. Towne beckoned to Cecelia. 'We need you.' He led her away from the building and Sydney followed. After a moment's hesitation so did Paul. As Lincoln led them a little way down the slope several figures became visible. Talbot, arms crossed in front of him and rifle carefully slung over his shoulder was standing silently. Close by was a teenage Kyrgyz boy sat on a small horse. The boy looked tanned and rosy cheeked from a life lived outdoors. Paul noticed a long leather whip coiled on the boy's belt which was tied at the waist over his thick sheepskin jacket. Talbot was making every effort to appear non-threatening, but he appeared to be having a side-eye staring competition with the huge pale-furred dog who was sitting between the rider and the Marine. The pony had dropped its head to snuffle in the snow looking for grass to chew on.

'We needed a translator – we think he speaks Russian,' said Lincoln as they approached.

'The boy or the dog?' asked a poker-faced Cecelia.

The corner of Lincoln's mouth twitched upwards. 'Both of them, probably. And the horse, too.'

The boy gave a broad smile and nodded politely toward Cecelia as she approached, but the way his eyes roamed around the group in front of him made it obvious he was astonished to find these strangers at the top of his lonely valley. Behind him a few dozen brown and grey woolled sheep huddled together, bleating occasionally.

He didn't seem surprised when Cecelia spoke to him in Russian though and seemed quite happy to strike up a conversation. After a while Cecelia broke off to translate for the others.

'This is Azamat.' The boy waved when he heard his name. 'He doesn't speak English, but his Russian is pretty good. I have told him we are on a hunting trip and got caught in the weather, so we are sheltering in the lodge for the night.'

'Did he believe that?' Talbot glanced at the dog who yawned, exposing huge teeth.

'Yes, I think so: he seems quite trusting. He obviously knows we aren't local. I told him we were all from Finland, but you don't speak Russian.'

'Hunters from Finland?' Talbot seemed offended. Paul thought it was quite a clever lie to explain the appearance of a group of well-armed foreigners in the middle of nowhere. Talbot sniffed. Did he say what he is doing up here?'

'Gathering his flock to take it down the mountain for the winter, he says.'

Talbot's eyes rested on Paul for a moment. 'Sicknote can help with that – you're good at finding sheep in the snow, aren't you Sicknote?' Talbot turned back to look at Azamat. 'Is the boy alone?'

After an exchange in Russian Cecelia answered, 'he says his grandfather is somewhere nearby, but that could be miles away or just over the hill, I can't tell. He seems surprised we don't have a local guide, but I told him the guides left us to organise safe passage out of the country. He doesn't seem to know too much about the conflict.'

'I don't suppose he has any reason to know about it, the lucky bugger. He'll get a hell of a shock when he tries to take his flock to market though.'

Standing still in the chill air Paul was feeling cold again.

'Has he seen anyone else today? Any other…foreigners? Talbot asked.

Cecelia posed the question and translated, 'No, no-one else. He tells me he and his grandfather were planning to head down the valley this afternoon, but the weather slowed them down. A lot of the sheep were hunkered down to get out of the snow.' Paul avoided catching Talbot's eye. Cecelia continued, 'He thinks they have recovered nearly all of the herd now so they will break camp tomorrow.'

'Ok.' Talbot, nodded, smiled, and waved politely at the boy. 'Tell him to bugger off now, would you ma'am?' With a final glance at the dog he headed back towards the lodge.

Cecelia spoke with the young shepherd for a little while longer and then followed. Azamat watched them go.

The warmth inside the kitchen hut was welcome after the cold air outside. Paul followed Talbot in. The Colour Sergeant was met at the door by Corporal Towne.

'Are Sicknote and the Great Dane with you, Colour? 'Cos we are two sheep short of a full herd.' Towne noticed Paul. 'Ah, there's one..'

'Ms Eriksen is following just behind, Corporal. Sydney is with her. We had an encounter with another local; hopefully, it won't cause us any problems, but warn the sentries we have locals in the vicinity, so they need to use discretion, ok?'

'Very good, Colour. '

Paul moved away from the Marines and unzipped his coat. Lincoln had come in and made a beeline for the stove, and Paul followed him hoping for a warm drink. He had to settle for a cup of melted snow water. Shortly after Cecelia and Sydney came in.

Tor had appropriated the centre of the room for herself and was running through what looked like extremely slow-moving yoga movements. Having removed her boots and outer layers of clothing she was stretching her unfurled limbs into a series of highly controlled poses; eyes closed in a passive face. Several of the Marines dotted around the room were watching her, as was Jordi who was sat at the table beside is parents. Hendrik and Agnes were engaged in a loud conversation in Dutch.

Tor opened her eyes and said to them. 'Do you mind being quiet? I developed this form of Tai Yoga Chi as an exercise of mind and body, and it takes a good deal of concentration. I can't hear myself meditate over you two gabbling on.'

Hendrik and Agnes broke off their discussion looking startled, but before they could respond there was an eruption of noise from around the room, with all the marines contributing – some were coughing, others yawning loudly, someone was whistling and in the corner Hamilton was now shouting into the radio 'This is Shepherd! Calling Gretel! come in, over!' All followed by a round of uproarious laughter. Tor looked furious, her usually ice pale cheeks flecked with a delicate pink flush, but she closed her eyes again and went back to her exercises.

As the noise died down Talbot muttered loud enough for everyone to hear 'Tai Yoga Chi my fucking arse…' which caused another burst of laughter. A level of conversation began around the room, louder than before Tor's outburst.

Cecelia looked at Talbot. 'You're not inclined to join in with 'Tai Yoga Chi' then, Colour Sergeant?'

Talbot glanced at Tor. 'Excuse my French Ma'am, but I'd sooner shit in my hands and then clap.'

Cecelia permitted herself a smile. 'I practice Yoga. Very beneficial for physical and mental wellbeing.'

'Yes Ma'am, I'm sure it is. But you don't insist on everybody else sitting quietly in the corner while you take over the room to do it, I don't suppose?'

While continued on with her exercises the rest of the Herd were seated around the table. Jasper was sighing dramatically, laying slumped across the table next to Charlotte. Campbell and the Van der Molen family were watching on as Annabel, Rachel, Belinda, and Moira were playing cards. After several rounds of rummy between the four of them Campbell asked, 'is there anything we can all play?' The card players looked at each other. Rachael shrugged. 'At uni we play Twenty-One with nine players and a dealer. We could give that a go?'

'What is 'twenty-one'?' asked Hendrik.

'Oh, you know, erm, everyone gets two cards, you can twist for another three cards, nearest to twenty-one wins...'

Jasper sat bolt upright. 'Blackjack! Count me in ladies!' He slapped his hands on the wooden table surface. 'I haven't played blackjack since that night Las Vegas two years ago, d'you remember Tor?'

'I remember you lost about ten grand of my money.' Tor tilted her head to stare at Jasper angrily.

'Oh, it's not like you can't afford that quite easily my darling.' Jasper sneered and waved a hand dismissively. Paul noticed he received a sharp dig in the ribs under the table from Charlotte.

'I do not approve of gambling. We will not play,' Agnes said, which elicited a wail of disappointment from Jordi.

Belinda held out a placatory hand towards the Van der Molen family. 'Oh, go on Mrs M; there'll be no money involved, this will just be for fun.' She reached further and patted Jordi's arm. Come and sit beside me, I'll show you how to play.' Jordi shot out of his seat and raced around the table to sit beside Belinda.

'It's not so much fun without a bet.' Jasper complained, but he also moved around the table to join in.

'Actually its Mrs Vee Dee Emm.' Agnes said. Hendrik looked at Agnes and raised his eyebrows imploringly. Agnes sighed and said, 'OK Jordi. But never for money, yes?'

'Yes mama!' he cried delightedly.

The atmosphere in the hut changed swiftly, with happy chatter emanating from the players and spectators of the card game. Belinda's friendly instructions to Jordi were occasionally drowned out by whoops and groans from Jasper reacting to each card he was dealt. The other players responded in kind, joking with each other and particularly teasing Jasper for each noisy reaction he made. Jasper was obviously enjoying himself enormously. Paul thought he suddenly looked very young.

In the corner of his eye Paul noticed Talbot walk across the room, deliberately moving through the space Tor had appropriated for herself and passing remarkably close to Tor. The model was sitting cross legged with her arms outstretched in a 'swan wing' pose. Paul though he heard Talbot mutter 'pack it in love, nobody's watching' as he moved off. After a moment Tor got to her feet and went and stood staring out of the far window.

As the raucous card came continued the light outside steadily ebbed away, the clouds and snowy landscape visible through the windows becoming filtered through deeper and deeper blue. The Marines set up four powerful torches around the room, their white beams pointed at the ceiling. A jiggling orange glow emanated from within the stove, the undulating firelight throwing shadows across the floor in the spaces below the torch light.

Just as the outside world was about to disappear from view entirely there came a call on the Marines comms device that made them all turn to the door, reaching for their weapons.

'Corporal Towne says we've got company.' said Talbot.

Chapter Twelve

Even as the marines hurried to take up firing positions around the room Talbot
motioned them to stop. He put his hand to his ear, listening on his comms device
to the message relayed from the sentries outside.

'Stand down; it's just the shepherd boy and an old man. Linc, open the door and
invite them in.'

As Lincoln reached the entrance Corporal Towne and two other figures passed by
the window and climbed the steps to the doorway. Towne stood to one side and
let the strangers enter first. In front of a wide-eyed Azamat came a short elderly
man with a long white goatee beard and thick handlebar moustache of the same
colour. He was wearing a tall white hat which had a sharp crease at the front and
a dark upturned brim, and a charcoal grey suit jacket over a blue woollen jumper.
Between them they were carrying a large cooking pot which steamed slightly.
The placed the pot onto the stove and then turned to look at the travellers who
had gathered in front of them. The old man slowly surveyed every face in front of
him, bowed politely and then spoke in a clear quiet voice. Everyone looked
towards Cecelia.

'That wasn't Russian; it must have been Kyrgyz, which I can't speak I'm afraid.'
She stepped forward, slowly bowed to the old man, and then addressed the boy.
After a few exchanges Cecelia translated again for the benefit of everyone else.
'This is Daniyar, Azamat's grandfather. He has come to offer food and a
welcome to the strangers in his valley that his grandson told him about.'

'And to check us over, no doubt.' Talbot growled.

'Oh, most certainly. But I think he is just curious about us. Can I suggest everyone follows my lead for the time being?'

Daniyar and Azamat moved away from the stove and sat cross-legged on the floor where Tor had been exercising a little while before. Azamat divested himself of a large leather bag and an even larger cloth sack that had been hanging across his back. Cecelia sat facing them and the rest of the party sat in a circle around them. After a look and a nod from Cecelia, Talbot instructed the Marines to join them, although he remained standing near the door.

Cecelia turned to Campbell. 'As the British ambassador's representative in the room - are there any Kyrgyz customs I need to know about? He won't be offended talking to a woman?'

No, not at all. Deference is given to the elders, so probably best you lead the conversation anyway. It may be worth noting the old man has dressed to impress, with his suit jacket and best jumper. And *that* is the kind of hat that is only worn on special occasions.'

Cecelia nodded and spoke to Azamat while maintaining eye contact with Daniyar. She translated back into English.

'I have said thank you for the welcome and for the lovely smelling mutton stew they have bought to share with us. We do not mean to get in their way, and we will be gone tomorrow.'

The old man nodded solemnly and turning to his grandson he held out his hands. The young boy hurriedly rummaged in his leather bag and pulled out a thick rolled up piece of heavy material.

The old man took it and unfurled it, placing it on the floor at Cecelia's feet. It was a small woollen carpet, intricately woven with a myriad of colours, about the same size as a door mat. Daniyar spoke for a while and Azamat translated. Cecelia repeated the message. 'This is a gift of welcome; a gift of friendship; a gift to wish safe travels.'

'Are you sure he's not just trying to sell us something?' Tor's voice sounded bored.

Cecelia didn't turn away from Daniyar. 'Ms Turner, this is not a commercial transaction, this is what genuine friendliness looks like. However, it would be polite to give a gift in return. Does anyone have something?'

The group looked at each other in silence for a while until Moira gasped 'Oo, yes!' She reached a hand under her collar and pulled a leather strap over her head. Dangling at the end of it was silver coloured pendant in the shape of an eagle.

'I bought this at a market when we first came into Kyrgyzstan. I thought it was pretty. Will it do?'

Cecelia reached out a hand and took the necklace, held it up to look at it and smiled. 'Very nice.' She extended her hand with the necklace to Daniyar. He bowed again, accepted the gift, and after studying it for a moment he turned and hung it around Azamat's neck. The surprised look on the boys' face made everyone laugh, including the old shepherd. Azamat studied the pendant for a while, then smiled and gave Moira a little wave.

Daniyar reached for the sack beside Azamat and pulled out two objects. One was a broad shallow drum which the old man placed in his own lap; the other was a stringed instrument that looked like an elongated mandolin. He handed this to Azamat. After a short speech Daniyar began to beat out a steady rhythm on the drum.

'This is a song about the shepherd and the wolf,' Cecelia translated. Azamat began to strum, carefully placing his fingers on the strings to create a simple melody. The young boy started to sing in a high-pitched voice using only a single note. After a while Azamat's voice stopped and the old man, still drumming, closed his eyes and began to sing instead. In contrast to Azamat, Daniyar's voice was a shockingly deep growl, emanating from the back of his throat.

'I guess he's the wolf...' Paul suddenly realised he had said this out loud, but no one around him seemed to have noticed. After a while Azamat began to sing again, louder now, more urgent. The song went on and on, the music became faster and louder as the two voices competed even as they stayed in close harmony. First one voice was louder, then the other, calling and responding, circling one around the other. Finally, with their hands a blur over the instruments the song reached a climax, with a groan from the old man followed by a shout of triumph from the boy.

The two shepherds bowed low to acknowledge the round of applause that followed their performance. Cecelia spoke to Daniyar via Azamat, then looked at Paul.

'He says yes, he was the wolf.'

Paul blushed, but Daniyar smiled and nodded at him, seemingly pleased. The old man spoke to Azamat and began beating another rhythm on his drum, more gently this time.

After listening to the young boy for a moment, Cecelia spoke. 'This is a song of sunset in the mountains.'

The two voices began together, Daniyar's still low and gravelly, Azamat still with a high soprano, but their tune was the same, the lyrics wistful and sad sounding. A few of the spectators began to copy the rhythm of the drum with gentle tapping on the floor and one or two tried to hum the tune as well. Paul noticed Rachel had put her head on Annabel's shoulder. He also saw Charlotte had her camera out again.

When the song finished there was another round of sustained applause. The old shepherd spoke to Cecelia and then looked expectantly at the group.

'Aah.' She looked around. 'I think we are expected to reciprocate?'

The group looked at each other for a while, not knowing what to do.

'Does anyone know any songs?' Cecelia asked, looking around. 'Anyone?'

The room was silent. Over by the door Talbot cleared his throat, stretched his neck to stare at the ceiling, and began to sing in a strong tenor voice -

'Men of Harlech, march to glory,

Victory is hovering o'er ye,

Bright-eyed freedom stands before ye,

Hear ye not her call…?'

Talbot's voice grew stronger and more confident as he continued with the song.
Around the room the Marines, clearly enjoying the performance, joined in with
rough choruses of "la-la-la" and "pom-pom-pom" to support their leader. By the
time Talbot reached the last line the whole room was filled with a raucous echo of
voices.

'…love of conquest hither bought them,
but this lesson we have taught the-e-e-e-e-em!
Cambria - ne'er - can yield!'

As the final note echoed around the hut the two shepherds clapped
enthusiastically and Azamat leapt to his feet in delight, rushing over to shake
Talbot's hand vigorously.

'You don't have to ask a Welshman twice to get up and sing,' he said gruffly. He
looked around. 'Now who's next? They gave us two songs; we owe them one
more.'

The civilians looked at each other again but still no one moved. From the back of
the room Jackson called out, 'What about that song we always had to do on the
yomps? What was it called – Over the Hills and Far Away?'

'Right then!' Talbot cried. 'Marines! Fall in, front and centre! Stand easy.'

The marines lined up in two rows in front of Talbot. The Colour Sergeant turned to Daniyar and pointed at the drum, then started to clap out a rhythm. The Shepherd began to tap on the drum skin. Talbot began to sing.

"Here's forty shillings on the drum.

For those who'll volunteer to come

To enlist and fight the foe today.

Over the hills and far away!"

After four beats on the drum all the marines joined in.

"O'er the hills and o'er the main

Through Flanders, Portugal, and Spain!

King George commands and we obey,

Over the hills and far away!"

The singing was rough and ready, and a few of the voices could be called enthusiastic rather than tuneful, but overall it was impressive. In the enclosed space of this room it was *loud.*

"When duty calls me I must go,

To stand and face another foe.."

As the singing continued Paul noticed the expressions of seriousness on the faces of this choir of military personnel. This song plainly held a deep meaning for all of them. As they continued they began to stamp their feet, marching on the spot. The thud of the floorboards matched with the more delicate drumming from Daniyar. The audience were by and large enthralled by the performance, but Paul noticed Cecelia show a flash of irritation when the Marines began singing.

Finally the song reached its finale and again the shepherds gave an effusive round of applause, as did most of the Herd. Jasper put thumb and forefinger into his mouth and produced a piercing whistle of appreciation. Tor leant away from him with a pained expression.

Daniyar stood up and with a graceful wave of his arm he indicated the stove.

'Let's eat,' said Cecelia. As everyone moved towards the kitchen area she picked up the mat, rolled it up and handed it to Moira. 'Fair exchange, I think.'

Although it was a large pot of stew it wouldn't have been enough to feed everybody on its own but combined with the remaining provisions from the Hotel there was still plenty of food to go round. The appetizing smell coming from the cooking pot gave Paul a slight conundrum. He was wary of upsetting his digestive system for a third time in two days, but the growls emanating from his stomach impelled him to try a little. He was glad he did; it was delicious. The mutton in the shepherd's pot was mouth-wateringly tender and the thick sauce was spicy but tasty.

Once the meal was completed Azamat set about cleaning the pot. Daniyar sat and talked with Cecelia for some time, occasionally pointing around the hut, sometimes gesturing outside towards the valley or the mountain ridge. Then he stood and walked to the door, turned, bowed, and addressed everyone in the room. Cecilia passed on the translation as the old man pulled the musical instrument bag over his shoulder.

'He thanks us for an entertaining evening; he hopes we have peaceful night; he wishes us safe travels tomorrow; and he promises us a warm welcome should we ever return.'

There was a murmuring of thanks from the group, although Paul heard Jasper muttering 'fat chance…'

Daniyar raised his hat in salute and putting his arm around Azamat's shoulders he left. The boy carried the stew pot under one arm and waved goodbye with his other hand. The youngster then reached into his leather bag and pulled out a short pink umbrella which he held carefully over his grandfather's head to protect his tall white hat. Through the open door Paul could see it had started to rain quite heavily. Paul watched them slowly move away into the dark.

'That was quite a long chat you had with the old boy,' said Campbell to Cecelia once the shepherds had gone. 'I thought you didn't speak Kyrgyz?'

Cecelia smiled gently. 'I don't. We spoke in Russian.'

'I thought…' Campbell began.

'Oh, getting the boy to translate at first was just a ruse while the old man sussed us out; he never actually said he couldn't speak Russian, but he was happy to let us think that for a while. Fortunately for us he actively dislikes the Russians because of how they used to run his country. Once he realised we were not from that part of the world he was happy to talk to me directly. My little cover story about us being from Finland and here on a hunting trip fell apart fairly quickly once he got a good look at us.'

'I suppose he recognised me and Tor,' sighed Jasper, running his hand over his lean stomach.

Cecelia didn't look at him. 'No, Mr Hood-Daley. However great your celebrity is in the rest of the world, the pair of you mean nothing to an old Shepherd and his grandson in the mountains of Kyrgyzstan. He kept pointing at you, Mr Campbell, and Corporal Towne, and asking if Finland had a long colonial history in Africa.'

Talbot snorted out a mirthless laugh. Cecelia looked at him coldly. 'You didn't help, Colour Sergeant. British military marching songs aren't much of a disguise, are they? You may as well have sung Rule Britannia and God Save the Queen.' Talbot's beard bristled as he pouted, but he said nothing. 'Anyway, he was happy to hear we were no friends of the Russians. I told him were trying to avoid meeting any Russians whilst we were here and that we didn't want to cause any trouble. I also told him that we would be leaving his valley tomorrow, which is true enough, one way or another. He did tell me that he hadn't seen any signs that there has been anyone else in the valley today, so hopefully our friends from the hotel are not in pursuit. Not yet at least.'

Talbot nodded and looked relieved.

'He said he would send us a signal tomorrow morning if he does see any Russians heading this way.'

'What kind of signal?' Talbot asked.

'He didn't elaborate. Best we just keep our eyes and ears open though.' Cecelia yawned. 'That's enough for me for one day; I'm off to bed. Good night everyone.' She stood up from the bench, stretched her back and headed outside.

The rest of the group decided to follow Cecelia's example. As they were gathering their belongings and shuffling towards the door Talbot called out 'We leave here at oh-eight hundred tomorrow morning, sharp. Don't be late!'

Jasper threw him a mock salute. 'Yessah!'

Talbot turned on him. 'Pretty-Boy, you are *such* a fucking twat. You haven't earned the right to salute me, dribbledick. Piss off to bed before I break your fucking kneecaps, you little WANKER!'

Paul was one of the last of the Herd to leave the hut, although several of the Marines were clearly staying there for a while yet.. As he reached the doorway Talbot spoke. 'You're looking pretty fuckin' rough, Sicknote.'

'Oh, thanks very much…'

'Your face I mean. Have you still got that moisturizer in your bag?'

'Um, yes, I think so.' Paul ran a hand over the stubble on his cheek.

'Well slap some on before you go to sleep tonight. Cracked skin is no laughing matter in this weather.' One corner of Talbot's mouth twitched slightly. 'Won't stop you being an ugly git though.'

Paul tried to joke along. 'I better get some beauty sleep then..'

'Oh, far too fuckin' late for that! On a serious point though, once you get the bandages off you need to put some of that lotion on your feet as well. The last thing we want tomorrow is burst blisters that you can't walk on, so soften the skin.' Paul glanced at Draws who was re-packing his medical bag. The medic looked up and nodded.

'It's good advice. They teach you all the tricks of the trade for looking after your feet in the military.'

'There you are then.' Talbot pointed his chin at Paul. 'Is that clear?'

'Yes, Colour Sergeant.' Paul had a strong urge to salute but managed to restrain himself.

'Very good. Now fuck off.'

Paul hobbled down the steps of the hut in the rain and headed for the dormitory building. At the insistence of a full bladder he changed direction and headed to the toilet block. Away from the torch light of the kitchen hut the darkness was actually a little less oppressive; the snow on the ground seemed to reflect some light, enough at least to let him find his way to the door. Inside the block it was considerably darker. Paul bumped into an open door with a grunt, made his way inside the stall, and closed the door behind him. The air felt chill on his bare skin as he fumbled to undo his belt and the zip on his trousers. Once he had dropped his trousers he sat down heavily over the hole in the wooden bench seat. Distressingly the wood was wet in a couple of places. As he began to urinate a bright torch light swept across the wall as someone entered the block. Paul couldn't remember if he had locked the stall door, so he stretched out a foot to push up against it, moving his bare skin into another cold puddle. Whistling tunelessly, the new arrival swept passed Paul's stall and entered the next one. Paul realised it was Hendrik. Paul heard the thump of metal on wood, and the beam of light illuminated the ceiling. In the newly lit up room Paul could see his steaming breath. He slowly realised the steam he could see was also rising from the hole underneath him.

'Need paper?' Hendriks' voice was surprisingly loud. A wad of toilet paper appeared over the side of the stall.

'No. No thanks.' Paul stood up, hurriedly dressed, pushed open the door and headed outside.

The continuous rain was starting to pummel the snow out of existence, but Paul was able to grab a fistful from a sheltered spot by the wall. He used it to scrub his hands clean. Shaking and rubbing his fingers to dry and warm them he limped in to the two-storey dormitory building. Entering the hallway he tapped the side of his feet very gently against the door to shake off the snow that was sticking to the soles of his boots. Glowing torchlight escaped from different rooms, reflecting weakly along the passageway.

He hobbled to the room with his pack in, wriggled out of his coat and sat on the lower bunk in the gloom. He slowly unlaced the walking boot on his left foot and placed it carefully under the bed. Nervously he eased the sock off and inspected his foot. The bandage was still mostly in place, although it was becoming frayed at a couple of points. Paul tentatively started to unwind the material. A couple of times the cloth stuck to his skin, and he had to tug a little more firmly to remove it. His foot was a mess. The blister on the back of his heel was large, but the ones on the underside of his foot were larger. Most of the blisters over the tops of his toes had burst and were bleeding again with the removal of the bandage. Keeping his naked foot hovering in mid-air Paul stretched out an arm to take hold of his rucksack and wrestled it onto the bed beside him. He burrowed an arm around inside until he found the moisturizer jar and dragged it out. Quickly unscrewing the lid he scooped out a generous dollop of the white ointment, carefully placing the lid and the open jar on the end of the bed. Nervously he smoothed a small amount of moisturizer onto the blister on his heel. To his relief he felt no pain when his finger came into contact with the swollen skin. He put a larger amount onto the sole of his foot, massaging the cream across the whole of the underside of his foot, and then across the top. Although it was a little cold the feeling was quite soothing. Finally he swiped his hand over the toes.

The flash of pain as the moisturizer connected with the raw skin under the broken blisters was startlingly intense, like a shock from an electric fence. With an agonised yell Paul flung his hands away from his foot and bounced upwards, smacking the top of his head on the upper bunk. 'Ow! Shit!' The world got a little fuzzy for a moment. He cradled his head in his sticky hands, still waving his left foot in the air. A few moments of vigorously massaging his skull helped ease the discomfort on his skull, but the toes continued to throb horribly, and Paul could only sway from side-to-side waiting for the pain to subside.

A bright blue-white light illuminated the room as Draws, torch attached to his jacket, opened the bedroom door. 'I just thought I 'd see how…what the fuck are you doing?'

Through gritted teeth Paul managed to mutter, 'banged my head…'

'Right, come here.' Draws stepped closer to the bed, rolled Paul into an upright position, and inspected the top of his head. 'No lasting damage, but you might have a lump there tomorrow. Now, how are the feet?' Draws surveyed the floating foot closely while muttering 'can't leave you on your own for five minutes…' He helped Paul remove the second boot and sock and then carefully unwrapped the bandages. The right foot was in a similar state to the left, large blisters across the foot and broken skin over the top of and between the toes. Paul picked up the moisturizer jar and began to add the creamy substance to the unbroken blisters while carefully avoiding the bleeding ones.

'Try and leave them unwrapped tonight if you can; an airing will do them good. I'll help you bandage them in the morning.'

Paul let out a deflating sigh. 'I just want to go home!' he wailed.

Now come on, get a grip. Here…' Draws reached into a top pocket of his tunic, 'take these, they'll help you sleep better tonight.' He passed Paul a couple of pills in a foil wrapped packet. 'They should stop the pain from keeping you awake.'

Draws left and the room descended into gloom again. Paul lay on his back staring at the underside of the bunk above him. He was almost disappointed there was no dent or bloodstain caused by his head connecting with it.

After a few minutes, the creeping chill of the air in the room caused him to raise himself and prepare to go to sleep. He realised parts of his trousers still felt damp, so he took them off and hung them from the end of the bunk above him. He retrieved his suit jacket from the rucksack, then placed the bag on one side of the mattress at the foot of the bed. He wrapped the jacket around his lower body from his waist to his shins, then draped his coat across the end of the bed and the rucksack to form a little tent which stopped the material from resting on his feet. He pulled the water bottle from his coat and put it by his head. He pulled the zip as high as it would go on the fleece then popped out the two pills Draws had given him. Maybe two pills was overdoing it a bit, but right now he just wanted to be in a deep painless asleep. He took a large swig from the water bottle to

swallow the medication which left a sharp taste on his tongue. He screwed the lid

back on the bottle and carefully stood it on the floor. As he lay back on the thin

mattress and pulled his hands inside the sleeves of his fleece he realised it was the

water that had tasted odd rather than the pills. Just before he spiralled into

unconsciousness he realised he had drunk some of Jasper's solution.

Chapter Thirteen

Dark. It was so dark. Paul stared into the noiseless void above his bed. So dark he couldn't see his own hands in front of his face. Were they his own hands? He stared into the dark again. The blackness began diffracting slowly into the darkest shades of colour, purples, midnight blues, browns, greys. Patterns emerged, spinning and dancing across his vison. He tried to turn his head to follow one large shape as it moved from right to left in front of him and heading towards where he knew the door to be.

Quietly he got out of bed to follow the shape, to keep it in sight as it beckoned him on. The shape became a vertical oval, and as it moved out of the room it morphed into human form. A red nailed finger reached back to beckon him on even as the form continued to move away from him, along the corridor and out of the building. Paul ran after it, after her, it was his wife Annie, she had come to take him home. Through the main door he followed her.

Outside was bathed in bright daylight with multicoloured shadows spinning across the ground as the sun raced impossibly fast around the rim of the horizon. The sky was smothered in bright stars pulsing and flashing. He was surrounded by people. Tor was floating motionless in a shallow pool of liquid gold with sunglasses covering half her face, her curved outstretched arms sprouting huge white feathers. Cecelia was seated in tall chair placed on a high platform; words and sentences scribbled across the skin of her face. She was staring intently at Paul, but he couldn't hear what she was saying. Orla and Chingiz danced past him, whirling around in a waltz, and all the Marines were dancing too, spinning clumsily in pairs as they slowly floated into the air, their feet twirling and kicking, their legs jerking as the ropes around their necks tightened and stretched. Charlottes was screaming from behind her camera. She clawed and pulled at the machinery covering her face, but it didn't come off. Jasper was floating face down in a deep pool of blood.

Still Paul chased after Annie, but she was getting ahead. He looked down at his bare legs and saw he had no feet; he was running on bloody stumps. Terrified, Paul stumbled and fell into a snowdrift, feeling the cold bite deep into his bare skin.

'We had to amputate,' Draws said kindly. A noose dropped over his head and dragged him into the air kicking and struggling, in amongst the other Marines who were now hanging limp and still. Orla and Chingiz lay dead beneath them; their bodies riddled with bullet holes.

Paul tried to crawl away, as his hands became frozen claws that started to shatter into tiny pieces of ice. His legs were cold and heavy, too chilled to move. He began to sink through the snow, through the soil beneath, into the liquid rock that solidified around him. He was held fast, nearly encased in granite, only one eye still above ground. Annie strolled away, heading for an enormous helicopter that had just appeared. She ignored him. He tried to call out to her but could make no sound.

'Time to go,' Morgan said in someone else's voice, backing away towards the helicopter. The ground began to shake. The rocks surrounding Paul closed in, squeezing him tighter. 'Time to go.' Morgan was shooting flames from his rifle as he climbed into the aircraft. Pauls bones began to break as he was crushed, his ribs snapping, bone shards piercing his lungs and heart, he could hear and feel his skull fracturing like an eggshell being trodden on. 'Time to go.'

When Paul awoke, it was Draws that was crouched beside the bed shaking him. Campbell was standing behind the medic staring anxiously at Paul. There seemed to be a distant thudding noise.

'Ffnffurgh…' Paul's tongue felt bloated and cracked. He tried again to speak. 'What is it?' He was suddenly overwhelmed with other sensations from his nervous system. His hands and feet were impossibly cold, his head was throbbing, and nausea was squirming in his stomach like an irritated eel.

'Time to go, I said. You were having a spectacularly noisy nightmare.' Draws reached out and pulled up Paul's eyelid. 'We are supposed to be leaving in about ten minutes. Your eyes are bloodshot, are you feeling okay?'

'I think my head is about to explode. I drank some of Jasper's solution by mistake.' Paul realised the thudding was his own pulse inside his head. Draws face had a pained expression.

'Ooh, that was not a good idea. At best you'll have quite the hangover today. It should only take a day or so to work its way out of your system though. Unfortunately for you…'Draws rummaged in his pack, 'you can't lie in bed all day recovering, we have a helicopter to catch. Take these.' He offered Paul two large tablets. 'Painkillers. Strong ones: they should cover up the headache for several hours and maybe help with your sore feet for a while too. Where's your water bottle? The clean one I mean.' Paul swallowed the pills with a large swig of water. 'Drink the rest of that now, you'll be dehydrated from your little pharmaceutical adventure.' Paul glugged the remaining water. Draws took the bottle from him and passed it to Campbell. 'Could you refill this from the spring out the back?' As Campbell left the room Draws nodded to the window. 'Mind you it might be as quick to just stand outside and hold the bottle up.' Paul could see the heavy raindrops hurling themselves continuously at the windowpane. Inside the cold dry room his breath was visible as a thin wisp of steam. Draws held out some fresh bandages. 'Let's get your feet sorted, shall we?'

Just as Draws finished dressing Paul's feet Campbell returned with a full water bottle.

'And this.' Campbell held out a small package. 'Too late for the full English breakfast, I'm afraid,' Campbell said with a smile. 'Some biscuits, a couple of apples. Just to keep you going.'

Paul nibbled at a biscuit and tried not to think about a plate full of greasy food. At least the painkillers were starting to whittle away at the sharpest edges of his headache.

'Finish getting dressed, we'll see you outside in two minutes,' said Draws, shouldering his pack. Draws and Campbell headed out of the room.

The only decision Paul had to make about what to wear was which pair of underpants to choose. The white boxers he'd had on yesterday were looking horribly grubby, so he opted instead for the navy-blue briefs decorated with lines of cartoon ducks coloured red and yellow. A joke present from his daughters last Christmas. As he pulled on the dry but tattered suit trousers he bent over to check as best he could that the ducks weren't visible through any of the torn seams. With extreme care he eased his feet into the thick woollen Royal Marine socks and then pulled on the walking boots. Shirt, fleece, and overcoat completed his attire – the suit jacket he folded and stowed carefully into his rucksack. As he left the room he paused at the door to double check he had packed everything. He caught sight of the bottle with Jasper's medication on the floor almost under his bunk. He stuffed it into his coat pocket, checked the room once again, and then left.

As he walked gingerly down the steps in front of the dormitory building he was greeted by Talbot's cry of 'well, about fucking time!' Everyone was gathered in front of the building, obviously ready to depart. The other members of the Herd were standing huddled in groups, coat hoods pulled down tight and shoulders hunched against the icy rain that was bombarding them. The base of the dark clouds seemed to be far above their heads, although thick eerie fronds of vapour trailed close about them. Paul made his way over to Jasper, Charlotte and Tor who were standing close to the wall of the dormitory building. Charlotte as always was checking her camera. Jasper and Tor were whispering fiercely. Paul held out the bottle of medication.

'Oh right. Yeah, thanks.' Jasper closed his large fist around the neck of the bottle. Paul wanted to tell Jasper about the nightmare he had had after just one sip, to tell the young man that he had some inkling of the discomfort he must be going through. But no words came, so Paul just nodded and let go of the container.

'Listen up, people!' Talbot's voice echoed back from the metal clad walls behind them. His beard glistened with rainwater. 'Pay close attention to what I am about to tell you! There will be no pissing about today! The helicopter will arrive at the pickup point…' he checked his watch '…within the next ninety minutes and it will depart no later than sixty minutes after that. Anyone not on the helicopter at that time will have to make their own way home, is that understood?' A succession of nods dislodged a spray of water droplets. 'We will return to the rendezvous using the same path we took yesterday to get here. This is a distance of approximately two miles, so that gives us plenty of time, there will be no need to rush, no need to panic. But this is difficult terrain, and the weather is not our friend! Slow and steady wins the race. Ok? Any questions so far?' The herd remained silent. 'We will walk in small groups again like yesterday. Stay close to your walking buddy and stay in sight of the groups ahead and behind. Corporal, you, and Lincoln will take point; Ren, Porky, I want you to follow and escort Ms Eriksen and Mr Campbell. Draws, Jackson, you're with the Van Der Molens. Smoke, Eeyore, you will babysit Ms Turner and her little party. Flo, Sydney, you stay with Legol...um...' he pointed at the group of four women.

'Legolas and the Hobbits,' called out Rachel. 'We gathered that's our nickname. Thanks very much, by the way.' Talbot shrugged. Sydney and Flo laughed.

'That leaves you and me, Sicknote,' Talbot threw an arm across Pauls shoulders, 'to bring up the rear. Right then! Let's get cracking.'

Towne and Lincoln set off, passing through the gateway in the loose stone wall surrounding the lodge, and headed towards the ridge to the northwest. Most of the snow that had settled yesterday had been melted away by the heavy rain which must have been falling for most of the night. Here and there were patches of white, either sheltered from the falling water or hammered into ice by the force of the rainfall. Elsewhere there were increasing numbers of puddles forming. The air was chill, and the rain hitting bare skin was painfully cold. Paul could hear

Lincoln crooning 'I'm siiiii-nging in the rain...' as he headed up the path. The rest began to move off.

'To infinity...and beyond!' Sydney called out.

'That's from Toy Story!' a voice shouted back.

Paul adjusted his backpack to sit more comfortably on his shoulders and tightened the straps. When the others had passed through the gateway Talbot summoned him forward and off they went.

'Draws tells me you had a bad night. How are you feeling? How are the feet?'

'I feel knackered, to be honest with you. My feet...I don't know how my feet are yet.'

'Well, you'll sleep in a proper bed tonight, and we will have you home again in a couple of days,' Talbot leaned in closer to Paul, 'as long as you make it onto that helicopter, eh? So, come on! Hurry up!'

With most of the snow removed the path between the bare rocks and grassy tussocks was easy to follow. Even as Paul began to be reminded of the blisters on his feet he was able to keep up with Talbot. Dozens of miniature streams had appeared on every slope as the rainwater and the snowmelt combined.

It only took a few minutes before they reached the scree slope where the path levelled out and disappeared among the loose wet stones. A few deep marks in the scree showed where the others had passed, like footprints on a shingle beach. Campbell and Cecelia were still within sight as Paul began to traverse the slippery surface with Talbot just behind him.

Above the 'pock-pock-pock' sound of continuous rain hitting his coat hood he heard a distant 'woosh' and the light around him took on a reddish hue. He turned his head quickly to look down the valley, only to find himself looking at the inside of his hood. He pulled it aside to see a red flare racing upwards, lighting up the underside of the clouds into a pinky brown hue before the ball of light slowed and then dropped towards the earth, fizzling out and disappearing from view.

Talbot was speaking on his comms, staring into the sky. 'Listen up, Marines. Our friendly old shepherd from last night has just given us a warning: we have the enemy on our trail again. So get moving!' Talbot turned and looked at Paul. 'Fuck!' he shouted.

The echoes of Talbot's expletive bounced off the surrounding mountains. Astonishingly it was answered; a deep bleat echoed from the very top of the ridge high above them. Paul twisted round to look up and just below the ridgeline he could see a huge mountain goat astride a rocky outcrop a hundred metres above them,. The animal looked extraordinarily large, the size of a pony, his shaggy wool hanging in long thick strands that swept his flanks as he moved. He stood at the apex of the scree slope, his huge, curved horns swinging as he turned his head to survey the humans beneath him first with one eye, then the other. It seemed to be the living embodiment of the statue on the gate of the Ala Aracha Hotel in the valley far below.

Paul detected a second movement above him, then another, then another. Behind and above the goat three wolves, no wait, four, eyes locked on the goat slowly, remorselessly, stalked closer to the unwitting beast. Paul was entranced, watching open mouthed at the wildlife drama unfolding above him.

The others turned to look at what had captured Paul's attention just as the biggest wolf began to run, large paws silently powering it over the wet ground. The other three wolves charged just behind. The goat suddenly sensed the danger, turned to look at the wolves, snorted steam, then turned to flee. It jumped from the rock onto the loose stones below. The lead wolf shot forward, shortening the distance between them in a fraction of a second, leaping onto the goat and sinking its teeth into the back of its neck.

The goat bellowed and twisted, still trying to run. A second wolf bit into the goat's rump, but a double footed kick into the wolf's belly sent it rolling and yelping away. The goat was considerably bigger than the wolf on it back and the two animals became conjoined into a single mass that flailed and thrashed. The other two wolves circled, snarling, waiting for an opportunity to strike. Because of the goat's size, the thickness of its woollen pelt and the position of the predator the goat was proving hard to kill.

For several moments, the creatures turned this way and that until finally the goat slipped and fell. The two animals tumbled over and over, sending pebbles and stones cascading down the mountain. Still the animals fought, they tumbled and shook, the goat screamed, and the wolves growled. The loose stones underfoot prevented either animal from keeping their balance and gaining an advantage. Finally the goat twisted and rolled, threw its body weight to one side, and flipped the wolf from its back. In doing so it stretched it neck up, and one of the circling wolves lept forward, closed its jaws around the goat's windpipe and killed it.

Paul found he had been holding his breath and exhaled heavily. Oddly exhilarated by being so close to this event, he turned to pass comment to Talbot but realised the Colour Sergeant was running towards him, strapping on his helmet.

'Landslide! Run! Get clear!'

Paul looked up again. Although the wolf and the goat were now lying still, the violent struggle between the two animals had caused a cascade of rocks and stones to drop onto the wet scree immediately below them which in turn had loosened many more stones and now the whole slope seemed to be sliding towards them. He broke into a hobbling run.

Most of the party had moved beyond the scree and were already walking where the path was shielded by a solid outcrop of bedrock. There were only four of them still on the open slope. Paul and Talbot were at the rear of the group and were about halfway across when the rockfall started. Annabel had stopped about fifty metres from the edge of the scree to tie an errant bootlace, blocking Sydney's path who waited patiently behind her.

It was the noises that Paul would always remember. It began with a pitter patter of clicks and snaps as small pebbles bounced and ricocheted down the slope. But as the quantity of stones moving increased, and the size of the stones and then rocks rolling and flipping downhill swelled, the noise became louder and more constant. As a tipping point was breached and the sodden fragile scree slope gave way and slid off the mountain there came a continuous deep rumble, as if the earth itself was protesting at its mistreatment by the elements. As a whole the scree slid downhill quite slowly but single rocks unconstrained by the weight of others around them bounced away dangerously fast.

He saw Talbot and Sydney both attempt to run over the scree even as it began to move, arms extended like tightrope walkers and digging in their heels to give them balance. Annabel set off downhill ahead of most of the falling stones, skidding and sliding over the scree. Sydney was still running when Paul lost sight of her, but he saw Talbot twist and fall as a rock the size of a football clipped his shoulder as another, smaller stone smashed into his leg. His balance gone he tumbled into the heaving waves of stone shards, rose to his hands and knees, and tried to get his feet beneath him but he was immediately swept away. Paul saw the Colour Sergeant's legs above his body as he cartwheeled once, twice, and then he was gone.

Paul could see Annabel moving at speed, running straight down the steep incline before suddenly changing direction to run to her right. She seemed to be aiming for a rock formation with a thick overhang which was just off the scree slope a couple of hundred metres below the path. He didn't see if she made it before the buzzing swarm of stones began to fly past him and blocked his sight of her.

Paul fell forward as the ground beneath his feet suddenly slipped away down the slope. He plummeted downhill, sliding at first on his stomach and then on his back, spinning in circles, then rolling head over heels, all movement totally out of his control.

Paul would have imagined that in a landslide the mountain side would slide uniformly away. You would almost think you could surf over the top of it unscathed. The reality was that he was engulfed in a blizzard of flying shrapnel as the ground beneath his feet heaved, bucked, and disappeared. Despite the falling rain there was cloud of rock dust ballooning around him. Stones bounced up at him and stones dropped on him as he tumbled and fell. Unable to stand or stop moving Paul tried to curl into a ball, arms protecting his head and legs pulled in as he abandoned any attempt to direct his movements. The absurd thought that he resembled a helpless ant caught in a cement mixer flashed through his mind. A pillar of rock the size of an upright piano rolled alongside him for several long seconds. It came to within a few inches from his head, swayed, and dropped mercifully away, disappearing with a creaking thud into a hidden crevasse. A rock fragment as thin as a dinner plate but as wide as a car tyre frisbee'd through the air just above him as he tumbled, catching the back of his left hand a glancing blow that made him cry out.

Suddenly he stopped, caught at the waist. The change of velocity caused his limbs to shoot forward as he bent double, chin thudding into his chest. A freshly exposed root from a long dead tree had speared into his clothing as he had slid past, narrowly missing impaling his flesh. The tip of the root had slid straight into his pocket and ripped through the trouser leg to push up against the opposite thigh. Paul's momentum caused him to spin on the root until his full bodyweight hung from it. He jerked and wriggled to free himself and the material tore and gave way, splitting and tearing the trousers in several places. Paul felt several pounding shocks as a trio of stones the size of cannonballs thudded into his rucksack and bounced away over his head. He let out a high-pitched cry of fear and frantically shook at the root again which snapped under the strain. He spun away downhill leaving much of the fabric of his trousers behind. The tumbling and sliding continued for endless terrifying seconds, until he passed over a rocky outcrop and dropped three or feet off a ledge. He landed heavily on the wet and stony soil beneath, knocking the breath out of him. Shielded from the stones still flying past above him by a large overhang he lay face down covering his head with his hands.

After another thirty seconds the noise of the rockfall began to subside. Paul could hear the trickle of water pouring around him and the hollow he was lying in began to fill up with muddy water. As the last few stones slipped down the hill Paul cautiously levered himself to his feet and looked around. He could see he was almost at the bottom of the slope, close to the glacier. The debris that had fallen down the mountain was fanned out below him. Peering over the lip of the outcrop, back up the hill, it was obvious there was no way to get back up to re-join the others. He could hear shouting voices, but he couldn't make out what was being said, and he could see no-one.

The dust cloud, so thick a minute ago, had been damped down to almost nothing by the still falling rain. Paul could feel the cold wind and rain stinging his bare skin. What remained of his trousers was hanging like a tattered scarf from two belt loops that still encircled the belt buckled around his waist. Looking down he was dismayed to see his bare legs, scratched and sliced by the rocks during his fall, were smothered in dozens of lacerations. None of the wounds that he could see were especially deep, but several were weeping with blood, leaving his legs stained with a red wash.

When the water in the hollow reached the top of his walking boots Paul decided he had to move. Slowly, awkwardly, he clambered out of his hiding place and began to make his way down the uneven surface. In a few places movement continued as the loose debris around him was summoned by gravity. Each step Paul took dislodged a trickle of pebbles which dribbled away. Much of the landslide material had come to rest in front of the glacier, disturbing the small lake of powder-blue water at the foot of the ice. Choppy waves ricocheted back and forth across the surface.

An odd movement close to the water's edge caught Paul's eye. It took him a second to realise what was peculiar – the movement was up, not down, the hill. An arm had emerged from under the pebbles and was scrapping at the stones around it. Paul scurried over as fast as he could, dropping to his knees beside the limb. The insignia on the camouflage tunic confirmed it was Talbot submerged in the soil and shingle. Paul began frantically scraping the loose material away from the marine's head, quickly uncovering his mouth, nose and one eye. Talbot took a deep rasping breath, coughed, and spat and then breathed again. He shook his head free of the stones and whispered 'Fuuuuuuuuuck…' He began to wriggle and shake himself, slowly forcing his way out of the ground like a butterfly emerging from a chrysalis. Paul grabbed hold of the straps of the Marine's rucksack and pulled and pulled until finally Talbot slithered completely free of the earth.

As Talbot lay prone trying to catch his breath Paul heard a clicking noise of something coming down the hill above them. Looking up he saw a small black rectangular object sliding over the stones and coming to rest almost at Pauls feet. He reached out and picked it up. It was a smartphone; the touch screen fractured into a spider's web of cracks. He slipped it into his coat pocket.

He looked down as Talbot. 'Are you alright?' Paul could see the Colour Sergeant had a gash under his right eyebrow that was dripping blood. The Marines helmet had a noticeable dent on one side, and a wire was dangling from the smashed coms earpiece. A shard of plastic from the comms unit had stabbed into Talbot's earlobe and was sticking out like a punk earring.

'Fucking goats. I fucking hate fucking goats,' Talbot said, then grunted in pain as he tried to sit up.

Paul put out a hand. 'Are you injured?'

Talbot grunted, 'My left leg.' He glanced at Paul, 'my foot is damaged…' He stopped. 'Why the fuck have you got no trousers?'

Before Paul could answer there came the click and rattle of more stones falling downhill. Paul looked up in alarm, worried a further rockfall was coming. With relief he realised these small rocks had been dislodged by two figures who were making their way down the slope directly above where he stood. Although they were still some way off recognised Sidney and Annabel. Sydney seemed to be supporting the taller women as they descended. As they got closer Paul could see Annabel was holding a bloodstained towel to her face.

'Both still alive then?' Sydney called out cheerily.

'Just about alive,' Paul answered glancing at Talbot.

'What the fuck happened to your trousers, Sicknote?' Sydney laughed, but on closer inspection she became more serious. 'You're bleeding?'

'Fairly superficial, I think. Stings a bit though,' he added, hoping to sound suitably brave. 'I'm worried about Talbot. He was caught under the landslide.' Sydney helped Annabel to sit down on a solid piece of rock and hurried over to the Colour Sergeant.

Paul looked at Annabel who was taking some beep breaths and shaking slightly. When she moved the towel he could see her nose was broken and bloodied. Her right cheek looked puffy, and her right eyelid was swollen. She looked at him with her good eye. 'How're you doing?' he asked gently.

'OK I guess. I-I smacked my face pretty hard when I fell. She dragged me clear.' She indicated Sydney with a trembling hand.

'Sicknote, I need your help.' Sydney's voice was authoritative. Paul scurried the dozen or so metres to crouch alongside the two Marines as Annabel unclipped her rucksack and started searching through its pockets.

Talbot's eyes were squeezed shut and his teeth were clenched, bloodied gums clearly visible through his face-stretching grimace. Tendons as taut as anchor cables bulged in his neck and a constant growl transmitted from his throat. 'Hold him still.' Sydney ordered. Paul knelt beside the prone figure and gripped the Colour Sergeants shoulders as Sydney swiftly unlaced Talbot's left boot. Having widened the opening as much as possible she eased the boot from the foot, then pulled off the sock. The outside of the left ankle bulged obscenely, with the foot itself slightly turned in.

'You've dislocated your ankle, Colour Sergeant.' Sydney looked up at Paul. 'Well that's a bit of a bugger. Any ideas? We can't linger around here for too long.'

Paul looked at the foot. 'Right. Right. Just thinking out loud now. I've done a First Aid course or two. Let's work this out. Right. The good news is the skin isn't broken, there is no bone sticking out, he's not about to bleed to death. There is no immediate discolouration and not too much swelling that I can see, so hopefully that might mean he doesn't have any internal bleeding. We should dose him up with whatever painkillers we have between us.'

Sydney nodded and said, 'We should pop his ankle back in.'

'I'm sorry, what?'

'There is no way of knowing if he has fractured anything without an X-ray, but we should reset his ankle. Like you would with a dislocated shoulder.' She shrugged. I've done that before.'

'Well maybe you have, but I certainly haven't. I wouldn't know how to…'

'Every day is a learning day, Sicknote. Look, he won't be able to walk on this foot for several days either way, but if this works he'll probably be in less pain, OK? We have to do whatever we can for him. Grab his leg.'

Paul shuddered. 'Shouldn't we wait? I'm not a doctor. Perhaps if we can get Draws on the radio…'

'My comms device isn't working, and Colour's is smashed to bits. I managed to shout up to Towne once the rockfall stopped. After the landslide I couldn't see a safe way of climbing back up to join them, and they couldn't get down to us either. Towne is taking the rest of them on to the rendezvous point, so it's just us now. Come on, no time like the present. Put one hand under his knee and lift it, grab his calf with the other hand, and hold them both steady when I say 'now'.'

'Oh God.' Paul moaned. He was suddenly feeling squeamish.

'Colour Sergeant!' Sydney called out. 'Brace yourself, this is gonna hurt.'

'Do it!' Grunted Talbot.

'Now!' Sydney grabbed the top of Talbot's foot with one hand and pulled the back of the heel down and across with the other. Paul could feel the grind of bones and tendons as he gripped Talbot's leg.

As the bones clicked back into place Talbot roared with pain, sat up and slapped Paul across the side of the head before falling back down again. Paul rolled away under the force of the blow and sat waiting for the ringing in his ears to stop.

'We did it.' Sydney said calmly. The correctly aligned foot looked a lot less disturbing now. Sydney was reaching into her Bergen for her emergency medical kit. 'Here, Colour,' she said and offered him a sip of water. 'I've got to bandage and splint this, then we will get your boot back on.' She looked at Paul. 'And then work out what to do next.'

'What about Annabel?' Paul rubbed the side of his head, thankful that Talbot hadn't punched him instead. Sydney gently wrapped the foot and ankle in bandages, then replaced the sock and boot. Talbot lay back and closed his eyes.

'I think she's got a broken cheekbone, probably a fractured eye socket and that cute nose of hers is quite a mess. Plus she has had a hell of a shock. But we can dose her up with some strong painkillers and she could march all day if she needed to. Nothing wrong with her legs. Unlike the Colour Sergeant here.'

Talbot was clutching his hands into thick fists. 'Painkillers?' Paul suggested. 'I have some morphine.' From his coat pocket he pulled out some of the vials he had picked up from Draws' medical kit the day before. Sydney took one, snapped off the top of the plastic tube and pressed it to Talbot's lips. He grabbed Sydney's wrist, tipped his head back and swallowed the liquid. Still holding onto Sydney he pulled himself up into a sitting position and unclipped his backpack. Slowly, painfully, he hauled himself up to stand on his good leg.

'Situation report,' he demanded.

'Yes, Colour. Four of us got caught in the landslide; I'm unharmed, these two are walking wounded. The rest of the team are escorting the civilians to the chopper as planned. The departure time deadline is approximately two hours from now. From this position we have to get over or around this glacier and then up the other side of the valley. And you can't walk.'

'We'll see about that. Now listen carefully, Muggeridge, this is a direct order. Take the girl and go. Leave Sicknote with me. You know what our mission objective is; we have to get her on that helicopter in time, no matter what. If Sicknote and me don't get there before the deadline, you leave anyway, is that clear? '

Sydney seemed to consider this for quite a long time before nodding.
'Understood, Colour. But I'll carry your Bergen, and Legolas over there can take your pack, Sicknote. Just to lighten your load a little.'

Talbot looked at Paul. 'All clear?'

Paul stared for a moment. A small angry voice at the back of his mind was telling him to say no, to demand to be taken to safety and to let the military man look out for himself. He was quietly proud of how easy it was to ignore that voice.

'Yes. I'll just grab my water bottle.' Paul shuffled over to where Annabel was sitting. He shrugged his way out of his backpack and sat down beside her. 'Did

Sydney give you anything for the pain?' Annabel started to shake her head and winced.

'No, not yet.'

'Here you go, take this.' Paul snapped open another of the vials from his coat pocket. Annabel poured it into the unbruised side of her mouth.

'I've lost my water bottle, and some other stuff,' she said.

'Have a sip from mine,' Paul offered. He passed her the drink. 'Sydney said you are going to carry my pack to the helicopter for me.'

'Really?' Annabelle sounded surprised.

'Talbot can't walk on his own, he's bust his ankle and God knows what else. I'll have to help him.'

Even through the injuries Paul could see the expression of doubt on Annabelle's face. Whether she was dubious about having to carry Paul's rucksack or his ability to help Talbot he wasn't sure.

Sydney tied Talbot's rucksack across the top of her own in a 'T' shape, strapped herself in and began trudging towards Paul and Annabelle.

'Come on lass, we've got to help these poor boys out by carrying their luggage!' she said brightly. 'Bloody lightweights.' Annabelle chuckled slightly, standing up and reaching for Paul's rucksack. After a few attempts to position it on her back alongside her own she strapped it across her chest instead.

Sydney looked over at Talbot who was trying to use is rifle as a walking stick, then spoke softly to Paul. 'You get him to the helicopter, Sicknote. I don't care how, but you get him there. We know our Russian friend is closing in, no doubt he would be delighted to find you still here. But anything the Russians do to you will pale by comparison to what I'll do to you if the Colour Sergeant doesn't get home.'

It was weirdly comforting to be threatened in this way. It felt as though Sydney hadn't given up on him completely.

'Why did he call you 'Muggeridge' just now?'

Sydney rolled her eyes and chuckled slightly. 'My first day with this squad I'm introduced to everyone in the barracks. Corporal says, 'this is our new recruit, Sylvia Muggeridge.' Colour Sergeant Talbot over there pretends not to hear and shouts, "What's that? Sydney Harbour Bridge?" And from that moment on I'm Sydney.' She sniffed and adjusted her packs slightly. 'He only calls me Muggeridge when he is deadly fucking serious. So come on...' she tapped Annabel lightly on the arm, '...let's get moving. Tell you what Sicknote, you get him to the helicopter, I'll tell you the story of why we call him 'Double Tap'.' Sydney and Annabel began to clamber over the last of the rockfall debris and headed towards the glacier.

Paul looked back at Talbot. The marine's efforts to use the rifle as a walking stick were not successful; it was too short and on the stones it slipped frequently or sunk into the loose material. 'I'm not sure I want to hear that story,' Paul muttered, but Sydney didn't hear him.

Paul clambered over to the Colour Sergeant. 'Try leaning on me,' Paul said, and stepped alongside him.

Talbot grabbed hold of Pauls shoulder and continued hopping forwards. Paul grunted and his whole body jerked with each jump Talbot took as the Colour Sergeants full weight pushed against him. After only a dozen steps Paul slipped and fell, causing Talbot to drop to his knees as well. By the time they had progressed another twenty metres and had managed to get clear of the rockfall they had fallen twice more, and Paul's shoulder felt like a punchbag.

'This isn't working, we need to try something else.' Paul flexed his back. 'I could try and carry…?'

Talbot cut him off. 'Fuck off Sicknote, you wouldn't get a dozen metres with me on your back.' The marine was trying to hop by himself, holding his injured foot off the ground behind him. Every step seemed to jolt his raised leg making him wince.

'Yeah, OK. But no matter how physically fit you are you can't hop up this mountain by yourself. And I can't be your walking stick; I can't stay upright with you shoving me in the back every step.'

With a grunt Talbot lowered himself down to sit on the ground. He turned his head from side to side, scanning the area around them.

'I guess this is as good a spot as any to make a last stand. I can use these rocks for cover if they come down from the ski lodge; I've got good line of sight if they stay up at the top of the ridge. I should be able to pin them down for a while.'

'What? No! We can't stay here; we've got to get to the helicopter,' Paul said, looking anxiously in the direction of Sydney. 'I'm not leaving you. She'd kill me if I ran away and left you behind.'

'What's the plan then, Professor Smartarse? How the fuck are we going to get up there…' he pointed to the top of the distant ridge, '…with only three good fucking legs between us? And two of those fucking fuckers are fucking yours.' Talbot shook his head. 'If you're staying, you need to go and hide some distance away from me. I'll be the focus of their gunfire, but they *probably* won't shoot a civilian, especially a half-naked one.'

'Three good legs,' Paul repeated. 'Three good legs! How about this? We do a three-legged race!'

Talbot glared at him. 'What the actual, bollock-slapping, *wankery* are you talking about now?'

'You bend your knee and keep your bad foot off the ground. We tie your that leg to one of mine and then swing it between us. We'll sort of balance off each other.'

Talbot tilted his head to glare ferociously at him from a different angle. His dented helmet shifted slightly on his head. Paul blinked nervously but managed to hold his nerve and maintain eye contact with the Royal Marine.

Talbot sighed. 'You arse fucking shitgibbon, that is a twattish idea that stinks worse than ten days old knob cheese. But it's better than waiting to be pissing shot at, and I can't think of any-fucking-thing else, so we'll have to try it.'

'Right.' Paul thought for a moment. 'Here.' He reached for the belt encircling his waist which still had the last tattered remnants of his trousers hanging off it. He unbuckled it, swiped away the remaining fabric and passed one end of the belt around the back of his own bare right thigh and Talbot's left. He pulled the strap towards the buckle and passed it through. The strap went past the premade holes by some distance before it pulled tight, which dragged Paul's hip painfully against the pistol Talbot wore in a holster on his fabric utility belt. The Colour Sergeant adjusted the position of the holster to his other hip.

Looking down at the long belt Talbot said, 'Jesus, what size trousers do you wear?'

'Really? Now? Comments about my waistline?' Paul said sharply.

Talbot grunted, 'Ya dipshit, don't be so fucking sensitive.' He opened another pouch on his utility belt and took out a tool that resembled a Swiss army knife, opened one arm on it that ended in a thick metal needle and stabbed it through the belt at the point where it emerged through the buckle. As Talbot put the multitool pack in its pouch Paul pushed the belt tongue through the new hole. He wrapped the loose end of belt around the buckle. Their legs now tightly bound together, they both swung an arm across the other man's back and took a grip on the outside shoulder. They moved off. Paul planted his right leg; he and Talbot swung their other legs forward in unison; then pivot Pauls right leg forward again. Swing, pivot; Swing, pivot. It worked. As long as they moved in unison, they remained balanced and upright and could make slow progress.

Carefully they made their way towards the edge of the glacier. Patches of bare rock underfoot were easier to traverse, the many dunes of loose gravel less so. Swing, pivot; swing, pivot. Fortunately, the incline was quite shallow. From the top of the ridge the ground in front of the glacier had appeared quite flat. Up close the area was wildly uneven, with huge boulders, jumbles of large rocks and tall deposits of pebbles and grey sand spread across the landscape.

By the time they reached the edge of the ice wall the tight leather strap was starting to chafe the skin on Paul's thigh. Swing, pivot; swing, pivot. Each bend and stretch of his legs was pulling on several of his cuts and grazes, causing them to re-open and weep blood. Paul barely noticed this; his blistered feet and sore muscles generated far more pain, and the bruising on his hand was starting to throb.

When they first reached the glacier the wall of ice to their right rose eight or nine metres above them. From a distance the glacier looked glossy and smooth, a stationary river of solid ice filling the top of the valley. As they had approached the leading edge they could see it was actually fractured and jagged, and it was huge; easily thirty metres high at the centre. Paul had expected the front edge to be a vertical wall of ice, or perhaps the thinnest part of a wedge but in fact it was curved, like the front end of an aircraft carrier but half a mile wide. The underside of the front of the glacier was scooped out, leaving the top looming alarmingly above them. In a few places this front lip had collapsed leaving a land locked iceberg out in front of the main body of ice. They could see the whole glacier was riven with cracks and crevices, large stones laying on the surface and suspended at all levels within the ice, giving the face of it a dirty mottled look. Up close there was a multitude of colours and hues, from yesterday's newly fallen pure white snow, to the richer creamy colours of the compacted ice, and the palest of blues and greys as the week daylight caught the different surfaces. What Paul hadn't expected was the amount of noise coming from the glacier. There was the splash and gurgle of melt water, running out from underneath and pouring off of the top in several places. There was the clink and crack of different sized stones and rocks falling from or being moved within the glacier. Most worrying were the loud rumbles and cracks from the ice itself as it shifted its position. Paul would have preferred not to get too close, but they had little choice. To their left, a broad lagoon of cloudy pale blue spread across the valley floor, fed by the streams running out of the glacier. In a couple of places fingers of blue water stretched back to touch the ice.

Sydney and Annabel had disappeared from view as Paul and Talbot reached the first expanse of water, only ten or twelve metres across, that blocked their path. Swing, pivot; swing, pivot. The water's surface was disrupted by rocks breaking through in a few places, and by weakening ripples bounced to and fro; a fading hint that Sydney and Annabel had passed through some time before. Paul and Talbot stepped down a loose shingle bank into the water. The first three steps were in water so shallow the water barely touched their bootlaces. Swing, pivot. Their third step however took them knee deep, and then another step and they were in up to their waist. Paul emitted a drawn-out high-pitched squeak in shock from the glacially cold water enveloping his bare legs and, worse, his groin. They stumbled forward. Talbot roared in pain as his damaged foot was dragged onto rocks beneath the water. Their heads collided as they lost their co-ordination, Paul's forehead clanging against the edge of Talbot's helmet.

'Stop, fucking stop!' Talbot growled. Paul managed to plant both feet, but his shivering was unstoppable. Talbot pulled his helmet from his head. The inside was coated with blood. Talbot threw the helmet into the lagoon. It floated, spinning like an empty coracle for a moment before turning over and capsizing, leaving a slick of bloody brown liquid on the surface of the water as the helmet disappeared from view. The bloodstain slowly dissipated. Talbot stood and watched it.

'C-c-come on,' Paul said. 'We've gotta move. Ooooh that's cold. Middle leg on three – one, two, three!' Swing, pivot; swing, pivot. The depth of water diminished again to shin high, and they moved ahead. A dozen more steps and at last they stepped free of the water. Now Paul felt the cuts on his legs. Although they had been somewhat rinsed by the icy liquid, the lagoon water was gritty, and Paul felt as if he had had wet sand rubbed into each scratch. The deeper wounds were weeping blood more profusely than before. Cold air drifted out of the glacier and seeped over them, tickling every part of Pauls anatomy above his boots and below his waist.

Anther twenty, thirty metres and Talbot stopped, causing Paul to lurch.

'Fucking foot,' Talbot said. Paul looked over his right shoulder. He could see that Talbot's damaged limb was hanging low, almost scraping the ground.

'What is it?'

'I can't…can't keep it held it high enough. We'll have to stop.' Talbot's head was drooping slightly.

'No! We have to go on. Look, let me think….'

'Fuck's sake, Sicknote. This won't work.'

'No, I've got it…' Paul bent over and loosened the laces on Talbot's left boot, unthreading them from four eyelets until a length of bootlace hung down from each side. 'Up, up, lift it up…' Paul urged Talbot, then twisting his body awkwardly he reached back, grabbed the laces, and passed them through a loop on Talbot's belt. Paul pulled them tight, winching Talbot's foot up close to the back of his leg and making the Marine wince. Paul tied and knotted the laces together as tight as he could. Once done he tried to give Talbot a smile of success, but he was too close to be able to focus on the Colour Sergeants whole face, so he grinned at his beard instead.

Talbot stared into the distance for a moment and then sighed. 'Well,' he said, 'just…oh fuck me, alright. Let's do it. Come on then.' Paul felt Talbot's body tense up, the Royal Marine suddenly radiating new determination. 'On three – one, two, three…'

They moved much faster now, Talbot's physical strength and willpower driving them on. Talbot was even supporting some of Paul's weight on each step. Paul began to puff from the exertion.

Halfway across the valley where the glacier was at its tallest they encountered a section of ice the size of a barn that had broken free from the ice wall. It had fallen forward and spread out from the glacier, a frozen barrier spilt across their path and reaching out into the lake beyond. They stopped in front of it.

'Sydney found a way through,' Talbot said. Paul looked dubiously at the lake, reluctant to go into the water again. Talbot was scanning the iceberg in front of them, but it was too tall to climb over. Paul Leant forward slightly to look past Talbot's head. The front edge of the glacier here was cracked and broken, with numerous fissures revealing the dark thick ice at the base of the ice sheet.

'What's that?' Paul pointed to the darkest hole in the wall. Talbot turned to look. Being so close Paul couldn't help but notice the thick dark hair at the back of Talbot's head was and slicked down as if he had just applied a huge dollop of hair gel.

'We'll go take a look,' Talbot urged. 'We are going to swing round to the right, one, two, three…'

Carefully they plodded over to the break in the ice. As they got close they could make out the space extended deeper into the ice at ground level with a bubbling stream running out of it. 'Yeah, this is the way through.'

Paul peered dubiously into the gap. The fissure was wide enough to accommodate four people walking in a line abreast, although it narrowed quickly. A few metres in the fissure began to close up completely.

'How do you know?' he asked.

'I have supernatural tracking skills,' The Colour Sergeant said, 'Plus, Sydney left us a bit of a clue.' He jabbed one finger towards the floor at their feet. Paul looked down to see, freshly scratched deep into the dirt, a large arrow pointing into the opening.

A few metres into the fissure a gap in the side wall appeared, through which the stream dribbled. The pair had to duck to go through the low opening but beyond was a huge ice cave three or four metres high and twenty metres wide. Gloomy as it was where they stood they could see that the cavity stretched away into the distance. Apart from the shallow stream burbling across the floor the area was surprisingly dry. Daylight beyond the thin front wall caused the glassy ice to glow with a neon blue. Above their heads puffy cloud shapes were embedded in the much thicker green ice. As the roof curved down to become the back wall the ice became smoother still, like polished marble, the colours darkening through royal blue to midnight black. The far end of the cave was brightly lit by a large opening at the front of the glacier, although the light seemed to flicker continuously. The noises of shifting ice and grinding stone together with the hiss of the running water echoed repeatedly within the space. Talbot had to shout to make himself heard. 'Onward! One, two, three…'

They made swift progress through the cave. Nearer to the large opening the ice had been shaped and honed by the wind as well as by the stream beneath their feet. Thick twisting pillars of frozen water resembling crystal trees spanned from floor to ceiling. Huge Icicle stalactites hung menacingly over their heads. Sharp edged chunks pushed out from the black back wall like flints in a salt mine. The hiss of water grew louder as they reached the opening, and the cause of the flickering light became apparent. A large waterfall poured down in a broad fluid curtain from the top of the glacier where the roof of the cave disappeared. Water droplets that had settled on nearby surfaces cooled to form a frost. Breezes caught the frost crystals and lifted them into the air again, dancing and glittering around Paul and Talbot as they stomped on.

They were moving comfortably as if one three-legged creature now, well balanced against each other. They found a sustainable rhythm to their movements which improved their balance, and this in turn increased their momentum. They approached the waterfall like a two headed troll in a nightmarish snow globe.

'Straight through, no stopping!' Talbot shouted and they stepped into the icy wave. Shockingly cold water cascaded briefly down Paul's neck, causing him to twitch. There was a wide pool at the base of the waterfall, but it was shallow, and they splashed through it in a few steps. The water ran off from the pool in a broad thin film over bare rock. They followed the flowing water until they were clear of the broken ice that covered the landscape beyond the ice cave, then they turned towards the ridge once more.

Chapter Fourteen

After ten minutes of steady plodding they reached the far side of the glacier where the thinning ice was buried under a thick crust of grey soil and stones. The rising incline was the only clear indication that they had left the glacier behind. The valley side ahead of them appeared to be a continuous slope without any signs of sheer cliff faces to negotiate, although the top of the hill looked a long way off to Paul. As he raised his head to try and pinpoint their destination, he caught site of two figures moving high above them. Sydney and Annabel had made good progress and were more than halfway up the mountainside.

As they reached the first tufts of short grass Talbot stopped suddenly.

'Listen!' Talbot cocked his head to one side. Above the noise of splashing water around the glacier and the buffeting wind rolling up the hillside Paul could just make out a faint mechanical sound. The low constant hum grew louder and was joined by a second noise, intertwined with the first – 'taka-taka-taka-taka.' The echoes bounced disconcertingly from all the mountains around them, but Talbot raised a bloodstained right hand to point at the ridge top above the glacier just as a huge grey-green helicopter swooped into view above it. The aircraft powered over the valley and reduced speed as it approached the top of the hill above them. The thinning rain clouds hanging listlessly overhead were sliced apart by the whirling rotor blades. The landing gear deployed as the vehicle slowed to hover, turned ninety degrees, then began to descend.

Paul felt a surge of joy and excitement. 'Brilliant, that's, brilliant! Yeah!' He waved enthusiastically, although the aircraft had quickly dropped from view.

Talbot was less pleased. 'Fucking shitty bollocks,' he muttered, shaking his head.

'What's wrong?' Paul, too close to Talbots head to look at him properly, stared up at the point the helicopter had last been visible.

'We have less than an hour to get up this pissing hill, that's what's wrong. If we're not fucking there, they will leave without us.' Talbot sighed deeply, shifting his weight on his good foot.

'Well, we will just have to do it in time, that's all,' Paul stated confidently. 'Come on, Colour Sergeant! Chin up! Let's plot a route, make a plan, then carry it out!' Paul could feel the sweat on the left side of his body starting to cool as they remained stationary, his right side remaining insulated by the solid bulk of the Royal Marine pressed against it.

'Fuuuuuck me, Major Sicknote! Are you the pansy-arsed bollock slapping little bitch that's giving me orders now?' Talbot took a deep breath and raised his head, surveying the hill. After a moment's thought he said, 'Climbing in a straight line won't work, it will be too steep; so we start by heading off to the east - that's to the left of you, Sicknote - then turn south again past that clump of rocks, OK? From there we go directly up, but where the slope is too steep we may have to tack. That means zig zag to you, Sicknote. Clear?'

'Yes, Colour Sergeant,' Paul nodded.

'Which should mean in an hour from now we will have a fucking lovely view from halfway up this mountain of that helicopter flying away. Come on then, on three - one, two, three...'

Even though the ground ahead of them was fairly even and solid, the rising slope immediately impacted the speed of their progress. The steady rhythm that had carried them across the valley floor now deserted them, causing them to stumble and clash against each other. After only a couple of minutes of this Talbot growled.

'Wait, wait! This is no fucking good. Smaller steps, see? Push off more with your outside leg, hold the centre leg steady when it's on the ground, then swing on again…'

'I'm trying…'Paul panted.

'Try not! Do…or do not. There is no try.' Talbot spoke is in a strange, strangulated voice. He seemed to be grinning to himself. Paul turned his head to stare incredulously at Talbots ear.

'Was that meant to be Yoda? Did…did you just quote Star Wars at me?'

'Fuckin' wise, that little green bastard.'

'I thought you only watched the film Zulu?' Paul adjusted his right arm across Talbots back. The Marines' tunic felt slippery at the shoulder under Paul's grip.

'Best film ever, but I have seen some others you know. Aaah, that's it! We need a song to march to! Follow my lead, one, two, three, four, "Men of Harlech, march to glory…"' Talbot sang quite softly, punctuating every other beat of the song with a step.

Paul tried to join in, but was soon breathing too hard to sing along, and anyway after the first line he barely knew any of the words. 'Dee,' (puff) 'da dee,' (wheeze), 'da dee,' (puff) 'da dee da…' he managed, gasping.

The singing seemed to have the required effect; the two men began to move together more easily, and they slowly continued their way up the hill.

By the time Talbot had completed the song three times a further fifteen minutes had gone by. Paul had been concentrating so hard on placing his feet carefully he hadn't been looking where they were going, leaving it to Talbot to guide them. Only when Talbot halted did Paul look up. Blocking their path was a sheer rock face about seven or eight feet high which ran off in both directions as far as they could see. Above it Paul could see a long swathe of grassy meadow rising steadily but evenly almost to the top of the ridge.

Talbot stooped to untie the belt around their legs. 'One at a time on this, I think. I'll go first, then you follow. Give me a leg up,' he said. As Talbot reached up to find cracks in the stone to grip onto Paul reached down for Talbots leg.

'Aaargh, the good leg, you dip-fucking-shit moron!' Talbot yelled.

'Oh, yes, sorry,' Paul said, reaching for Talbots other leg. The Colour Sergeant quickly pulled himself up as Paul pushed the good foot from below. Once Talbot was over the edge of the embankment Paul reached his arms up and searched with his fingers for something to clutch onto. Even with solid handholds Paul struggled to lift himself more than a few inches up the wall on his own, his bruised and swollen left hand barely able to grip at all. Talbot reached down, grabbed Paul by the collar, and heaved, dragging Paul most of the way up. Paul's feet wriggled against the rock, and he managed eventually to bellyflop on to the grass, gasping for breath like a landed trout. Slowly he sat up, painfully trying to flex the fingers on his left hand.

Talbot glanced over. 'You need to get your wedding ring off,' he said.

'What? No!' Paul shook his head.

'Take it off now before the swelling gets any worse, or they'll have to cut it off,' Talbot said.

'They'll cut my ring off?'

'No, Sicknote, they'll have to cut your finger off to remove the ring.'

'Oh. Well, bugger that.' Unable to pull the ring straight over the middle knuckle because of the swelling, Paul began spinning it, trying to corkscrew the golden band past the knuckle. Teeth bared in a grimace, finally he succeeded in pulling the ring from his finger. For a moment he held the ring up, angling it to and fro until he could clearly read the single word engraved on the inside. He considered it for a moment, then awkwardly managed to force the ring onto the fourth finger on his right hand. He clambered to his feet and reached out his right hand towards Talbot.

Looking up the mountain Paul could see Sydney and Annabel still plodding on although they no longer seem so far ahead. It was difficult to be sure from this distance, but Sydney seemed to be leading Annabel by the hand for a few steps before stopping for several seconds, then going again.

The leather belt creaked as Talbot pulled it tight around their thighs once more. Paul tried to stifle a wince as the buckle pinched his bare skin. The hole Talbot had made had begun to tear and stretch, but it held. The Royal Marine was breathing heavily through his nose as he straightened up and grabbed hold of Paul's left shoulder with his left hand.

'On,' was all he said.

The hill was steeper now, and the effort to ascend it on three legs was punishing. The burning in Paul's thigh muscles was matched by the fire in his lungs. Talbot had started singing a marching song again, but after several minutes or so this dropped to a mumble before stopping entirely. Unnoticed until Talbot became silent, each breath in that Paul took was accompanied by a high-pitched squeaking noise. The thick grey pillows of raincloud that filled the entire sky had lifted clear of the mountain tops, but drifting threads of water vapour draped over the hillsides and brushed across the two men as they ascended, chilling Paul's sweat.

They managed to keep moving for another twenty minutes before Paul stumbled to a halt once more, gulping wheezy lungfuls of air. He bent over at the waist, hands on knees, but Talbot gripped his left shoulder to pull him upright.

'Don't sit down now. You won't get up again,' Talbot said slowly. 'Sixty seconds to get your breath.' Paul couldn't imagine how long sixty seconds was any more. 'Take a big slug of water. Now we go on.' The Colour Sergeant was leaving long gaps between each sentence, as if he had to summon words in a foreign tongue each time he spoke.

On they went. Paul's visual focus became entirely fixed on the ground in front of them, trying to ensure each step was onto the flattest ground possible. Even as the world around them became less noticed, a quiet part of Paul's mind was assessing the different pain messages his body was sending to his brain. He had become weirdly accustomed to the constant discomfort of his blistered feet. Similarly, painful knee and hip joints had been with him every waking hour for the last two days, so these too were commonplace. The cuts on his legs didn't produce pain, and if anything the seeping blood covering his limbs was lessening the effect of the cold wind on his bare skin. The belt around his thigh was intensely uncomfortable, bruising and chafing with each step. His left hand throbbed horribly. Worse still was the muscle pain, the stretch and flex of every movement hurting his legs and his back. Hardest of all to bear was the burning in his lungs, the punishing effort of getting up the hill making every breath searingly difficult.

Paul's strength ebbed away with each step; the next one had to be the last. But Talbot moved again, so Paul moved with him. Swing, pivot. And again. Then once more. Stopping would have been harder than taking that one more next step, so they moved on.

After uncountable minutes Paul managed to raise his head to look up. Talbot's head was nodding even as his feet still plodded on. Paul could see the top of the slope was suddenly much nearer, and just over the ridgeline poked a sharp metallic object.

'A rotor blade...I can see it!' Paul wheezed excitedly. Talbot didn't answer. Paul leaned his head away to look at the other man. Talbots eyelids drooped; his mouth slackly open as his head hung down. Paul noticed the other man's right hand, swinging loosely, was coated with thick, oily blood. Glancing at the back of Talbots head he realised it was blood that was greasing the dark hair into a single lump that now resembled bitumen on a flat roof.

The realisation that Talbot was bleeding heavily shocked Paul like wet fingers touching a live wire. Paul couldn't hold back tears of fear, but he gripped Talbots tunic more tightly and muttered 'nearly there! Keep on! Please!'

With each tiny step more of the rotor blade became visible, then a second blade tip, then all five. The top of the ridgeline rolled away and the ground began to level off. The dangling shrouds of rain drifted away too, revealing the curve of the mountain they had walked round yesterday at the head of the valley. Paul tried to move faster but the barely conscious Talbot only had one speed. Swing, pivot.

The top of the helicopter was just about visible now. Paul tried to shout but his inflamed lungs couldn't spare the breath to make a noise beyond a pitiful squeak. Swing, pivot.

Paul looked up again, hoping to be able to see anyone, to be able to wave, but they were still too low over the horizon. No-one could see them.

The rotor blades began to turn.

Paul sobbed in despair. They were so close but not close enough.

Blinking through the tears Paul noticed distant movement away to his right. Peering hard, he could just make out several tiny figures on the mountain path, at least one of them moving fast, running.

The rotor blades were turning faster now, the tips beginning to rise. The helicopter was side on to them, and the tail of the helicopter coming into view. The tail rotor was beginning to spin. Paul could see the glass of the cockpit and the main fuselage with small oval windows along it. He tried to wave his left hand, hoping someone might be looking out, but this unbalancing action nearly toppled the pair over. Paul grabbed Talbots left sleeve as best he could with his own swollen left hand.

The noise of the helicopter engine was building, echoing off the mountains around them. Even if Paul could shout he wouldn't be heard now. Swing, pivot. Every muscle on each of Paul's limbs was tense, bulging as he shuddered and trembled, trying desperately to muster the last iota of strength left in him.

With a moan of terrified hope Paul could see the ramp at the back of the helicopter was open. He could make out a figure standing on it. Paul prayed for them to turn their head in his direction.

An insect whizzed past them. Paul heard it rather than saw it; the first one he had encountered all day. Then a second one flew past, except this one ricocheted away off a rock just in front of them with a sharp 'ping.' Paul glanced instinctively to his right and could make out the leading figure on the mountain path standing still, legs apart, arms raised.

'He's shooting at us,' Paul said to himself. Without thinking Paul let go of Talbot's right shoulder, reached down to the pistol holster on Talbots belt, and pulled out the gun. Swing, pivot. He pointed the gun at the far distant figure and pulled the trigger. Nothing happened. Swing, pivot. Another bullet flew harmlessly over their heads. Paul tried again with the pistol, but still nothing. Swing, pivot. He looked back at the helicopter and the buckle on the belt tying his leg to Talbot's snapped.

Talbots full weight dropped onto Pauls shoulders. Paul managed to keep Talbot upright, even drag him forward a yard or two, but he couldn't lift him any further. They were done. He looked despairingly towards the aircraft.

Charlotte stood at the bottom of the ramp, pointing her camera in his direction. Paul saw her head turn to shout at someone inside the helicopter, then point towards him.

Six Marines came running towards them. Towne deployed himself and two others into shooting positions, aiming towards those approaching on the mountain path. Preston and Hamilton eased Talbot from Pauls grasp and carried him towards the helicopter. Relieved of his burden Paul exploded into noisy tears. He swayed, his knees buckled, and he would have collapsed to the ground except Lincoln swooped him up into his arms and carried him like a baby.

Through stifled sobs Paul managed to squeak, 'Talbot...head wound...he's bleeding...'

Lincoln glanced down at Pauls legs. 'You're bleeding on me, Sicknote. And what the fuck happened to your trousers?' He gently took the pistol from Pauls unresisting hand. He had to shout to be heard above the roar of the helicopter. 'Don't worry, Draws will sort him out.'

The inward curve of the ridge at the top of the valley obscured the view of the helicopter to anyone approaching on the path from the ski lodge. The slope up from the glacier was clearly visible though; Paul and the Marines were out in the open.

Towne shouted into his comms. 'Hansel, this is Corporal Towne; we've recovered the Colour Sergeant and the civilian and we are on our way back. We have eyes on twenty, maybe twenty-five hostiles approaching on foot from the west, about four hundred metres from your position. Prepare for take-off.'

A few of the hurrying figures approaching on the pathway paused to raise their firearms and take aim and a crackle of shots echoed from the surrounding mountains. Lincoln dropped to his knees, lowering Paul gently to the ground before lying flat. He turned his head to Paul. 'Can you crawl?'

They set off towards the helicopter, Lincoln flat and lithe like a snake, speeding across the damp grass. Paul dragged himself along on hands and knees, head down, bottom up. He only managed to get a further twenty yards or so before his strength gave out again and he slumped face down on the earth. 'Corporal!' Lincoln yelled after noticing Paul had stopped. 'I need cover!' Lincoln stood and grabbed Paul, lifting him effortlessly into his arms once more and beginning to run. Paul saw Towne ahead of them leap to his feet and start running towards the attackers. After a few paces he drew back an arm and hurled a small object ahead of him before he dropped to the ground again. After a brief second the grenade began to emit a thick white smoke which swirled and drifted across the mountainside

'Go, go, go!' Towne shouted as he jumped up again, hurled a second smoke grenade, fired three shots through the smoke, turned, and ran. Preston and Hamilton with Talbot suspended between them had reached the ramp and were moving inside. Lincoln ran past Ashton and Jackson, still in prone firing positions. Occasionally bullets pinged through the air around them but, robbed of clear targets, the approaching soldiers seemed wary of firing indiscriminately.

Paul began to feel the downdraft of air from the rotor blades as Lincoln brought him closer to the helicopter. The breeze became a blast as they arrived underneath the spinning blades and Lincoln had to slow to a walk. Paul could see Towne,

Jackson, and Ashton, some fifty yards from the aircraft, slowly backing towards it as Lincoln stepped onto the ramp. The smoke from the grenades had begun to dissipate, blown apart by the mountain winds. Several figures had come into view at the end of the path, but they ducked out of view as Jackson fired a volley in their direction.

Lincoln manoeuvred Paul past the large machine gun which was positioned on a pivot at the top of the ramp. It was manned by someone Paul didn't recognise, dressed in a military green jumpsuit. Their face was hidden beneath a large visor attached to a bulbous helmet.

Paul caught a glimpse of shocked faces as he was carried into the helicopter cabin by a stooping Lincoln. The other members of the Herd, all wearing large ear defenders, were strapped into seats along both sides of the cabin. Annabel sat near the ramp wearing a neck brace and with one side of her head swathed in bandages. Rachel was sat next to her, her fingers intertwined with Annabel's, staring at the far end of the cabin with an expression of fury on her face. Paul was laid gently onto a stretcher on the floor next to Talbot. He felt rather than heard a *clunk* from the bodywork of the helicopter which then swayed very slightly – the brakes were off. The helicopter began to move.

Paul reached over to grab hold of Draws arm as the medic was examining the Colour Sergeant. Draws looked at Paul. 'Nice of you to join us. You don't appear to have any trousers on.'

'Dislocated ankle!' he yelled, pointing at Talbots leg. Draws nodded.

'Sydney told me, but why is he…?' he began. Paul continued shouting as the helicopter began to rise. The ramp came up but didn't close entirely; the noise level inside the aircraft increased.

'Deep scalp laceration on the back of his head - must have been bleeding since the avalanche! Possible rib damage too…'

Draws reached up and ran his fingers across the back of Talbots head, drawing back bloody fingers.

Looking down past his feet Paul could see outside the helicopter the three marines turning to run towards the ramp. The crewman on the machine gun waved frantically at them. The Marines dropped to the ground, and the machine gun began to fire in short bursts over their heads. It made a huge noise, which temporarily drowned out the sound of the engines. The sound was strangely similar to the 'taka-taka-taka' of the rotors Paul had heard earlier. Paul could see huge clods of earth and chunks of rock being thrown into the air where the bullets struck, close to where the attackers had last been. After a final long burst of fire the helmeted figure signalled to Towne again and the three marines were up and running. Jackson reached the ramp and leapt inside, turning to reach out to the marines behind him. Ashton stretched out a hand to grab Jacksons but then stumbled and fell. As he went down Towne stopped, grabbed Ashton's shoulder, and pulled him upright again as the helicopter moved on. The two sprinted forward. Paul could see Ashton gritting his teeth with the effort as he ran ahead of Towne.

'Ashton! We are LEAVING!' roared Jackson, gripping a strap on the edge of the ramp and stretching his arm out again towards the two Marines. Ashton reached the ramp and threw up an arm again and caught Jacksons hand. Jackson heaved and catapulted Ashton forward into the helicopter. Through the shreds of smoke at the end of the mountain path a figure in a black leather jacket ran forward and raised a rifle. Towne reached the ramp just as the helicopter began to rise. He jumped, landing on his stomach on the end of the ramp. Before Jackson or the machine gunner could reach down to grab him he rolled forwards, twisted himself up onto one knee, stood upright and casually walked into the helicopter cabin.

Jackson turned to join him. 'Hey, did you hear that one? "Hudson, we are leaving!" That's from 'Aliens,' that is…' He broke off and dropped to the floor as several sharp pings echoed around them. Bullets hit the underside of the tail of the helicopter, sparks flaring across the riveted metal and puncturing a row of small holes. The machine gunner shouted something into his headset and the helicopter rose sharply, nose first, giving Paul a clear view of the ground below. The helicopter machine gun fired again, a longer sustained burst, the barrel swinging to and fro to sweep the whole area. There was no sign of anyone returning fire. The plateau rapidly shrunk away until the aircraft turned, and the flat piece of ground disappeared from view. Paul had a brief glimpse of the glacier as a flash of pale blue and white and then it was gone.

As the helicopter levelled off and began to accelerate forwards Draws hurriedly set up an intravenous drip into Talbot's arm, then tightly bandaged Talbots head.

Paul didn't notice someone kneeling on the other side of him until their hands pulled a clear plastic oxygen mask over his face. Cecelia leaned down until her mouth was close beside his ear.

'Bravo, Mr Huggins. Bravo.' She patted him encouragingly on his shoulder before draping ear defenders over his head. She stood up and moved back to a seat near the cockpit between Sydney and Ren. Sat beside Cecelia was Tor, huge sunglasses covering the top of her face. Looking back down past his feet Paul could see Campbell sat next to Charlotte and Jasper at the tail of the aircraft. The diplomat looked enquiringly at Paul, raising one thumb, almost as a question. Paul responded, raising two thumbs close to his face and grinning through his mask. Charlotte pointed her camera towards him. The seated Marines were staring grimly at Talbot lying unconscious.

Paul laid back and closed his eyes for a moment.

Sometime later a sharp sting in his arm woke Paul. 'Ow, ow,' he mumbled, looking up at Draws kneeling next to him. He felt a cool tingle drifting up his arm from the syringe, then the world went a bit fluffy.

'A decent painkiller for you,' Draws said. 'You must be dehydrated as well, so I'll get some fluids into you.' Hearing the medics voice clearly through the speakers in the ear defenders struck Paul as comical. He smiled up at Draws as the Marine set up an intravenous needle and fluid drip for Paul.

'Just like my pal over there! Good ol' Double Dutch, Tap Dance Talbot!' Paul flapped his right hand in the direction of the Colour Sergeant still laid out on his stretcher.

Draws grinned. 'I think you mean "Double Tap."' Having set a fluid pouch hanging from a hook in the ceiling Draws started gently cleaning the cuts on Pauls legs.

'That's the fella. Watcha doin'?' Paul raised his head to look down at his legs. 'I'm all bloody. And muddy. And look at the little ducks!' He pointed at his underpants. 'Muddy ducks. And bloody ducks. Bloody muddy ducks if you ask me! Why is that funny?'

Draws laughed again. 'I think that painkiller I gave you has really kicked in.'

'Ok. My hand was hurting, and my feet were hurting, and everything was hurting, but now it doesn't. Yippee!' Paul put his head down. He put his head up again. 'Draws! Who's the bloke in the funny hat?' He pointed behind him.

Draws chuckled, still working on dressing Pauls wounds. 'That's not a funny hat; that's a flying helmet. He's part of the aircrew for the helicopter.'

'Oh.' Paul twisted his head back and gave a little wave. 'Hello!' the helmeted figure grinned and waved back, before turning back to the console on the wall.

'Draws!' Paul called again.

'Now what?'

'Is everybody else OK?' Paul's good hand waved all-round the cabin.

'They're all here and they can all hear you, ask them yourself, I'm kind of busy right now.' Draws started wrapping tight bandages around Paul's leg.

'Hey everybody!' Paul called out excitedly. There was a mixed chorus of 'hi's and 'hellos in return. 'Everybody OK?'

'Just about – no thanks to *madam* over there.' Rachel's voice was dripping with venom even through the slight distortion of the microphone. She was staring towards the cockpit.

'Whaaaaat?' Paul couldn't work out who she was looking at.

'A certain SUPERSTAR was too important to wait for you and Annabel.'

'Whaaaat?'

Rachel was shouting now. Annabel was clutching her arm tightly to keep her in her seat. 'That BITCH was throwing her toys out of the pram as soon as we got to the chopper, demanding we take off immediately. Fuck everybody else, eh Tor? Well FUCK YOU, you heartless COW!'

'Leave it, Rachael. We're here now.' Sitting beside her sister, Belinda's voice crackled through the headphones.

Rachel wasn't done yet. 'When Annabel and…and…Sydney came storming up the hill, THAT heartless arsehole laughs - she fucking *laughs* - at Annabel's face.'

'Whaaaat?' Paul couldn't quite find anything else to say.

'She's got a broken cheekbone and fractured eye socket, and God knows what else and she could have *died* – it's a bloody miracle she made it back up that mountain at all…'

'Ok, sweetheart, that's enough.' Tors Australian accent sounded stronger than it had before. 'We were bloody lucky that everybody got here in time, weren't we? Now maybe your girlfriend had what it takes to make it in the modelling industry before, but not now she won't, not with a busted-up face. Broken bones don't give you a jawline and cheekbones like mine, do they? You might think its harsh, but I was just being honest.'

Angry tears were flowing from the corners of Rachels eyes. 'Who the fuck asked you anyway, You shitty BITCH!'

There was silence for a while.

'Well. Um. How's everybody else?' Paul asked brightly. No one answered for a while. The Aircrewman at the rear of the helicopter raised the ramp into the fully closed position.

'I'm very glad you made it Mr Huggins,' Jordi said quietly. Paul twisted his head to look at the Van Der Molen family, seated near the cockpit opposite Cecelia. 'But please – why have you got no trousers on?'

Before Paul could answer a new voice buzzed through the headphones. The helicopter had levelled off and reached a steady speed. 'Good morning everyone, this is Lieutenant Commander Glaven, I am the pilot and senior officer on this flight. It's good to have you with us; I am glad you all made it onboard, most of you in one piece. We will be flying for about three and a half hours, travelling at a speed of about one hundred and thirty knots, heading south southwest out of Kyrgyzstan, then over Tajikistan before we make a refuelling stop in Northern Afghanistan. After that we will head south to Kabul to the British military base by the airport; there the Marines detachment will get a full debrief before we put the civilians amongst you on a plane home. We are not expecting any trouble during the flight - We are flying away from the battle zones, and the Kyrgyz air traffic control is somewhat distracted currently.

For your own safety I would ask you to stay seated and strapped in as much as possible during our flight; we will be flying at low altitude in a mountainous region so we may encounter some turbulence, and I would prefer not to add to the list of walking wounded we already have on board. With regards to the wounded, your medic informs me that although Colour Sergeant Talbot will require hospital treatment he is out of immediate danger. I am sure that will come as a relief to you all.' There were a number of sighs and smiles from the Royal Marines around the cabin. 'Talking of relief - if anyone needs to relieve themselves, well, we can open the side door and you can pee out of that, otherwise, you'll have to hold onto it I'm afraid.' Paul could see the Royal Marines, lifted by the news about Talbot, grinning at this weak joke. However, Agnes looked quite concerned. Glaven continued, 'This is a brand-new Merlin mark four helicopter, only commissioned into active service in the last six weeks, so please, try not to make a mess in our brand-new aircraft. This thing has a range of over nine hundred miles which is not quite enough to get us into Kyrgyzstan and then get you to Kabul in one trip, hence our little pit stop in the Afghan mountains. For now, sit back and relax and enjoy the flight, courtesy of Naval Air Squadron Eight Four Six, Commando Helicopter Force, and the Royal Navy.

Corporal Towne, report to the cockpit, we need to get on the comms and inform Gretel of our progress. As Talbot remains incapacitated, they may have some questions for you.'

For a while Paul surfed through the woolly fluff the painkiller had put inside his head, giggling gently. Outside the windows thinning grey clouds swished past and splashed water droplets across the Perspex, until the helicopter passed through into open sky. Without the camouflage of the clouds the pilot dropped the helicopter lower into the valleys turning south, then west, then south again to follow the course of the rivers below.

'We're flying underneath the mountains now! Weeeeee!' Paul chortled happily, looking up through the window nearest to him at the landscape racing past.

After a few minutes Towne returned from the cockpit. Agnes stopped him.

'Please, Corporal, the pilot said three hours…?'

'Yes, Mrs. Van Der Molen.'

'I cannot wait three hours,' she said anxiously.

Towne smiled. 'It's fine, we'll be there before you know it…'

'No, you don't understand. I cannot hold on for another three hours.'

Towne looked at her for a moment until comprehension dawned. 'Oh. Oh, I see.' He said softly. He looked around. 'Aircrewman!'

'Yes Corporal?' The man by the cabin side door replied.

'I can't do it out of the door!' Agnes wailed. Jordi pulled his coat hood so far down over his face it covered his chin and groaned with embarrassment.

'Don't worry Mrs V, we can figure something out,' Towne responded. He turned back to the Aircrewman. 'I need an empty jerrycan, a funnel and a couple of blankets,' he said. 'Ren, Sydney: another guard duty for you…'

As the aircrewman recovered a large round tin funnel and a clanging metal container from a storage locker under a panel on the floor Towne shooed Hendrik and Jordi out of their seats. Towne hung a blanket like a curtain with corners tied to the wall and ceiling, then positioned a second one at right angles to enclose a single seat in the corner of the cabin. He then held out the jerrycan and funnel towards Agnes.

'Your very own latrine, Mrs V!' He grinned.

Cecelia reached into the rucksack at her feet, then stood up. 'Good effort, Corporal, but I think we can improve this still further.' She reached out a hand towards Agnes and handed her a small pink plastic funnel with a narrow, curved aperture at the top. Agnes smiled gratefully, took the device and the can, and stepped behind the blankets.

Towne laughed again. 'Well, I ain't never seen a thing like that before!'

'Corporal?' Ren raised her hand as she stood up. She held out a similar device, but this was painted with camouflage green colours. Sydney waved another one. 'Standard issue for front line female personnel, Corp,' Ren told him. She and Sydney took up guard positions standing with their backs to the blankets. After a minute or so Agnes called out above the rattle and hum of the helicopter, 'I cannot go with everybody listening!'

The other occupants of the cabin exchanged glances, unsure of what to do, but Paul had a fuzzy brainwave. He began to sing. 'God save our gracious Queen, long live our...' he warbled, until he was interrupted by Cecelia.

'I don't think that's an appropriate song in the circumstances, thank you very much.' She looked down at him sternly. Her expression softened slightly. 'Perhaps a different tune? What song does everybody know?'

After a moment of silence a soft, high-pitched voice began to sing, 'Si-lent night... ho-oly night... aaaall is calm... aaaall is bright...' Jasper stretched his neck and widened his mouth as he sang.

In amongst a burst of grins and giggles a dozen other voices took up the refrain, raising the volume to drown out all the other noises around them. The constant "taka-taka-taka" of the rotors became a sensation rather than a sound. Unconsciously the singers followed the rhythm. As the second verse began Paul could distinguish Hendrik and Jordi singing in Dutch - "Stille Nacht...heilige nacht..." It rapidly became clear that most people only knew the first verse, so they were singing it again. Halfway through the third repeat Agnes, face red with embarrassment, emerged through the blankets, wiping the she-wee with a wet wipe. She received a cheer and a round of applause that made her blush even more.

'Anyone else?' Towne asked. A hand went up from every female civilian except Tor.

No-one else asked to be serenaded. As the women took turns filing into the makeshift toilet a buzz of conversation began to vibrate through the speakers as the marines began to relax into the journey. Jackson nudged Preston who was sat next to him. Jackson pointed to the large machine gun at the back of the helicopter, now neatly folded away against the bulkhead. 'Here, listen – "*say hello to my litl' friend!*" Get it?' Preston looked blank. Ashton laughed.

'That's from Scarface; Al Pacino firing an M16 as big as that with a rocket launcher on it,' he said.

Preston shook his head. 'I'd sooner have that GPMG over an M16 thank you very much.'

'Oh, go on, you could barely lift that on your own, never mind shoot it,' Jackson mocked.

Ashton looked puzzled. 'How come Scarface gets shot about a dozen times at the end of that movie and doesn't die?'

'He's so full of cocaine he doesn't realise he's dead yet,' replied Jackson.

'Would that really happen?' asked Ashton.

'Dunno. If only we knew somebody with experience of class A drugs.' Jackson slowly turned his head towards the tail end of the helicopter. 'Hey, what d'ya reckon, Jasper…?' The Marines roared with laughter.

Jasper grinned widely, 'Yeah, that's right, eh boys? Great movie - he must have been off his tits on Charlie! There was this chap I knew at Uni, Lyndon his name was, he was an absolute *demon* for a bit of the old blow. There was this one time, him and his girlfriend on a night out got fully coke'd up, decided it'd be a great idea to watch the sun come up over Glastonbury Tor. Before he'd even got out of Bristol he wrapped his Audi TT around a tree – broke three ribs and his collar bone, he didn't feel a thing, hahaha!' A few of the Marines exchanged glances. Jasper ploughed on regardless, 'He's standing on the side of the road, yeah, shouting abuse at this oak tree he's just crashed into, the girlfriend, forget her name, she's unconscious in the passenger seat, me and a friend happen to drive past, so we drag them into the Maserati and race off to A&E. He didn't even realise he was hurt until the doctors' showed him his X-ray. Hahaha!'

Charlotte gave Jasper a dead-eyed stare for a long moment before stomping off to the latrine. Paul dropped his head back to the floor, staring up at the ceiling, watching the way the light and shade ebbed and flowed with the changing landscape outside as the helicopter surged on.

Chapter Fifteen

'Ladies and gentlemen, we have just left Kyrgyz air space. Welcome to Tajikistan.'

Paul found his right eyelid far too heavy to lift. The left one was marginally lighter, allowing him to open it just enough to peer out. Most of the civilian passengers within his line of sight seemed to be sleeping. The Marines were more alert, giving a muted cheer to the news from the pilot.

'We are not quite out of the woods yet – we didn't exactly file a flight plan with the Tajik authorities for our top-secret hush-hush rescue mission, so they might be a bit iffy about a foreign military aircraft abusing their hospitality. It's only a small country though, so we should reach our refuelling point in Afghanistan in a little over an hour.'

'Corporal Towne,' Tor called out, 'I'll have my mobile phone back now, thank you very much.' She extended a long thin arm and held out a large hand, palm facing up, towards the Royal Marine.

Towne grunted. 'I don't think so. You'll wait until we are safely on the ground in Kabul, along with everybody else.'

'Oh for God's sake, what is wrong with you people?' She folded her arms angrily across her body, turning her head away to stare at the blankets still hanging from the ceiling around the chair opposite her.

In the seat next to Tor was Cecelia. Paul noticed the grey-haired woman was sitting comfortably upright, reading a small hardback book as calmly as if she was sat in her local library. Seen in profile, Cecelia's eye flickered rapidly side to side as the pages of the book turned regularly. In the bright light flooding the cabin from the helicopter windows Paul could clearly see a lattice of fine lines across her forehead and a fan of more pronounced wrinkles spreading out from the corner of her eye. Her hands cradling the book in front of her had multiple skin blemishes, as if dozens of freckles had huddled together, but the fingers were smooth and straight and her fingernails were carefully manicured.

'Watchya reading?' Paul asked.

Cecelia smiled slightly, gave Paul a glance, and looked back at her book. 'It's an anthology of poems. I carry this book with me everywhere I go. I find poetry can stir the emotions or soothe a mind in torment. It can inspire, it can impart wisdom, it can make you laugh and cry in the space a few words. Poetry is one of the greatest achievements of human civilisation.'

Paul blinked his one open eye slowly. 'Oh. What's your favourite?'

'My favourite poem? Oh, I couldn't pick just one. There are dozens…' She scanned the index at the back of the book, then flicked to a particular page somewhere in the middle.

'Here is one that I know well, and perhaps it is appropriate for our situation…the last verse…

"I shall be telling this with a sigh.

Somewhere ages and ages hence:

Two roads diverged in a wood and I ,

I took the one less travelled by,

And that has made all the difference."

It's by an American poet, Robert Frost. I often have cause to bring this to mind.'

Ashton said quietly to Hamilton, 'Not many poems about helicopters then?'

Hamilton shook his head. 'I'm more of a limerick man myself. "There was a young Royal Marine…"'

a chuckle of recognition ran around the Marines and several voices joined in -

"..who tried to fart 'God save the Queen.'

When he reached the soprano, out shot the guano, and his trousers weren't fit to be seen!"

The Marines roared with laughter.

The bubbles of conversations continued to float out of the headphones, but Paul let them drift away without paying them any attention. As the flight went on he guessed from the way the sunlight angled in through the Perspex that it was mid-afternoon, but he had no idea what day it was. He shifted uncomfortably on the stretcher as the painkiller began to wear off. He glanced to his right; a slight rise and fall of Talbot's chest indicating steady if shallow breathing. Draws had disconnected Paul from the drip and did the same for the Colour Sergeant.

Eventually there came a change in the noise of the engines and the helicopter began to decelerate and change direction sharply. Sunlight and shadow spun giddily across the walls and ceiling. Gaven addressed them once more from the cockpit.

'In two minutes we will be touching down in the village of Jamarj-e Bala, our refuelling stop before we travel on to Kabul. Strap in and prepare for landing.'

Draws leaned over Paul, tightening the straps across his stretcher. He smiled encouragingly at Paul before turning to check Talbot. There was a clunk and a hydraulic whirring noise as the landing gear deployed. Seconds later there was a gentle bump as the helicopter landed. The ramp began to slowly open.

'Everyone will need to disembark while we check the aircraft for damage and refuel her. The Landing Zone Commander will find a safe location for you; Aircrewman Tiffey will organise your exit in small groups.'

The crewman stood feet slightly apart and planted on the edge of the ramp. 'When you exit the aircraft walk straight out past the tail before you turn to the side; that way you will avoid the worst of the down draft from the rotors. Wait until I point to you before you try and leave the aircraft. Corporal, stretchers first please.'

'Wait, wait!' Paul struggled to sit up, fighting the straps across his chest. He had a sudden urge not to be carried off the helicopter. 'I can walk.' He raised himself up on his elbows but the tight bandaging around his legs made it difficult to bend at the knee. He slipped and rolled onto his stomach before and levering himself upright using the seat frame next to him and grabbing hold of Jacksons knees. He dropped into an empty seat, his legs sticking out in front of him.

Preston and Ashton picked up Talbots stretcher and headed down the ramp proceeded by Towne with Draws following behind. Tiffey pointed at Cecelia and Tor, who exited followed closely by Ren and Sydney. Next the Van der Molen family, then four of the Marines, then Jasper and Charlotte. The departures continued calmly as the rotor blades slowed, and the engines powered down. Paul removed his headphones as Tiffey waved at him and Annabel and Rachel, the last three passengers still on board. As Paul struggled to his feet he overhead Tiffey say

'Final three now leaving Lieutenant Commander – it's the walking wounded: the tall lass with her girlfriend and the weird little guy in his underpants.'

Paul pretended he hadn't heard. As he couldn't bend his knees properly he tried to descend the ramp with small steps, but he went waddling down the slope quicker than he had intended to.

The helicopter had landed on an exposed clearing halfway up the hillside of a deep river valley. A dirt road wound away from the landing site down towards a small town that fanned around one end of a large bridge that spanned the wide shallow waterway. A number of modern buildings three or four stories high formed the centre of the town on this side of the river. A smaller settlement consisting of single-story dwellings squatted at the other end of the bridge.

Paul hobbled after the rest of the herd who had congregated beside a collection of khaki tents set up on the town side of the landing zone. A faint smell of wood smoke hung in the warm still air, mingling with the odour of aviation fuel emanating from a sandbagged enclosure several metres away. The Marines were chatting with some of the military personnel manning this site. Although the uniform colour and camouflage design was different to that worn by the Marines, Paul could hear British accents exchanging gentle banter with the new arrivals. The soldiers from the base, whilst uninterested in most of the civilians that had disembarked from the helicopter, were all straining their necks trying to get a good look at Tor. She ignored them with a display of bored indifference.

Paul looked around for somewhere to sit, but he decided the fold up chairs dotted about were too low for him to get into whilst bandaged up, so he tottered over to the corner of the tent where Talbot's stretcher had been laid on a camp bed. The Colour Sergeants face was turned towards Paul as Draws was busily changing the dressing on the back Talbot's head. As Paul tilted his head to look more closely, Talbots eyes sprung open. They glared at Paul for a moment; one eye winked very deliberately at Paul, and then both eyes closed again.

'He looked at me,' Paul croaked. Draws looked up at him, then back down at Talbot.

'Really?' He sounded doubtful.

Ten minutes after their arrival Lieutenant Commander Glaven came over to the group, accompanied by a young army officer and Corporal Towne. Glaven spoke first.

'Here's the situation report. Our aircraft sustained some damage from small arms fire when we took off – nothing too serious but we need to spend a little bit of time repairing it, then we can refuel and be on our way.'

'How long will we be here?' Campbell asked.

'Two hours at most.' Campbell nodded. Most people seemed relieved they weren't going to be staying overnight. Glaven continued, 'This is Lieutenant

Crane, he is officer commanding this outpost; he can brief you on what you can and can't do while you are here.' Glaven headed back to the helicopter.

The young officer stepped forward. Paul guessed he had to be in his early twenties. 'Thank you, Lieutenant Commander. Welcome to Afghanistan, everyone. This site is a forward operating base that we use occasionally when we have British or Allied troops on manoeuvres in the area. The rest of the time it is a helipad for the Afghans. In the town below is a government hospital and an Afghan army base, so the locals are used to seeing military helicopters dropping in and out of here. However, as a group you are quite conspicuous, so it would be best if we can keep you out of sight. Fifty yards down the track is a community centre. It's a bit more sheltered from the view of the town and I suggest you would be more comfortable waiting in there. So, if you would like to follow me.'

'What about the Colour Sergeant?' asked Campbell.

'Probably best he stays here with your medic, I think.'

Draws looked up and nodded. He looked at Annabel. 'You better stay put too. The less running around you do for a while the better.'

Crane set off and the rest of herd followed him. The Marines and about half of the soldiers formed an escort surrounding the civilians.

'This is a fairly close protection detail you've given us, Lieutenant. Are we not safe in this area?' Cecelia asked.

'Safety is a relative term in Afghanistan, ma'am. Away from the major cities the peace can be fragile at times. There is a bit of a power struggle going on between the regional Governor and a local tribal chief, Amu Zemar, who aspires to be something more. Allied troops can be a bit of a pawn in that game sometimes. I would rather avoid giving either side an opportunity to use you in this dispute.'

The track descended the hill in a gentle curve. As they headed down the road the roof of a single-story stone building came into view. In front of it was a large playing field.

'Belinda, look!' Moira cried gleefully.

In the centre of the field was a cricket pitch with three stumps set out at one end of the wicket, and a single stump at the other end. The outfield was covered in lush green vegetation, but the strip in the centre was bare creamy coloured earth, compacted so hard that the surface was shiny. Three girls and two boys, all appearing to be under the age of twelve, were out in the middle of the field.

As they approached the community centre from the rear it had resembled a brick-built cow shed, but from the front it looked like an English village cricket pavilion, with a covered veranda bordered by a carefully carved and painted wooden fence. On a fold up chair at the far end of the veranda sat an elderly local man watching the children play. He wore a soft brown hat which had a thick rolled brim. His clothes consisted of multiple layers of rough linen and wool which contrasted with the modern military boots on his feet. He slowly raised an arm in greeting and muttered a welcome; Crane responded in kind. The old man's gaze darted around the crowd of people but his unchanged expression registering no surprise at this pack of strangers appearing before him.

Out on the cricket pitch the young batter wielding a full-size bat that stood taller than his waist. The only protective equipment he had was a huge pair of batting gloves. The wicket keeper had large green gloves and a white pad on one leg. She stood close behind the three stumps with her bare leg hidden behind the padded one. As the Herd approached the edge of the pitch the young batsman took a huge swipe with the bat and set off running, his sandals slapping noisily on the hard ground. Moira ran forward to collect the ball as it stopped in the thick grass. Instead of throwing it back she ran out to the centre of the pitch.

'Hey, just a minute…' Lieutenant Crane complained, but she took no notice of him. As the other civilians filed towards the building doorway Belinda stood at the edge of the pitch. Cecelia stopped to watch Moira as she approached the players. After a few moments of voiceless pointing the Afghan girl politely urged Moira to bowl. Moira took two steps towards the single stump, gave a little skip, twirled her arm over and sent the ball fizzing towards the other end. Before the young batsman could complete the swing of the bat the ball landed, spun prodigiously, and bounced away past the young boy's shoulder. The wicketkeeper set off in pursuit of the ball as the batsman looked at Moira in wide eyed amazement.

Belinda glanced at Cecelia. 'Moira starts a Sports Science Degree at Loughborough Uni later this month on a cricket scholarship. She isn't going to miss the chance to play on a cricket pitch somewhere like this.'

'Ha! Quite right too. Carpe Diem.'

'Yes!' Jordi ran out onto the cricket pitch as well. Agnes moved to call him back, but Hendrik laid a gentle hand on her shoulder and shook his head. They stood and watched Jordi for a while before turning through the pavilion doorway. Belinda followed after Jordi.

Paul remained standing on the veranda. He had glanced inside the pavilion into what appeared to be a large, richly carpeted space with whitewashed walls and many broad fat cushions spread around the room for people to rest on. Paul didn't fancy trying to lower himself down onto the cushion, or worse, have to try and get off one, so he remained outside. Just inside the door Campbell and Cecelia seemed to be having an intense discussion with the young British Army officer.

The old man called out to him and having got Paul's attention he waggled a finger at Paul's legs and spoke again, clearly asking a question, even if Paul couldn't understand the language. Paul spread his hands and shrugged, before acting out the tearing of cloth and making a ripping sound. The old man nodded and smiled before turning back to the cricket match. Moira seemed to have turned the game into a coaching session; Paul could see her showing the Afghan children how to grip the ball. Jordi had taken the bat and was practicing defensive shots.

The old man spoke again, but when Paul turned to look at him Paul could see he was speaking into a mobile phone.

Lieutenant Crane hurried out of the pavilion and began to brusquely order his soldiers to take up guard positions around the pitch perimeter and along the track towards the town. It occurred to Paul that the Marines, whilst seemingly relaxing on the edge of the field, had in fact positioned themselves in a ring around the pavilion, with Sydney and Ren positioned either side of the door.

Campbell stood in the doorway, watching Lieutenant Crane deploy his men.

Paul looked at him quizzically. 'What did you say to the Lieutenant? He looked a little put out.'

'We just thought…that is, uh, Corporal Towne and I suggested he needed to be a bit more careful.'

Paul looked past Campbell through the open doorway. Corporal Towne was in discussion with Cecelia, with Tor seated nearby next to Charlotte reviewing pictures on the camera screen. Jasper, Agnes, and Hendrik stood at the window, watching the game.

'You and the Corporal, huh? Alright, if you say so.'

An Afghan teenager came sprinting along the track from the town, clasping a small bundle to their chest. The youngster ran past the British soldiers who made no effort to intercept. The child began yelling excitedly as they headed straight to the pavilion. Half a dozen rifles were instantly aimed by the surrounding Marines and the small figure skidded to a halt, their cries turning to shrieks of fear. The old man leapt up from his seat, and hurried over, waving his hands at the Marines.

Lieutenant Crane ran over. 'Stand easy! This is the old man's great granddaughter, or something. We see her up here all the time!'

'What is she holding?' Towne's rifle was still firmly aimed at the girl. The old man was shielding the youngster behind his legs while waving his skinny arms frantically at the guns around them.

Crane seemingly spoke a few words of the local language and indicated to the teenager to hold out her hands. As she did so the old man grabbed the bundle and held it up. The material unravelled like a newly raised flag. The marines lowered their weapons and turned away, grinning.

Paul stiffly stepped forward, and nodded slowly and politely to the old man, then grabbed the teenager's hand and shook it firmly. 'Thank you.' The girl began giggling nervously as the tension flowed away. Paul looked into the old man's face. 'Thank you.' The old man nodded and handed Paul the pair of trousers.

The sandy coloured voluminous garment was elasticated at the waistband and at the ankles, allowing Paul to easily pull the trousers on over his boots. Although the clothing was extremely baggy, it was lightweight and comfortable, and put no pressure on his bandaged legs. Paul heaved a sigh of relief. He grinned and nodded again at the old man. The girl ran off towards the cricket pitch.

More children had made their way up the hill to join in the game, most of them teenage girls. Moira was still acting as coach, giving each newcomer a bowl at Jordi who confidently hit most of the deliveries around the field. The growing number of fielders chased after the ball, their yells and shrieks of laughter growing louder.

Agnes and Hendrik had stepped onto the veranda and were encouraging Charlotte to take pictures of Jordi.

'Jordi is doing very well,' Paul called out. The couple smiled proudly.

'Yes. He plays for the school team with boys much older than he is.' Hendrik replied.

'Oh, really? I didn't know you played cricket much in Holland,' Paul said.

'Yes! It's very popular.' Agnes told him. 'Hendrik played for several years, didn't you dear? Our local cricket club is one of the oldest in the Netherlands.'

'Oh, I play too! I keep wicket for my local Sunday league team. It's always a real family event – my kids used to come and watch, and Annie always helps me make the sandwiches when it's my turn.' Paul glanced down at his bandaged hand.

Hendrik smiled at him slightly. 'When I played I was semi-professional; we were in the national league. We would travel all across the country for our matches.'

Still angling her camera towards the pitch, Charlotte muttered, 'I never understood cricket. Hours and hours of standing around doing nothing, and then you stop to have tea. How can you have a sport with meal breaks in it?'

Jasper had stepped out onto the veranda and was rapidly tapping his fingers on the wooden rail, eyes glued on the players on the field. After pacing up and down for a few minutes he seemed to come to a decision and stepped onto the grass.

'It looks like they are having fun!' he shouted as he ran out to the middle. He held a requesting hand to the girl holding the ball as he ran.

'He always suffers from FOMO,' said Charlotte.

'From what?' Hendrick asked her.

'FOMO. "Fear Of Missing Out." He can't bear not being in the middle of things.'

Jasper had walked a long way back from the stumps before turning and running in at full pelt. He swung his arm over wildly and let go of the ball. It bounced halfway down the pitch. Jordi calmly took a step back as the ball bounced high over his head. Three fielders set of after the ball as it bounced away towards the boundary.

'Gimme another go!' shouted Jasper. Moira seemed to try and intercept the ball as it was thrown back by the fielders, but Jasper swooped forwards and grabbed it before running back to begin his run up. His second attempt at bowling was better than his first, the ball travelling fast and pitching close to the batsman's feet. Jordi leaned forward and flicked the ball away to the boundary.

Jasper demanded a third attempt and was starting his run up again when a commotion on the road caught everyone's attention. Paul could hear a squawking noise from the army radios, a warning from the sentries posted on the road towards the village. A large black Toyota SUV hurtled up the track followed more slowly by an open topped truck carrying half a dozen men armed with Kalashnikov rifles.

'Oh, great,' muttered Lieutenant Crane. 'We are getting a visit from Amu Zemar, the local chief I was telling you about.'

The car came to a halt close to the pavilion. As the doors began to open the Marines quietly ushered the Herd that stood nearby inside the building before taking up inconspicuous positions close to the doors and windows. Campbell remained outside and walked over to stand beside Lieutenant Crane.

A tall man wearing dark clothes and a black hat with a thick rolled brim stepped out of the SUV, removed a heavy pair of sunglasses, and looked around. Three armed bodyguards got out of the Toyota as the men on the truck jumped down to join them. The tall man smiled as Crane and Campbell approached him.

'Good afternoon Lieutenant!' Amu Zemar placed the palm of his hand to his chest and gave a little bow of the head. He glanced briefly at Campbell.

'Hello Mr Zemar, my name is Fitzroy Campbell, I work for Her Majesty's Government in the Diplomatic Service…'

Zemar ignored Campbell completely and addressed Crane. 'I heard you were organising a game of cricket, so I thought I would come and show my appreciation for your kind efforts to entertain our children.' He spoke in clear English, with only the faintest hint of an accent. He waved a hand towards the cricket pitch where Jasper, Jordi, Moira, and Belinda stood staring at the new arrivals. 'But it seems you and your soldiers are not alone?' The fingers of one hand idly tended the curling ends of his black beard.

'Good afternoon, Zemar.' Crane nodded politely, then looked pointedly at the Afghan militia men standing near the truck. 'Just like you, we are not alone today either. But our guests are only here very briefly – just to refuel their aircraft before they continue their journey. The cricket is just, er, a little distraction.' The Afghan children on the cricket pitch had run off down the hill as soon as the militiamen had exited the truck.

'Mr Zemar, if I might…' Campbell tried again.

'I cannot allow strangers to pass through my territory without offering my hospitality. You will bring them to my home. We will have a feast, and they will stay with me for a while.' Amu Zemar folded his arms across his chest and stuck out his chin, raising the end of his beard to point threateningly at the soldier.

'Oh, no, that's very generous, but there is no need. They will be leaving very shortly…'

'I insist Lieutenant. It would be an insult to me personally if you were to refuse.'

There was a long silence. Lieutenant Crane's eyes flickered towards the pavilion. Everyone seemed to be holding their breath.

Cecelia suddenly stepped towards the door, grabbing one of her walking poles and ruffling her hair until it stood up at all angles. she hunched her shoulders and bent her neck forward, changing her gait into an awkward shuffle. By the time she stepped onto the veranda she somehow looked ten years older. Leaning heavily on her stick she waved her free hand and called out,

'I say, Lieutenant! Do you mind if I interrupt your chat?' She had changed her voice too – it was thinner and more shrill, and at the same time more aristocratic and superior. She shuffled slowly towards the tall Afghan and squinted myopically at him. 'Hello there! Salaam alaikum! I hope I said that right.

Zemar turned to face Cecelia and bowed deeply. 'Wa alaikum assalam,' he said in response. Even as he drew breath to speak, Cecelia spoke loudly.

'My name is Dame Cecelia Eriksen, Mr...Zemar, was it? Delighted to meet you. Delighted.' She waved her free hand. ' Now listen here young man, it really is most awfully decent of you to invite us round for tea, and we are greatly honoured, really, we are but it just is not possible I'm afraid. Completely out of the question, in fact! We are in quite a rush, d'you see? We must get to Kabul tonight. We'll have to beg your forgiveness on this occasion; it is terribly rude of us, but it simply can't be avoided. Great shame, great shame. Afghan hospitality is legendary ya know - legendary! – so any other time I would have been delighted to accept, but sadly, it is not to be. So thank you again, but most unhappily, we must decline. Well! We best be getting back to the helicopter,

Lieutenant Crane, don'tcha think?' She started hobbling slowly towards the track to the helipad.

Her words carried an irrefutable certainty; there was not the faintest possibility of any other course of action being taken after she had spoken. Zemar stared at her in disbelief.

'Would you do me the honour of walking with us, Mr Zemar?' Cecelia said loudly. For a moment Zemar stared at her before nodding in agreement. 'Just you, I mean. It would be lovely to have a little chat. I'm sure your group of fine fellows have got better things to do than watch me stagger up a hill.'

Cecelia spoke softly to Campbell as she walked past him, 'Get everyone rounded up and loaded onto the helicopter, would you Fitz?' Campbell nodded, then hurried towards the pavilion. Cecelia returned to her eccentric old woman voice. 'Mr Huggins! Would you be so kind as to give me your arm? That track is quite steep; I don't fancy a fall at my age…'

Zemar turned to shout a few brief instructions to his men. The men with rifles clambered back on board the truck which performed a jerky three-point turn and headed back down the track towards the town. The bodyguards waited beside the SUV.

Zemar finally found his tongue, 'Dame Cecelia, we should take my car...'

'No, no! I do need the exercise after all, but I just get a bit wobbly nowadays.' She put an arm through Pauls and carried on walking, talking over her shoulder to Zemar until he hurried over and began walking alongside her. 'My Great Grandfather on my mother's side was a Brigadier in the British Army in India, ya know; he was stationed on the Northwest Frontier. I remember when I was a small child he would tell us tales about battles in the Khyber Pass. He always said the Afghan people were ferocious on the battlefield, ferocious! But absolutely the most generous hosts in the world. They'd give you the shoes off their feet and the shirt off their back he always said! Oooof…' Cecelia paused, puffing out her cheeks. 'Just need to catch my breath…'

Paul and Zemar stood politely either side of Cecelia as she made a show of filling her lungs. The Herd and the Royal Marines streamed around them, following Campbell up the hill. Paul noticed Zemar do a double take as Tor and Jasper strode past him.

'Shall we continue?' Cecelia straightened and extended her free hand towards Zemar. He smiled and offered her his arm to lean on. Slowly they made their way up the track. Sydney and Ren were at the back of the Herd, urging them up the hill, although both kept glancing back towards Zemar.

'I'm afraid my Persian is a little rusty; 'Amu' means 'uncle,' doesn't it?' Cecelia asked.

Zemar pushed out his chin, making his beard bristle. 'My language is Dari; this is one of several different Persian languages. But yes dear lady, you are correct - 'Amu' means 'uncle.' It is not only my family who call me by this name; I am an uncle to everyone in this region.'

'Ah, I see. I must say, your English is excellent.' Cecelia plodded on, carefully watching her feet. Paul found he was barely supporting any of Cecelia's weight at all, but he got the sense she was leaning more heavily on the Afghani. 'So what does 'Zemar' mean in English?'

'It is an ancient name; it means 'Lion'; the most dangerous animal in the wilderness.'

'Well, quite.'

Paul glanced over his shoulder. Lieutenant Crane and his troop, along with Amu Zemars' trio of bodyguards were following a little way behind. Standing beside the track near the cricket pitch Paul could see the old man and his granddaughter watching him. Paul waved farewell. The old man raised an arm in response. The girl was squinting up the track, holding the cricket ball and bat.

Zemar was talking freely now, detailing how his parents had come to name him and his four siblings. He continued reciting his family history.

'My father and two of my older brothers were killed fighting the Taliban in the south. I became the head of the family…' He broke off and looked up the track ahead of them. 'That handsome couple that walked past us – I recognise them…who are they?'

'Why don't we go and introduce you?' Cecelia smiled sweetly. Beyond the crest of the hill in front of them the afternoon sun hung low in the sky, the softening light turning the bare soil on the track to a caramel brown.

By the time Cecelia, Paul and Zemar reached the top of the track the rest of the Herd had gathered in the large tent and were grabbing a drink of water.

'Miss Turner, Mr Hood-Daley – could I borrow you for a moment?' Cecelia called out. Jasper ambled over, looking slightly wary. 'Let me introduce Amu Zemar, a very important man in these parts, and he was very keen to meet you.'

She turned to Zemar. 'Of course you recognised them – this is Tor and Jasper, two of the most famous people on the planet.'

Jasper's face broke into a dazzling smile as he extended an arm for a handshake. 'It's always a pleasure meeting a fan.' Zemar shook Jaspar's hand vigorously.

'Yes, yes of course! Your picture is in every English magazine… you were the face of Roloberry Watches – see? I have one!' Zemar pulled up his sleeve to display a chunky wristwatch.

Jaspar admired the watch for a moment, before turning away slightly and extending an arm. 'This is Tor,' he said.

It was as if a spotlight had been turned on Tor as she moved towards them. Her head was tilted slightly down; her shining eyes fixed on the newcomer from under her lowered eyelids. She stepped forward with a catwalk stride, extending a languid arm with fingers and palm facing down, inviting a handshake.

'Delighted to meet you, I'm sure,' she purred. Zemar nodded politely then stared admiringly at her as he briefly grasped her fingertips before turning back to Jaspar.

'She is beautiful. You are a lucky man Jasper! How did you capture a woman such as this?'

'Ah, well! We met at a party in Paris…' he paused. 'You tell the story better than me, Tor, why don't you…'

Zemar cut him off, 'No, I wish to hear it from you, not from her.' Tor's smile froze into a static mask. 'You will tell me, but first – photographs!' Zemar pulled out a mobile phone and held it at arm's length, while hugging Jasper by the shoulder. 'Smile!' Zemar commanded. After poking the screen several times with his thumb Zemar beckoned Tor with quick flicks of his fingers. 'Now you as well.' Tor stood motionless, but Jasper made a sidestep to stand beside her and Zemar turned to get all three of them in the picture. 'Very good!' he cried.

Zemar kept on tapping the phone screen, collecting picture after picture. He summoned his bodyguards to join in. The gaggle of men gathered tightly around Jasper and Tor, throwing their arms around their shoulders. Zemar began waving his arm around to capture pictures of the group from different angles. The men began to chatter and laugh, changing places and positions, turning Jasper and Tor this way and that to face the camera as it was passed from hand to hand. Tor's expression was stony and unmoving, while Jasper kept trying to laugh along with gang surrounding them.

Cecelia turned to the tent opening, muttering, 'time to leave I think...'

The helicopter rotors were beginning to turn as Campbell came scurrying back from the helicopter, waving a beckoning arm. As the remaining civilians began leaving, Jasper and Tor were still at the centre of the group of bodyguards who were now using their weapons as props in the pictures. Draws supervised four of the Marines carrying Talbot's stretcher to the helicopter, and Moira, Belinda and Rachael grouped around Annabel as she walked stiffly across the open ground towards the aircraft ramp. The Van Der Molen family, Charlotte, Cecelia, and Paul walked out with the rest of the Marines from the tent.

'Hey, wait...' A nervous cry came from Jasper, still surrounded by the armed men who were effectively blocking his and Tor's exit.

Without turning around Cecelia said to Corporal Towne, 'you probably better rescue those two.' Towne grinned, summoned five of his team and turned back as Cecelia, Charlotte and Paul paused. The Marines walked calmly into the tent and Towne and Lincoln gently but firmly inserted themselves in the middle of the final photograph huddle either side of Tor and Jasper. Towne took hold of Tor's elbow, turned her around and walked her outside. Lincoln put a long arm around Jasper's shoulder, grinned widely at the bodyguard next to him, and led Jasper away.

A few moments later Jasper and Tor were jogging hurriedly towards the helicopter. Cecelia waved to Zemar who stood smiling in the tent doorway. Then Paul and Cecelia walked on with the Marines acting as escort once more. The rotors were gaining speed, and the engine noise was increasing. At the foot of the helicopter ramp Lieutenant Crane was waiting. He saluted and shook Cecelia's hand as she climbed on board. 'Thank you ma'am. Have a safe trip home!' he shouted. Cecelia nodded and moved inside the aircraft. As the last Marine strapped themselves into their seat the aircrew closed the ramp, and the helicopter rose into the afternoon sky.

Tor was incandescent with rage. 'I am sick of it! Sick of men treating me like a dumb animal - I can't stand it! All my life I've had men leer and paw at me, then talk over me as if I'm deaf, or stupid, or both. I swore it wouldn't happen again. I swore that I wouldn't be mute and docile any longer – I would be the one in control of my body, in control of my voice. And then that fucking medieval arsehole treats me like a piece of fucking furniture!'

Jasper held up a placatory hand. 'Tor, sweetheart, it's over and done with now. Calm yourself…'

'Don't you fucking DARE tell me to calm down, ya useless piece of shit! What the fuck were you doing, letting him treat me like that, eh?'

Jasper looked shocked. 'What? Now, hang on…'

'You were bloody pathetic. "Pleasure to meet a fan!" You dickhead.' Tor snarled.

'What was I supposed to do, punch him?'

'Yes! You fucking saw him grab my arse!'

'He had armed bodyguards…' Jasper protested. Tor cut him off.

'WE WERE SURROUNDED BY SOLDIERS AND MARINES! WHO WERE ON OUR SIDE!!!' She screamed.

'Miss Turner?' Cecelia called out. Tor turned to look at the older woman. 'You might not fully realise the value of what you did. Amu Zemar is an unpredictable, ambitious, and possibly dangerous man. He came looking for a trophy to show off to his followers. Your distraction of him with the photography session was exactly what was needed to prevent him interrupting our escape.'

'Oh…well.' Tor seemed caught off guard. 'Alright then. But I stand by what I said. I won't be treated like that again.' Tor crossed her arms angrily.

'No, indeed, you shouldn't have to. In this instance though - you may have prevented a difficult situation escalating out of control.'

Tor still looked irate, but said nothing further, seemingly mollified by Cecelia's words. Paul happened to glance at Corporal Towne as Cecelia finished speaking.

Towne was staring intently at the ceiling, his broad mouth clamped tightly shut as if holding something in.

<u>Chapter Sixteen</u>

The globe of the sun was melting into the line of the horizon as the helicopter approached the outskirts of Kabul. They remained at an altitude of several thousand feet until they cleared the perimeter fence of the airport before dropping so quickly Paul thought his stomach was trying to flip over. His hands became momentarily weightless as the aircraft descended rapidly, before dropping into his lap once more as the helicopter began to hover fifty feet or so above the ground. Through the cabin window Paul could see military transport planes moving to the end of the main runway. Two ground crew in camouflage clothing, ear defenders and orange hi-vis tabards were directing the helicopter to the landing point close to a huge hangar. With a soft bump the wheels touched down onto the concrete and they began to taxi forward towards.

Lieutenant Glaven spoke to them through the intercom. 'Welcome to Kabul International Airport. We are being directed to hold station for a couple of minutes while they get the doors to the hanger open. We have been asked not to disembark anyone until we are undercover as a safety precaution, so sit tight for just a little bit longer.' The helicopter became stationary, the rotor blades gradually slowing and the noise from the engines lessening as the crew powered them down.

The Herd were getting fidgety and restless. Paul looked down at Talbot still laid out on his stretcher looking for all the world as if he was having a nap.

'Sydney?' Paul called out. 'You said you'd tell me why the Colour Sergeant has the nickname 'Double Tap,' didn't you?'

Sydney looked doubtful. 'Well, I'm not sure I should…'

'Annabelle says you did promise,' Rachel called out. One side of Annabelle's face was uncomfortably swollen now, causing her to speak out of only one side of her mouth in barely more than a whisper. She leaned awkwardly towards Rachael's ear again.

'You said if Mr Huggins got Sergeant Talbot to the helicopter, you'd tell him,' Rachel said.

Corporal Towne chuckled. 'If you are going to tell this story, best to tell everyone while the Colour Sergeant is unconscious, I'd say!' the other Marines grinned.

'Oh, alright then.' Sydney sighed, but she began to grin as she recounted the story. 'So, you've heard how we all get nicknames right? You don't get to pick your own, it gets given to you by the rest of your squad. Some get their nicknames on their first day as a squaddie – isn't that right, Porky?' Hamilton laughed and nodded. 'For others, it can take a while. I didn't get called Sydney until I joined the Colour Sergeant's squad eighteen months ago, and I 'd been in the Marines for three years by then.' Everyone's eyes where now pinned on Sydney, who was enjoying her role as a teller of tales. 'Colour Sergeant Talbot had avoided picking up a nickname for *seven years* in the Royal Marines, though god knows how.'

''Sweary Welsh Git' is not much of a nickname is it?' chuckled Ashton. 'It doesn't really roll off the tongue.'

'I've always thought of him as a bit of an old softie really,' said Lincoln, straight faced.

'Whaaat?!' cried Orlando; the other Marines looked round in open mouthed astonishment.

'An old softie who every now and then can go full 'Turbo Nutter Bastard,' to be fair,' Lincoln grinned. The Marines laughed.

Sydney pounded her foot on the floor to get everyone's attention again.

'*ANYWAY* - Talbot kept getting promoted, and moved into new teams, so he was never in one place long enough for a nickname to stick. *Until…*!' She paused, checking all eyes were on her again. 'He gets sent on a deployment to Belize for six months of jungle training. Now this bit of the story is a little bit hazy – apparently something went a bit wrong while Talbots troop from Forty Commando were on manoeuvres in the jungle near the border and they get caught up in a night-time firefight, there were some casualties…anyway, it all gets hushed up; but to avoid an international incident Talbot and his troop are shipped back to Belize City and sent on leave for a four-day weekend. Being Royal Marines, they set off to drink the pubs dry…' - the Marines cheered - '…but on the first day Talbot meets this local woman. By all accounts they hit it off big time, getting on like a house on fire.'

'What, huge flames, people running around screaming, property damage – that sort of thing?' Lincoln laughed.

'Shut up, you idiot! They get on great, just drinking and talking for hours. The rest of the troop bugger off to the next pub and leave him behind, and they don't see him again for the next three days. Eventually he staggers back into camp on the Monday, so they sit him down and demand all the gory details. So he says..' Sydney adopted a passable Welsh accent to impersonate Talbot, 'I spent the entire weekend plumbing her a new bathroom!' Now that's a euphemism they'd never heard before – what does it mean? Has he been shagging her up the arse, or is it some convoluted sex position from the Kama Sutra, or what?' Sydney broke off for a moment as Jordi giggled and Agnes tutted. The Marines roared with laughter, but Sydney wasn't done.

'So they ask him again what he had been doing, and whether he had been shagging this woman and he says 'I told you – I wasn't having sex with Maria, I spent the weekend installing a bathroom in her house; I put in the toilet, shower and basin, rigged up the pipes and I spent two days grouting all the tiles.' Then he said, 'the hardest part...the hardest part was getting the pipework aligned for the double tap in the sink,' and from that moment on he was known as 'Double Tap.'

The audience cheered and clapped as Sydney reached the punchline. 'He found out later she really was a prostitute. I'm told they still exchange Christmas cards.'

'How do you know this story?' Draws demanded of Sydney.

'My old Sergeant told me. He was in Belize when this happened; he was just a lowly Marine back then,' Sydney said.

The helicopter lurched slightly and began to roll slowly forward as it was towed into the hangar. The Marines busied themselves preparing to disembark, removing headphones, and adjusting the straps on their kit. Paul stared through the window, watching the dark dusky sky as it was replaced by the blue-white glare of LED lamps illuminating the inside of the building. As soon as the helicopter was stationary again a heavy rumble and a clang denoted the closing of the hangar door, and the rear ramp immediately began to open.

Waiting at the foot of the ramp were eight soldiers dressed in beige camouflage. In contrast to the drab uniforms, on their heads they each wore a green beret sloped over the right ear with a large red feather on the left side and a woollen bobble on the top. Corporal Towne led the Marines down the ramp; at the rear came four of them carrying Talbot on his stretcher. Towne approached the soldiers, came to attention, and fired off a sharp salute. The senior officer took a few steps forward and gave a precise, measured salute in response.

'Well done Corporal; mission accomplished. We'll look after the civilians from here.'

'Sir,' Towne replied, staring slightly over the officer's shoulder.

'The Lieutenant here will escort the wounded to the Medical Centre. You and the rest of your team can find a temporary billet in the main barracks. The 'sneaks' will want to do a full de-brief with you shortly but get some chow in you first.'

'Thank you, Sir. I'll send my medic with the wounded; he can debrief the medical personnel here.' Towne glanced at Draws.

Four of the soldiers moved to take hold of Talbot but faltered at the stony glares the motionless Marine stretcher bearers directed at them. It was only after a direct order from Corporal Towne that they surrendered their precious cargo.

'Very good.' The officer nodded. 'Lead the rest of your team your team on, Corporal.'

Without looking back, Towne followed another of the soldiers across the hanger towards one of several exits. The Marines trooped after him; a few gave a brief farewell wave to the civilians but mostly their eyes were on Talbot as they moved away. They soon passed through the double door in the nearest wall and in a matter of seconds they were gone. The enormous hanger was abruptly much quieter.

The Senior Officer addressed the civilians as they hesitantly descended the ramp. 'Welcome to Kabul; I am Lieutenant-Colonel Gibbs, Officer Commanding the British deployment in Afghanistan. You'll be glad to know the rescue mission is officially over! You are on safe ground now - we will get you fed and watered, patched up where necessary, and we'll get you shipped home to London in a day or so. If the walking wounded would care to go with the stretcher, I'll ask the rest of you to follow me; we have some VIP quarters arranged for you.' Gibbs beckoned them and strode off towards a doorway on the far side of the hangar.

Paul was about to step off the ramp when he felt a firm hand on his shoulder. Aircrewman Heacham gently removed the headphones from around Paul's neck. The cable which stretched back into the helicopter was nearly drawn tight.

'Best leave them with me before you garotte yourself,' Heacham grinned.

'Oh. Yes. Haha.' Paul failed to achieve a smile. He felt strangely bereft at the unceremonious dispersal of the group that had only formed two days before. He hobbled after Talbot's entourage. Rachel was clutching Annabel at the waist, glaring at everyone in case they tried to suggest they shouldn't both go to the Medical Centre. Nobody tried to stop her.

The Lieutenant led them through a third doorway, down a grey painted corridor past workshops and offices and out of the building. Two sandy coloured ambulances were waiting for them; Draws and the stretcher bearers loaded Talbot into one, and Annabel, Rachel and Paul were ushered into the second. The two vehicles set off at high speed, but barely thirty seconds after starting the vehicles took a sharp right turn and came to a stop in front of a large single-story building.

'Here we are,' called the Lieutenant, urging them out again. There was bustle and noise as they were met by more military personnel in camouflage uniforms. Some of them had red cross emblems attached to their sleeves. The medics were obviously prepared for Talbots arrival – several staff converged on the stretcher and began tending to him even as he was carried in. Paul was put in a chair in the reception area and a medic with a clipboard began to fire questions at him about his injuries. Paul stumbled through a series of answers for several minutes until Draws re-appeared, took the clipboard and pen from the orderly and set about making several corrections.

'Fractured left hand is Sicknote's most serious injury – it needs an x-ray. Blistered feet and skin lacerations have had a field dressing, and a bit of de-hydration needs treating as well. OK?' He returned the clipboard to the surprised looking medic. 'Now, where's Legolas?' Draws looked around. He spotted Annabel sat in a chair nearby and moved towards her.

The orderly looked at the clipboard, then at Paul. 'I'm so sorry, we had your surname down as Huggins. So, how do you spell 'Signode'?'

For the next two hours Paul was guided to various different locations within the medical centre to receive treatment. At each location he seemed to accrue additional personnel to treat him. The surprisingly small X-ray machine in a huge room at the back of the hospital made quick work of confirming fractures in several bones in Pauls left hand. In a second, smaller room his shirt was removed, his arm was bandaged and then plaster was added from his forearm to the knuckles at the base of his fingers. Half his thumb was plastered too, positioned to show him giving a constant 'thumbs up' sign. Whilst the plaster was left to dry a doctor decided to re-assess his feet and leg wounds in a consulting room with frosted glass windows. Paul reluctantly removed his trousers again. Three of the lacerations on the back of his legs had begun to bleed at some point in the afternoon so he was laid face down on a hospital bed whilst stitches were put in. His legs were re-bandaged so tight he could barely bend at the knee. He was relieved to be told the dressings on his feet were good enough for now.

Finally he was escorted into a room with four bays separated by curtains with a bed in each one. He was directed to a bed with the curtain pulled back. From the hidden bed opposite there came a click-click-clack sound.

'Here you go Mr Huggins, we'll let you get some rest now…' began the medic, but he was interrupted by a howl from the curtained-off bay opposite. The curtain billowed and shook as if being poked by sticks.

'Is that Sicknote? Let me see that fucker!' the curtain was torn back to reveal Talbot sitting upright in a bed in neatly buttoned up pyjamas, his head tightly bandaged. His damaged ankle was encased in a heavy-duty medical boot. 'There he is! My old pal! Thank you Doctors, you can go now; Sicknote and I have got some serious catching up to do…' Talbot made a shooing motion with his right hand.

The senior medic smiled and shook his head. 'Not quite yet, Colour Sergeant; we'll just get Mr Huggins settled first.' Unable to bend at the knee or move his left arm Paul found himself incapable of getting into the bed unaided, so two of the medical team had to lift him gently in. The clicking noise continued. After arranging the bedsheets, checking Paul's pulse for the umpteenth time that evening and then giving him some painkillers, the doctors finally retreated out of the room.

Paul looked over at Talbot who grinned at him. In Talbots lap was a large ball of bright red wool; the two knitting needles he held lightly in his hands were a blur of movement. Click-click-clack.

'Now then,' Talbot said, 'They tell we got everyone back safe enough; just about the last thing I remember from our little jaunt is climbing up that pissing hill, then some shit-stained twatwanker was shooting at us and you were in your ducky underpants. So, fill me in – what the fuck happened next?' Talbot asked.

Paul laughed so hard a nurse ran in to check that he wasn't having a seizure. It took a while for Paul to get enough breath to convince them these weren't tears of pain rolling down his cheeks, and that, no, really, everything was fine.

It took Paul fully half an hour to describe the events that had occurred between the two of them reaching the top of the mountain in Kyrgyzstan and Talbot waking up in the bed he currently occupied. Talbot would fire off occasional questions at Paul or interject with cries of 'shit coloured fuck!' for things he didn't like of 'Brammer Rice!' for things he did.

'What on earth does 'brammer-ice' mean?' Paul queried.

''Rice' means 'effort' in the Royal Marines, Sicknote; and 'Brammer' means 'outstanding.' So Corporal Towne and that rotorhead pilot getting us away safe under fire was 'brammer rice,' you see? Especially without me around to get things sorted.' Talbot grinned.

The Colour Sergeant seemed delighted with the tale of Cecelia's role in the encounter with Amu Zemar. He was less impressed by Tor's diatribe on the helicopter shortly after. 'She's a precious fucking snowflake, that one,' he muttered. Mostly Talbot seemed concerned that his Royal Marines had acquitted themselves well, especially in comparison to the other British military personnel they had encountered along the way. Paul tried to give Talbot a reassuringly positive response, although he felt sure Talbot would be scrutinizing every report made about his team. Paul made sure his praise of Draws was effusive.

Food was brought to them on bed trays. The meal consisted of tomato soup with a bread roll, Spaghetti Bolognese with large lumps of cheddar cheese melting on the top, and this being a British military establishment, a pot of strong tea. They both ate in silence, wolfing down the food as if they hadn't eaten for a week.

As the plates were being cleared away there was a knock at the door. Cecelia entered, dressed in the dark trouser suit she had been wearing on the flight from Seoul. Following behind her was Sydney, Ren, and a bespectacled army officer.

'Good evening gentlemen, I thought we should come and see how you were getting on.' Cecelia said.

'Thank you ma'am, doing fine now,' Talbot replied, sitting bolt upright. 'Army Surgeon says he'll have me under the knife tomorrow to sort out my ankle, and they'll be shipping me home by the end of the week.'

'Um…what day is it today?' Paul asked. 'I seem to have lost track.'

'It's Monday,' Cecelia replied. 'Now Mr Huggins, you will be flying home tomorrow, along with several others from our group of companions. Captain Powell here has a request of you before you leave.'

The young officer stepped forward. 'Ah yes, well, hello! I'm in charge of the SPS team in the Adjutant Generals office here in Kabul. I was rather hoping you could help us out of with a ticklish little problem.'

Paul looked at him blankly. 'I don't know what that means,' he sighed. Cecelia stared directly at him.

'Ah, well, er…let me start again. I work in the Staff and Personnel Support team, reporting to Lieutenant Colonel Gibbs, I believe you have meet him already. Among my other duties I handle any media matters for the British Army in Afghanistan - although we haven't really had anything unusual like this for absolutely yonks.'

'Unusual like what?' Paul asked.

'Well its normally the press that come to us with interview requests, but this time, it's the other way round.' As Powell turned his head to look at Cecelia his spectacles reflected a bright flash of light from the bedside lamp. 'Miss Turner has requested that we organise a press conference for her. I, we, er…I mean I, was rather hoping we could put you in front of the media as well, an extra bit of grist to the mill, so to speak. It will be quite an event for us, you see. A bit of celebrity glam and glitz; every journalist in the country will want to be in on it. We thought we could put someone else from your party in front of the cameras as well, give it all a bit more context, as it were… '

'I'm sure with your experience in Whitehall you will have done press briefings before Mr Huggins,' Cecelia said.

'Well, yes I have…' Paul replied.

'Splendid! Well, we'll get it arranged then!' Captain Powell clapped his hands together. 'Awfully decent of you, thanks very much! We'll plan to start at around ten am. Your flight is due to take off at around midday, so that all ties together nicely.' The captain half turned towards the door, then stopped. 'There is just one thing – you can't actually talk to the press about the military operation or the military personnel involved. Technically speaking it's still an ongoing mission until you are back in the UK, and we want to avoid any accidental complications, you know, with China and Russia as they fight a proxy war in central Asia, so best to keep schtum about all that. Just stick to your personal experience and that of the other civilians; then you'll be fine. Righto, I'll see you in the morning!' Powell hurried out of the door.

Talbot grinned. 'It sounds like you've just been invited to a cake and arse party,' he said.

'I don't know what that phrase means either, but I'm guessing it's not good.' Paul grumbled.

'We've bought both of you a gift.' Cecelia said. She reached into her handbag and pulled out a large ball of blue wool which she tossed to Talbot. The Colour Sergeant almost purred with delight before clearing his throat and thanking Cecelia gruffly.

'And for you Mr Huggins, something to read on the flight home,' she said, handing him a paperback. He expected it to be a poetry book, but it turned out to be a thriller by John Le Carre.' 'It's surprising what the Quartermaster can find in the Army Stores if you take a Lieutenant-Colonel with you,' she said.

'Have you heard how Annabel is getting on?' Paul asked.

Cecelia nodded. 'She is in a room up the corridor; she's heavily sedated. The medical team have done a full assessment, and the X-rays have indicated she has multiple fractures of her right cheek, her jaw, and the skull behind her ear. She is destined for multiple surgical procedures once she gets home, I'm afraid.'

'She's a tough one, that girl,' Talbot said. 'Isn't that right, Syd?'

'She's a bloody superstar, Colour. She went up that mountain like a sodding gazelle, and she was carrying two rucksacks and with half her face smashed in. Despite all that, she easily beat you and Sicknote up that mountain in a footrace, Colour Sergeant. I'd have her on my team any day.' Sydney said proudly.

'High praise indeed! But you're not wrong,' Talbot said.

Sydney grinned at Paul. 'She even kept her trousers on through the whole day, which is more than some of us managed, eh Sicknote?' She held out her arm bent at the elbow, her thumb upraised to mimic Paul's plaster cast digit.

 Cecelia said, 'Colour Sergeant, your squad has been billeted in a barracks nearby; we passed a wheelchair on the way in, perhaps we could escort you to a short reunion?'

'Too bloody right you can ma'am.' Talbot threw back the bedclothes and motioned to Ren. 'Come on Marine, bring me my chariot!' He swung his legs off the bed as Ren positioned the wheelchair beside him. 'Hasta La Vista, Sicknote! "I'll be Back."

'Ooh, that's easy, that's from 'Terminator'!' said Ren.

'Sydney, you're driving; Ren, you're on guard duty.' Ordered Talbot.

'No need to tell the doctors where we've gone, eh Sicknote?' Sydney smiled as she began pushing Talbot across the room, 'You can keep our little secret for a while, can't you?'

'Hey Colour Sergeant!' Paul called out as the wheelchair reached the door, 'We heard where you got your nickname 'double tap' from. A Belize bathroom, wasn't it?' As the door swung shut Paul got a glimpse of a wide-eyed Sydney staring at him. Talbot's exclamation of 'what the fuck...?' was cut off by the door closing noisily. Ren remained in the room, waiting for Cecelia.

'I have a request, Mr Huggins.' Cecelia was looking at him closely. 'Regarding the press briefing tomorrow.'

Paul nodded. 'I think I can guess. Would it be 'don't mention Dame Cecelia Urquhart was here'?'

Cecelia smiled, then turned to Ren whose gaze was flicking between Cecelia and Paul as if she was watching a tennis match. 'Would you mind waiting for me outside? I'll only be a moment.'

Once the door had clicked shut behind Ren, Cecelia turned to Paul again. 'My late husband's surname was Eriksen, God rest his soul; it seemed prudent not to use the name I was known by publicly while we were at risk. But yes, I am Dame Cecelia Urquhart, and there must be no mention of me tomorrow to the media. I can rely on Miss Turner to talk about no-one but herself, but I need to instruct you on this directly. I assume you have worked out why?'

Paul considered the question for a moment, and then said, 'I think so. This whole thing, this whole operation was always about rescuing you and ensuring your safety, wasn't it? The rest of us who happened to be at the airport when the Marines arrived were just, well...'

'Please don't say 'expendable,' that wouldn't be true.' Cecelia sighed.

'No, I was going to say we were just lucky. Right time, right place; we happened to be standing next to you when your rescue party showed up. Lucky too there was only eleven of us so we could all fit on that bus. If there had been eighty or ninety Europeans on that plane, well, who knows what would have happened?'

'Oh, I think you know the answer to that – the Marines would have evacuated me and the rest of you would have been left where you were. We would probably have had to take Jasper and Tor with us, just for the look of the thing; abandoning a global celebrity in a warzone does generate such bad press after all. I suspect Mr Campbell would have volunteered to stay behind and try and get everybody else out somehow. He's a brave and resourceful man. And yes, there were probably a thousand Western Europeans in Kyrgyzstan when the war started, and perhaps a hundred of them British; we would never have been able to evacuate all of them in one go. When did you work this out? You seemed to have an inkling at the mountain hotel.'

'It took a while. Lots of little clues that all began to add up. The soldiers that chased us to the hotel and then up into the mountains as well; they went to a lot of trouble to capture a little group of civilians, celebrities notwithstanding. I can see now they were after a much bigger prize than a supermodel and her boyfriend. I think I realised when we were at the mountain hotel - you were never on your own once the Marines had arrived. There was always a Marine close by you at all times, especially during the battle; you always had a bodyguard,' Pauls eyes flickered to the doorway; Ren's outline was visible through the pane of frosted glass in the door. 'At the bottom of the landslide, Talbot told Sydney not to wait for him and me; he was very insistent. 'A direct order,' he said. 'The mission objective is to get her on that helicopter;' I thought at the time he meant Annabel, but of course he was referring to you.'

'Yes I expect he was. Have you worked out the final piece of the puzzle? Why I am so important to Her Majesty's Government?'

Paul's eyes flicked towards the door again. 'The way all the other military personnel treated you – the helicopter crew, Lieutenant Crane at the refuel point, Lieutenant-Colonel Gibbs when we got here – they all seemed deferential. Come to think of it, Talbot and Campbell have been too. The name Cecelia seemed vaguely familiar when we met on the plane, but I didn't recognise your face. I wondered briefly if you were connected somehow to the Royal Family, but that isn't it.'

'No, definitely not part of the Royal Family.' Cecelia smiled. 'Very much a commoner.'

Paul spoke more confidently now. 'Gibbs made refence to a de-brief by the 'sneaks' when we were in the hangar which must have reminded me of something. It finally came to me when you mentioned Whitehall a few minutes ago; I've seen your name on high security clearance documents at work. Not often, mind you. Department of Health files don't usually require vetting by MI6.'

'Ah, yes. That would have been an old file.' Cecelia said. 'I retired as head of the Secret Intelligence Service five years ago. In as much as you can every really retire from the Service, that is.'

'Even so, the government couldn't run the risk of you being taken captured by the Russians or the Chinese on foreign soil, so they sent in a rescue party.' Paul waggled the paperback Cecelia had given him. 'Nice touch with the final clue by the way. "Tinker, Tailor, Soldier, Spy"?'

Cecelia shrugged. 'Just my little joke, but it seems you pretty much worked it out by yourself. One small correction though; the deference thing. Technically, I do out-rank all the military personnel you referred to. I was in the Royal Navy for thirty years before I joined SIS; I reached the rank of Commodore in the Defence Intelligence Staff before hitting the glass ceiling. So I transferred to SIS but retained my rank. Only Generals outrank me in the Army.' She smiled. 'But you see why I have to remain out of the story you present to the world? I am still a security risk until I get back to home soil. You told me yourself you have signed the Official Secrets Act.'

Paul nodded.

'Lots of people carry secrets with them, Paul, you won't be alone tomorrow. There will be personnel on the flight home with you that I happen to know are hiding significant secrets, but I will let you picture that out for yourself. Well, farewell then. I won't be travelling home with you; separate arrangements are being made for me. I wish you the best of luck.' Cecelia turned to leave. 'Oh, I nearly forgot.' She reached into her bag and withdrew a mobile phone. 'Yours I believe. I doubt you will get a signal here.' She handed it to Paul. 'Arrangements are being made for your family to be at the airport tomorrow evening to meet you. They know you are safe and sound.'

'Goodbye. I must say – I'm glad we all got out.' Paul said.

'Yes; so am I.' Cecelia reached the doorway and looked back at Paul. 'In case no-one else remembers to tell you – your behaviour throughout these last few days has been exemplary. In particular the way you helped Mr Hood-Daley at the hotel, and Colour Sergeant Talbot on the mountain; bravo, Mr Huggins.'

After Cecelia left, Paul switched on his phone and spent a long time trying, without success, to get a signal so that he could call home. Eventually he gave up, rummaging in his bag for the charger cable. He found it at the bottom of his rucksack, along with the mobile phone he had picked up after the landslide. He pressed the on button and the screen lit up with a kaleidoscope of colours through the cracked glass. Unable to get past the pin code screen, he turned it off again. He spent some time straightening out the charger cable that had become twisted up in his rucksack.

Paul had been carefully repacking his bag when Talbot zoomed back into the ward, alone, over two hours later. The Colour Sergeant seemed energized by being reunited with his squad, talking rapidly and at high volume about how proud of he was of the successful conclusion of their mission.

'Great bunch of lads, but don't fucking tell 'em I said so. No, only joking, I told them so myself, just now! Ha ha! Poor old Sydney nearly shat herself when you dropped her in it, mind! She thought she was in for a right old bollocking. You should have seen the look on her face! I made out I was furious with her; she went bright red and was gaping like a goldfish. I couldn't keep it up, as the actress said to the bishop, and I just burst out laughing, and so did everyone else. I think she nearly fainted with relief.' Talbot bellowed with laughter again, slapping the arm of the wheelchair in delight. 'She's lucky she's got a nickname already, or she'd be called 'beetroot' from now on.'

'You don't mind being called 'double tap' then?' Pau asked.

'Nah, not at all. I've heard much worse. In basic training when I first joined up there was a cadet that was always talking back to the instructors, so they called him 'Alf,' even though his name was Michael. When he asked why they told him its cos he's an Annoying Little Fucker.' Talbot chuckled. 'There was another lad who became known as 'The Submarine Door' cos he was so incredibly fucking thick. And one of the instructors at the training centre in Devon is known to everyone as 'Spray-paint,' 'cos his real name is Matt Grey. Hahaha!' Talbot wiped a tear from the corner of one eye.

'So that Belize story – was it true?' Paul asked.

'Which bit? The part where I spent a weekend plumbing in a bathroom for some hussy I'd only just met? Yeah, that's true. We thought we were about to be sent home in disgrace, you see; I didn't want to spend the last few days either getting into trouble in the barracks or getting as tight as a boiled fucking owl in the town, so I decided I was better off distracting myself with something productive. My uncle is a plumber; he runs a business fitting kitchens and bathrooms. I spent a couple of summers as a teenager earning pocket money working for him. Uncle Austin showed me all the trade skills, plumbing, tiling, even electrics; but what I mostly learnt is, I didn't want to spend my entire life with my head underneath someone else's shitty toilet.

At the end of the road I grew up on was the local pub, the Green Dragon. My Da and Uncle Austin would spend every waking moment in this place at the weekends, and they'd drag us kids along with them. They loved it in there, but all I remember is the old boys, the pensioners, who would shuffle in at the same time every day, sit in the same seat, sup on the same beer, and stare at the wall with nothing to say like they had for the last forty fucking years. I realised I had to get out; I had to find some way to leave that town, so I didn't stagnate and rot, the way my Da and uncle were doing. So I left school at the earliest opportunity and joined the Royal Marines. I'll say this for my uncle though, he does have cracking sense of humour. He had an old fella working for him who had one leg shorter than the other; it made his head bob from side to side when he walked. Uncle Austin named him 'the sniper's nightmare'.' Talbot threw back his head and laughed uproariously. Paul chuckled too, enjoying the happiness of the other man as much as the joke.

The medical orderlies bustled in shortly after, escorting Talbot back to bed and encouraging them both to get ready to go to sleep. As the lights were dimmed Talbot resumed his knitting, deftly introducing threads of blue wool into the woven fabric he was creating. Click-click-clack. After a while Talbot began humming a tune to accompany the percussion of the knitting needles. Click-click-clack. Eventually he began to sing, 'Men of Harlech, march to glory…' began to echo around the room. Click-click-clack. Paul drifted off to sleep.

<u>Chapter Seventeen</u>

Paul was woken from a dreamless slumber by the touch of a hand on his arm and someone loudly and repeatedly calling out his name. Paul barely had his eyes open before he had a couple of pills pressed into one hand and a plastic cup of water placed in the other. Almost without thinking Paul swallowed the medication.

Talbot was stoically allowing himself to be checked over, the medic turning the Marine's head from one side to the other to assess the stitches on his scalp. When the orderly took hold of the boot containing Talbot's damage ankle the Colour Sergeant grimaced and closed his eyes but laid still and said nothing. Paul recalled the slap Talbot had given him at the base of the landslide in Kyrgyzstan when he and Sydney had reset Talbots ankle.

Once he had finished with Talbot the orderly helped Paul out of bed and escorted him to the bathroom, peppering him with constant instructions on how to wash his face and brush his teeth. Paul had to shoo him out so that he could use the toilet alone.

A breakfast tray was waiting on Paul's bed, although none was provided for Talbot. Even as Paul stirred a spiral of golden syrup into the bowl of creamy porridge the orderly was fussing around him, arranging fresh wound dressings on the bedside cabinet, straightening the bedclothes and even attempting to remove the pyjama jacket Paul was wearing, before an angry 'Hey!' from Paul made the orderly hesitate. 'When I'm ready, I'll tell you,' Paul said. Once the meal finished Paul allowed the medic to check his wounds.

'The dressings on your legs should stay on for now; you can take them off once you get home. You don't seem to be bleeding from any of those cuts as best as I can tell, which is good. Let's get your feet unwrapped, shall we? Those bandages have done all they can for you; a bit of a clean-up and some fresh air are what these blisters need now. We'll get you some compression socks for the flight home to stop them swelling up but keep them uncovered until you get on the plane.' The orderly pointed under the bed. 'There's some slippers for you to wear until then.' Paul merely grunted in response.

'Bit tetchy this morning, Sicknote?' Talbot asked. 'Cheer up man, you'll be home before the end of the day.'

'I know, but it all seems…oh, it doesn't matter.' Paul sat on the edge of the bed, awkwardly pulling the voluminous trousers over his bandaged legs.

'Spit it out, for fucks sake, you old twat.'

'Well, there are lots of things bothering me really. But look, I don't want to make a fuss.' Paul said.

Talbot settled back on the bed and picked up his knitting again. 'Too late for that, you whinging little git. Come on; the psychologists always tell me it's good to talk, it might do you good to get all this bollocks off your chest. Not that I give a shit…' Talbot grinned widely.

Paul sighed. 'Alright. Yes, I can't wait to get home, that's part of it. I miss my wife, my daughters. I really want to spend the night in my own bed. I'm tired and sore and bruised and I've got to wear this bloody plaster cast for God knows how long. I've had enough of danger and excitement – I just want to go back to my ordinary life. This building we are in, I don't really know where this place it even is, and I've got to do this stupid press conference and it's all a bit much...'

Talbot rolled his head back and emitted a loud snoring noise, then opened one eye to look at Paul. 'Oh sorry, were you still talking?'

Paul blinked rapidly, then snorted out a laugh, 'Ok, I know, I said I shouldn't complain.'

'No! Complain all you like but just face up to these things and deal with them, man. One fucking problem at a time. You're in pain? Take a painkiller. You want to sleep in your own bed? Get on that aeroplane and go home. You are worried about that media thing? Don't do it. Or do it and just get it over with. Whatever, it's an event that will pass. Just deal with it.'

'Thank you, oh wise one.' Paul bowed in Talbots direction.

'Fuck off, you little prick,' Talbot said. Paul laughed. 'No seriously, fuck off. They've got to get me ready for surgery, and you've got some fucking media shit to go and do.' Paul looked round as Captain Powell appeared in the doorway.

'Good morning! Ready to go?' Powell said, swinging his arms excitedly.

Paul gathered his belongings into his rucksack, carefully tying his boots to the back of the bag by their laces. He swung the bag onto his back, then shuffled over to Talbots bed.

'Goodbye then, Colour Sergeant.' He held out his hand.

'It's Morgan to you, Sicknote,' Talbot said gruffly. He took Paul's hand, pulled him forward and gave him a not too gentle slap on the cheek. 'Now; piss off.'

Captain Powell led the way through a zigzagging series of corridors before exiting the building into bright sunshine. Once Paul's eyesight had adjusted he noticed the horizon in every direction was punctuated with a seemingly continuous dark mountain range. A swirling wind flicked sand over Pauls bare toes as they hurried to a waiting land rover. The drive once again lasted barely more than a minute as they rumbled past a number of identical single-story warehouses. They pulled up next to an ornate older building which had several stiff regimental flags on display outside crackling in the breeze. Powell strode inside, pausing at the reception desk to collect a large badge marked 'visitor' which he hung on a lanyard around Pauls neck.

'We've set up the ballroom for the press conference; it's the only room big enough to accommodate all the media who had requested to attend.' Powell was on the move again, beckoning Paul to follow him through a double swing door. 'Miss Turner had a number of very...ah...*specific* requests about how we set this up. We've done our best in the time available.' He paused beside another door which he held open slightly for Paul to peer into. A rumble of busy voices wafted across a large high-ceilinged room. Rows of fold up seats had been arranged facing a low stage which had a huge canvas screen stretched taut behind it. On the stage an oblong table was smothered in a bouquet of microphones. Off to one side of the stage was a plain wooden lectern. Half a dozen TV cameras were set up behind the press chairs and two large sets of TV studio lights were being arranged on tripods.

Paul pulled his head back from the doorway. 'Why does the British Army need a ballroom?' he asked.

'Well, it's traditional isn't it? Each regiment hosts a least one Ball each year, and we have half a dozen regiments posted here. And we host several diplomatic functions as well, you know.' Powell leaned towards Paul and whispered theatrically, 'To tell you the truth it's really a gymnasium.' Powell pointed at the floor near the door. The carpet that covered most of the floor surface stopped two metres short of the wall all the way round the room. The polished wooden flooring had a series of painted lines of various colours visible at different points. Paul glanced down then looked up at the ceiling.

'Most gymnasiums don't have that many chandeliers though, do they?' he said. The sloping roof was topped off with a long cupola which had small windows set in it. Hanging from the central beam were three enormous crystal chandeliers, all faintly moving, brushed by the breeze squeezing through the high windowpanes.

'Rather lovely, aren't they?' Powell smiled proudly. He pulled the door to the ballroom closed. 'This way, come on.' The captain set off along the corridor again, leading Paul down a stairwell and through a dark of passageway underneath the ballroom before climbing up a spiral staircase into a room originally intended to be the gym locker room. It was now laid out as a reception room with brightly painted walls covered in military banners and randomly selected paintings. A large table was placed at the centre of the room displaying plates of fruits and pastries, and numerous bottles and cups. Several sofas and cushioned chairs were distributed around the room; seated in them were Jasper, the Van der Molen family, Moira, Belinda, and Fitzroy Campbell. Tor was on the other side of the room, prowling relentlessly across the floor close to the door. A large television on a wheeled stand was displaying a live feed from one of the cameras in the ballroom, currently showing an image of the empty stage. Charlotte was sat next to the TV, hunched over her phone.

'Mr Huggins!' An excited cry went up from Jordi, who spotted him first. Paul was rapidly surrounded by most of the people in the room who bombarded him with questions and seemed genuinely pleased to see him.

'Can I write on your cast?' Jordi held up a pen.

'Um, OK.' Paul shrugged. Jordi held the cast with his right hand began scratching letters into the plaster with the pen in his left.

'Have you seen the Marines?' Moira asked him. 'We haven't seen them since we left the helicopter.'

'Or Cecelia; they've taken her somewhere else, and they won't tell us anything.' Said Agnes. Campbell avoided catching Paul's eye.

'I was with Talbot in the hospital; they were getting him ready for surgery on his ankle today. I saw Sydney and Ren; they came and took Talbot to see the other Marines who are in barracks somewhere on the base. Cecelia came for a chat last night too; don't worry, she is being well looked after.'

'Why isn't she here though?' Charlotte had crossed the room to join the conversation. Tor was still pacing by the door. Charlotte had renewed her make up to be heavier than ever, the foundation powder making her face almost orange, her eyebrows painted black in two thick straight lines.

'Er, I think perhaps she already knew that Colonel - Gibbs, was it? - he must have found her alternative quarters for the night.' Paul glanced at Campbell again, who gave an almost imperceptible nod.

'Oh, of course; Five-star accommodation no doubt,' Jasper grumbled.

'Oh, come on, your room last night was fine.' Campbell protested.

'How is Annabel?' Paul asked quickly.

Belinda gave a one shoulder shrug. 'Her face is swollen, and her eyes are all bloodshot. They want to send her home for an operation rather than do it here though, so they've put her in a head brace, she's all strapped up and heavily sedated. They can't peel Rachel away from her though.' Belinda grinned. 'They had to physically restrain my big sister yesterday from getting under the X-Ray machine as well.'

Captain Powell re-appeared and clapped his hands together. 'Right then! Just about time to get underway. We are all set you for you Miss Turner; take as long as you want with the press.'

'Obviously.' Tor carefully put on her enormous sunglasses.

'Ah, yes. And Mr Campbell, and Mr Huggins, if we need you, we will bring you out after Miss Turner has left the stage, so if we could have you on standby…? I'll just go and make the introductions.' Powell hurried off.

'Oh, you're doing it as well? I thought it was only me they wanted.' Paul addressed this to Campbell, but Tor reacted instead.

'Oh, please; I hardly think the world's press are waiting for you, darling. Come on Charlotte, let's do this.'

Paul stuttered over a response, but Tor was heading for the door. Charlotte scurried after her, fingers flicking over her mobile phone screen.

As Tor curled her fingers around the door handle she looked back at everyone in the room. 'I just wanted to say a few words to you all before I go do this. It was quite the adventure we've been on for the last few days, wasn't it?' she said softly. 'We've been through a lot together.' There were a few smiles and nods. 'And now the Press are waiting for me next door, and they'll want to know every last little detail. This story is going to fill every newspaper and TV screen around the world for months. I've been doing this a while and I know how to play the game; I'll have those boys eating out of my hand from the moment I walk out there. But I want you all to remember this – my brand, my whole career, is entirely dependent on my public image. So if there is a single negative word about me in the press that originates from anyone in this room, I will sue each and every one of you into oblivion. Is that understood?' She paused for a moment, surveying the horrified faces in front of her; then opened the door and stepped through, followed by Charlotte.

'Jasper?' Moira said quietly.

'Hmm?'

'Do you remember yesterday when Rachel called your girlfriend a shitty bitch?'

'Hmm.'

'She wasn't wrong.'

'Hm hmmm.' Jasper stared despondently at the television.

On the TV screen they could see Captain Powell standing behind the lectern on the stage already addressing the crowd. A small speaker attached to the wall relayed the sounds picked up by one of the microphones arranged on the table.

'You've all had the briefing pack with the details of the evacuation, or as much as we can release to the public at this time. I'm sure you appreciate that much of the military detail is still classified; we will be providing more information in the coming days.

However, here to give you a first-hand account of her personal experiences through this successful rescue mission…it gives me great pleasure to introduce 'The Swan' herself – Miss Victoria Turner!'

A hissing noise came spitting out of the speaker, then loud music with a thumping bass line erupted as Tor emerged from behind a curtain at the side of the stage, moving with a slow sinuous stride to the table. Mobile phone and camera flashlights flickered around her as she paused beside the centre of the table. Gradually she turned her head from left to right as if scanning the audience. She reached up and slowly removed her dark glasses, then unflinchingly swept her eyes across the room from right to left. She gracefully lowered herself into the chair. The camera operator steadily zoomed in for a close up, the camera emphasizing her flawless features as she stared directly down the lens. The music stopped.

'Hello boys. Did you miss me?' Tor blinked as if in slow motion, then a forest of hands shot into the air and a clamour of voices called out her name, desperate to be called on to ask a question.

'I just want to make a short statement, then I'll take your questions, Ok?' Tor turned her gaze briefly to the side of the stage, at which point the screen behind her lit up with a famous picture of Tor in front of the Eiffel Tower in her signature pose with arms spread wide and head lowered. The picture changed to another of her in the same posture in front of Buckingham Palace, then another on top of the Empire State building in New York, and then finally a less polished picture of Tor, standing in her famous pose on a mountainside next to a wooden sign that Paul remembered said 'Welcome to Ala Archa National Park' in Russian.

'I am the star child of a random universe; I live at the whim of fickle chance, blown through space and time by the arbitrary muse of aimless fortune. I have been remarkably fortunate in my life; I have been blessed with the opportunity to travel the world and enjoy incredible experiences and then share those experiences with my friends and followers on social media. However, I do have to exist within the prism of global celebrity, and that can bring about risks to my safety and to those around me. I am immensely grateful to the British Royal Marines for their rescue operation in helping to get me to safety.'

The pictures changed again, becoming a rolling montage of photographs of Tor trekking through the valley mountains in Kyrgyzstan, serving food at the Alpine Hotel, distributing water bottles to the other civilians, collecting wood at the ski lodge, and finally on board the helicopter. Jasper was included in several pictures. Paul was startled to see his own face a couple of times; Cecelia didn't appear once.

Tor raised a languid finger and pointed to a journalist on the front row.

'Robert Spindle, the Times. Miss Turner, how dangerous was your situation in Kyrgyzstan? Were you actually being shot at, at any point?'

'I was shot at a few times, actually; I can't say too much,' (she flicked her eyes towards Captain Powell) 'but the military guys got us through it. We just had to do our best to keep everyone's' spirits up and to keep going, you know?'

Every move and gesture Tor made was measured and deliberate. Occasionally her head would turn from side to side, and her hand would sometimes twitch, but mostly her body was still. She would fix her gaze on the person asking a question, but her answer was always directed into the camera.

'Bruce Filbert, Daily Express. Tor, did you encounter many people trying to flee the fighting in Kyrgyzstan?'

'Yeah, the main roads were chocka with civilians trying to get out. It was really scary.' Tor gestured to another journalist.

'Elliot Tetrandra, Fox News. Tor, your online fans have been frantic with worry about you as you have been absent from social media for more than three days now. How did you cope?'

'Elliot, my fans mean the world to me. I am so pleased they can see I am safe and well thanks to you guys, and I'll be joining them again soon. Watch this space!'

'Mohammed Kaj, Afghanistan Times. Is this your first visit to Afghanistan? Are you enjoying it so far?'

The questions kept coming.

'Once the fighting stops, would you consider going back to Kyrgyzstan as a holiday destination?'

'Do you think you were emotionally traumatised by the events of the last few days?'

'Will you be reducing the amount of traveling you do in the near future because of this dangerous experience?'

Tor's response to each question was brief and banal, presented as the perfect soundbite. Only question caused Tor to hesitate for a split second.

'Magnus Wattle, The Australian. So why isn't Jasper with you right now? Did he not cope with this ordeal very well?'

Tor took a deep breath before answering. 'He's safe and sound nearby. Jasper was a brave boy, he coped as best he could with what was, after all, a very traumatic situation.'

There was a buzz of interested murmurs among the journalists. In the back-room Jasper raised his hands to his head.

'Oh, no, no, no, you didn't…you didn't just do that…' he moaned.

Tor leaned forward towards the microphones. 'Jasper has been going through a lot, OK? I'm just glad I was there to help him with it all.' The pictures on the screen behind Tor disappeared abruptly. The flash of camera lights intensified as several voices yelled questions at Tor. She resumed turning her head from side to side, her gaze scanning the rows of faces in front of her, impervious to the tumult.

Charlotte burst through the door of the locker room. 'Jasper, did you see? She just totally threw you under the bus! You can't let her do that!'

Jasper was frozen in his seat; his fingers threaded through his blond hair. Moira and Belinda were staring at each other with expressions of horrified delight on their faces. All three of the Van Der Molen's were sat with a hand over their mouths.

Paul tugged Campbells sleeve and whispered, 'what just happened?'

Campbell whispered back, 'Tor just told the worlds press that Jasper has a problem which they will all assume means he is a drug addict.'

'Which he is.' Paul looked puzzled.

'It wasn't public knowledge, though, was it? A lot of his lucrative advertising deals will have dried up by the time he gets home. I'm just not sure why Tor has chosen now to set this story running,' Campbell said.

Captain Powell appeared in the doorway and frantically signalled to Paul and Campbell to come over.

'Miss Turner has given me the signal – she wants to wrap up, so I'll need you two to go out there in a minute. Just wait by the curtain.'

From the side view of the stage it looked as though Tor had stopped answering questions and was posing for an impromptu photo shoot. After a minute or so, she turned on her heel and walked off without a word. A few of reporters tried to follow her but a couple of Powell's men blocked their way and sent them back to their seats. It took Powell a few moments to make himself heard over the shouts of the press, even with the aid of a microphone.

'I'm sorry gentlemen, I'm afraid that is all from Miss Turner; she has to go and prepare for her flight home to the UK. We do just have time to present another two members of the party that were rescued along with Jasper and Tor – let me introduce Fitzroy Campbell, and Paul Huggins.' Campbell strode confidently forward onto the stage and took up a seat. Paul scurried after him, trying not to stumble on the lip of the stage.

'Mr Campbell is the Diplomatic Service Officer from Her Majesty's Embassy in Kyrgyzstan who co-ordinated the rescue on the ground. Mr Huggins is a UK citizen who happened to be in Kyrgyzstan when the current situation began.'

Campbell sat upright with his hands in his lap. 'Good morning gentlemen.'

Paul shifted in his chair, trying to get his legs comfortable on the wooden seat. He plonked the plaster cast covered arm heavily on the table in front of him. 'Ow. Um…hello.' The bright spotlights trained on the stage made it difficult to see the faces of the journalists in the crowd, lit only by the red lights on top of each TV camera.

Even as Powell drew breath to make another statement Spindle called out, 'You've spent the last three or four days in close proximity to Jasper and Tor, has it been noticeable that Jasper has been struggling physically and mentally?'

'Has Japer given signs of going through withdrawal?' called Flibert.

In a loud voice that cut through the restless noise from the crowd, Campbell said, 'Gentlemen, perhaps I can start by giving you some context to these events? Last Wednesday, the Ambassador at the UK embassy in Bishkek received instruction from the Foreign Office that due to the impending crisis he was to evacuate the staff and to temporarily close the building as a safety measure. Within forty-eight hours we were packed and ready to leave the country when we received word there were a group of UK, Commonwealth and EU citizens stranded at the airport. I was tasked with co-ordinating the safe extraction of these individuals in conjunction with a detachment of UK military personnel. We successfully located the group and were able to withdraw from the city. As the borders had by then been closed off we travelled to a safe rendezvous point from where we could be airlifted out.' Campbell had softened his voice as he had been speaking, causing the press to quieten as they took in what he was saying. 'We arrived in Kabul last night. I would like to pay tribute to the professionalism of the military team that have been involved in this operation; both the team directly involved with the rescue and the support teams here in Afghanistan.'

As Campbell had been speaking Paul could hear a faint noise coming from the room behind the hall. It sounded like shouting. He tried to resist turning his head to look.

A journalist raised a hand. 'Douglas Alderson, Daily Mail. How did the UK soldiers get into the Kyrgyzstan warzone? And how many were directly involved in this operation to rescue Tor and Jasper?'

'I can't really comment on military issues for reasons of security, but we do of course have military personnel protecting the UK embassy. I have to tell you; I didn't know Ms Turner and Mr Hood-Daley were involved until I met them at the airport.' Campbell said.

'Yeah ok, sure,' Alderson laughed. 'You "have to tell us you didn't know." We get it.' Campbell smiled politely back at him.

'The operation was risky at times, and we had some problems to overcome. The rendezvous point was high in the mountains, and as you can see,' Campbell indicated Paul's arm, 'We had a couple of injuries along the way, but ultimately everyone was safely evacuated.' Campbell said calmly.

'So, what happened to your arm then?' Wattle shouted.

Paul blinked at the bright lights. 'Ooh, er, well, I, er, I fell down. Off a mountain.' The nervous jiggling of his left leg caused the sole of his slipper to tap rapidly on the stage floor.

'You fell off a mountain?'

'Ah, yes, a bit.' Paul gulped and stared wide eyed at the eager faces in front of him. He tried not to think of all the things he had to avoid saying. Finally he managed to stutter, 'The whole thing was very tiring. We had to do a lot of walking you see. Except when were on the bus. Or on the helicopter, obviously. But the rest of the time we had to walk. My feet got lots of blisters.' There was a long silence as the journalists glanced at each other.

'So, you fell off the mountain because you had blisters and were a bit tired. How dangerous was this whole thing? Were there any life-or-death decision moments?' Spindle asked. Out of the corner of his eye Paul could see Campbells hand hidden from the journalists under the table making a sharp slicing gesture.

 Paul thought of the bodies laid out on the lawn in front of the Alpine Hotel. 'It was a bit scary at times, but the rescue team got us through.'

'How did Tor and Jasper keep everyone's spirits up?' Filbert asked.

Slightly louder now Paul could hear shouting from behind him. 'I didn't really speak to them that much. I guess they are very private people.'

'Is there anything else you can tell us?' Images flashed through Paul's mind - the wreckage of the cars hit by artillery shells on the motorway; the avalanche; marching under the glacier tied to Talbot. Instead, he said,

'It was very cold. And windy. Very windy. When we were up on the mountain.'

'It was…cold *and* windy…when you were up on a mountain? I better write that down.' Filbert said. A couple of the other journalists chuckled.

'Oh, there was something else! I found a sheep under a snowdrift.' Paul said. Then flushed red as he remembered that he had had his trousers around his ankles at the time. Many journalists were laughing now, some shaking their heads.

The light in the room suddenly changed as the screen behind Paul flickered into life again. Campbell glanced at it, and without a further word stood up and rushed off the stage, tapping Paul's shoulder urgently as he went past. In front of Paul the press instantly changed from grinning and joking to open mouthed astonishment. Through the speakers came the sound of moans and repetitive squeaking sound. Paul slowly turned to look. Projected on to the screen, three times life size was a scene Paul had seen before from a slightly different angle. It was the inside of a yurt at the Alpine Hotel and naked on the bed were Tor and Jasper. The squeaking was coming from the bed frame that was rocking backwards and forwards. In the bottom corner of the screen was the entrance to the yurt, and even as Paul watched, the silhouettes of two heads pushed through. Paul's squeal of horrified recognition was drowned out by uproar from the audience.

'Mr Huggins! Mr Huggins!' Tetrandra was waving frantically to get his attention. 'We are broadcasting live on Fox News. Was this filmed in Kyrgyzstan?' Paul stared at him dumbly. 'Did everyone in your group know this sort of thing was going on?'

'Were the lovebirds going at it like rabbits the whole time?' shouted Alderson.

Several Afghan journalists were shouting angrily and gesticulating at the screen. A couple of them took off their shoes and threw them, making the screen billow and the figures rock back and forth even more quickly. When a chair was hurled just past Paul's head he dived to the floor. His slippers flew up in the air and spun in a gentle arc towards the exit. Paul crawled rapidly off the stage, scrabbling to recover his footwear as he went. Captain Powell rushed in front of the screen, making angry hand signals to his technical team who finally managed to cut the power to the projector, although Tor and Jasper's moans and groans were heard for a while after through the speakers.

'Gentlemen, please! There is no need for this hostility! This was an honest mistake, and we never meant to cause offence!' He turned to a junior officer, 'Turn that bloody sound off!'

Paul hurriedly shuffled into the locker room. Jasper and Tor stood at either end of the room pointing at each other like duellists with pistols drawn, shouting.

'Oh Jasper don't be such a prick about this. This will be an absolute bloody goldmine for both of us!' Tor's hand pointing at Jasper flicked towards the ceiling as if caused by a handgun's recoil.

'You've made me look like a complete pussy time and time again!' Jasper's face was flushed and the tendons in his neck bulged as he yelled. 'You treat me like an accessory! I get pushed into the background or cut out altogether; it's like I don't matter to you!'

'Oh get over yourself. You know it's in the nature of our business; it's just the way things work. Don't be so bloody soft,' Tor sneered.

Charlotte, Moira, and Belinda were gathered around Jasper preventing him approaching Tor while the Van der Molen family seemed to be trying to pacify her. Campbell stood by the door, looking from one to the other.

'Sorry to dash off and leave you back there. I couldn't have my picture taken in front of that film,' he said to Paul.

'Yeah,' said Paul vaguely. He was staring at Jasper. Paul could see the young man's outstretched finger was trembling, and there was a sheen of sweat on his forehead. Paul walked over to Jasper and slapped him hard on the chest with both hands. 'Jasper! Look at me! Look at me!' Paul slapped him again. 'Listen to what I am saying. Have you had your medication today? Have you taken it?' Jasper, still breathing hard, shook his head. 'You are dipping, I can see it. If you don't take it now you will crash again, like you did at the hotel. Have you got it with you?' Jasper nodded. Paul stretched his head up to whisper in Jasper's ear. 'Don't prove her right. Go and take your medicine.'

Jasper glared at Tor for a second, then turned and strode over to his rucksack and began rummaging inside it.

Tor turned her attention to Charlotte. 'I suppose you think putting that fuck tape up on screen was supposed to hurt me, somehow? I would have had that uploaded on my website within the week anyway, you stupid bitch. Now it's just got more publicity. And there is no such thing as bad publicity.' Tor looked defiant. 'Listen, Jas, this was the perfect time to get your drug story out. All the worlds press is focussed on us, we can get out ahead of the story and control it, and it will keep us on the front page for months. It'll put us in the broadsheets as well as the tabloids. She was so right.'

'Who's "she"?' Paul asked.

'That old girl Cecelia. "Don't bury the bad news – make it the headline." She said. 'The press will lap it up.' Damn right they did. As soon as I mentioned setting up the press conference to Colonel Gibbs last night she gave me the idea, and good on her; she's done me a solid favour.'

'She's a clever one, alright,' said Paul.

Captain Powell put his head round the door. 'Well, that could have gone better. There is still a bit of a hullabaloo going on in the ballroom so it's probably best if we get you on your way. Gather your things and follow me. We'll use the back door I think.'

A decrepit looking bus was waiting for them at the rear of the building. Jasper and Tor sat as far away from each other as they could. The deafening roar from the bus's engine made conversation with the person on the next seat virtually impossible. Paul reached into his rucksack to rearrange the contents again.

The breeze twirled small eddies of brown grit across the open airfield as the bus rumbled away from the cluster of buildings and headed towards one end of the runway. A huge grey transport plane sat off to one side, dwarfing the cluster of vehicles gathered around it on the tarmac. A fuel tanker sheltered under one wing, hi viz wearing crew members detaching the fuel line from the aircraft. The bus came to a stop underneath the tail of the plane. Beside the lowered rear ramp was a large van with a red cross painted on the side. Moira and Belinda rushed to the door of the bus, tugging at the handle even before the vehicle had fully stopped. Once the door opened they leapt out, sprinting towards the ambulance. As they approached the rear door swung open and two camouflage wearing medics emerged, lifting out Annabel who was strapped into a stretcher chair. A third figure dressed in camouflage fatigues followed them. They carried the chair onto the ramp and headed inside. Rachel clambered down from the ambulance, grabbed Belinda and Moira by the hand, and hurried to catch up with Annabel. The rest of the Herd followed more slowly.

Paul was the last to alight from the bus, stepping stiff legged onto the tarmac. Campbell had waited for him as the others followed Powell towards the ramp. Campbell looked at his mobile phone, and Paul saw his shoulders sag and his face crumple into tears.

Paul awkwardly patted Campbells arm. 'What's wrong?' The fuel tanker engine thundered into life, and the vehicle began to move away from the aircraft. Campbell watched it move off, wiping his eyes one at a time with the heel of his hand. Once the noise had abated slightly he looked back at Paul.

'I've had a message from Talaay. He got through to his parents' village. He's safe.' Campbell sniffed loudly and puffed out his cheeks.

'Oh, brilliant!' said Paul, although he immediately felt embarrassed by his clumsy response. Campbell smiled.

'Yes it is. But time for us to go.' Campbell headed for the aeroplane. Paul pulled his phone out of his pocket but was disappointed to find he still had no signal.

The inside of the aircraft was vast. There was little in the way of décor, and no exterior windows except for a small porthole in each of the exit doors on either side of the cabin. The top of the walls and the ceiling were festooned with cables, wires, and pipes. A dozen pallets piled high with crates and boxes were heavily strapped to the floor near the ramp. Beyond a curtain of cargo netting at the front of the cabin were ten rows of seats. Annabel's stretcher was being bolted to the floor beside the last row. A metal stairway led up to the cockpit. A narrow doorway to one side at the base of the steps had 'LAVATORY' spray painted across it. On the other side was a cramped galley kitchen.

There was a bustle of military personnel inside the aeroplane preparing the aircraft for the flight. Most of them were paying no attention to the civilians who were shepherded into the seats by Captain Powell. The two medics who had carried Annabel in were leaving as Paul hobbled towards the seating but the third was still kneeling beside her chair.

'Hello Draws. Are you coming home with us?' Paul asked him, hopefully.

The Marine medic grinned at him and stood up. 'I'm afraid not, Sicknote. You guys will just have to manage without me. I have something for you though.' He reached into a pouch on his belt and withdrew a blister pack of pills. 'Two of these, every three hours should keep you comfortable on the flight home.'

'Will Annabel be okay? I didn't think you were supposed to fly with a head injury like that.' Paul glanced at Annabel who seemed to be sleeping. She was clutching Rachel's hand.

'Nah, don't fret. Combat wounded with much worse head injuries get repatriated on flights like this all the time.'

'What about Jasper? Is he…?' Paul wasn't sure exactly what question he was trying to ask. Jasper was slumped in a seat in the row in front of Annabel.

'He'll be fine. The pharmacy at the base have made up enough of your magic potion to last him a couple of days.' Draws grinned again. 'Look at you, watching out for everybody else even though you're wrapped up like an Egyptian mummy yourself. I'll have to make you an honorary medic for the flight home.'

'Is there a first aid kit on board, then?' Paul asked.

'Jesus, man, I was kidding…!' Draws said, shaking his head.

'Oh, right. How did Morgan's surgery go this morning?'

Draws raised an eyebrow. 'Morgan, is it now? Well, I'm not surprised. He was singing your praises last night, you know. He kept banging on about how it was you that got him up that mountain. I'd say you've got a friend for life. To answer your question - *Colour Sergeant Talbot* hadn't come out of surgery by the time we left, so I don't know.'

Paul stuck out his good hand. 'Thank you for everything. I wouldn't have…well, you know.'

Draws grasped Paul's hand and shook it. 'Oh, no need to thank me Sicknote, I'll be dining out on barrack room stories about you for years to come. Have a safe journey home.' Draws headed down the ramp.

Captain Powell had worked his way round each member of the Herd, shaking hands and saying goodbye. When he reached Paul he gave a half smile, patted Paul's shoulder, and walked off towards the exit. Paul slumped into a seat, reached into his rucksack to retrieve the paperback Cecelia had given him and began to read.

Eventually a loud whirring sound heralded the ramp being raised. As the interior of the aeroplane became darker, strip lighting in panels on the wall flicked on. After the ramp closed with a clang a tinny voice came over the tannoy.

'Ladies and gentlemen, welcome on board this RAF flight to London. This is your pilot Flight Lieutenant Rumbold. Our flight time to RAF Northolt is expected to be around seven hours, thirty-eight minutes. We have a crew of three on board this C17 Globemaster aircraft…'

Paul stopped listening and turned his attention once more to his book. The aircraft began to roll gently forwards.

<u>Chapter Eighteen</u>

Shortly after take-off Paul had switched his slippers for shoes and socks as the cold air began to bite at his exposed toes. The inside of his rucksack had a slight aroma of damp clothing and toothpaste - on investigation he found the lid had come of the tube in his washbag. The air in the aeroplane cabin had complex layers of smells, the scent of the wooden pallets mixing with the clean metallic tang from the walls and floor, and a slight taste of jet fuel. Oddly, there was also a hint of lemon.

For the first couple of hours of the flight Paul remained buried in his book. When he did glance up, he noticed the Herd were all still, as if they were all drained of energy. Most of them were dozing in their seats. Tor was alone on the front row wearing a glittery silver eye mask, her head tipped back on the headrest. The Van der Molens were in the row behind her, Agnes and Hendrik sitting side by side with their heads together while Jordi laid out flat across three seats. Only Jasper seemed to have moved since the aeroplane had become airborne. He was lounging against the frame of the exit door, staring out of the porthole.

Campbell emerged through the kitchen doorway carrying a tray of plastic cups. He offered one to everyone who seemed to be awake. After passing Paul a cup he sat down next to him. 'Feeling ok?' he said.

Paul thought for a moment. 'No,' he replied.

'Is it your legs?' Campbell asked him, frowning.

'No not really, although now you mention it, they are stiffening up a bit. Its more the fact that I feel like a right pillock after I've made a massive tit of myself on national television.' Paul grumbled.

'I think you would have to say we were on global television rather than national.'

'Well thanks, that makes it so much better.' Paul sipped his water angrily.

'Look, it wasn't your naked body on display on that screen; it won't be you that is remembered from that whole PR disaster,' Campbell said.

'I was sat right in front of it!' Paul said.

'And nobody was looking at you once that started,' Campbell replied. 'Trust me. Think of it like this; we provide a perfect distraction for Cecelia's exit. Her plane took off just as Tor walked out on stage with every member of the international press corps in Afghanistan in the room.'

'Why was that so important, then? Her being in Kyrgyzstan, I get that that was a problem, but why did it matter that she was in Afghanistan?'

'International politics is all about signals, Paul. It's all about non-verbal communication, the divining of intent by interpreting the actions of friends and foe alike. So, it's in our national interest not to reveal the activities of our senior intelligence service personnel, even the retired ones. Other countries might interpret her being in Afghanistan when she wasn't expected to be as a signal of new activity by the UK, or a threat, which could lead to unforeseen consequences. And we like to avoid unforeseen consequences.'

'That seems a bit far-fetched, though, doesn't it?' Paul said.

'Did you see the huge statue outside the airport in Kyrgyzstan, Paul?' Campbell clutched the plastic cup in his hand. Paul shook his head no. 'The great leader Manas, who united the forty tribes and created the Kyrgyz republic, astride his war horse, sword raised triumphantly above his head? The Airport was named after him.

There are statues of him everywhere in that country; every town and village square has his image displayed one way or another. Put up by the government in the last ten years or so to remember a mighty leader from the history books. Now, at home we would likely think nothing of it, just remembrance of times past and all that, but here – here it is a symbol of future aspiration, independence from past oppressors, a country ready to throw its weight around in the region.' He paused to sip his drink. 'I'm not saying the civil war was caused by a statue, but it was a clear political signal of the government's objectives. Other countries read the signals, and some of them didn't like it at all.' Campbell glanced around the cabin. 'At the base of every statue, under the hooves of Manas' mighty steed are the mangled bodies of his defeated foe. They included that element for a reason. What doesn't get mentioned much in Kyrgyz school books is that it is entirely possible that Manas never existed – his story may have contained elements from several tribal chief's tales across a hundred years, or the character may just be a legend like King Arthur or Robin Hood is in England.'

'Everybody needs a hero I suppose,' Paul said.

'Paul, you have to remember, that with great power comes great responsibility.' Campbell smiled slightly.

'Well, we can't always know what the response to our actions will be. Sometimes other people…' Paul broke off mid-sentence. 'Did you just quote Spiderman?'

Campbell laughed. 'I picked up the habit from the Marines, I guess. But really, I am just your friendly neighbourhood diplomat.'

'No, stop it, the phrase is "Friendly Neighbourhood Spiderman," not "something, something, diplomat" …you're doing it again.' Paul wasn't sure he could cope with Campbell the comedian.

Campbell chuckled. 'OK, ok, I'll leave you alone. If you need anything – just send up the Bat-signal.' He put on a deep voice, 'because I'm Batman!'

'Oh, stop it,' Paul said again, but laughed despite himself. Campbell drained his cup and stood up, moving round the seats checking on the other civilians. Paul returned to his paperback. He had only read through a couple of pages before he felt a tap on his shoulder. He looked up to see Jordi smiling at him. The boy waggled his mobile phone at him.

'I want to start a WhatsApp group. Can I add your mobile number?' He said hopefully. Paul reached for his phone.

'Have you got everyone else?' he asked. He showed Jordi his phone number and the boy punched the numbers into his device.

Jordi shrugged. 'Most. Moira and her friends; Charlotte and Jasper, even Mr Campbell. I haven't asked *her* yet.' Jordi nodded towards Tor.

Paul thought for a moment. 'Didn't Tor use your phone a few days ago?'

Jordi's eyes widened. 'Yes, that's right!' He tapped quickly at his mobile phone screen. 'I can use the call history to tell me her number!'

'She might not accept the invite,' Paul said.

'We'll see.' Jordi smiled happily.

Paul ignored a growing feeling of pins and needles in his feet until he had successfully completed one hundred- and fifty-pages of his book. He bent the corner of a page as a marker and set the paperback on the seat next to him. He heaved himself out of the chair and stretched back before taking a few hobbling steps up and down the aisle, grimacing as the prickling feeling intensified, then died away. He limped over to the doorway and spent some time staring out of the port hole window. Mostly all he could see was a canopy of deep blue sky above and a blanket of white cloud beneath them, but occasional breaks in the cloud revealed leaden grey water far below.

'We've got some food for you guys!' The shout came from the airwoman stood by the kitchen door. Paul hobbled over and joined the queue. When his turn came he was presented with a plastic serving tray that was divided into six sections. In the biggest was a smaller tray covered with a clear plastic film. The airwoman pointed at this. 'Vegetable lasagne, I hope that's OK,' she said, in a tone that suggested there wasn't any choice in whether it was ok or not. On the rest of the tray was a small pale bread roll with a tiny packet of butter and sachet of cheese paste, two crackers also wrapped in plastic with a thin slice of bright yellow cheese also wrapped in plastic, a tub of chocolate mousse and a carton of orange juice. A plastic knife, fork and spoon were wrapped in a serviette.

'Thank you very much,' Paul said, and went back to his seat. Eventually he worked out how to extract the tray table from the arm of the chair and warily poked at the food. Although he usually avoided vegetarian food, the lasagne was surprisingly pleasant, and he ended up wiping the inside of the container with the bread roll to capture every mouthful. One spoonful of the mousse was sufficient to tell him he wanted no more of it, and he left the two types of cheese untouched on the tray. The crackers and juice carton he slipped into his coat pocket in case he was peckish later.

He carried the tray back to the kitchen. 'Thanks again. Where are we?'

The airwoman looked at him carefully for a moment. 'Where do you think we are?'

'What? Oh, God...I know we are on a plane, I meant, what are we flying over? When I looked out a little while ago I could see ocean.'

'Right. I was told some of you had had a fall recently, I thought you might have banged your head. That was the Black Sea below us.' She checked her watch. 'We should be just about over land again by now. Romania first, then Hungary, Austria, Germany, Belgium, then home.' She made to walk past him.

'How long?' Paul asked.

'Three and a half, maybe four hours.'

As Paul headed back to his seat again, he noticed Tor had risen from her chair and was removing layers of clothing. When she got down to knickers and thin strapped vest top, she laid out a towel in the middle of the floor, set her phone to play ambient music on loudspeaker and began doing yoga exercises. Paul saw Jasper turn away to talk to Charlotte, but Jordi was stretching his neck to get a better view.

Paul tried to concentrate on his book again, but with the combination of repetitive music, the rumble of the huge jet engines, and the hot food, Paul found his eyelids getting heavy. He carefully clicked on his seat belt and put his head back and dozed.

Paul awoke with a shudder from dreams of flames and wreckage, his heart juddering in his chest. Campbell was stood over him. 'Paul, are you OK? You were shouting something.' Several concerned faces were turned towards him.

'Sorry, sorry,' Paul stammered. He forced some deep breaths in and out.

'We are only about half an hour away from London,' Campbell told him. 'Are you sure you are ok?'

'Yes, I'm fine.' Paul fumbled for the pills Draws had given him. 'Bad dreams. I'm fine now.' He tried to stand up, forgetting he was wearing a seat belt. The image of the burning cars on the road in Kyrgyzstan still sat behind his eyes; the dead woman in the passenger seat was staring at him. He blinked repeatedly to shift the image. Campbell patted Paul on the shoulder. Once he had clipped open the belt Paul stumbled to the lavatory to splash some water on his face from the tiny sink.

Several of the Herd were taking it in turns to peer through the windows on either side of the aircraft, although Tor had resumed her position on the front row with eye mask pulled down and ear buds in place. Jordi hurried up to Paul. 'They let me go and sit in the cockpit for a while! It was really cool.' The boy suddenly looked incredibly young.

'That is cool.' Paul agreed.

As the aircraft began to descend Campbell tapped Tor on the shoulder, pointing to his ear as she removed the mask. She took out the earbuds. He then picked up the tannoy microphone. 'Attention please everybody. We will be landing at RAF Northolt in a few minutes. For those of you staying in the UK we have arranged some transport for your onward journey; for the Van der Molen family, there will be representatives of the Netherlands embassy waiting to greet you and they will help get you home.'

'I was expecting to arrive in Heathrow, why aren't we going there?' Tor asked loudly.

'The RAF doesn't operate from Heathrow. RAF Northolt is northwest London. You could get to Heathrow in about twenty minutes by taxi, or central London in about thirty.' Campbell replied.

'What about Annabel?' Rachel shouted.

'There will be an ambulance waiting to take her to the Royal London Hospital.' Campbell said.

'It will take both of us.' Rachel answered. Campbell didn't contradict her.

The landing was smooth. The large aircraft quickly came to a halt after taxiing in front of the low buildings away from the main runway. The airwoman stood at the back of the plane, large headphones on, tapping at buttons on a large panel on the wall. The rear ramp descended with a hydraulic whine and three ground crew hurried up the ramp. The Herd began lining up to disembark, but the airwoman held up her hand.

'Wounded first!' she called out. The ground crew detached Annabel's chair from the floor and carried it down the ramp, followed by a determined looking Rachel. Paul stood waiting, until he realised everyone was looking at him.

'Oh, yes, sorry,' he said, and set off down the ramp.

The tarmac was wet, large puddles spread thinly over the surface, although the rain had now passed through. The familiar smell of summer rain in England told Paul he really was on home soil. The green and yellow ambulance for Annabel was waiting on the roadway in front of the nearest building. A figure in camouflage fatigues and a pale blue beret by a double door waved at him. He headed in that direction. He hadn't got halfway to the building before Tor strode past him. Most of the rest of the group had caught up with him by the time he got inside. Tor had disappeared already; Jasper and Charlotte were deliberately loitering at the rear to ensure they were the last to go in.

Paul was clutching his passport as the group passed through a waiting area. 'Not needed today, Mr Huggins!' Campbell said. He stuck out a hand. 'Goodbye then; it's been a pleasure.' Paul put his passport between his teeth and shook Campbells hand. Campbell hurried over to Moira and Belinda, guiding them towards the exit door. Paul waved goodbye, and the two women waved back.

Paul was suddenly engulfed in a hug, two arms reaching around his neck. It was Agnes, who looked teary. 'Goodbye now!' she said and let him go. Hendrik smiled and shook Pauls good hand. Jordi raised a hand for a high five, and Paul gently tapped the boy's palm.

As the exit door opened there was a hubbub of voices. Paul hobbled through behind the rest of the herd. Through the crowd of strangers he could just see Annie craning her neck. When she saw him her face lit up with a beaming smile. 'You silly bugger, where have you been?' she laughed, before noticing the plaster cast and his bruised hand. 'Oh my God, what did happen to you?' she exclaimed. Paul enveloped her in a huge hug, clutching her tightly with his good arm and burying his face in her neck. He gasped, not trusting himself to speak. 'Oh. It's OK, honey,' Annie whispered softly into his ear. 'You're home now.' Paul closed his eyes and took a deep breath. For an endless moment, the world was still, and perfect, and he needed nothing else. Annie kissed him lightly on the cheek. Paul pulled back slightly, straightened up and stared into her eyes before kissing her lips. He cupped the side of her face with his right hand. 'I love you so much,' he said, then kissed her again.

A line of taxis was driving into the car park once they got outside. Paul and Annie were in the queue behind Moira and her parents. After some awkward introductions Paul said, 'I hope Annabel will be OK.'

Moira's mum looked indignant. 'She should sue them. Being treated like that. It a disgrace.' Moira flushed a deep pink colour.

'Who would she sue, exactly?' Paul said.

'Well the travel company for starters. And the Government of course, they were responsible for her. I'm just so grateful Moira wasn't hurt…'

'Get in the taxi, mum,' Moira said. She opened the door and pushed her mother inside. Moira gave Paul an exasperated grimace, then climbed in after her mother.

A black cab pulled up and Paul and Annie climbed in.

'Where to, folks?' the driver asked.

'Harbut Road, Battersea, please,' Annie said.

As they set off Paul started to tell Annie what had happened to him, but he had barely begun when the taxi driver interrupted him.

''Ere that's you, innit? I saw your face on the telly this morning. You've been hanging around with that supermodel, wassername, Tor, that's it. You've just been rescued from Afghanistan, or something. What's it like?'

'Er, which bit? The being rescued bit?' Paul asked.

'Nah, hangin' around with a supermodel. Aw, she is well fit,' The driver said.

'It's not as much fun as you'd think,' Paul told him.

'Oh, right. Still, you've got a hell of story to tell now, eh?' said the driver.

Paul went back to talking to Annie. He spoke continuously for the rest of the journey home, describing all the events and the people involved as best as he could remember them. He knew Annie would see through any fabrications or embellishments he might add so he stuck to the facts. Annie let him speak, occasionally asking a question or two but mostly just listening. The drive home took nearly an hour.

When the taxi pulled up outside the family home, Paul reached for his wallet, realising he had virtually no cash. The driver waved him away.

'All paid for on the governments' account, guv. Cheerio then. Be lucky!'

A rich smell of cooking food greeted them as they stepped into the hallway. As the front door closed behind them Annie said 'Right, get those boots off; let's take a look at your feet.' Once Paul had kicked off his footwear, she took Paul by the hand and lead him to the lounge. 'Let's get these ridiculous trousers off as well.'

'I quite like them actually,' Paul said, stepping out of the trousers. 'I lost my own trousers in the avalanche that did this,' Paul waggled his cast.

Annie put her hand to her mouth. 'Oh, love,' she said, looking at the bandages. 'Right, let's get these off too, then I'll run you a bath, OK? The girls will be home in an hour or so, you relax until then. It's beef for tea; I put a stroganoff in the slow cooker this morning before I came out.' She started to slowly unwind the bandages on each leg, Paul wincing as dried blood and the few hairs were pulled away. He sat down on the sofa. 'Oh, your poor feet!' Annie said.

'Any chance of a cup of tea?' Paul said.

Whilst Annie bustled around in the kitchen Paul picked up his mobile phone, switched it on and plugged in the charger. Instantly various apps began to ping, and messages flashed up on the screen. He looked at the missed calls. Several numbers he didn't recognise, but the work switchboard number came up several times.

He quickly scrolled through his contacts list for his boss's number, found 'Kieran Mills,' and pressed dial. 'Kieran, its Paul - Paul Huggins.'

'Paul! At last, I've been trying to reach you. Are you okay? We've all been dreadfully worried about you since you fell off the face of the earth last week.' From the wind noise on the phone it sounded as if Paul's boss was on the move.

'Well…' Paul began but was cut off.

'It sounds like you've been through a terrible ordeal. I understand you've suffered some serious injuries, is that right? What a nightmare for you!' Kieran's voice had a slight Scottish burr.

'Well, I don't know if you can call my injuries that serious. I've got some broken bones - my left hand is in a plaster cast – but apart from that it's just cuts and bruises. Looking forward to getting back to work though,' Paul added as Annie bought in two mugs of tea.

'Now just slow down there, laddie. Our number one priority has to be to look after you. We've got to have you fully recovered before we let you back in the office. Duty of Care, and all that. We've got to make sure you are in the right state of mind as well. You've been through an horrific experience. ' Kieran said.

'Oh, but really, I feel fine. We've got that interdepartmental presentation at the beginning of next week, haven't we?'

'Don't concern yourself with that for the time being, Paul. We've got it covered.' Kieran replied.

'Well look, I can always dial in on the laptop, even if I can't get into the office...' Paul said.

'No, we don't want you to do that. We think it's probably best for you to stay at home on sick leave for a week or two, just while all this fuss dies down. And stay off your laptop as well. We can't have you working during your recovery. Remember, we do have your best interests at heart.' Kieran said.

'I don't understand, what fuss?' Paul said.

'It's nothing for you to worry about.' Kieran said. 'I'll call you in a week or so, see how you are getting on. We'll talk again then about arranging to get you back in. In the meantime, just keep your head down and stay home. And get better of course. Bye.' Kieran hung up.

Paul turned on the TV and scrolled through the news channels. In less than ten minutes he saw footage of the RAF C17 he was on departing Kabul and then landing in London, a rerun of Tor's press conference in Kabul, and a clip of him sat in front of Tor and Jasper's sex film as shoes were thrown at the screen. This programme content was repeated with slight variations across at least three different channels. Different presenters would give a short description of the recent events in Kyrgyzstan, offset with a limited description of Tor and Jasper's rescue. On one occasion the images of the Kyrgyz civil war were replaced by a montage of pictures of Tor's modelling career.

'I think I'll go and have that bath now,' Paul said.

Although the warm water made some of the cuts on his legs sting, the bath was soothing once Paul had got his left arm into a comfortable position. He tried to let his mind drift off, but an image of dead bodies kept re-appearing unbidden in his mind's eye. When the water cooled he pulled out the plug, levered himself upright using one hand and stepped gingerly onto the bathmat. He wiped the condensation from the bathroom mirror with the edge of the towel he had wrapped around himself, which caused it to drop off him. He peered closely at the reflection of his face as Annie came through the door.

'Oh hello cheeky,' she said, giving him a gentle slap on his left buttock. Paul yelped slightly. Oh, sorry love, you've got a bruise there, I didn't see it. And is that a burn mark?'

'Probably – I got a bit close to the stove in the mountain hut.' Annie shook her head in disbelief. Paul chuckled, then looked at the mirror again. 'Is there more grey hair than there was a week ago?' he said.

'Hardly,' Annie scoffed. The front door slammed. 'Oops, better get some clothes on, your daughters are home.' Paul scurried into his bedroom.

Three minutes later, dressed in a clean tee shirt and shorts he opened the bedroom door and was engulfed in hugs from both daughters. He laughed. 'Hey! Careful with the old man, he's a bit fragile.'

'We were worried about you!' said Jessica. 'Oh my god, what happened to your legs?'

'Yeah, we were properly worried. Then you were on TV.' Sophie said. She tapped his plaster cast, making him wince slightly. 'What have you done there?'

'Come on, I'll tell you all about it over dinner.' Paul said and kissed them one after the other on the forehead. 'I love you both very much.'

'Oh, Dad! Love you too,' said Jessica.

'Soft git.' Said Sophie. 'Love you.'

It took a long time for Paul to finish his meal as he went over the details of his adventures for the benefit of his daughters. The story telling continued through the washing up and once they had all settled into the sofa and armchairs in the living room. Paul did omit some of the moments that he told Annie – his daughters didn't need to know the most graphic details of the deaths he had seen. He had hurriedly explained the sex tape appearance to Annie in the taxi, and he gave his daughters this explanation of some of this too. Secretly he quite enjoyed the way his whole family were hanging off his every word, although the focus of their questions wasn't quite what he was expecting.

'So you injected Jasper with homemade heroin?' Sophie gasped.

'Well no, it wasn't an injection, it was liquid solution he had to drink, and it wasn't heroin...'

'OK, but you were the one who mixed up his drugs to keep him going?' demanded Jessica.

'Yes, me and the Marine medic, whose nickname, this is funny...'

'Wow!!! Our Dad can make class A drugs! Wait until we tell all our friends...'

Paul waved his good hand. 'No, no, no, you can't tell anyone that...'

His daughters laughed. 'Easy, Dad, we're kidding!' said Jess. The girls shared a glance. 'You can bet your arse we'll tell them you know Tor and Jasper though.'

Annie twirled the wine left in her glass. 'So, what is the world-famous Tor *really* like?' she asked, stealing a look at her husband out of the corner of her eye.

Paul looked at her directly. 'Actually, I found her to be...quite horrible.'

Jessica and Sophie gasped. Annie looked into her wine glass. 'Thought as much.' She finished her wine.

'Jasper's not so bad. He's just like a big puppy dog really,' Paul told them. 'There is a bigger secret though.' Paul had refrained from mentioning this before but decided on the spur of the moment to trust his family with it. 'The real reason the Marines came to get us.' Three faces stared at him intently.

'Go on then, what?' Annie said.

'The elderly woman I mentioned, Cecelia? Her full name is Cecelia Urquhart-Eriksen, and she...'

'I've heard that name!' Jessica shrieked.

'Really?' Paul leant forward.

'At school. Social studies, I think it was.' Jessica looked a bit sheepish. 'Can't remember why though.'

'Well I'll tell you. She used to be head of MI6. That's why they sent in the Marines to get her home safely.' Paul said.

'Yes! We did a piece on "Female role models in public life," that was it.' Jessica remembered.

'It wasn't on the news,' said Annie dubiously.

'I told you; it was a secret. That's why they want Tor and Jasper all over the front pages, to keep that bit quiet.' Paul sat back.

'Ooooh! A conspiracy!' sad Sophie.

'International espionage comes to Battersea!' Jessica giggled.

'Oh, hush you two. Put the telly on, I want to see the news. Especially if your dad is on it again,' Annie said.

The girls laughed.

After a bit of channel hopping Annie chose the Channel Four news programme. After showing again the film of the flight arriving at RAF Northolt and clips from Tor's press conference in Kabul there was a more in-depth report on the Kyrgyzstan civil war. A journalist wearing a dark blue helmet and bullet proof vest described how an impasse had been reached with the two sides having consolidated their positions but neither showing much appetite for launching attacks against the other. There was footage of the reporter picking his way through a roadway covered in rubble. Paul pointed at the screen.

'I've been there!' he said excitedly. 'That's just outside the airport.'

The journalist finished his piece to camera saying, 'United Nations envoys are expected to arrive here tomorrow; they will be hoping to begin negotiations that can bring about first of all a ceasefire, and ultimately long-term peace to this war-torn nation. This is Jason Huntley, for Channel Four news.'

In the studio the presenter said, 'Thank you, Jason.' He turned to the camera. 'We are joined now by the Cabinet Minister, the Minister for Health.' He turned towards his guest.

'Hello! Thanks for having me on, it's a pleasure to be here as always,' the Minister said smiling widely. Annie pulled a face and was about to press the remote to change channels when Paul stopped her.

'That's my boss's boss! I was with him a week ago. I want to hear what he has to say.'

'Oh, dad, you do hang out with some important people,' Sophie said.

The interviewer began, 'Minister, your recent trip to the Far East has been overshadowed by events in central Asia, wouldn't you agree?'

The Minister smiled into the camera. 'I led a high-level team from my department on an important visit to Korea and Japan which I am proud to say was a huge success. We were able to show the world that Britain, and this government in particular, leads the way in Health Innovation. I am delighted to be able to present this big win to your viewers.'

'It wasn't a complete success, was it, Minister? There was something of a row about the ongoing dispute with Germany and the rest of the EU over Intellectual Property Rights on some of the biotech solutions you've been promoting,' said the interviewer.

'Well, um, that was unfortunate…' the Minister began. Normally he was quite animated when answering questions, with lots of hand gestures and nods of the head, but he now became still.

'That legal dispute could drag on for years, couldn't it?' the interviewer asked.

'We will have to wait and see on that…' the Minister shook his head. 'I am completely confident we will be able to come to a resolution that can deliver wonderful benefits for our country.' The minister launched into a monologue listing all the achievements he expected to deliver following his appearance at the summit. The interviewer let him speak for thirty seconds before interrupting him.

'You mentioned the trip to Japan. That was all very rushed, wasn't it? It wasn't on your itinerary when you left London at the beginning of the month,' the interviewer continued.

The Minister's blinked, then answered energetically, 'Ah…an opportunity arose to meet with our colleagues and, indeed, allies in Japan to further discuss…um…greater co-operation in Health projects across a range of…matters. You see, sometimes in politics you can't be afraid to seize the moment, when the chance presents itself, and at the end of the day…'

The interviewer cut the Minister off again. 'Speaking of colleagues, one of the delegation that was with you in Korea, Paul Huggins, was part of the group that was rescued in Kyrgyzstan and flew home today.'

Paul sat bolt upright at the mention of his name. Annie grabbed his shoulder and shook it.

'Well, I don't really know much about that…' the Minister was becalmed again.

'We understand Mr Huggins was on his way home after being with you on your trip to South Korea. Why didn't he travel to Japan with you?'

'Um…well…Mr Huggins was a fairly junior member of the team…'

The interviewer lent forward. 'He's a Special Policy Advisor with particular expertise on drug rehabilitation programmes, isn't he? One of the very projects your press release says was discussed in Japan. Seems odd not to take him with you?'

'Well, as you say, the Japan trip was quite short notice, and we decided that to give the British taxpayer best value for money, we had to reduce the size of the party…'

'Who went with you then, Minister? What was the selection criteria for those people?' the interviewer persisted.

'I don't think…'

'It was just you, your personal assistant and judging by your press release it would seem there was a photographer as well, is that correct?' the interview continued.

'I don't think your viewers are really interested in that, I'm sure they would rather hear about the success we had in preparing the way for more trade deals with our global partners.' The Minister carried on.

'This trip to Japan was just a glorified photo opportunity for you personally, wasn't it? Is it reasonable for the British taxpayer to have to stump up for what is effectively an extended holiday trip for you?'

'That's completely preposterous; as I've already said, this was an important diplomatic trip which delivered significant success for Great Britain. It is highly irresponsible of you to suggest it was anything else.' The Minister replied.

We will have to leave it there I am afraid; that is all we have time for today. Thank you, Minister.' The interviewer turned away to face the camera. 'Join us again for Channel Four news, same time tomorrow. Goodnight.'

Annie looked at Paul.

'Oh dear,' he said. 'He won't be happy with that.'

The announcers upbeat voice spoke over the rolling credits on the TV screen.

'If you enjoyed our interview with the Minister for Health then tune in tonight at ten pm for - "In the Raw on Channel Four," the cutting-edge chat show with Duncan Jay. Duncan's guest tonight is supermodel and international celebrity – Tor! And what links the Cabinet Minister with the glamorous world of jet-setting supermodels?' A picture of Tor in a TV studio flashed onto the screen.

Tor will be telling Duncan about her recent death-defying adventures, life on the road with Jasper, more details on *that* sex tape, and, presumably, all about her new best buddy, and close advisor to the political elite, the English civil servant, Paul Huggins!' Paul sat bolt upright in the armchair. 'Coming next, "In the Doghouse" takes you to Battersea Dogs Home where rescued mongrels wait to be adopted. I wonder if Paul Huggins is in this one, too?'

Chapter Nineteen

Paul began to feel besieged in his own home. The next day his phone rang constantly, a multitude of different media organisations trying to arrange interviews or just get a soundbite quote. Whilst refusing to respond to these requests he couldn't stop himself from scanning the news websites. The lead story in most of them was Jasper and Tors' relationship, but every website also had Paul's picture on it, mostly taken from Kabul press conference, several with a pixelated image of Tor and Jasper copulating over his shoulder. The Evening Standard managed to get hold of his civil service ID card photo and used that as well. He was described in the Mirror as a 'medical expert' which pleased him, and as a 'hapless civil servant' by The Times, which pleased him less, and as a 'Bumbling Bureaucrat' by The Sun which he actively disliked. The Sun also listed some of the projects Paul had worked on relating to drug dependency and labelled him a 'Lefty Do-gooder.' The Health Minister's TV appearance barely got a mention on any of the sites.

Trying to distract himself, Paul set about polishing all his shoes stored in the rack under the stairs.

It didn't take long for the press to track down his address, and on the second morning after Pauls return home news camera crews and reporters were camped on the street outside. Paul left the curtains drawn at the front of the house. After breakfast Jessica and Sophie chose to climb over the fence in the back garden to get to school rather than fight through the scrum at the front. By the middle of the afternoon they were still there and showing no signs of leaving. Paul intended to ignore them and hope they would go away. Annie was more positive.

'I've had an idea,' she said. 'Let's try and change the way the Press are portraying you; we'll give them something positive to write about.'

Annie pushed him gently towards the kitchen.

'How?' Paul said, miserably.

'Let's show them a different version of you. We'll start by being nice to them. You don't have to give any interviews, just go out and show your face. A couple of nice pictures might be all they need.' She said firmly. She reached for the kettle.

'It feels like I've had my picture taken quite enough,' Paul said. As Annie bustled about in the kitchen Paul headed upstairs to get changed. Following his wife's instructions he put on a pair of trousers that Annie approved of and a large jumper that would fit over his plaster cast. After carefully brushing his hair he re-joined Annie in the kitchen. She held out a loaded tray for him to carry. Paul balanced it carefully on his plaster cast.

'Just smile and be nice and don't answer any questions you don't want to,' Annie told him.

'That's what the Minister would do. I'm not a politician,' Paul protested.

'Just for now, pretend you are,' Annie replied.

When the front door opened there was a flurry of clicking cameras and shouts from the waiting journalists at the front gate. They were surprised to see Paul emerge in his slippers carrying a kitchen tray loaded with a dozen mugs, and

Annie following behind with a second similarly loaded one. Paul walked stiffly up the path and said loudly, 'Hello everybody! I'm Paul, this is my wife Annie. I won't be giving any interviews, and I won't be taking questions about recent events, but as you've been out here all day we thought you might need a cup of tea or coffee. Tea on this tray, coffee on that one, milk in the jug and sugar in the bowl. Here you go.' Paul held out the tray towards the person nearest to him, a TV reporter who was holding out a microphone. Behind her the cameraman from the same station angled his camera towards Paul. The red light on top of the camera came on. Annie took her tray to the other side of the garden.

'Mr Huggins, how do you feel…' the TV reporter started to say.

'No, no questions remember! No tea for you.' Paul said, moving along the low garden wall and offering the tray to the next person who was clutching a pen and notepad.

'Paul, it was quite risqué footage of Jasper and Tor in that film, were you embarrassed to be seen…?' the journalist began.

'Oh, that turned into a question didn't it?' Paul said, shaking his head and moving the tray out of reach of the journalist. He moved on again.

The third reporter hesitated, glanced at the first two, then said to Paul, 'Um…is the tea PG Tips?'

'Typhoo, actually,' Paul answered.

'Oh, go on then, I've been gagging for a cuppa.' The journalist grabbed a mug and picked up the milk jug.

The second journalist leaned forward, reaching sheepishly for a cup. 'So am I. Could I, please? I'm really thirsty.'

'Of course. But no more questions, now!' Paul smiled. The cameraman had lowered his camera and was whispering to the reporter. She raised her hand. 'Any chance we could have two coffees over here? If it's not too much trouble,' she added politely. Annie headed over.

'Have you got any biscuits?' Someone shouted.

Paul and Annie spent twenty minutes distributing hot drinks and making small talk before collecting the empty mugs, all the while politely refusing to answer any questions. As they turned to go back inside one of the journalists shouted, 'Can I come in a use your loo?'

Paul smiled. 'Absolutely no, you cannot come into our house. I'm not quite as dumb as I look.' There were a few wry chuckles from the crowd.

'Can't blame me for trying!' the journalist shouted. There were more laughs.

'Yeah, good effort. Look, seriously folks, I know you've got a job to do, but please, try not to disrupt the neighbours too much. This is a nice community, we try and look out for each other, and they've done nothing to warrant any intrusion in their lives. Now, our daughters will be coming home from school soon; we will take a very dim view of anyone who tries to ask them any questions.' The teacups rattled as Paul tried to balance the tray on his cast covered arm. 'As they are under the age of consent I want to state for the record I most emphatically do not give permission for their photograph to be taken, OK? Just keep them out of all this. Have a good afternoon everybody.' Paul headed indoors.

The crowd at the front gate remained in place for the rest of the day, but Annie and Paul began to notice a change in the online reporting within a couple of hours. As the news websites updated their stories pictures of Paul in Kabul started to be replaced by photographs of Paul and Annie in their front garden distributing mugs of tea. The text of the stories started to change too; a few of the sites now referred to Paul as a 'loyal family man.' Even The Sun now described him as 'charmingly eccentric.' 'That's an improvement, I suppose,' Paul said.

Even though Annie texted Jessica and Sophie they still chose to come home from school by climbing over the back garden fence. They hurried in clutching their phones.

'Dad look! You're on TikTok!' said Sophie.

'I don't even know what that is,' Paul said. The girls showed him their phones. On a social media app a short film clip played of the Kabul press conference. A censored image of Tor and Jasper having sex played on the screen with Paul sat in front, seemingly unaware. The soundtrack was taken from a Scooby Doo cartoon – 'Huuuuh?' – then Paul turned, and the sound became the chorus of the song by Oasis, Don't Look Back in Anger. A second clip using the same footage had animated eyes popping out of Pauls head and comic book steam coming out of his ears as he turned around. He waved the girls away from showing him anymore.

The next day, Friday, Annie went back to work. After breakfast Paul made hot drinks for the press on his own. Their numbers had diminished significantly from the day before, and it only took one tray load to dispense drinks to everybody.

Paul still refused to speak about his experiences, and hardly any of the remaining journalists tried to question him anyway.

Once back indoors Paul tried, despite the instructions from his boss, to log in to his work laptop. He couldn't get past the login screen. The password must have expired while he was away. Not knowing what else to do, he laid out on the sofa and turned on the TV, looking for a film to watch. Just as he found a classic film channel that was about to show an old Michael Caine film, his phone chimed. He looked at the screen to see a message from Jordi on a WhatsApp group named 'De kudde.' The message said, 'Hi Everybody! We got home yesterday. How you all doing? Stay in touch!'' Jordi then sent a picture of him, Hendrik, and Agnes at Schiphol Airport, then a second one in what was presumably their home kitchen. The phone pinged again seconds later with a message "Hi!" from Moira, "Hello" from Belinda, a waving hand picture from Charlotte and a thumbs up and smiley face emoji from Campbell. Paul typed in "Hi All" then "Jordi, what is "De kudde"?"

"This means 'The Herd' in Dutch," Jordi answered.

Campbell sent a message addressed to Belinda & Moira – "How is Annabel?" A series of updates game through, one sentence at a time. Annabel would be in hospital for several weeks; she was expected to undergo a series of operations; she would be left with a number of scars across her face and head. Moira promised to get Annabel to join the WhatsApp group when she was planning to visit her on Sunday.

Around lunchtime there was a rat-a-tat knocking at the front door. 'Go away!' Paul shouted.

A voice from outside called out 'Mr Huggins, it's the Mail!'

'I'm not giving interviews to any newspaper!' Paul yelled.

'The Royal Mail, I've got your post,' came the reply.

When Paul opened the door the postman winked at him and handed him a package. It was addressed to "Mr P. Huggins (Sicknote)." He tore off the wrapping paper and pulled off the lid of what had previously been a shoe box. Inside, neatly folded was a mostly red handknitted scarf which had one end finished in blue. The word 'Sicknote' was roughly embroidered at one end. A handwritten note was folded at the bottom of the box. It was dated the day they had flown home.

"Dear Sicknote" it began, "Greetings from Kabul. I write this having returned from the surgery on my ankle this morning. I am still full of painkillers; it is fucking lovely. The doctors say I should make a full recovery, but I will need lots of physio to make it fighting fit again. Those fuckers better believe I will come back fitter than ever.

Me and the whole squad are being shipped home in a couple of weeks before redeployment. I INSIST you and your family will come down to the barracks in Devon when we are back so I can host a dinner in your honour. I will get you so pissed you will throw up again. Ha Ha.

Please find enclosed this shitty scarf as a token of my esteem.

Your Friend

Morgan

Colour Sergeant Talbot, RM."

Paul stared at the scarf for a while, blinking.

By Saturday morning there were no press waiting outside the house, and Paul was no longer on the front pages. Instead, the media interest was focussed on Jasper having been spotted signing in at an exclusive rehabilitation centre in London, while Tor, after a whirlwind series of interviews with the glossy fashion and celebrity magazines, had flown to Paris to open a new branch of her international modelling agency. The press was highly critical of Tor and her seemingly heartless behaviour. At the same time, a carefully edited and produced version of the sex tape became available to watch online behind an expensive paywall. Although Tor made no mention of this publicly, a link to the payment page was added to the contacts section of Tor's own website.

On the WhatsApp group Charlotte shared a single angry face emoji. The rest of the group sent messages of sympathy and good luck to pass on to Jasper.

Paul had unpacked the rucksack on his first day back, putting the remaining clothes into the wash, and carefully laying out the remaining items giving them all a thorough cleaning, before wiping the rucksack inside and out. The cracked mobile phone he had recovered from the landslide he had put in his bedside table after wiping it down and left it there, having no immediate idea of what to do with it. After reading the headlines on Saturday he copied Charlottes contact details from the WhatsApp group and sent her a private message.

"I think I have Tor's mobile phone. If it is hers, how can I return it?"

A few minutes later Paul's phone rang. It was Charlotte.

'Hi Paul, how are you? How's the hand?' She said.

'Hi Charlotte. It's getting there I guess. The swelling has gone down a little, and the bruises have started to change colour. Look, I need your help. I – I seem to have a mobile phone which I think may belong to Tor, and I wanted to, maybe, get it back to her, but I don't want to put it in the post, it could end up getting lost. Could you help me with that?' Paul said.

'I might be able to, although that could be a little tricky just now.' Charlotte replied.

'Oh, is she not speaking to you because of what happened in Kabul?' Paul suggested.

'That's not exactly it,' Charlotte said. She paused for a moment, then said, 'To be honest I am trying to stay incognito for the moment, you know, flying under the radar sort of thing, but I would like to help you with this. You've been in the papers a lot these last two days…'

'Oh, a lot,' Paul said with feeling.

'…so, I am a bit wary of meeting up and us being pictured together.' Charlotte continued.

'Well, the press was camped outside my house for two days, but they've all gone now. You could come here if you like?'

'Where is "here"?' Charlotte asked. Paul spelt out his address. 'I'll be round about four pm, okay? I read in the papers you make a cracking cup of tea, so put the kettle on.'

At about three forty-five Charlotte texted Paul, asking if the coast was clear. He peered out of the window, then messaged back there was no press in sight. Ten minutes later there was a knock at the front door. Paul swung it wide open with a smile, then faltered. 'Charlotte?' Paul stared at the young woman on his doorstep. Smartly dressed in a dark blue trouser suit and high heeled shoes and bereft of make-up, she looked both much younger and much older than the last time Paul had seen her. She smiled at Paul, the corners of her eyes crinkling slightly. The smattering of dark freckles across the bridge of her nose stretching upwards slightly as her mouth widened. Her unpainted eyebrows looked half the size they had previously.

'Can I come in?' If Paul had had any doubts that it was Charlotte standing in front of him the London accent was unmistakably the same.

'Of course!' Paul waved his cast inside the house and led her into the living room. He directed her to the sofa, then lowered himself into a chair. After a moment he blurted out 'You look so different!'

'You saw me once without those blue contacts in, do you remember?' Charlotte said. Her dark brown eyes stared intently at Paul.

'Oh yes! At the Hotel Alpine. I'd quite forgotten. But...you're different in so many other ways. I'm so sorry! That is awfully rude of me,' Paul stammered.

'Hello! I'm Annie. You must be Charlotte. Cup of tea, dear?' Annie said from the doorway. Charlotte stood to greet her. 'No need to stand on ceremony in this house. How do you take it?'

'Milk and two sugars please,' Charlotte said. Annie headed into the kitchen. 'It is useful not to be recognised sometimes,' Charlotte said to Paul. 'Now, tell me about this phone that might be Tor's.'

Paul told Charlotte how he had overhead Tor and Annabel talking at the airport hotel in the stairwell when Tor had asked Annabel to hide something for her; and then how after the avalanche he had found this device sliding down the hill before Annabel and Sydney had climbed down. Paul took the mobile out of his pocket.

'I can't conclusively prove this is Tors - it might be Annabel's own, or Sydney's, or even someone else's, but that all seems unlikely. I saw Annabel surrender her own phone to Talbot, why would she have two?'

'Can I see it?' Charlotte reached out her hand and took the device as Annie came back in the room with three mugs. She closed the living room door behind her and sat next to Charlotte. 'Top of the range iPhone – Tor certainly has one of these.' Charlotte said. She pressed the power button. The screen lit up beneath cracked glass on the cover, revealing the numeric keypad. The screensaver image behind the numbers was of Tor in her swan pose. 'Yes, this one belongs to Tor.' Charlotte punched a pin code into the device, and it unlocked. 'She uses the same code for all her devices so that she doesn't have to remember too much.'

'How is Jasper?' Annie asked suddenly.

'I read he has gone into rehab, have you seen him?' Paul asked.

'No, I'm not allowed in just yet. Immediate family only for supervised visits for the first week. I have messaged him, but his use of his phone is strictly limited, at least at first.' Charlotte looked at Annie and smiled. 'Jasper would be much worse off if it wasn't for your husband. He really saved his life I think.'

'You don't look like Jasper at all, do you? I can see it now, up close.' Annie said. She plucked the mobile phone out of Charlotte's hands and enfolded it in her lap.

'Annie…!' said Paul, shocked.

'So, explain why Paul should entrust someone else's property to you. Because I don't think you are who you say you are.'

Charlotte gave a little cough, then smiled again. 'You're right, I don't look like him. At all.' She picked up her mug of tea and took a sip.

'You said you are only half siblings, though, right?' Paul said, looking confused. 'Same Dad, different mothers?'

'Tell people what to see frequently enough, and, mostly, that's what they will see.' Charlotte replied. 'Alright, I'll tell you why you should give me the phone. But for now, this is confidential for legal reasons. Is that understood? No running to the press with what I am about to tell you.'

'We've done an excellent job of not talking to the media this week I'll think you'll find.' Annie said.

'I've noticed, that's why I'm taking the risk of telling you this. But it has to stay secret – for now, at least. It is going to be announced in the next couple of days that Tor is under police investigation for fraud and tax evasion. Parts of her modelling agency are a scam; around the world hundreds of young girls and boys who dream of being models pay thousands of pounds as a sign-up fee, they sign a non-disclosure agreement, then ninety nine percent of them never hear from the company again. Tor has been getting away this for a long time, but it looks like she has been getting bolder, or perhaps greedier; the business has been ramping up its global operation. Jasper wasn't involved in the agency, but he was close enough to realise that something was wrong, and when Tor tried to get him tied up in the scheme he decided he wanted to get out. Unfortunately, his addiction was becoming a massive problem, so he need help.'

'Oh my god.' Paul said. 'Is that where Annabel came in? She was signing up for the agency, wasn't she?'

'I believe so,' said Charlotte. 'Carrying the phone to curry favour with the boss isn't too much of a burden for Annabel. But it might suggest there is some information on there that Tor wanted to keep secret from those around her; Jasper especially.'

'That doesn't explain your role in all this,' Annie said pointedly.

'No, it doesn't,' Charlotte replied. She reached into her jacket pocket and pulled out a small wallet and flipped it open. On one side was a silver crest with a crown on it, on the other side a laminated card which read "Metropolitan Police" across the top. Beneath a picture of Charlotte was the name "Naomi Crawford" and the words "Detective Constable."   Paul's mouth dropped open slightly. Charlotte continued, 'I had been working on the investigation team for six months already, but we didn't have enough hard evidence to take the case to court. Then Jasper reached out to a senior officer he happened to meet at a posh do at the Savoy

Hotel. He was interviewed without Tor knowing and agreed to help in return for immunity from prosecution. I had done undercover work before, so it was decided I would become Jasper's long lost half-sister Charlotte. This let me get close to Tor and gather the evidence we needed. I had gathered just about enough good stuff by the time we were headed home from Seoul. I suspect whatever is on that phone will confirm what we already know, but the fact that Tor wanted to hide it gives us more proof of knowledge and intent.'

Annie tossed the phone back as if it were red hot. "Charlotte" tucked it into her jacket pocket with the warrant card.

'Oh,' Annie said. 'Well, that is not what I was expecting, I must admit. I had just assumed you were his drug dealer.'

"Charlotte" burst out laughing. 'Definitely not. Hopefully, this means Jasper can get the help he needs now; Tor can't drag him off somewhere else around the world. He's not the sharpest tool in the box, but he is harmless enough. Now, Annie, I have to tell you something about your husband.' Paul's mouth opened wider, and Annie's eyebrows shot up as she turned to stare at Paul. Charlotte reached into another jacket pocket and pulled out another mobile phone; Paul recognised it as one she had had during the rescue. 'In fact, I need to show you something,' she said, flicking through the photograph gallery. She found the one she wanted and passed the phone to Annie who looked at it, then raised a trembling hand to her mouth.

'What did I do?' Paul said. Annie turned the camera. The photograph was taken from the ramp of the helicopter on top of the mountain in Kyrgyzstan. It was slightly out of focus, but in the centre of the image it was clearly Paul, splattered with blood and dirt, his face screwed into a grimace of effort and pain, brandishing a pistol, and carrying a seemingly unconscious Talbot. Paul's right leg was forward, the thigh muscle taught and stretched. Annie looked at Paul, her eyes brimming with tears.

'You silly sod! You didn't tell me about this!' she cried.

'Well, I …sort of did,' Paul answered. He looked again at the image. 'You can't really see them there, but that's just me in my ducky underpants, and me and Talbot are tied together like we're in three-legged race.'

'That's the Marine who sent you that scarf?' Annie asked. Paul nodded.

"Charlotte" reached over and flicked over the subsequent photographs, showing the six royal Marines running out to bring Paul and Talbot in.

'We were under fire by then, so we were seconds away from taking off when you came over the hill. Sergeant Talbot...'

'Colour Sergeant,' Paul said automatically.

'Colour Sergeant Talbot was bleeding heavily from a scalp wound and wouldn't have made it on his own. So, you see Annie, your husband...'

'I know,' said Annie. 'I've always known what he is and what he can do.' She sniffed. 'But you can send me that photograph, if you don't mind.'

"Charlotte" stood up. 'Right then, I have to be going; I have some work to do. Thank you for the tea, Annie. Paul, I will be in touch.'

'I have one question, er, Naomi?' Paul said.

'Stick with calling me Charlotte for now,' she replied. 'Just to be on the safe side.'

'Did Cecelia now who you are?' Paul asked.

'Oh, so you know about her. I wasn't sure anyone else, but Campbell did. I recognised her straight away – it was a bit of a fangirl moment to be honest - but being undercover I couldn't really say anything to her. I figured she was the real reason we were being rescued, whatever Tor or even Jasper thought. Cecelia approached me when were up in the mountains, asking if I needed any help. She'd obviously sussed me out. I just shook my head, so she winked at me and walked away. I'd love to get a chance to talk to her properly once this is all over.' "Charlotte" smiled at the memory. 'Now remember, everything we've talked about this afternoon is confidential until it goes to trial. Not a word to anyone.'

'Understood. If you do get to speak to Jasper, say hi from me,' Paul said.

Shortly after "Charlotte" had left, Paul had a call from Kieran Mills. 'Paul, you need to come into the office tomorrow. You'll need to be there from ten o'clock sharp.' Without waiting for a reply Kieran hung up.

Chapter Twenty

They had been in the meeting room for more than thirty minutes.. The small

space had no windows but was lit by bright lights in the ceiling. The large table

that took up most of the space had six chairs arranged around it. At one end of the

room a large TV screen was hung on the wall with cables hanging down to a

control box on the wall below it. More cables trailed out of the box across the

floor. The screen was black apart from a tiny red light glowing in one corner.

Three people were sat on one side of the table; Paul was seated opposite them. To

Paul's left was Kieran Mills, who had mostly said nothing, and had kept his eyes

averted from meeting Paul's gaze. In the centre of the three was the imposing

figure of Sir Julian Willoughby, the Senior Solicitor from the Government Legal

Department. To Paul's right was Beatrice Lowe, who had been introduced as

Senior Officer for Personnel Security in the Department of Health which was a

role Paul hadn't previously known existed. Beatrice had made regular notes on a

pad on the desk in front of her, although Paul had barely said anything other than

'yes or 'no.' Sir Julian had done most of the talking. Laid out on the table were

photocopies of numerous tabloid newspaper front pages, a copy of the letter Paul

had written at Bishkek airport, and invoices for the books thrown into the river in

Kyrgyzstan.

'So, in summary, we have direct evidence of numerous incidences of your

misconduct. Repeated instances in the last seven days of collusion with the press

for illicit personal gain, at the risk of the release of highly classified government

information. Written proof, in your own handwriting, of theft of clothing goods in a foreign country. Your admittance of negligence in losing government property, namely three books valued at over six thousand pounds, paid for by her majesty's government.

'Mr Huggins, it is the decision of this disciplinary hearing is that you have bought the department, and in particular the Minister of State, into disrepute by your actions during your little, ah, foreign *adventure*. You are extremely fortunate that you are not being dismissed outright, but you will be demoted from Senior Policy Advisor to the role of Executive Officer with immediate effect. You will be put on garden leave for a month while a suitable position is found for you, far away from Whitehall and most likely out of London altogether. You could of course, choose to resign. If you were to do so, and I would strongly urge you to consider this, we might be persuaded to permit you to retain some of your current pension privileges. We will also require you to write a statement for release to the press.'

Paul looked up at the trio sitting opposite him. He thought for a moment of Colour Sergeant Talbot being swept asway by an avalanche on a mountainside thousands of miles away. He sighed, then slammed his right palm down on the table. Kieren and Beatrice both twitched.

'Is that it?' Paul said.

'Yes, I think that concludes the meeting. You have to decide…' Sir Julian began.

'No, no, I mean, is that all you've got?' Paul said.

'Mr Huggins, this is most serious,' Beatrice said.

Paul laughed. 'It really isn't. This is a joke.' Sir Julian opened his mouth to speak but Paul raised a hand and waggled a finger at him. 'I think you've had your turn speaking. Now it's my go. I haven't released any top-secret information, and you know it. If I had done that I would be in a prison cell by now. As for the books and the clothes – at worst those are unfortunate, but hardly a sackable offence. The real problem here is I've been in the spotlight in the last few days, haven't I? Just to be clear, I haven't been paid by any media company or done any in-depth interviews with the press, so your use of the word 'collusion' is stretching the truth somewhat.' Paul stared at the blank screen on the wall.

'Mr Huggins, this isn't for you to…' Sir Julian began but Paul ignored him and addressed Kieren.

'I honestly thought when you called me in at short notice it was because they were going to give me a *bloody* commendation.' The civil servants opposite him looked startled. 'Going above and beyond, and all that. But it would seem that the Minister's nose is out of joint because of some bad publicity and what you actually want is a scapegoat. My head was above the parapet so I'm the obvious target.'

Paul recalled the banter amongst the Marines, the nicknames, the jokes, and for a moment he wished he could experience that again. 'I get it. You know? I understand what it is that I am not. I know I'm not special. I know my role in life is not to be the champion who gets the girl, the superhero who saves the day. I'll always be just in the crowd, in the background. So, I'm expendable. When my superiors need a fall guy, I'm the obvious choice. But you know what? I'm a good dad. I'm a good husband. And I am really good at my job. *Really* good. All I've done wrong is to be in the wrong place at the wrong time and because of that,

I've become a nuisance to be got rid of.' He suddenly reached across the table and grabbed Kieran's wrist. 'I've seen things you people wouldn't believe…'

Paul remembered a Mercedes Benz on fire off the hard shoulder of a Kyrgyz motorway. He thought of 'C' company Royal Marines dancing under a glitterball in the dark near the Hotel Alpine fireplace grate. 'All those moments will be lost in time, like tears in rain…' he said, staring at Kieren.

'What the hell are you doing?!' Kieran pulled his arm away.

Paul smiled at him unnervingly. 'It's a movie quote – oh, never mind, you wouldn't get it.'

The panel of three looked at each other in confusion. This really wasn't going as planned at all. Paul thought again of the dash to the helicopter on a frozen hillside with an unconscious Talbot strapped to him. He could almost hear the machine gun fire as they took off. 'I think it's fair to say I have been remarkably discreet up until now. With my picture in the papers, I have a certain - *notoriety* - at the moment, as well as several contacts in the media.' Paul was improvising at this point, and probably overreaching, but it struck him he had nothing to lose. 'So, I am sure they would be interested to hear some of my stories. If you try and demote me or fire me, there will be a flurry of articles in the tabloids about how the Minister *really* behaves when he is on one of his jolly little trips.' Paul recalled several pieces of gossip in the department which previously he had ignored. The Minister could be over-familiar with some of the female staff, and there had been gossip of an extra-marital affair; but Paul's statement today was pure invention. He had not a scrap of evidence of misbehaviour from the visit to

Korea. However, judging from the worried exchange of glances between the trio on the other side of the table he appeared to have hit a nerve.

'You don't really want me to make a fight of this, do you? If this goes to a tribunal there will be witnesses, statements, all the gory details splashed across the newspapers. If the minister finds me embarrassing now, imagine how he will feel after I drag this out for several months. Which I will. Given how much negative publicity this would generate I doubt the Prime Minister would be particularly pleased.' Another thought occurred to him. 'And as for the way you have tried to bully me into silence today, well if that came out it wouldn't look particularly good for you three, would it? I can promise you I will put in a formal complaint, and your names will be all over the press as well.'

'Now steady on…' Beatrice began. Paul cut across her.

'Here is what is actually going to happen. You are NOT going to demote me by three grades and cut my pay in half; In fact, I will retain my current salary, my job grade, and my existing security clearance. I realise that the Minister considers me too much of a nuisance to have around, so I suppose I have to accept I cannot stay in my current role. In which case I will be on indefinite garden leave *on full pay* until a suitable alternative position is found for me. Provided I choose to accept the new position, of course. In return I will leave the department quietly, with no fuss and bother. Nothing embarrassing for the Minister, or the Department, or you personally, will come out from me as long as everyone stays true to this agreement. There will be no reference to this in my employment record, and no black mark against my name. Is that understood?'

Kieran began to splutter 'I have never heard anything so preposterous…!' but Sir Julian waved him into silence. Looking thoughtfully at Paul, he nodded.

'You realise you are running the risk of a very public personal humiliation Mr Huggins? However uncomfortable you make it for the Minister, it would be much more embarrassing for you.'

Paul smiled widely. 'Oh, it seems I have a remarkably high tolerance for public embarrassment. I have had a lot of practice at that lately. However, I would prefer not to put my family through any more scrutiny if I don't have to. That is your guarantee that I will keep my end of the bargain.'

After a moment's consideration and with a quick glance at his colleagues, the senior man spoke again. 'Very well; for the sake of a swift resolution to this matter we will go along with your selfish and, frankly, rather unprincipled demands. You will however sign a binding non-disclosure agreement that will ensure your continuing silence *and* will absolve the staff of this Department from any liability for unfair dismissal or wrongdoing, is that understood?'

Paul noted he didn't mention protection for the Minister. Interesting. 'I will indeed sign a *mutual* NDA, with a clause that clearly states that any breach that doesn't emanate from me will invalidate my obligation. I will sign that just as soon as I have written approval for what we have discussed, signed by the Head of the Civil Service. Just to avoid any deniability issues.'

'Now then, I am not sure I can promise you that.'

'Of course you can deliver that. You knew before you walked into this room exactly what you could and couldn't offer me.'

The senior managers eyes flickered towards the TV. 'Well, um, we will have to see about...'

'Why don't I wait here while you go and sort that paperwork out? In the meantime, I would quite like a cup of tea and a cheese and chutney sandwich. I can go and wait in the canteen if you like?'

'No! We will have that bought up to you. Just...wait here.'

Paul turned to face the blank TV screen. He smiled and gave it a little wave. 'Hello!' he said. The other three heads in the room all turned to stare at the screen and then turned back at Paul. 'I've learnt what that little red light means. It means the camera is on, doesn't it?'

The Permanent Secretary at the Department of Health and Social Care was seated in his plush office in Victoria Street in London. On a large screen on the wall was the video image of a cramped meeting room with Paul waving to the camera. Both the Permanent Secretary, and the Head of the Civil Service who was seated beside him, turned away from the screen to look at the third occupant of the room. The white-haired woman dressed in an elegant business suit had started to laugh. 'Bravo, Mr Huggins. Bravo.' she said.